ROYAL MAGES

THE GIRL WHO SHATTERED THE SEA

EVELYN PUERTO

THE GIRL WHO
SHATTERED THE SEA

ARDEBIL

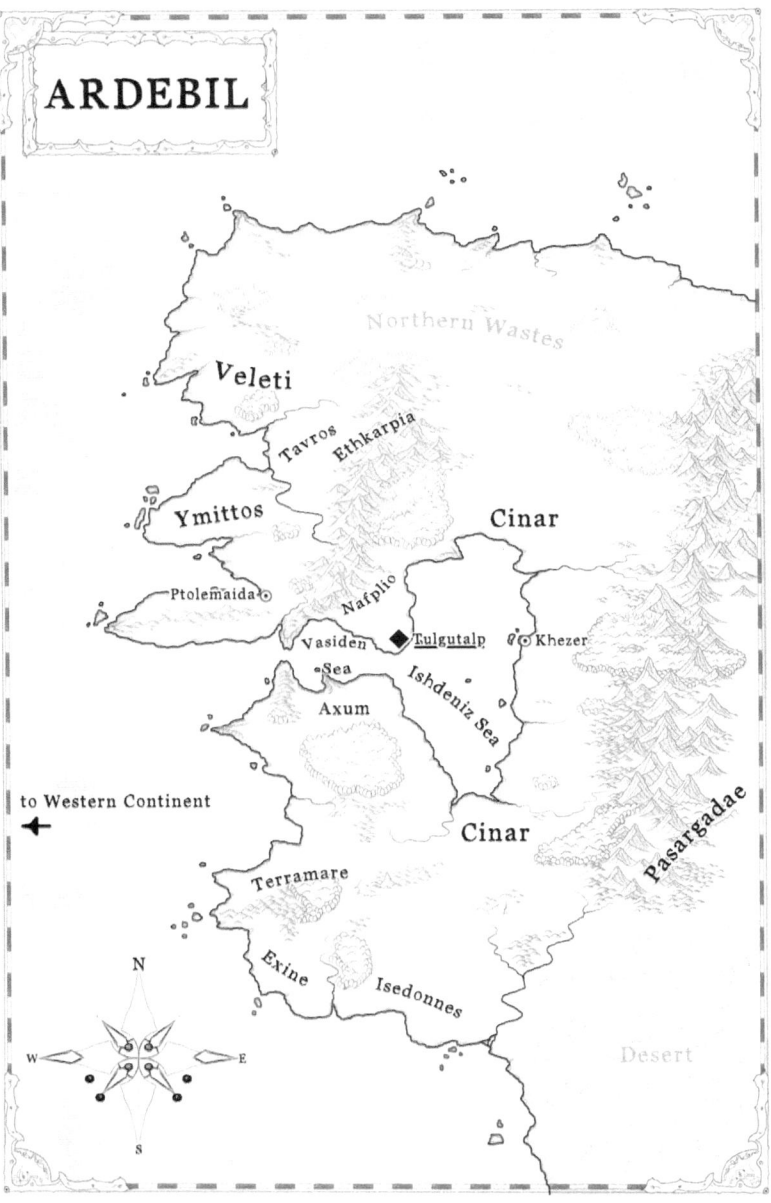

Veleti

Northern Wastes

Tavros

Ethkarpia

Ymittos

Cinar

Ptolemaida ⊙

Nafplio

Vasiden
◆ Tulgutalp

Khezer

Sea

Axum

Ishdeniz Sea

to Western Continent

Cinar

Pasargadae

Terramare

Exine

Isedonnes

Desert

N

W E

S

CONTENTS

THE STORY SO FAR...

BOOK 1: THE GIRL WHO BROKE THE DARK

Princess Eliana of Ymittos has long anticipated the day she gets to make the rules — and use her magic without fear of penalty. But until she ascends the throne, Eliana's days are devoted to practicing diplomacy on inconsiderate guests and weighing the merits of her latest suitors.

The most recent visitor, the obnoxious Princess Derya of Cinar, makes Eliana's life a trial. But when the girls use their magic to rescue trapped workers, they somehow become friends. Then Istvan of Nafplio arrives, intending to woo Eliana. Derya takes a distinct dislike to him, much to Eliana's annoyance.

Then, on her 18th birthday, Eliana's parents reveal her true destiny: she must venture to the monster-infested under-world of Malkh to wake a sleeping prince from his hundred-year curse. Terrified, Eliana refuses. But the terms of the curse are clear: only the heir of Ymittos can break its spell. If she fails, the evil sorcerer Cetus will begin his reconquest of the continent.

Banished and stripped of his power a millennium ago,

Cetus has lain dormant, rebuilding his strength and amassing his armies. Now, his carefully laid trap is about to spring destruction on the first realms in his path.

After considering that if she fails, Eliana realizes that nothing will hold Cetus back from invading the continent to restore his reign of terror and slavery. Remembering that a ruler must be willing to sacrifice for her people, she agrees. She sets off, accompanied by Istvan and a large party of guards. Derya accompanies her to the rift and continues back to Cinar after Eliana descends to the underground world.

Once in the underworld, Eliana discovers the legends she'd heard of half-fish, half-goat monsters were false. She meets the Tavkatseen Shirdona, a sometimes kind, sometimes mocking clan leader who explains that after the cataclysm that sent the realm of Malkh underground, the name changed to Chorokha. And that the Chorokhese survived all these centuries by raiding cattle, grain and beer from the people of Ymittos.

Horrified, Eliana wants to find another guide. But knowing time is running out, she agrees to Shirdona's terms: her help in exchange for Eliana's assistance raiding cattle from a Ymittosian farm. With no other option, Eliana agrees.

After the raid, Shirdona leads her to Prince Adakizh, where Eliana is stunned by how attractive she finds him. With nothing to guide her in breaking the curse but old fables, she kisses him. He awakens and shouts at her to flee. There's a second curse, he explains, and now he's compelled by it to kill her. He'll die if he doesn't do so within three days.

She flees, seeking help from Istvan. Her maid, meanwhile, found a letter Istvan received, and based on conversations she'd overheard, suspects that Istvan had Eliana's parents killed, planning to rule Ymittos through Eliana. And that he may have had his own family killed as well, intending to take over his own realm. Her suspicions are intensified when Istvan suggests that the way out of the second curse is simply to kill the prince.

Eliana realizes while she's committed to a life of self-sacrifice, blindly trusting Istvan is a sacrifice too far. She decides to find Adakizh and work with him to break the second curse. This begins a cat-and-mouse game through the tunnels and caverns of the underworld, where Eliana is fleeing Istvan, other Chorokhese who would sell her to Cetus, and the prince intent on killing her.

In her encounters with Adakizh, he tells her he's doing all he can to resist the curse, even knowing he'll die. Eliana can't help but notice his self-sacrificing attitude in contrast to the selfishness and treachery of Istvan.

Reluctantly, Eliana agrees that the only way forward is to kill Istvan before he kills the prince. They seek him out, and discover he'd cut off a finger from Eliana's maid's hand while torturing her for information about Eliana's whereabouts. This decides it for Eliana. Adakizh fights Istvan and kills him.

Then the prince shares knowledge of an ancient spell that could break all the dark curses on Chorokha. Together they figure out a way to use the spell but fear they might die in the attempt.

They pronounce the spell and cause a great cataclysm that brings all the people of Ymittos down into the underworld. They nearly die and fall unconscious. When they awaken, they are faced with the consequences of overusing their magic. Eliana is blind and lost her sense of smell. Adakizh is deaf and has lost his sense of balance. They find a way to communicate and agree to sleep off the aftereffects, hoping they won't be permanent.

Meanwhile, Princess Derya has reached the foothills of the mountains on Ymittos's border. She and her entourage watch in horror as a great earthquake rocks the ground, the land turns to white sand that sucks everything below it. One of their horses panics and runs onto the sand, and is pulled below. Convinced Eliana has failed in her quest and has now perished, Derya realizes it's up to her to warn her father, the emperor of Cinar, of the coming threat of Cetus.

Eliana and Adakizh are awakened by Shirdona, who is impressed by the magic they performed but not the destruction that's taken place. And she understands that Cetus won't give up his ambition to conquer the continent. She tells Eliana and Adakizh that the only way to prepare for the inevitable invasion is to unify the terrified Ymittosians and the ravaged Chorokhese, and the only way to convince the people to do that is if their rulers marry. Eliana feels trapped by Shirdona, and even though Adakizh is still deaf and can't hear the conversation, she agrees to wed him and unite their peoples.

BOOK 2: THE GIRL WHO WROTE ON WATER

As dust settles over the buried kingdom of Ymittos, Princess Derya is faced with a grim revelation: her friend, Princess Eliana, has perished while trying to break an evil sorcerer's curse. That means the next target in Cetus's quest to enslave the continent is Derya's own father—the Emperor of Cinar.

En route to Cinar, Derya and her entourage arrive in the realm of Nafplio, only to find its royal family had been massacred in their sleep. The ruling nobles, paralyzed by fear, scramble to uncover the assassin's identity. When someone tries to drown Derya in her bath, she understands their terror firsthand.

The shaken Nafplians, threatened by Cetus, refuse to ratify a treaty with Cinar unless Derya proves herself. They demand she retrieve the ancient magical scepter Cetus lost a millennium ago—a weapon that could make him unstoppable. The scepter lies deep in barbarian-controlled territory, and the Nafplians give her fifty days to return with it, or they will submit to Cetus themselves.

Unbeknownst to Derya, Eliana has survived the cataclysm and is now queen of the Ymittosian remnant. As queen, she fights to unite her people with the Chorokhese. But when Adakizh learns she publicly agreed to marry him without his knowledge, he's enraged, threatening the fragile alliance between them even as they prepare for Cetus's inevitable attack.

Back in Nafplio, Derya sends word to her father, unaware that he views her actions as reckless and plans to delay naming her co-emperor. A second assassination attempt—and the discovery that someone attempted to bribe Bahadir, her own military commander—convinces Derya that Cetus has embedded an agent within her retinue. She can no longer trust anyone.

The emperor responds with cold pragmatism: Derya must choose between hunting the scepter or staying in Nafplio to solve the murders and secure the alliance. Whichever task she declines will fall to her cousin Nazif—a rival for the throne. Derya chooses the scepter, but warns Nazif of the attempts on her life before departing.

Her first stop is the kingdom of Ethkarpia, where Queen Moesia rebukes Derya's diplomatic missteps but offers vital intelligence: the scepter may be hidden in the far north, and the Rorvikians—a tribe of cunning warriors—often speak in deceptive riddles.

As Derya's party heads north, she begins relying more strategically on her advisors, listening carefully but trusting her instincts. After rescuing a village from barbarian raiders, she discovers a wounded winged horse. She heals it, and in gratitude, it promises to carry her to three places of her choosing.

Continuing north, Derya's group battles wyverns in a haunted wood before encountering King Stigandr Tyr of Rorvik. He dismisses the scepter as myth, but Derya suspects he's lying. Eventually, she gains his cooperation, and he reveals his ancestors hid the artifact in one of three places.

Derya tries a new use of her water magic—writing on water to purify a lake Cetus befouled. In gratitude, a flock of enchanted swans grant her a magical sword: Hrathung, forged to slay the fiercest dragons. She and Stigandr fly on Habeci, the winged horse, to search the three potential hiding places.

The first two—a wyvern's lair and a frost giant's cavern—have already been destroyed by Cetus's mutant water fae, confirming he too is searching. The final location is a dragon's stronghold.

There, Derya uses her water magic to blind the dragon while Stigandr wounds it with a magically enhanced spear. Wielding Hrathung, Derya decapitates the beast. After searching the dragon's hoard, they find the scepter. Distrustful of each other, they split it—Derya keeping the ruby capstone, Stigandr taking the body of the scepter.

That night, Stigandr betrays her, stealing the ruby and attempting to flee. But Derya anticipated his treachery and had swapped the real gem with a decoy. Using her magic, she induces uncontrollable vomiting in Stigandr, reclaims the ruby, and calls Habeci for their escape. She deceives Stigandr's men into chasing a false lead, while she heads south.

At the Veletian port of Sundsvall, Derya attempts to secure passage home. When Stigandr arrives with his forces, Derya unleashes her full magical strength, conjuring massive waves that launch her ship from the harbor. She escapes with the scepter in hand, humiliating her enemies as she sails into a brewing storm.

Now, with only days remaining, Derya races to return to Nafplio before the deadline expires—or before Cetus catches her with the one weapon that could stop him.

1
_____

Seventy-eight days after the winter solstice 29th year of Emperor Vural Tzimiskes

PRINCESS DERYA OF CINAR yearned to scream, to shout, to fling herself overboard and swim for shore. Towering sails flapped overhead, and the wind seemed to hold its breath as the ship crested a wave at the mouth of Nafplio Bay. After almost a month of fighting one winter sea storm after another, she had despaired they would never return.

The storms, she suspected, had been sent by Cetus, the evil sorcerer whose ambition to enslave the continent raged unabated through the centuries. She shivered, clutching her sea cloak tighter around her shoulders. *What terrors would he send if he knew I stole his scepter?*

The Nafplian diodochi's palace loomed over the harbor, as gloomy and foreboding as when she saw it last. But this time, instead of brooding gray clouds that threatened snow, somber ashen masses hung low in the sky, portending rain.

She pushed against the wooden rail of the *Barden's* bow as if she could hurry the ship along. The Nafplians had given her fifty days to retrieve Cetus's magical scepter. If she failed, the Nafplians, cowed by Cetus's threats, would capitulate to him in hopes he wouldn't destroy them as he rampaged over the continent. If they did, Cinar would lose a valuable ally in the war. The suffering and death of millions would rest on her shoulders.

And this morning marked the fiftieth day.

Derya cast a glance over her shoulder at Chiliarch Bahadir, who was deep in conversation with the ship's captain. Would he notice if she used her water magic to hurry them along? Better not. Weeks of short rations had left all of them weak, and she needed her strength for the confrontation to come. *Patience, Derya.*

The captain strode to the bow and shouted orders. Two sailors lowered the flapping mainsail. Others scrambled belowdecks. Within a few moments, a drum began to beat, and the sound of splashing oars reached Derya's ears. *At last.*

Bahadir turned to rest his back against the rail. "I don't know about you, but I'm grateful those clouds are hanging onto the rain like a miser grips a coin. I've had enough of storms for a lifetime."

Derya laughed. "And I thought you enjoyed the patter of rain."

"Not on a ship tossed by waves higher than the mast. I'm looking forward to a little quiet."

"You think we'll find it in Nafplio? I'm wondering if anyone else was murdered while we were gone." *Including my dear cousin Nazif.*

Bahadir chuckled. "Let's hope—"

His words were lost in a gurgle.

Derya jerked her head towards him. A water fae was perched on the ship's rail. It gripped Bahadir's throat with long, bony fingers. But this creature wasn't a normal water fae.

An icy hand clenched Derya's heart. She recognized these monsters. Others like them had slaughtered frost giants. Cetus had mutated water fae, giving them fish heads and needle-sharp teeth that protruded from gaping jaws. A pair of long tentacles extended from the fae's shoulders, tentacles that ended in barbed hooks. One of them raked Bahadir's torso, slicing through his outer leather armor like it was fine silk. Fear froze her feet to the deck while her heart galloped, spurred by panic.

Over Bahadir's shoulder, she saw a long-fingered hand clutch the ship's rail. Another water fae pulled itself up and over the rail. It thumped onto the deck and snarled.

"Kiral!" Bahadir shouted.

She jerked her attention back to the chiliarch. He was struggling to free himself from the hissing water fae's grip. One tentacle wrapped around his leg. The other lashed towards Derya.

The princess flung herself to the deck to avoid the spiked hook. *Raging waters, where did they come from?*

From a distance, she heard the captain's cursing. "Cetus's monsters!"

Derya yanked a dagger from her boot. She scrambled to her feet. Frantically, she slashed at the flailing tentacle.

Her blow swished through the air. The water fae howled and jerked its tentacle out of her reach. It jumped from the rail, still clutching Bahadir by the neck. A scarlet trail of blood trickled along the straining muscles under the chiliarch's wide eyes and reddening face.

Derya lunged and stabbed the fae in the side. Gray blood spattered her arm and face. The fae snarled and smacked the side of her head with its hook.

Pain shot through her skull, and dark spots danced before her eyes. She stumbled back, staggering as the ship rolled.

Bahadir stomped on the fae's foot. When the creature bellowed, the chiliarch dug an elbow into its abdomen.

The fae gasped and bent over, releasing its hold. Derya

darted forward and slashed at a tentacle, severing it. The hooked end fell to the deck with a clatter.

Bahadir grabbed Derya's arm and shoved her behind him. He drew his sword and, in a single blow, sliced off the water fae's head. A fountain of gray blood spewed over the deck. "Are you hurt, Kiral?"

She shook her head, sending a stab of pain across her forehead. Blood trickled down the side of her face. "No. What about you?"

Bahadir tore a piece of cloth from his tunic and pressed it to his bleeding neck. He looked down. There was a gaping tear in his leather breastplate. The claw had slit his tunic underneath but hadn't done more than leave a deep scratch on his torso. Scarlet stained the cloth he'd twisted around his neck and dripped on his tunic, leaving dark spots on the turquoise.

Derya breathed a sigh of relief. He didn't seem badly injured.

Around them, soldiers shouted. Metal clashed against metal. Some of the fae were armed with spears, others with long daggers. Tall and willowy, like most fae, they resembled humans except for their cold-eyed fish heads and lashing tentacles.

A violent shudder shook Derya. She gritted her teeth and gripped her dagger, her fingers slick with the water fae's blood. Twenty or more of the water fae had clambered over the rail.

A water fae jumped on Bahadir's shoulders, hissing angrily. It beat the chiliarch about the head with its tentacles' hooks. One hand clutched a long knife. It raised the blade high, preparing to plunge it into Bahadir's throat.

Rage drove away Derya's pain. She sprang forward and stabbed Bahadir's assailant in the back. It lashed her with one tentacle, scraping her arm and shoulder. Searing pain shoved a scream from her throat. A second long tentacle wrapped around her abdomen and tightened.

She clenched her jaw and slid her dagger under the tentacle. With one arm, she fought off the first tentacle's lashing while she sawed at the one cinching her waist.

Inexorably, the tentacle constricted, cutting off her breath. Her lungs screamed for air, and her head swam. With a final effort, she sliced through the tentacle's muscle. Its hooked end fell to the deck. Derya sucked air into her aching lungs.

The fae tipped its head back and howled. Seizing the moment, she darted forward. With one quick motion, she slit its throat.

Bahadir shoved the dead fae off his back. "Thank you." He raised his sword and faced a charging water fae. Its tentacles whirled over its head like a pair of whips. The creature's cold, black eyes were fixed on a sailor who'd slipped in a pool of blood. Bahadir ducked underneath the spinning tentacles and plunged his blade into the creature's heart. The tentacles dropped. One hook struck Bahadir on the head. He staggered but kept his footing as the fae crumpled to the deck with a thump.

Derya stood panting, clutching her dagger. The shouts of battle died down, replaced by the splashing of the waves and the creak of the ship. Bahadir's men, it seemed, had fought off the water fae, or at least the ones that had climbed on board.

She picked her way through the pools of gray blood and peered over the rail. She heard shouted commands, and the drumbeat resumed. The oars swept back and forth in a smooth, rhythmic motion, propelling the ship through the harbor. She squinted at the water. No sign of anything lurking in the depths.

Halting footsteps approached her. Bahadir made his way over the slick deck, his gait unsteady. His olive skin was a pallid yellow, and the old scars on his cheek were vivid white. He pulled the cloth from his neck. The deep gouges streamed with blood.

Derya's breath caught. She darted to him and grabbed his arm. "Sit down and let me see."

"No, Kiral, I need to—"

"Let one of your sub-kentarchs deal with it." When he resisted, she flashed him a smile. "Don't make me overrule you in front of your men."

He rolled his eyes but lowered himself to sit leaning against the mast.

The princess called to one of the soldiers. "Bring me hot water and a towel. Quickly." She frowned at Bahadir's wounds. She'd rather wait to clean them, but there was so much blood. Was that a white tendon she saw? She summoned her magic and sent it into the deepest gouge, where it touched the torn flesh and began to knit the severed veins, muscles and nerves.

She'd finished repairing two gouges on the left side of his neck by the time the water arrived. Gently, she daubed away the blood and surveyed her work. *Good.* The two she'd healed already looked like half-healed wounds from a week ago.

Sweat pooled on her forehead, and she took a deep breath. At least the healing part of her water magic wasn't as taxing as other uses of it. Perhaps she could ignore the numbing in her toes long enough to finish healing Bahadir.

While she worked, soldiers dumped the bodies of dead water fae over the side. Then the motion of the ship slowed.

Heavy footsteps approached. "Highness, there's a problem."

2

————

DERYA FROWNED INTO the captain's face. "What is it?"

"You need to look."

Her eyes narrowed at the man's wobbling voice, wariness spreading through her like a rising tide. She hauled herself to stand, moving gingerly on her numb feet. She'd have to take a break from her magic or she wouldn't be able to walk.

She scanned the dock, unsure at first what she was seeing. A horde of mutant water fae overwhelmed the dockhands. Among them were about ten men in Cinarrian black and turquoise.

"Chiliarch!" she exclaimed. "Can you stand?"

With a grunt, he clambered to his feet and leaned on the rail. "More of them," he muttered. "But the Cinarrians? Are those your cousin's men? Or are they some of ours?"

She gripped his arm. They'd sailed from Rorvik on three ships. Their first night at sea, a storm drove them apart. They never caught sight of the others again and feared they were lost. Could it be that one survived? Now her desire to be on shore increased to a frenzy. "We need to help them."

"Highness." The captain appeared at Derya's elbow. "I'm

not taking my ship into that fight. We need to find another harbor."

She stared at him. "No. We have to land here." Desperation tightened her voice. Unless she returned to Nafplio this evening, all the hardships of the past fifty days would be for nothing. The Nafplians would ally with Cinar's greatest enemy. And she couldn't leave her countrymen on shore to fight monsters unaided.

The captain folded his arms and scowled. "Those beasts killed three of my crew. I won't risk any more."

"I'm sorry about your crew." Derya tried to maintain a soft tone instead of allowing her anxiety and impatience to prevail. "But we can't turn back. What about the dockhands? We must defend them."

"Looks like they have help." The captain shook his head.

"Can you dock us away from the fighting?" Bahadir asked. "Then we could see about avenging your dead crew."

The captain hesitated, then huffed. "See that you do." He stomped off, shouting to the helmsman to steer to starboard.

Frustration at her helplessness burned Derya as she watched the battle on the dock, yearning to join the fray. Another Cinarrian toppled, his throat torn open by a water fae's hooked tentacle. Then a fae lost his head. A second fae fell face forward when its legs were severed above the knees. But there were still so many. Her head throbbed where the water fae had hit it, and her spent limbs begged her to sit down. But she couldn't rest, not while her people were in danger.

At last, the ship reached the dock. Dockhands secured the lines and sailors lowered the gangplank. Bahadir led the charge, twenty armed soldiers racing toward the battle a quarter mile away.

Derya followed, accompanied by four guards. She studied the fighters, looking for an opportunity to use her magic to help. She took a gulp of water from her flask, hoping that would revive her flagging strength.

Three water fae converged on Bahadir. He slashed a tentacle. Another lowered its head and lunged at the chiliarch, aiming its green, spiked horn at his throat. Derya's heart skipped a beat. She needed to eliminate all three before they overpowered Bahadir. But how?

She clenched her shaking hands and gathered her magic. With a twitch of her finger, she pulled a bucket's worth of water from the bay. Then she shoved more power at the water hovering in the air. When it boiled, she hurled it into the faces of the water fae attacking Bahadir.

They sprang back, clutching their eyes. Their howls chilled Derya's bones. But scalding the fae gave Bahadir the chance he needed. He sliced the head off one and let his momentum spin him around to stab a second in the throat.

The third lashed at him. Bahadir dodged to the side as the stroke hissed in the air. Derya hurled more boiling water at the fae. It screamed and fell to its knees. Bahadir brought his sword down on its head. Bone crunched. The fae lay dead in a spreading pool of gray blood.

Derya raced to the chiliarch. They stood without speaking, both panting hard. Even though he'd lost a lot of blood earlier, he wasn't showing any sign of weakness. Numb toes and fuzzy hearing told her she was feeling the effects of using her magic more than usual. *Comes from weeks of short rations.* And a nasty bump on the head.

She glanced about, seeking enemies. It appeared the water fae had either all been killed or the survivors had fled. A few dockhands lay on the dock amid the corpses of dead water fae and, she noted with a pang, three men wearing black and turquoise.

She stumbled toward the knot of Cinarrians, Bahadir on her heels. Most had slashes on their faces and hands, splatters of gray and scarlet blood on their clothing.

One man lay moaning on the dock. A crimson torrent surged from the stump of his forearm. Derya sucked in a breath, tears stinging her eyes. No magic could regrow a severed limb. Even if he survived, his life was over. No one missing a limb could serve the emperor. He'd be pensioned off with barely enough to survive on. Assuming infection didn't take him first.

Still. She knelt by the man and sent her magic into the limb. The bleeding ebbed to a slow ooze, and she grew the skin to cover the wound. She was breathless and dizzy by the time another healer joined her.

"I'll take over, Kiral," the woman said.

Derya thanked her with a nod and staggered to her feet. She gasped for breath. *I need to rest before I fall over.*

"Sezgin!" Bahadir's anguished cry arrested her attention. He was kneeling by the kentarch who lay still on the deck, pale as sea-foam.

The pool of scarlet under Sezgin seemed to be spreading, merging with puddles of seawater and gray blood.

"You can't die," Bahadir said. "You're my right arm and leg." His shoulders slumped.

Derya's heart constricted. Bahadir rarely showed any emotion other than anger or excitement. She wanted to help, she really did. But she was so tired already. After using her magic to fight the monsters and healing Bahadir and the handless man, she couldn't feel her feet.

This is no time to go limp, and I'm halfway there. I need to be wise. Prudent. Cautious. All the things I'm not.

So what would be the wise course? Find another healer? A quick glance around the dock showed her they were all busy with others. Derya scooted to Sezgin's side through puddles of seawater tinged red. His face turned the color of milk, and his breathing was slow and shallow. He might not have time for her to rest.

Had he been Bahadir, she wouldn't have hesitated. But she

didn't know Kentarch Sezgin well. Still, he was one of her entourage and important to Bahadir. Especially if Kentarch Farooq was lost at sea.

A glance at Bahadir's tight face made her decision. *To dust with prudence.*

Derya fumbled in her bag for some bitter herbs. She slipped them into her mouth, hoping their amplifying effect would give her the power she needed. With a light touch, she laid her hand on Sezgin's seeping neck wound.

The kentarch opened one eye. He gripped her wrist. "No, Kiral."

Was he whispering, or was her hearing that far gone? She bent toward him in an effort to hear. "I'm trying to heal you."

"Don't. I don't deserve it."

"But you're one of my people."

"I'm not worthy." This last was muttered, and she wasn't sure she understood.

"Nonsense." She summoned her power and pushed it into Sezgin's neck.

The torn skin heated, then the edges knit together as if sewn by invisible thread. She pressed her fingers into his neck, willing her power to find any lacerations and to mend them.

Sweat beaded on her forehead and her knees went numb. *This is what I get for using so much magic after no sleep or food. But if I can save him, it will be worth it.*

It grew harder to draw a breath, but she still sensed some damage in the tendons of Sezgin's neck. She eased her power into them, knitting the sinews together.

Her hearing was a little muffled, like she was watching the pounding waves from a distance. The men's voices faded into hushed whispers.

Fatigued tugged at her limbs. But she wasn't finished. She pushed magic into his bones, not knowing why, but sensing that was how to make blood to replace what had pooled in a scarlet puddle beneath him.

A seagull landed on the dock in front of her and opened its mouth. Its squawk was as faint as the cries made by a bird circling overhead.

Derya pulled her hand back. "I'm sorry. I can't finish." She slumped over Sezgin and allowed herself to sink into sleep.

3

T HE ROCKING MOTION was soothing, Derya thought, but it lacked the familiar sway of ocean waves. Instead of the salty tang of sea breezes, the odors of stale sweat and horse mingled with a whiff of fresh bread and rotting fruit. As she shifted, her cheek grazed a leather breastplate. A muscular arm tightened around her waist. The faint clopping of horseshoes on cobblestones reached her ears. Why was she on horseback, cradled in someone's arms?

Memories flooded her mind. The water fae who attacked their ship. The battle on the dock. Healing Sezgin. The princess stiffened and opened her eyes. She stared up into Bahadir's concerned brown eyes.

"Kiral, how are you feeling?"

She smiled, relieved she could hear well enough to understand his question. "Better. How long was I asleep?"

"About two hours. It took that long to care for the injured and to unload enough horses for fifty of us to ride to the palace. We've got another half an hour before we get there."

"How many did we lose?"

"Four, and thirty wounded."

Sorrow pricked her eyes. "Four. So many."

"It could have been worse."

The horse's shoes scraped the stones. The ground seemed to tilt, and she rested her spinning head on Bahadir's shoulder. Sudden movements weren't a good idea.

But she'd glimpsed spiky spires and domed turrets, confirming she was in Ziyamet, Nafplio's capital. Unlike her first visit, when the population was reeling from the assassinations of the entire royal family, the streets bustled with activity. Market vendors called their wares, a group of laughing children chased a dog with a string of sausages in its mouth, and loud clanging announced a blacksmith hard at work.

That's right. We made it to Ziyamet and fought off mutant water fae on the docks. She shivered, thinking of the monsters who nearly killed Bahadir. She grazed her fingers over her throbbing head. Someone had bandaged the wound left by a water fae's hook. "Is Sezgin…"

"He's going to live, Kiral. Thanks to you."

"I'm so glad. And delighted he's not lost at sea. Did he tell you when he got here?"

"Yes. Apparently, they sailed from Veleti just in time to avoid the storms. They caught up with Farooq's ship in Jiknas Bay and waited for us for five days." He scowled. "I ordered them to wait for only three." With a shake of his head, he continued. "Both ships arrived here a bit over two weeks ago. Other than three hands washed overboard, they're all here."

A surge of relief swept over Derya. She closed her eyes while she took a deep breath, the tension of worry for her lost ships easing. "And what of the Nafplians?"

Bahadir snorted. "The same as when we left. They still don't know who slaughtered the royal family. Because of that, they haven't appointed a new diodochi."

Derya rubbed her forehead. "Well."

"There's more. The people are grumbling that Lady Aspasia and the others are helpless to fight off Cetus's monsters."

Derya pressed her lips together. That didn't bode well.

A rider rode up beside her. "Kiral!"

The princess turned to look at Danisman Safiye and smiled into her advisor's creased face. "Safiye, I'm glad to see you. Is Oikeios Kelebek with you?"

The woman frowned. "Whatever you want to discuss with him can wait. You need rest, food, and a healer."

"We all do," Derya replied. "But if I'm counting correctly, today is the last day the Nafplians gave me to return with the scepter. Once I present it, I'll rest and eat." She raised her hands and clasped them together. "I promise. No more magic until tomorrow."

"If I may, Kiral," Bahadir said, "I agree with you. We show them the scepter and push for an alliance. I'm sure the oikeios will agree."

"Safiye, would you find Kelebek? I'd like to confer with him."

Safiye glared at Derya but turned her horse to obey. It squealed in protest, as if voicing its rider's disapproval.

The sharp sound cut through Derya's throbbing head, and she winced. Safiye's mount was generally placid. The danisman must have jerked the reins hard, communicating her irritation to her mare.

The princess watched her go until she disappeared behind a pair of black and turquoise clad soldiers. "You brought a mount for me, didn't you?"

"I'm afraid not. But when we get closer, I'll have one of the soldiers give you his."

A few moments later, Oikeios Kelebek rode up, his horse's hooves clattering over the rough cobblestones. Unlike the blood-spattered soldiers, Kelebek's tunic, trousers, and cloak were pristine, the black and turquoise vivid and crisp. Somehow the diplomat looked fresh, even after their long sea voyage.

Derya explained the debate between Safiye and Bahadir. "What do you think?"

Kelebek replied immediately. "By all means, complete your mission. Don't give them another heartbeat to consider the alternative."

Which was allying with Cetus. Derya's breath hitched at the thought. Not only would that give Cetus an easy staging point for invading Cinar, it would mean the dangers she'd faced down the past several weeks would be for nothing. "Thank you, oikeios."

He tipped his head. "Although you look less than royal, I think you shouldn't clean up first."

Derya put a hand to her hair. Her fingers met a mass of tangles, some stuck together with what she assumed was blood.

"I mean," Kelebek continued, "have someone tidy your hair. But meeting the Nafplians looking the part of a battle-tested, victorious warrior will emphasize you are heir to an empire strong enough to defeat Cetus, and powerful in your own right. That will strengthen your case that they need to ally with Cinar."

Derya stifled her smile of relief. He wasn't criticizing as was his wont; instead, he was actually implying he thought she'd been tested by battle and acquitted herself in a manner worthy of the Heir of Cinar. *Does this mean he doesn't hate me anymore?* She pointed at a white stone building with narrow windows. Raucous singing and laughter spilled out of the open door to the road. "Then shall we stop at this inn? Just to tidy up, as the oikeios says."

The smell of roasted goat, beer, and freshly baked bread teased Derya's nose when she entered the inn, leaning on Bahadir's arm. Her mouth watered, and her stomach rumbled. *Maybe we have time for food. The Rider knows I need it.*

The singing halted abruptly as if the trio of roughly

garbed and unshaven singers had turned to brick. Every eye was trained on the Cinarrians, food and drink forgotten.

Bahadir wove his way over the rush-strewn floor, skirting the wooden tables that filled the dimly lit room. Derya clung to his arm, unsteady on her numb feet. She stepped gingerly on the rushes, not sure what lay under the small humps. Abandoned crusts of bread? A dropped tankard? A lurking mouse? She shuddered and set her jaw.

Within a few moments, the stocky innkeeper with a black mustache that draped over the sides of his mouth produced surprisingly clean basins of hot water. He wiped his hands on his greasy, splattered apron. "My daughter will bring tea and bread." He vanished into the kitchen before anyone could ask for anything else. The other patrons turned back to their food, and the singers resumed their song.

While they waited, Safiye combed and braided Derya's dark hair into a coronet. She worked around the bandage on the side of the princess's head, saying it was better to leave it to emphasize the idea of being wounded in battle but emerging victorious.

Derya had no argument for that. She amused herself trying to understand the song a trio of workmen were singing, even though her hearing was still slightly muffled. Their words sounded slurred, no doubt, by copious amounts of ale. So different from the sullen, suspicious people she'd encountered two months ago.

But their changed demeanor had no effect on Bahadir. He demanded that the innkeeper taste the tea and bread before he'd allow any of them to eat or drink. The man complied with an impudent grin. "Only Cinarrians who have the stomachs of rabbits would fear a little poison."

Derya gulped the tea greedily, ignoring the sticky substance on the outside of the cup. When she'd drained the tea, she tore a piece of bread from the flat loaf and shoved it in her mouth. With every mouthful, her strength returned, a tiny bit of the numbness receded and the sounds around her sharpened.

Bahadir found a mount for Derya, and they proceeded to the palace. Word of their arrival had outpaced them, Derya assumed, since the Nafplian guards opened the gates as soon as her party approached, allowing them to ride through the high, peaked arch.

The approach of spring had done little to alleviate the palace's gloom. Rather than a shining blanket of snow, the courtyard was damp and barren. Derya glanced around, hoping to spot some of her soldiers who'd sailed with Sezgin or Farooq, but the only guards wore Nafplio's scarlet and gold.

Derya strode up the stone steps into the palace, planting her numb feet hard on each step. She fixed a stern look on her face. Kelebek thought she should play the triumphant warrior. The bread and tea had taken the edge off her shakiness enough that she could act her part, at least for a while.

Bahadir, Safiye, Kelebek, and ten guards followed her through the drafty, echoing great hall. Fires roared in the massive hearths at either end, doing little to combat the chill of late winter. The only occupants were maids sweeping the floor.

Derya headed for the chamber where the Nafplian council met. She paused outside the wood doors, carved and painted scarlet with a twelve-pointed golden sunburst. Shouts from inside drifted into the corridor. A guard moved to open the door, but Kelebek motioned for him to wait. Derya and he huddled close to the threshold, listening.

A reedy tenor voice yelled, "We have no choice."

That's Yiannis.

A smooth, sensual voice responded, and she strained to make out the words. "You gave the Heir of Cinar fifty days. Word came that her ship docked a few hours ago. She'll be here presently."

Thank you, Nazif. Her cousin was at least trying to support her.

The tenor snarled, "It doesn't matter. Cinar failed us. It's a dying empire. It's powerless against those monsters."

Powerless? Derya's face heated. She pulled the scepter from her boot and motioned to the guard to open the door. She strode into the room, her footsteps muffled on the thick carpet, silent as a jungle cat stalking its prey.

The Nafplian guard coughed. "Princess Derya, Heir of Cinar," he announced.

The room's five occupants jerked their heads toward her. Derya heard a few startled gasps and what sounded like a muttered curse. The princess raked her gaze over them, assessing their reactions to her appearance. Some smiled, others scowled, all were shocked.

Whether they were pleased or not, she'd returned on time. Sweat stained, blood splattered, battle weary. And triumphant.

D ERYA SCANNED THE FACES of the Nafplians seated
around the long table. Lord Calix looked genuinely
relieved, a slow smile spreading across his face as his
gaze slipped over hers. Lord Yiannis was scowling, his heavy
black eyebrows knitted together over hard, flinty eyes. Lady
Aspasia's countenance was inscrutable, her lips pursed and her
gaze fixed on a point over Derya's head.

So much for the three Nafplians. Oikeios Zeki, Cinar's
ambassador to Nafplio, betrayed his surprise only by his wide
eyes.

That left her wily cousin Nazif. He'd agreed to work with
her, for the good of the empire. But what about his own ambitions? If he was hiding any conflicting feelings about her
return, she couldn't read it on his face. Instead, he gave her a
broad grin that resembled a hungry shark's.

Derya brandished the scepter, allowing its colored gems to
flash blue, green, and scarlet in the afternoon sun that poured
through the windows. "I return as promised."

Lady Aspasia stood up. "Princess Derya, we welcome you
in freedom. And are delighted you've returned."

Are you?

Aspasia wrinkled her forehead. "You look a little . . ."

"Battle weary?" Nazif said. "You were so eager to see us, you came bloodstains and all." He ran a hand down the gold embroidery on his emerald green tunic. "So . . . spontaneous of you."

Derya shot him a look. Was that an insult? "I'm delighted to see all of you." She strode to the foot of the table, forcing her weary shoulders to refrain from slumping. All the hardships of winter travel, the chapped face and frozen toes, the battles with wyverns and a dragon, all of it worth beholding their stunned faces. "This"—she extended the scepter, giving her spellbound audience a closer view—"is the fabled scepter of Cetus."

Yiannis scoffed. "That's the scepter? It's missing a part." He curled his lip and shook his head. "Tell us the truth. When you realized you couldn't find Cetus's scepter, you raided a tomb and plucked that from the debris."

Bahadir stiffened and muttered a curse.

My thoughts exactly. This is going to be fun. Derya quirked an eyebrow. "It's missing a part, you say?" She dug in the bag hanging at her waist until her fingers closed around the ruby. With an innocent smile, she held up the massive gem, easily twice the size of an egg. "You mean the finial?"

This time, she didn't try to suppress her grin. Yiannis's eyes bugged out, and Calix appeared as though he was drooling. Aspasia stared at the ruby's twinkling red light as if spellbound.

Nazif chortled. "I sense you've a long story to tell."

"I do," Derya said. She stared pointedly at the scattered teacups and platter of half-eaten pastries on the table. "I'll tell it better after a little refreshment."

"I apologize, highness," Lady Aspasia said. "Please, sit, all of you."

In a few moments, Derya and her three advisors were sipping steaming tea and nibbling fresh bread drizzled with honey, Aspasia having given orders for stew to be brought as soon as it was ready.

Calix had volunteered to be the food taster. She'd have to find out why he'd volunteer for such a task. Later.

Meanwhile, she took her time eating. *Let the Nafplians wait a bit.* She was still a little shaky, and presenting the scepter had sapped her. After only a few bites, her hands stopped shaking and it was easier to sit straighter. Good. The fainting spell earlier was probably more exhaustion and hunger than magic overuse. She chuckled to herself, anticipating how shocked the Nafplians—and her cousin—would be when they heard her adventures.

Kelebek, thankfully, filled the time by questioning Nazif and Zeki for news from Cinar. Both of them played along, offering only trivial court gossip such as the death of a circus performer in addition to reports of decreased wine production (a matter of great concern to Nazif, Derya noted) and a border skirmish with Pasargadae.

While they chatted, Derya observed the three Nafplians. Every time Lady Aspasia set down her teacup, her shaky hand clinked the porcelain against the saucer. Lord Yiannis sat back in his chair, arms tightly folded, his scowl deepening. When Lord Calix wasn't pulling at the neck of his scarlet tunic or rubbing his chin, he was tearing a piece of bread into shreds.

The three Nafplians were jittery, that was sure. A slight chill of unease drifted over Derya. *I hope it's just impatience for my story.*

Derya dropped her spoon into her empty bowl with a clatter. When the others ceased their conversation, she straightened. *She needed to remind them of how daunting a task it had been.* "I suppose you want to hear how I retrieved an item that had been lost for a millennium."

Calix, Aspasia, and Nazif stopped eating and leaned forward, their eager faces turned to Derya. Oikeios Zeki's face wore his usual neutral expression. Yiannis narrowed his eyes, and his lips twisted into a sneer. Clearly, he'd be the hardest to win over.

The princess told them of traveling east from Ethkarpia and their battle with wyverns. Kelebek gave her a nod of approval when she skipped the part about healing a winged horse. And riding its back to a wyvern's lair, the realm of frost giants, and a dragon's den. The pegasus had requested her silence, and she wasn't about to break her word to it.

Other than Derya's voice, the only sound in the room was the crackling flames in the fireplace. The princess recounted her meeting with the king of Rorvik. And how, with great difficulty, she persuaded him to help her track down the scepter.

She took a sip of tea. Now for the tricky part. "The king thought a wyvern guarded the scepter. We found its lair, but there was no scepter." *Let them think we dueled the beast.* She shuddered at the memory of the blown-out mountain and the shattered den. Only Cetus could wield such power. No need to talk about that. The Nafplians needed no reminder of his might. She had to impress on her listeners that she and Cinar were the powers to ally with. Not Cetus. "So we went to the frost giants." She said it as lightly as if she were talking about a banquet. "No scepter. Which left the dragon."

Derya hurried to the next part of her tale before anyone could ask awkward questions, such as how they were able to venture into the frost giants' territory and survive. She delved into great detail of how King Stigandr and she killed the dragon, and how he used his wood magic powers and she used her water to find the scepter. And that they split it into two pieces so no one could use it accidentally.

Derya hoped they didn't ask why she ended up with both parts. She was reluctant to confess to having been duped by the king of Rorvik and how she filched the scepter from him. *I should have asked Kelebek to prepare a convincing explanation.*

She slid her gaze over the three Nafplians, all as silent and motionless as carved pillars. "So, I've returned in time with the scepter, as you requested. What is your reply? Will you keep your word? Can Cinar count on your alliance?"

"Well, highness, you see . . ." Lady Aspasia stared at her empty teacup.

"We are reconsidering," Lord Yiannis said.

"Oh?" Derya kept her tone bland, hiding the rage that surged within her. She risked her life to retrieve the scepter, and they wanted to slither out of their part of the bargain.

"What Yiannis means," said Lord Calix, "is there have been some developments since you left."

"Developments? Pray tell." Derya forced an expression of mild interest onto her face. As painful as that was, it was far better than screaming at the man to demand he get to the point.

"Highness, last week we were visited." Aspasia's voice shook.

"I know about the water fae attacking the harbor."

"Kiral," put in Oikeios Zeki, "it's worse than that. Cetus sent messengers."

Derya stiffened. *No. Tell me they didn't ally with Cetus.* The stew in her stomach turned to stone. "What kind of messengers?"

Calix's normally mocking eyes bore a somber, stricken tightness. "Two monstrous hawks with the heads of men. They carried the heads of two Cinarrians."

"Do you know whose?" Bahadir asked in a choked tone.

"Yes, Kentarch Farooq identified them as two who'd fallen overboard during the voyage here. He buried them according to your customs." Calix rubbed his forehead. "The hawks said the same fate awaited us if we didn't ally with Cetus. After they flew away, men with sharks' heads were spotted in the Vasiden Sea. We presume they, too, were sent by Cetus." Calix let out a long sigh. "The water fae have been harassing the docks for a week."

Lady Aspasia wrung her hands. "So, highness, please understand. It's in our best interest to align ourselves with the side most likely to prevail."

Derya's fingers tingled, and her heart thumped erratically. She was right to conceal how Cetus destroyed the wyvern and defeated a score of frost giants in his own quest for the scepter.

She longed to tell them of riding the winged horse, an honor rarely extended to humans. So rare that myths declared only the gods could ride a pegasus. Would that persuade the Nafplians of her power? But she was bound to her promise of silence. How could she prove an alliance with Cinar was the wiser choice?

"Perhaps if you'd returned sooner, our people wouldn't have fallen into a state of terror," Yiannis said. "As it is, we can barely keep them from surrendering every time one of those monsters shows up."

A log on the fire broke with a pop, shooting sparks that burnt out like Derya's hopes of success. Maybe she could have done better. Forced Stigandr to reveal the location of the scepter sooner. Or overruled her advisors and used her water magic to combat the storms that delayed them. A hundred moments collided in her mind. Perhaps Nazif should have gone instead of her.

"Only a fool would refuse to yield to invincible enemies," Yiannis said.

Whatever her errors in the past, she had to seize control before it slipped away like mist in the morning. A shout built in her throat. They wanted to see power? She'd show them power. She shrugged off the heavy cloak that had suddenly grown too hot.

"Invincible, you say? But we've already defeated Cetus's minions," Derya said. "Who do you think repelled the last bunch that attacked your harbor?" She raked the Nafplians' faces with a glare. "I've done all you asked. Tell me you kept your part of the bargain."

The three Nafplians bent their heads, staring at the table. After a long moment while the fire hissed, Calix looked up. "We've made no new alliances. Yet."

Yet? Did that mean they intended to ally with Cetus? She had to stop this immediately. Her magic thrummed inside her as she considered how best to display her powers.

"Please, highness," Lady Aspasia said. "Legally, we can't make any new treaties until we name a diodochi. Since we don't know who killed the old one, we're reluctant to appoint his successor."

Derya stifled a gasp and tightened her jaw. A glance at Oikeios Zeki told her Aspasia's words had no more substance than air. If Cetus marched in at the head of his army of monsters, they'd make a treaty faster than a hummingbird's wings beat twice. She clenched her fist and considered her reply.

Kelebek leaned forward. "As the Heir of Cinar stated, she has already fought many terrors and won. This is not the time to debate the matter. The princess has much to discuss with her cousin and will grant you an audience tomorrow. She will, of course, expect you to be prepared to ratify your existing treaty with the empire."

Irritation surged in Derya's veins, and she thought about rebuking him. Then she leaned back in her seat, allowing her ire to dissipate. Kelebek was right. She needed to learn what Nazif had to say about affairs in Nafplio. And she craved a hot bath and a long sleep. She'd be better able to wrangle with the fractious Nafplians in the morning. Not to mention Kelebek's tone emphasized she was of higher rank than all of them and shouldn't be trifled with.

The princess met Aspasia's eyes. "Thank you for the supper. Have you prepared rooms for us? The ones we occupied last time were quite comfortable and will do nicely. I'm sure you won't mind if my chiliarch posts ample guards."

Lady Aspasia pressed her lips together and nodded. "Of course. I understand. I'll see to it all."

"Kiral," Zeki began.

"Oikeios Zeki," she answered. "I believe that Oikeios Kelebek is correct. We should discuss this in the morning." *After I discover what Nazif's been up to in my absence. And figure out how to keep Cetus's poison from rotting all the fish in the Nafplian barrel.*

5

DERYA EYED NAZIF, who winked. "Will you join me in my chamber?"

Oh, Nazif. Do you never stop? "You want to talk now?" Her head was pounding. Bath, then sleep. Or maybe sleep first. *That's what I need.* "Wouldn't the library do?"

"Highness," Lady Aspasia said, "perhaps you could meet with Lord Nazif in the baths."

"Where?" Derya's eyebrows shot up, and she made no effort to hide her surprise.

Aspasia smiled. "The diodochi's private bath. It's a small pool divided by a movable screen and a tiny viewing window. The diodochis used it for their most confidential meetings. I can arrange for you to use it."

Nazif snickered. "One can only imagine what kind of confidential meetings." He raised a suggestive eyebrow at Derya.

She rolled her eyes. Zeki caught her gaze and nodded emphatically. Kelebek was also nodding. What did they think Nazif had to reveal that was so important? She let out a sigh. "Baths it is."

"We'll search them first," said Bahadir.

"Of course," Lady Aspasia said. "If you will follow me . . ."

Derya stood and pointed to the door with her chin. "Well, Nazif? Shall we?" Ever since she heard of the famous Nafplian baths, she longed to try them. Whether she ended up using them this evening remained to be seen.

To her amusement, Bahadir brought a full squad of ten guards to accompany her, four of them women. Lady Aspasia led the way down gray stone steps to a lower level of the palace. The air grew hot and steamy, warmed by the bubbling water from underground springs.

At the bottom, they emerged into a long cavern. Skylights had been chipped into the natural ceiling, allowing shafts of light from above. The cavern's far wall was a row of lead-lined windows, providing a view of the ocean and the scarlet and vermillion sky dominated by the setting sun.

A rectangular, tiled pool filled the middle of the cavern. Blue, turquoise, and sea-green tiles created a patterned mosaic at the bottom of the basin and the surrounding area. Brick-red stone pillars edged the pool and the cavern.

"The women's side is to the right," Aspasia said. "I'll make sure it's empty."

She slid her shoes off before stepping onto the tile. Bahadir followed suit, nodding to two of the guards to do the same. Aspasia led them into the shadows. A pair of Nazif's guards had accompanied them, and they headed for the corridor on the left.

While waiting, Derya admired the carved pictures on the walls, all depicting scenes of Nafplians at war. The gory events were a jarring contrast to the tranquil lapping of the water.

By the time Aspasia, Bahadir, and the guards returned, Safiye and Rasheda had joined them, the latter carrying a change of clothing for Derya.

"No one's there, Kiral," Bahadir said. "Six will stay at the entrance, and the others will go with you as far as the changing room."

Derya couldn't help but shiver at the memory of the assassin who tried to drown her in a bathtub during her last visit to Nafplio. *If anyone gets past Bahadir, I'll be ready.*

She followed Aspasia down a tiled corridor lit by flickering flames the woman said were candles spelled by light mages to burn without creating smoke. Aspasia led the way to a white-tiled room. Wafts of steam rose from several large wooden buckets.

"Wash here, then go through that arch"—Aspasia pointed with her chin—"to the bath. I left towels and made sure the screen that divides the women's half from the men's is shut. Don't worry, it can only be opened from this side."

Aspasia had barely left the room when Derya jerked her blood-spattered tunic off and dropped it on the floor. Within a few heartbeats, she stood under streams of warm water Rasheda poured over her head, rinsing the blood and sweat of the day's battles down the drain. Citrus-scented soaps cleaned the grime from her hair and body. The princess scrubbed her face, feeling she'd never lose the heat of the water fae's blood on her cheeks.

Safiye handed her a linen robe. "Do you want me to accompany you?" she asked.

"Stand at the door. Don't let Nazif see you but try to hear what we say." She dug in her discarded clothing and handed Safiye the bags that contained jewels from the dragon's hoard, the scepter, and its ruby finial. "Hold on to these." She unsheathed a dagger. "I'll keep this."

"Do you think you'll need it?"

"No. But I thought I was safe the first time I took a bath here." Derya's feet slapped against the tiles as she strode through the arch.

She gasped when she entered the next chamber. A tiled ceiling arched over a shimmering pool, which was roughly the size of a small bedroom. The water reflected the magically produced lights like a field of stars. Teal tiles turned the water the rich blue green of a tropical sea. Carved columns of red granite supported the ceiling. Other than a small walkway along the edges, the pool filled the entire area.

A fine metal lattice screen stood in the middle of the pool, obscuring the opposite side. Squinting in the dim light, she studied the screen. The metal strips forming the lattice were slimmer than her smallest finger, and the gaps in between were even narrower. She could see a few glimmers of light through the tiny openings, but not much more.

The lattice extended nearly to the ceiling, bisecting the chamber. No, Nazif wouldn't be able to walk around it.

A tiny rectangle that looked like a moveable shutter was placed low on one side of the screen. That must be the window Aspasia mentioned. "Nazif?"

No answer. Derya huffed, wondering what was keeping him. The Rider knew she hadn't hurried while she was washing. She wrinkled her nose thinking about getting into a bath with Nazif. Her pounding head put her in no mood to fend off his innuendoes. It was bad enough to deal with his idea of wit fully clothed. But naked, in a bath?

But she was here, and the rippling water beckoned, calling to her weary limbs. Derya pursed her lips. The water, the darkness, and the flickering shadows provided almost as much covering as clothing. And in the faint light, he'd barely see more of her than a shadowed outline. If he uttered more than three sentences without saying anything worth hearing, she'd leave.

Derya let the robe slide from her shoulders and dipped a toe into the water. Soothing heat caressed her foot, penetrating the lingering numbness. How many weeks had she endured frozen toes? Too many.

Tiny waves lapped against her skin as she descended the steps. Her knotted muscles relaxed. Oh, she could get used to this. If she lived here, she'd never leave this bath. No wonder the Nafplians were so proud of the hot springs that fed these baths and the marvel they created from them.

She moved through the waist-deep water and sat on an underwater ledge next to the screen. After a moment's consideration, she placed her dagger on the rim of the bath. She trailed her fingers down the screen and discovered it reached to the bottom of the pool. *Good. Nazif won't be able to take advantage of the situation.*

Derya slid down until the water nearly reached her chin and rested her head against the edge of the pool. This was bliss, sheer bliss. The heat and jasmine-scented water eased the tension in her head. Gentle dripping and gurgling accompanied the flow of the natural spring through the pool to the drain. Yes, the Nafplians had a brilliant idea, this secluded pool for lovers.

A tingling warmth fueled by heat that had nothing to do with the water she lay in spread through her. This would be romantic with the right person. *Will I ever have such joy? Or will I be forced into a marriage that's all political alliance?*

Muffled voices rumbled on the other side. Derya shoved aside her wayward thoughts. She closed her eyes and focused on the sounds. Yes, that was Nazif's smooth voice. He'd clearly brought his own guards.

Bare feet slapped the tile. Ripples lapped against Derya's skin as someone descended into the water on the other side. A dark silhouette approached the screen, making soft swells rise and fall.

Water splashed through the lattice. "Enjoying yourself?" Nazif asked.

Derya splashed him back. "I was."

He chuckled. "It's been a long time since we bathed together."

She snorted. "I was what, ten months old? Not that I remember anything of the incident." Derya glanced at her dagger, its closeness reassuring. She could never let herself forget how many Cinarrian emperors ascended to the throne by assassinating their predecessors. "What was so important that it couldn't wait?"

"Ever the impatient one."

"Ever the annoying one." She bit her lip. She needed Nazif as an ally. No sense antagonizing him.

The water sloshed, and she could see by Nazif's silhouette that he had settled back, his head resting on the tile rim of the bath.

"So, cousin, you succeeded. The Nafplians thought you'd certainly fail."

And what did you think? "If that's the case, why haven't they allied with Cetus yet?"

"With me here, they couldn't go back on their word, could they? They promised to wait seven weeks and a day but fully expected to ally with Cetus in the end. When you didn't return in six weeks, I imagine they hinted as such to his messengers, promising an alliance when the final day expired." He shifted, the water rippling gently against Derya's skin. "And word spread in the city that you were dead."

Derya tapped a finger against her lips. "Which explains their consternation that I succeeded." And the guard at the gate's reaction. She let out a long breath. "Nazif, I need to send a bird to my father so he knows I returned successfully."

"Your father." Nazif snorted. "About him."

Derya stiffened. "What? He hasn't named anyone else co-emperor has he?" *Like you?*

"Not that I know of. But his health is failing. Taking a young wife seems to be sapping his strength. Although now that she's with child, he might not be as attentive as before."

"What are you saying?" Ice filled Derya's heart. While she'd never been close to her father, she'd adored him from afar, desperate for his approval. If he died without naming her co-emperor, she'd go to her grave wondering if she'd been a disappointment to him, that he regretted that his oldest surviving child was an incompetent girl. She wrapped her arms around herself.

Nazif's voice tightened. "He's dying. And our other cousins, well, you can imagine."

His words cut through her like a winter wind whipping through the mountains. Her father couldn't be dying. Her vigorous, wise father approaching the end? She longed to see him, to hear him say for once he knew—rather than hoped—she was worthy to rule Cinar. She swallowed hard, and the tension the warm water had soothed away returned at a gallop. *Our cousins.* "Swarming around the throne?"

"All of them constantly making their case that they should be co-emperor. Not the girl gallivanting all over the continent creating diplomatic incidents."

"Or the libertine who believes every woman is his possession by right?"

Nazif laughed. "Oh, you heard that one, did you? It's one of the more flattering things they whisper about me to the emperor."

But the gossip is true about you. It's not about me. "Seriously, Nazif, what should we do? I can send a bird to my father, and also to one of my old tutors, to make sure my message gets through. But that's not enough to counter the words of those close at hand."

"No, it's not." Nazif sighed. "I send daily birds. But from the emperor's responses, I suspect many were intercepted. Maybe one of us should go back."

His idea had merit. "Well, he gave us two tasks. Find the scepter, and solidify the Nafplian alliance. I succeeded in mine, so I should be the one to go home."

"No, you can't. You told the Nafplians you can defeat monsters. They won't agree to anything if you plan on heading east, away from Cetus and his invasion."

She let out an exasperated huff. She was far too tired to

play games with Nazif. "I suppose that means you should return."

"Of course."

"And you'd have me believe that you'll rush to my father's side and fill his ears with tales of my exploits in retrieving the scepter and slaying Cetus's monsters, and that I should be named co-emperor."

"Of course." His low chuckle echoed over the dripping water.

"What kind of fool do you take me for?"

He snorted. "A naïve one if you think I'd give up the crown of Cinar that easily."

She glared at him through the screen, clenching her fists until her knuckles ached. "You're as vile as Cetus himself."

"Cousin!" After a pause, he continued in an icy tone. "That is a little extreme."

Her anger shoved down the thought that perhaps she'd gone too far. Scores of power-hungry nobles longed to wear the crown of Cinar and would do anything to seize it. Many weren't even related to the royal family. Nazif, at least, followed her in the line of succession, if two other cousins were overlooked. She should never forget he was as ambitious as she was.

She rubbed her forearms and crossed her arms tightly over her chest. Every time the Heir of Cinar failed to become emperor, their life got cut short, their end nasty. And their closest associates followed them into the grave. If Nazif prevailed, would he put her to death?

Derya shook herself, letting the water splash against the screen. She needed him as an ally, now and if—no, when— she inherited the crown. Pride surged in her veins. He thought her lesser since she was a girl. That he would be the better ruler. He needed to be taught a lesson.

She took a few deep breaths of the steamy air, striving to calm her racing heart. She'd figure out how to keep him on her side later. All she required was his help with the Nafplians. But how to secure it without appearing weak?

If he chose now to openly challenge her for the throne, she'd most likely lose. Many men of the court had favored Nazif for years. She dunked shaking hands under the water and twisted her fingers together. Browbeating him wasn't the answer. A move to push him off balance was.

"Cousin. Nazif." She spoke softly. "You are right. My words were thoughtless and cruel, spoken in anger, which, in my fatigue, I failed to contain. I was wrong. Please forgive me."

Nazif started, sending more ripples her way. His silhouette shifted as he straightened and turned toward her, shaking his head.

Derya pressed her lips together and bowed her head, glad he couldn't see the amusement in her eyes. She'd spoken sincerely. But she was sure he'd never expected a humble apology from her.

The magical light in one of the sconces sputtered. Long minutes filled with gently lapping waves and gurgling water passed before Nazif spoke. "Cousin, I apologize as well. In retrieving the scepter, you served the good of the empire. I should do the same."

Derya tipped her head. "At least until Cetus is defeated?"

"Precisely. In the meantime, I'll support your claim in the interest of stability in the succession. If we don't work together, there won't be an empire to inherit. Once we conclude the mission here, both of us can return to Tulgutalp and chase away the interlopers, leaving your father a much simpler choice regarding his heir."

The choice should be simple already. She was the Heir of Cinar. But that, it seemed, was only a pebble blocking the way of Nazif's ambitions. "And my father's new wife?"

"Five and a half months along. But sickly." His voice took on a hopeful tone with his last words.

The new child, if a boy, would assume her place as Heir of Cinar and push all the other contenders down a notch. Nazif might be ruthless enough to hope for the death of an infant, but she wasn't that heartless. *Rider let it be a girl.*

In any case, Nazif's eyes were fixed on the throne, and he wasn't attempting to hide it. "Well, now we understand each other."

"There's one more thing you need to know." His tone was somber, very unlike him.

"What?"

"My spies tell me our scheming cousins are trying to convince your father that whoever inherits must prove himself worthy."

"But I did that. I retrieved the scepter."

"I know. But I've heard our cousins have poisoned your father against us and persuaded him to devise a new mission to get us out of the way."

Derya's heart shrank, and her ribs felt as though they would trap the breath in her lungs. *I did what he wanted. Wasn't that enough?* She clamped her jaw shut to keep from saying the words aloud. *No whining in front of Nazif.* Her chin trembled. *Maybe my critics are right. I'm not good enough. I'll never be good enough.*

"It's not fair," Nazif said.

"No." She spat the word out, oddly touched by his sympathy. The princess blinked a tear away and squared her shoulders. *I am the Heir of Cinar. I will not be shaken.* "What is this new mission?"

"My spies didn't know. Does it matter?" He snorted. "If you and I go off on a dangerous quest and perish in the attempt, well, that just makes things easier for Yildiz and the rest."

The princess shuddered. Yildiz. That ruthless cousin wouldn't hesitate to lop her head off if he ever became emperor.

Derya narrowed her eyes. Was Nazif telling the truth? Perhaps Zeki and Kelebek heard the same rumors, which was why they thought a conference with Nazif was so urgent.

If she didn't return to Cinar soon, someone could worm their way into her father's good graces. But if she failed at the quests her father assigned her, she'd be out of favor faster than a rotting fish.

"As I see it," she said slowly, "we must conclude the missions my father entrusted to us. I'll notify him I have the scepter. Then we secure the Nafplian alliance."

"A few tales of your dragon fight might help."

She nodded. "True."

"But your father expects us to conclude a treaty with the new diodochi. He won't welcome us back until we do. And until the Nafplians know who killed the royal family, they won't name one."

"Have you any idea who did it?"

He sighed. "No."

"Then we need to find the guilty party. As if our lives depend on it." *Which might be the truth.*

6

DERYA SLID THE SCREEN'S tiny window open. She pressed her face against the small opening and studied Nazif's face, his strong cheekbones and regal, straight nose sharply defined despite the dim light. The perfect visage of a ruler. His ebullient confidence drew admirers like desert wanderers seeking water. But was he more capable than she? "Surely in all the time I've been gone you've learned something."

He winced and held up his hands. "These are the cagiest people. You ask them one question, and they throw four at you. It was all I could do to figure out which question was most important to them and least dangerous to me." He dropped his hands into the water with a splash.

Which was exactly how Derya felt about conversations with him. She flicked a few drops of water from her face. "You learned nothing? What about the men who attacked me on the stairs?"

"Oh." Nazif paused. "I tracked them down. They'd abandoned their property here in the capital, sold their estate, and fled to a mountain stronghold with their families and a herd of goats. It took all my charm to get them to even talk to me.

They claimed they had only wanted to tell you who they suspected and meant you no harm. That one of them died was a pure accident."

"Who did they suspect?"

"They refused to say, steadfastly insisting they must have been mistaken."

Derya frowned. "Do you believe them?"

"No. Someone terrified them. Or they feared they'd end up like the royal family if they spoke out."

Derya blew out a long breath. "Did any of your other questioning lead anywhere?"

"Not that way."

"Oh, so you discovered something interesting another way."

He brought his face close to the window and peered into Derya's eyes. "I did."

His smirk made Derya suspicious. "I suppose I don't want to know just how you learned this?"

"I employed a method I'm sure you wouldn't approve of."

"How many maids did you seduce?"

He pulled back from the opening, an expression of mock horror on his face. "Cousin, I'm hurt. Surely you don't suspect me of such sordid behavior."

She snorted. "When every maid I had either avoided you or sought you out? It's been many years since I understood why."

He gave her a rueful smile. "You know me too well. It was only two maids, both widows. They were willing and knowledgeable participants."

Derya scoffed. "I'd love to ask them to verify that." She curled her lip. "And inquire of your wife what she thinks of your activities."

"I'm not sure I care. Is it so wrong to seek a little joy in life to compensate for the political marriage forced on me, wedded to a woman who despises me? After the birth of our third son, she told me she'd done her duty, and I was to stay out of her bedroom."

Derya stared in his direction. That was the most vulnerable thing he'd ever shared with her. And there was no mistaking the bitterness bleeding through his tone. While she couldn't excuse his behavior, she felt a tug of sympathy. "Nazif, I—"

"Do you want to know what I learned?"

Derya blinked, startled but relieved by his abrupt change of subject. She clicked a fingernail against the metal lattice that separated them. "Out with it, then. What did they tell you?"

"Nothing. It's what one of them sold me that's so intriguing."

"Are you going to tell me, or listen to yourself congratulate yourself all night?"

"Patience, young Derya." He paused. "Hm. Maybe you are too young to be named co-emperor."

His words stung, and she restrained a curse. "I'm eighteen. Have you forgotten Empress Aynur, who took the throne at fourteen and fought off Tarhuntassian invaders?"

He chuckled, and she frowned. She knew better than to let him needle her.

Nazif tapped the lattice. "Can't you guess?"

"I'm going to bed." She put her hand up to close the window.

Nazif sighed. "You used to love to play games. You're getting crabby in your old age."

"You'd be crabby too if you hadn't slept in a real bed for two months and your fool of a cousin was delaying your rest."

He snickered. "Letters. Seven, to be exact. Tied up with a pink ribbon."

"You've read them?"

"Not exactly. They were written in Old Nafplian. I told Oikeios Zeki some story about finding them in the back of the wardrobe in my room, and he obligingly translated them. He said it was the most stimulating work he'd done in a while."

He sucked in a breath. "As I recall, one of them starts like this . . ." He recited a handful of words.

"Stop." Just that fragment of a sentence was enough to make her blush.

Nazif's laughter echoed through the cavern. "Quite bawdy, and very descriptive. All of them. Unfortunately, all unsigned."

"Who did the maid steal them from?"

"Lady Nuura."

"Nuura?" Derya scoffed. "Yiannis's wife, who creeps about, looking like a scared rabbit, afraid of every shadow that moves? You can't imagine someone wrote erotic love letters to her."

"Actually, I do." He snickered. "After some nauseating declarations of undying adoration and the multiple ways he'd prove it to her, he expressed a wish that the recipient's husband would be conveniently removed."

Derya jerked her head up. "Removed? Perhaps they were written to the diodochi's wife, or one of his son's wives."

Nazif scoffed. "They're dead, remember? Later, the writer says since he's far down in the line of succession, he could only take power by some catastrophe, natural or otherwise."

"He could be one of the diodochi's younger sons. But all of them were married, except Istvan." When she uttered the name, a shiver ran through her. *Istvan.* She'd never trusted him.

Derya let out a long breath. She scooped up a handful of water and let it trickle through her fingers. "Anything else?"

"Another letter encouraged the recipient to do what she needed to do so they both could be happy. Then he—the writer—would inherit his rightful birthright, usurped by the Kastellanos family." Nazif shook his head. "It doesn't make sense. The Nafplians weren't in the line of succession for the throne of Ymittos. Or were they?"

They were. Kelebek once mentioned that after Eliana and another relative, the old diodochi of Nafplio was fourth—or was it fifth—in line. She nearly told her cousin but decided to keep that tidbit to herself. Those who held the most information wielded the most power.

"The final one was short and scribbled, as if the writer was in a hurry. All it said was 'Thank you for giving me my heart's desire.'"

Derya's heart lurched. "Nazif," she said slowly, "what do you make of all this?"

He put his face closer to the screen, speaking so low she could barely hear him over the trickling water. "That Nuura conspired with someone to kill the royal family to give her lover his heart's desire, namely the throne of Nafplio. She must be the one who slaughtered them in their sleep."

"Or hired the assassin."

He nodded. "True. But given how the murders were committed, I think Nuura herself did them."

"Would she be that cold? She's always been rather kind to me."

Nazif shrugged. "She never warmed up to me."

Derya shook her head, a smile tugging the corners of her mouth. "She just might not have been interested. Can you compete with the promises her lover made?"

"I'd like to think so, but let's stick to the point. If we agree Nuura is the murderer, then who is her accomplice?"

Derya's dry tongue made it difficult to pronounce the word. "Istvan."

"Who? The one promised to the heir of Ymittos?"

"Yes."

"Zeki said the writer was arrogant. Every sentence, even the erotic ones, was all about him."

Derya snorted. "That sounds like Istvan. He was his favorite topic."

"He was dallying with a married woman while betrothed to Eliana?"

"So it seems." A memory flickered through her mind. The night they'd all reached the rift. The next day, Eliana and Istvan were to descend into Malkh to find the cursed prince. Rasheda told her Istvan received a message from Nafplio that made him grin. A message that said, "They're all gone." She counted back in time. That had been eight days after Eliana's birthday.

"Nazif, what day was the royal family killed?"

"The eleventh of Ocakis."

Raging waters. Ice crept down her spine, ice that chilled her despite the heated water she lay in. Now she knew her suspicions of Istvan were justified, but she felt little triumph. *Oh, Eliana. What did he do to you after you went to Malkh? I'd kill him if he wasn't already dead.*

She leaned closer to the screen. "You're certain Nuura was the object of Istvan's passion?"

He nodded. "Word is she's been inconsolable for the past few weeks. Most people put it down to her sorrow over the royal family. But I suspect her grief is more the agony over a lost love."

Derya peered through the window and gave him an appraising look. "That's very insightful of you. I didn't know you had it in you."

"Why do you think women flock to me?"

"Oh, stop." She nibbled her lip. "What do we do now?"

"Prove it, of course."

She sighed. "We can hardly accuse the wife of one of the ruling council members not only of adultery but of murder and treason. The problem is proving Nuura was complicit. The letters aren't addressed to her. She could always claim she found them and didn't know what they were."

"The maid I bought the letters from was new. The three maids who served Nuura before quit and moved away."

"That's a little too convenient, don't you think? Are we sure they're alive? If Nuura could wipe out the entire royal family, babies and all, what difference would three maids make?"

"But if all her maids died, that would draw attention to her."

"True. What about her husband? Does Yiannis know any of this?"

Nazif sucked in a breath, then released it. "I doubt it. He doesn't seem like the type who would be too happy with his wife dallying with a younger man. He's the kind who's content with his estate and his family."

"Too bad for him his wife didn't share his views."

"Right. What objections are there to our theory?" He scooped up water and splashed it over his face. "Why did Istvan believe he deserved Ymittos?"

Derya paused. *I have to tell him.* "Oikeios Kelebek told me the king of Ymittos's grandfather's sister—or was it cousin— married a Nafplian. Her son's daughter married the diodochi who was murdered. So the diodochi's sons were in the succession, just far down in the line."

"I'm not sure I followed that, but if I understood you, the diodochi's sons could feel that they had a claim to Ymittos's throne."

"Yes. But the difficulty is that Ymittosians allowed women to inherit, as in the case of Princess Eliana being the undisputed heir. Nafplians don't count women in the succession, meaning in their minds, the old diodochi was second in line, after the king's nephew Ormolai."

Nazif stared at her. "So if one of the diodochi's sons married the princess of Ymittos and then assumed control of the throne, he might believe he was justified?"

When she didn't answer, Nazif said slowly, "You think Dochan Istvan had designs on Princess Eliana's throne?"

"Yes." A sour taste filled her mouth. Maybe it was better Eliana died in the cataclysm rather than suffer a lifetime in Istvan's hands.

Nazif fell silent, and the chamber was quiet except for ripples lapping against the sides of the pool. He slapped a hand against the water. "Istvan had plans to rule both Ymittos and Nafplio."

Derya nodded. She recounted the message Istvan received at the rift. "It arrived one day after the royal family was killed."

Nazif turned his face to her. "The final letter states, 'It brought great joy to my heart to know you kept your word. After I descend, I'll do my part.' I never understood the bit about descending, but now I do."

"That sounds like he's answering the message about 'they're all gone.'" She gulped, her stomach clenching, wondering what Istvan had planned for Eliana.

"I agree," said Nazif. "However, he promised whoever he was writing to that she would reign with him. What did he intend to do with Princess Eliana?"

Derya clamped her mouth shut and swallowed the bile that had surged up her throat.

Nazif shrugged. "The smart move would have been to keep Eliana until she bore a son. He'd put this woman off on that pretext. If Eliana allowed him to rule as king, he'd probably keep her to placate the Ymittosians and do away with the one here. If Eliana proved to be a problem, he'd end her like he did his parents."

"That's horrible," Derya said.

"But the logical conclusion," Nazif answered. "The recipient of these letters most likely was the assassin, or the one who paid whoever did the actual killing."

"Care to guess who that might be?"

"In one letter he says, 'I knew you would do anything for me.' And later pens a few lyrical passages about how secrets held close are the safest. I think she did the deed herself or did away with the assassin."

"Then we need to find out if anyone either died or left shortly after," Derya said.

Nazif shook his head. "I made inquiries about that. No one died, but several servants quit, saying they were afraid to stay."

"Understandable," said Derya. "Who wouldn't be after such an event?"

"This doesn't help us much," Nazif said.

Derya let out a long sigh. "No." She waved a hand back and forth in the water, letting the ripples push outward. "We need samples of Istvan's writing. That will prove he's involved."

"And Nuura?"

She rubbed her pounding head. "Let's sleep on it." The exertion of the day, combined with the water's relaxing heat, was making her thought processes sluggish and dull.

If we don't find the murderer, then we will fail to secure the alliance. And I'll end up dead. Whether by a Nafplian assassin, Cetus, or a rival for the throne, it didn't matter. Her own failures would have killed her.

7

Seventy-nine days after the winter solstice 29th year of Emperor Vural Tzimiskes

DERYA FROWNED thoughtfully at the tiny green sprouts thrusting through the dirt toward the sunlight. The new growth signaled that spring was finally trying to arrive in Nafplio. Were these cooking herbs? Flowers? Or potential poisons? In this bloody realm, they could be any or all. Every time she thought she was making progress with the Nafplians, a fresh trouble surfaced. Like last night . . .

"What is it you wanted to discuss?" Kelebek asked.

She spun to face him, startled out of her musings by his question. His impatient tone suggested he'd spoken more than once.

He stood a few feet away at the corner of a path in the palace's kitchen garden. He'd resumed the robes of a Cinarrian diplomat, long and flowing with a ruby-encrusted hem and a high turban, most likely borrowed from Oikeios Zeki. This was more like the Kelebek she tormented when she was a child, the man who'd despised her. Not the aide she'd come to value for his knowledge and wisdom.

She smiled through the flash of childish fear that spread through her. "Thank you for coming so promptly. Now if my cousin was as courteous . . ." She rubbed her chilled hands together. Last night, she felt certain of their conclusions. Would Kelebek agree?

Crunching gravel heralded Nazif's approach, tailed by no less than ten guards. He left them with Derya's eight, who had positioned themselves on the six approaches to the center of the garden, where she and Kelebek waited.

Derya didn't waste time on pleasantries. She filled Kelebek in on the conversation she and Nazif had the night before. "Are we correct about Istvan? That with his father and brothers dead, he'd be third in line for Ymittos's throne?"

Kelebek nodded. "Yes, by the Nafplian reckoning. His marriage to Princess Eliana would have solidified his position, effectively nullifying any claims the princess's cousin Ormolai entertained."

Derya's heart sped up. *We're getting close.* "This morning Safiye got samples of Istvan's writing and is fairly sure he wrote the letters."

"All we need to do is pin the actual crimes on Nuura," Nazif said.

"But how?" Derya asked. "Try to trace the servants who left?"

"I'm not entirely certain that will be necessary." Kelebek paused so long that Derya thought he wasn't going to continue.

"Why not?" Nazif asked.

Kelebek gave him a condescending stare. "Years ago, the ambassador—the one before Oikeios Zeki—sent strange tidings to the emperor. A cousin of the diodochi's wife had a daughter who enjoyed dismembering small animals. While they were still alive. When the girl was thirteen, she attacked her younger brother, nearly slashing off his thumb."

Prickles rose up Derya's spine and she shuddered. Nuura

was more capable of murder than she'd suspected. "Let me guess. She married Yiannis." When Kelebek murmured his confirmation, she continued. "But if she had such a grisly reputation, why would he wed her?"

"After her brother died, Nuura inherited an enormous fortune. Between that and her connection to the royal family, she was considered a brilliant match for an obscure nobleman. Yiannis most likely thought that since he was much older than her, he could control her."

Nazif snorted. "We've seen just how wrong he was."

"More than you know. Oikeios Zeki mentioned to me that under the facade of marital harmony, Yiannis seems terrified of his wife." Kelebek pressed his lips together. "I believe the small girl who enjoyed ripping the legs off squirrels is now a woman quite capable of murder."

Derya let out a long breath. She hadn't wanted Lady Aspasia to be the guilty party. But Nuura? "Are you sure? She looks so mousy, so much like a scared rabbit."

"Rabbits have sharp teeth," Kelebek said. "She wouldn't be the only person to hide her true nature behind an act."

He spoke blandly, but Derya thought she detected a barb against her under his tone.

"Too true," Nazif said. "But how to prove it? The letters attest to an affair, and possibly a conspiracy, but no more."

"Accusing her without proof would convince the Nafplians that Cinar is not their friend," Kelebek said.

Derya studied his face. He was right. They couldn't afford any missteps. But time was running out. She twisted her hands together. "I don't think they'll wait much longer," she said.

"Kiral, you have insufficient evidence." Kelebek crossed his arms, a frown of disapproval creasing his sharp features.

"We'll just have to get her to confess." Derya jerked her head up with a smug smile. "And I know just how to do it."

DERYA SURVEYED the plates heaped with Cinarrian pastries, her mouth watering. The noon sun glinted on the silver tea service that stood on a cornflower-blue tablecloth.

Nazif, she had to admit, had a stroke of brilliance when he suggested convening in the old diodocheen's solar, a room halfway up one of the castle's larger turrets. Its smaller size made it the perfect place to hold a cozy chat, which was what Derya wanted the Nafplians to believe was the sole intent behind her invitation.

And Safiye had outdone herself, spending the morning helping the cooks prepare a traditional winter Cinarrian noon meal, with stew and bread and mounds of pastries. The stuffed grape leaves and salads of the summer would have been welcome additions. But fresh vegetables were merely last summer's memory, and it would be months before she tasted them again. If she lived that long.

Derya shoved away her gloomy thoughts and fixed a bright smile on her face. "Please, help yourselves."

The four Nafplians gazed warily at the platter of honey-drenched pastry.

With an effort, the princess prevented a frown from destroying her smile. *They ate the stew and bread with no hesitation. Surely they don't think I'm going to poison them now.*

Nazif laughed. "This is a Cinarrian delicacy. You'll love it." He picked up a sticky triangular pastry and bit into it. He closed his eyes and moaned. "There are few pleasures that rival it."

Derya repressed an annoyed glare. He just wouldn't stop with his innuendo. But perhaps it would be helpful. Now if the others would play their parts. Kelebek and Safiye, she knew, could be counted on. Oikeios Zeki and Bahadir, probably. Nazif, as unpredictable as an earthquake, was the wild card.

The eleven of them were seated around an oval, wooden table. Following Kelebek's advice, they'd seated Lady Nuura and her husband where the sun would illuminate their faces, while Derya and Nazif were seated opposite, their faces obscured in the shadows.

Lady Aspasia sipped her tea before setting the mug down precisely on the table. "We know why you invited us here."

"And it wasn't to get our fingers sticky," Lord Calix said.

For an instant, Derya froze, thinking they knew the real reason for the meeting. Then she remembered. "Yes. Have you further thoughts on your position?"

Aspasia and Yiannis exchanged glances. Calix examined the pastry in his hand. He set it on the plate in front of him. "We have," he said. "But came to no conclusion."

"I remind you," Kelebek said, "retrieving the scepter was your condition. The Heir of Cinar fulfilled her obligation."

"At great danger to herself and our entire troop," Bahadir said. "She killed a dragon and more than one wyvern in the process."

Derya pressed her lips together. She wanted to brandish Hrathung, the enchanted sword given to her by magical swans she'd rescued from Cetus's trap. But her advisors were adamant that she keep it secret if she could. The fewer who knew of it, the less likely word would trickle back to Cetus. Better to let him think others posed a greater threat. "Yes. My water magic defeated the dragon."

"What did you do, drown it?" Yiannis crossed his arms and shot a scornful glare at Derya.

The princess lifted her chin. "I froze the fluid in its eyes and pulled them from the sockets. The king of Rorvik stabbed it in the head, and I quenched its fire." *Not exactly how it happened, but close enough.*

Lady Aspasia had gone pale, the dark blue of her gown making her face look even more ghostly. Zeki, Yiannis, and Calix stared at Derya as if they'd never seen her before. Lady Nuura licked her lips, and her face was unreadable. Was that anger? Fear? Or . . . envy?

Derya gave them a smile as if she'd just recounted the plot of a children's book. "More tea, Lady Nuura?" She refilled the woman's mug and settled back in her seat. "Think on it, will you?" *Consider what a powerful mage I am.*

"Kiral, that reminds me," Safiye said. "There are strange tidings from Ethkarpia."

"Oh?" Derya made her eyes wide, as if eager for the story she'd heard the night before.

"Yes. It appears the king of Tavros wants his younger son to marry the queen."

Derya was saved from having to make a suitable response by Lord Calix spitting out his tea. "What? She's well past the age of bearing children. What could he possibly gain?"

"A political alliance, perhaps?" Zeki said.

"That would be my thought," Kelebek said. "Those kinds of intrigues go on everywhere." He launched into a recitation of the maneuvering of several of Cinar's minor nobles and generals, elaborating on the complicated web of genealogies and feuds.

Derya waited until Calix began fidgeting and Nuura's face took on a strained look. Derya noted the hardness in Nuura's beady eyes. She'd never noticed it before, barely looking past the mousy hair and rabbity mouth. "It gets so confusing," Derya said. "All these people taking lovers for reasons other than love and respect. Or even just passion. Power seems to be a greater motivation."

Nuura crumbled the pastry in her fingers, letting the broken pieces scatter onto her plate. She folded her sticky hands on her lap and stared at the table.

Derya took a bite of pastry and chewed reflectively while Kelebek told of another court scandal, of a pair of lovers who killed their king. The princess watched Lady Nuura. The woman's breath came in quick jerks, and her eyes darted from her plate to the door to the stairs. She was getting tense, like a tightly coiled spring. But would she break when confronted?

If our conclusions are wrong, we will have alienated the Nafplians forever.

With her head bowed, Nuura looked even more like a timid rabbit, someone who couldn't bear to tread on a cockroach. What if the rumors Kelebek heard were false? *We should have confirmed them first.*

Nazif touched Derya's arm. "More tea?" When she nodded, he flicked his eyes at Nuura and nodded.

I'll just have to spring it on her. After all, shocking people is what I'm good at.

Derya smiled. "Please." She waited for her cousin to finish pouring, then looked around the room brightly. "Did you hear the story about Lady Jorawar from a few centuries ago? She married a minor noble. Somehow, she attracted the attention of one of the princes. She used him to kill her husband, and the Heir of Cinar, along with a few others who stood in the way. Meanwhile, she'd seduced the king's nephew, and married him when he took the throne. Some people will do anything—or trample anyone—for power." She paused, her heart pounding. "Isn't that right, Lady Nuura?"

8

"WHAT?" THE COLOR FLED from Nuura's cheeks, her brown eyes twitching from side to side. "Oh, yes, I've heard such tales. Horrible people to do such things. Horrible."

"And to think you harbored such a schemer here," Derya went on. "I'm amazed no one has uncovered the culprit."

Nazif made a rueful face. "I did my best. The only certainty is the guilty party is close to Nafplio's ruling power." He said the words gently, as if to soften the blow he delivered by speaking the shameful truth out loud.

As he spoke, Derya studied the Nafplians. Aspasia looked resigned, Calix speculative, and Yiannis angry. Nuura shrank into her chair and hunched her shoulders. Was she truly frightened? Or was that part of her deception? Perhaps a veiled insult would rattle the woman enough to crack her facade.

Derya let out a long sigh. "I'm sure this has been difficult for you. Danger from within. Threats from outside. Whoever did this is clever and full of guile. That narrows the field a little. After consideration, we decided that Lady Nuura, for example, doesn't fit that description."

Nuura jerked and her lips tightened. "That's right. I'm just a simple woman."

Derya wasn't certain but thought she detected a hint of scorn in Nuura's tone.

Yiannis scowled and jumped to his feet. His chair toppled over, crashing with a dull thump on the blood-red carpet. "Why would you even suspect her?" He raised his voice to a shout as he waved an accusing finger at Derya. "This is an outrage!"

Lady Aspasia stretched a hand to him. "Please, Yiannis. Sit down."

Calix leaned back in his seat and spoke to the ceiling. "By all means, sit. No need to get excited. We could be murdered in our beds. Or enslaved by a crazed sorcerer. Nothing to worry about."

Derya forced her curling lips to still. Maybe someday, if they all survived, she and Calix could be friends. The Rider knew she needed someone she could laugh with.

Calix picked up Yiannis's fallen chair and gestured toward it with a mocking bow. Yiannis thumped into his seat and crossed his arms. "It's absurd," he said. "We weren't even in the castle when the murders were committed."

Derya's heart skipped a beat, and her breath hitched. *No. That couldn't be true.*

Lady Aspasia nodded thoughtfully. "As soon as we discovered the murders, we sent birds to all the prominent nobles. Only Yiannis and Nuura came, arriving two days later. Everyone else was too afraid to come."

Derya tightened her jaw. Raging waters, how could she have not known that? A dim memory of Aspasia—or was it Calix?—telling her this months ago flittered through her mind. Her stomach sank, pulling her spirits with it.

But Kelebek—had he known? He sat, his face still as granite. Surely he hadn't withheld this from her. Had the all-knowing Kelebek forgotten something? *This is a fine time for him to prove he's fallible like the rest of us.*

Derya glanced at Bahadir. The scars in his cheek jerked, a clear sign he was troubled.

The princess narrowed her eyes. Nazif. He must have known. Her cousin was staring at something in the distance, avoiding Derya's gaze.

"This is insulting," Yiannis said. "And ridiculous. We asked for your help. But expected much more from Cinar. All you've done is waste time deliberating over the one clearly innocent person."

Calix snorted. "I wouldn't have been surprised if you tried to pin the crime on me. Or even my cousin. But Nuura?"

Disappointment soured Aspasia's tone. "If this is the best Cinar can do, perhaps a different alliance . . ."

Maybe we were mistaken. We should have checked Nuura's movements more carefully. I didn't want to suspect Aspasia. I could have misinterpreted Calix's signs of grief and allowed myself to be fooled. Never, never will I allow a man's charms to deceive me.

As she sat, stunned into silence, Derya's dreams of writing a triumphant letter to her father detailing how she'd solved the murders and secured the alliance all crumbled like a house whose faulty foundation cracked. She dug in the rubble of her thoughts, seeking anything to salvage.

A flicker of doubt in Calix's eyes made her pause. Maybe she wasn't wrong. Then she spotted the gleam of triumph in Nuura's.

She is guilty. How to get her to admit it?

"Perhaps the Kiral didn't mean——" began Safiye.

Derya waved for her to be silent. "I apologize if I went about this badly. I should share with you some new information. We've uncovered what we believe is a clue to the identity of the culprits." She leaned toward Aspasia, who she thought was the least angry of the Nafplians. "It may help you understand why we started thinking about Lady Nuura, whom none of us, I am sure, suppose is capable of concocting such a complex scheme. Maybe you'll come to a different interpretation." *Let's hope they don't.*

Calix rubbed his chin. A vein pulsed in Yiannis's temple, and he muttered a curse.

At least they're willing to listen. Derya gestured to Nazif. "My cousin found some interesting letters."

Nazif smirked. "Interesting? Is that what you call them?" He pulled out the packet of letters. "I'll just read the relevant parts."

"Who wrote them?" Calix asked.

"You tell me." Nazif untied the pink ribbon, chose a letter, and pushed it toward Calix. "Do you recognize the writing?"

Calix frowned. "It's a strong, masculine hand. Could be anyone."

"What about this?" Derya handed him the sample Safiye had obtained.

"No. But it is the same hand."

Nazif dipped his head, indicating the papers Calix held. "The second was written by Dochan Istvan."

Nuura blinked but otherwise kept her face as still as the stones in the tower's walls. She bowed her head and picked at the gold embroidery on her scarlet dress.

Lady Aspasia took the letters from Calix. "It pains me to admit it, but this is the dochan's handwriting."

Yiannis jerked back. "Are you mad? He was nowhere around when the murders occurred."

"That's true," Derya said. "But the letters suggest he had an accomplice. Let my cousin read."

Nazif, surprisingly, covered only the key points, skipping the lascivious parts. When he finished, stunned silence settled on the room like dust after an avalanche, the stillness broken only by wind rattling the windowpane.

Calix was the first to speak. "I knew Istvan was ambitious, but . . ."

"But he was so charming," Aspasia said. "I can't believe he plotted to kill his family. I won't."

Derya and the other Cinarrians remained silent as the Nafplians argued, debated, and eventually, Aspasia and Calix agreed. Istvan had schemed to rule Nafplio and Ymittos.

Aspasia slumped, disbelief and disillusionment etched into the lines in her face. "Hearing this, my ears have dropped with sadness."

"I am sorry to bring such news to you," Derya said. "The next question, I'm afraid, is who he was working with."

"That's despicable," Yiannis said. "First you accuse my wife, then you implicate our dochan. You Cinarrians might be used to family members killing each other, but we're not."

Kelebek pushed the plate of pastries toward Yiannis. "Identifying the true culprit requires grasping the thorns as well as the roses."

Aspasia drummed her fingers on the table. "I heard rumors he had a lover but never a whisper of a name."

Calix looked up from the letter he was perusing. "Who was the object of his passion?"

Nazif answered. "A woman—"

"How do you know that?" Nuura asked.

"Because of the line where he wishes the recipient's husband would die."

Aspasia narrowed her eyes, flicking them toward Nuura. *She's catching on.*

"And," continued Nazif, "he employs some rather bawdy language to describe what he'd like to do with her—"

"We don't need to hear that," Derya said.

"But what woman of the court would behave so wantonly?" Yiannis asked. "Certainly not my wife."

"Oh, no," Nazif said. "I hardly think Lady Nuura would be the type to attract the dochan's attention."

Nuura compressed her lips, and she crossed her arms, a hard expression in her eyes.

"Perhaps," Derya said, "we need to read some more." She rested her shaking hands in her lap.

Nazif continued. "He talks of how their falcons had flown together, working as one to bring down their prey. Do we know any women here who love falconry?"

Nuura's olive skin flushed.

"Many women love the hunt," Yiannis said.

Nazif grinned. "And there's the unforgettable line about a claw-shaped birthmark like a finger beckoning—"

Yiannis whirled in his seat, his face darkening and his teeth bared. He raised a hand, his fist clenched as he glared at his wife. "You—"

Aspasia gasped. "Is it true?"

Nuura sneered. "That Istvan and I were lovers?" She laughed. "Of course we were." She leaned forward and grinned, exposing her sharp, white teeth. "Fooled all of you. Mousy, dumpy Nuura. I knew what you thought of me. You never imagined I could inspire passion from a man like Istvan. Everyone wanted Istvan." She sat straight in her chair and lifted her head proudly. "But he chose me."

Yiannis slumped, a look of defeat on his face. "How could you?"

"How could I?" Nuura curled her lip. "Wed to a shriveled fossil like you, of course I'd desire someone with a little more vigor." The scorn in her tone intensified as she spoke. Nostrils flaring, she glared at her husband, whose face had turned from crimson to purple. "Once I'd borne you two children, I decided I was free to find satisfaction wherever I pleased. The dochan was delighted to oblige. And offered me a more enticing life than dull obscurity in the country."

"This only proves her infidelity," said Lady Aspasia. "As troubling as that is, it doesn't prove the murders."

Calix shook his head. "But the bit about removing obstacles . . ."

"Whoever killed the diodochi did us all a favor," Nuura

said. "The dochan was the best of them. He would have led us to greatness."

Derya scrutinized Nuura with narrowed eyes. "Why do you say that?"

"He was the brightest of the sons."

"But, Nuura," Aspasia said, "his brothers were no fools. Any of them would have been competent."

Nuura muttered a curse. "Competent? Is that all you expect from your diodochi?"

"What else is there?" Calix asked.

"Strength. Cunning. Courage. All of which Istvan had in greater measure than his brothers."

"But our laws . . ." Aspasia began.

"What are laws in times of turmoil?" Nuura spat out. "With Cinar in decline, we need bold rulers."

Derya frowned. "Why do you think Cinar's in decline?"

Nuura snorted. "What else happens to an empire that puts an empty-headed flirt on the throne?"

9

H EAT SURGED UP DERYA'S cheeks and she clenched
her fists, staring into Nuura's mocking face.

"Everyone knows you'd lead the empire right
into ruin." Nuura smirked.

Derya blinked at Nuura, stunned speechless.

"Lady Nuura," Oikeios Zeki said, "the Kiral's ascension to
the throne is a potential future event, but you claim the
empire's already in decline."

*Raging waters. I almost took the bait and let her trap me into defending
myself.* She took a slow breath, trying to calm her racing heart.

"Everyone knows Cetus has plans for Ardebil." Nuura
folded her arms.

"That was true when he first tried to conquer the continent a millennium ago," Nazif said. "But until the cataclysm,
no one knew he'd returned for another try. Or did you?"

Nuura shifted in her seat, the wood creaking under her.
"The dochan believed Cetus had regained his power."

"He thought that?" Calix asked. "Why?"

"The cataclysm . . ."

"Happened after Istvan went to Ymittos." Calix raked his

gaze over Nuura's face. "Was he in contact with Cetus? Is that how he knew?"

"He knew the Malkhian prince was cursed for one hundred years," Nuura said. "Knowing that, anyone with more sense than a stone could guess Cetus was getting ready to make a move."

Calix furrowed his brow. "True." He inclined his head in a reluctant nod.

"When did Istvan inform you about the curse?" Derya asked.

"Shortly after the marriage with Princess Eliana was proposed," Nuura replied.

"Hm." Derya rubbed her chin. "The king of Ymittos didn't reveal the curse to Istvan until he arrived to formalize the betrothal."

"You're wrong." Nuura glared at Derya.

"No," Derya said. "I was there. The Ymittosians kept it secret. Istvan didn't know before." *Unless he lied to Eliana.* She twisted her sweaty hands in her lap.

"If that's the case," Calix said, "how did he learn about it?"

Nuura shrugged. "What difference does it make?"

"Well," Calix said, "perhaps Istvan hired a spy?" He fixed his gaze on Nuura's face. "Hmm?"

"That's what happened," she snapped.

"How do you know?"

"How else would he have known?"

Derya leaned forward. "From Cetus himself."

Nuura's eyes flared wide, and for the space of a breath she was immobile. "No."

Derya clenched her jaw to keep the relief from showing on her face. Nuura's flicker of surprise betrayed the truth.

The princess wasn't the only one who'd noticed. Yiannis was scrubbing his hands over his face, muttering. Calix's countenance darkened, and his eyes hardened. Aspasia looked stricken.

Kelebek spoke into the tense silence. "Someone who would do the unthinkable and engage with Ardebil's ancient enemy has crossed a line. Having done so, believing he deserved the throne, he might be willing to cross other lines."

"Such as abandoning any scruples about patricide?" Nazif asked.

"Are you all fools?" Nuura asked. "Istvan wasn't here."

"No, he wasn't." Calix's harsh tone cut the air like a lash. "He must have had an accomplice. And you're the one he was writing to about removing obstacles."

"I didn't do it," Nuura whined.

"She couldn't have," Lady Aspasia said.

"You're right," Derya said. "She's not clever enough."

Nuura's reddening face made Derya hope the woman was about to break. The princess continued. "Dochan Istvan devised the plot, and you provided the cold nerve to kill the royal family."

"I would never do such a thing." Nuura's high-pitched voice sharpened with anger.

"Wouldn't you?" Kelebek asked. "You attacked your own brother."

Nuura glared at him and cursed. "I was a child when he died. He deserved it." The glare she raked over Derya's face bore a threat laced with malice.

"What are you saying?" Aspasia asked. "That Istvan used Nuura to commit the murders?"

"He loved me!" Nuura snarled.

Derya gave Nuura a pitying smile. "Did you really think Istvan would marry you?" Derya scoffed. "He pledged himself to Princess Eliana. A more powerful match, and one more likely to help him hold the throne of Ymittos." She shook her head. "He would have married Eliana."

"And kept you on the side," Nazif remarked. "If he didn't throw you aside like old bath water."

"He promised me——"

"What?" Calix asked. "That you would be Queen of Ymittos and Diodocheen of Nafplio if you helped him?"

Aspasia waved a dismissive hand. "I can't believe it. Maybe Nuura would succumb to Istvan's charms, but she's not clever enough to plan these murders."

Nuura's face turned a dusky plum shade, and her nostrils flared. "Are you all that stupid?" she spat. "I'm not clever, am I? I had you all fooled. Of course I did it. Everyone knew Istvan was by far the most capable of the diodochi's sons. The one who could lift Nafplio from between the shadows of Cinar and Ymittos and restore its former glory. And he had a powerful ally to make it all happen. No, the diodochi deserved to die for not recognizing Istvan's greatness. And his other sons, as well, for not standing aside for their brother."

A chill swept through Derya, and she shivered. She had hoped the woman would confess. Relief made her want to sag in her seat. But shock kept her upright. She'd expected at least some remorse. Not this. Most chilling was Nuura's reference to an ally. Who had to be Cetus.

"So you don't deny it?" Lord Calix asked. "It was your hand that killed the diodochi and his family, and no other?"

"Of course it was me." She spit out a curse. "I'm not a fool who would hire an assassin only to have him turn on me. Why let someone else have all the fun?" She waved a hand. A knife leaped from the table and flew toward Derya.

The princess lurched back. The knife soared past her ear and lodged in the wall with a thwack. Several other knives rose into the air.

Derya reached for her magic, scrambling to use it to defend herself. Before she could, Bahadir vaulted from his seat and raced to Nuura's side. He grabbed her arm and twisted it behind her back.

Nuura cried out and the knives fell, clattering on the table. "You brute!" She writhed in Bahadir's grasp and let out a string of foul curses.

Lady Aspasia stared. "But you were in the country when the murders happened."

Nuura smirked. "No, I was in Ziyamet. With an aunt."

"But you said—" Calix turned to Yiannis.

"I was at my estate, that's true," Yiannis said. "Nuura was visiting her mother's sister, who was ill. When I received your bird informing me of the murders, I left right away, concerned for Nuura's safety."

"Why didn't you tell anyone she'd been in the capital?" Nazif asked.

Yiannis shrugged. "No one asked. Besides, I thought she'd been helping her sick aunt. And had no reason to think otherwise."

Nuura laughed. "Yiannis collected me from my aunt's house, and we arrived together. You all assumed I'd been with him the entire time."

Kelebek gave her an appraising stare. "And if anyone ever asked, you could refer them to your aunt, whom I presume would say you'd been with her all night."

Nuura smirked. "After a few glasses of wine, the old cow was out for the night."

Lady Aspasia summoned a pair of guards. "Take her to the wooden holding cell. And be wary about your weapons. She's a metal mage."

Nuura thrashed like a feral beast when the guards seized her arms. She spewed venomous threats as the guards dragged her out, her scarlet dress trailing on the floor.

Aspasia closed her eyes and waited until the echoes of Nuura's bellows died away. The rest sat without speaking, Yiannis with his head in his hands.

Finally, Oikeios Zeki spoke. "I never knew she's a metal mage."

"Maybe that's why she likes knives so much," Calix said.

Aspasia dabbed her eyes with a napkin. "I still can't believe it."

Calix rubbed his temples. "But she confessed. We'll have a public trial so the country knows what happened."

Aspasia raised her tearstained face. "What will the people think when they learn the truth?" She shuddered and took a deep breath. "I'm relieved to know who the guilty party is. Maybe now we can sleep a little more soundly."

"Yes, this is a relief," Calix said. "But it raises another more troubling issue."

"Istvan's ally?" Derya asked. "That bothered me, too."

Oikeios Zeki nodded. "Dochan Istvan often took long, solitary rides along the coast. At the time, I assumed he was hunting or pursuing some kind of dalliance. Now I think he was meeting with agents of Cetus."

"Your dochan was willing to sell you all out for his own ambition," Derya said. "You don't have to let his plan succeed. Ally with Cinar. We will protect you."

Bahadir leaned forward. "You've heard how the Heir of Cinar fought a dragon and retrieved the scepter. Her magic is potent. Imagine having her, along with the might and mages of Cinar, at your defense."

Aspasia and Calix looked at each other.

"Besides," Nazif said, "we have met all your conditions, and more. Retrieve the scepter. Help keep order. Find the assassin. If you don't ally with us, we'll be forced to tell the emperor you reneged on our agreement. I'm not sure how he'll react. He may just leave you to your own devices. And if an alliance with Cetus doesn't work out the way you expect it to . . ."

Lady Aspasia held out a hand. "Please don't think we're ungrateful. We're shocked by this news about Nuura and Istvan. I'm not certain we should agree to anything binding until we can deal with it."

Derya gripped her hands together under the table. She couldn't let the Nafplians wiggle out of their agreement. That would be a failure worse than not finding the scepter. She opened her mouth to speak, but at a nod from Kelebek, subsided.

"What do you think, Lord Calix?" Kelebek asked. "You did forge an agreement with the Kiral."

Derya drummed her fingers on her leg under the table while Calix and Aspasia deliberated the implications of Nuura's guilt and Istvan's treachery, with Kelebek and Zeki subtly directing their discussion. Yiannis sat glumly silent, giving no sign he heard the conversation around him. Several times Derya wanted to press them for a decision, but each time, Kelebek's twitching eyebrows made her wait.

I hope he knows what he's doing. Her palms were sweating. She had to secure the alliance with Nafplio. If they didn't agree now, they never would.

When the Nafplians had talked themselves out, Aspasia said, "I still don't know. Maybe we should allow the new diodochi to decide."

Kelebek raised his eyebrows at Derya, who took the hint. "I'm afraid you don't have the luxury of time, Lady Aspasia. You need a powerful ally, sooner than later." *And Cinar needs to keep Cetus from waltzing to our capital through Nafplio.*

Derya fixed her gaze on Aspasia. "Do you think it's honorable to alter the conditions for your loyalty as often as you change your guards? It's making me suspicious. Perhaps Nuura isn't the only untrustworthy one."

Aspasia's eyes widened. "Surely you don't suspect me or Lord Calix?"

"Why do you delay in ratifying our agreement?" Derya spoke as calmly as she could. "Do you presume Cetus will honor his promises? Based on what I've heard out of the western islands, you're more likely to end up dead, if not enslaved."

Calix sighed. "I think you're right."

Aspasia turned to him. "Lord Calix, do you agree we should ally with Cinar?"

"I do." He put a hand on Yiannis's shoulder. "And you?"

Yiannis nodded without raising his head.

"Then it's settled," Aspasia said.

Derya kept her spine straight, fighting the urge to slump in relief, and barely heard Aspasia's next words. "Ambassador Zeki, will you work with our chamberlain and draft a new treaty?"

Kelebek leaned forward. "If I may suggest, make this agreement contingent on the emperor, the current Heir of Cinar, or Lord Nazif holding the throne. If any others rule, they'll need to renegotiate."

Derya pressed her lips together and blinked to keep her eyes from widening in surprise. Kelebek was supporting her claim to the throne? *Thank you, thank you, oikeios.* This would keep the scheming cousins in line a little longer and allow her and Nazif more time to solidify matters in Nafplio.

"Of course," Lady Aspasia said. "And in our letter to the emperor, we'll clarify that both Princess Derya and Lord Nazif have proven their worth and have our full trust."

Derya bowed her head to hide her relieved smile. "Thank you, Lady Aspasia," she said, keeping her voice calm. "My cousin and I are grateful for your kind words." *Too bad you can trust him more than I can.*

10

ERYA WATCHED LADY ASPASIA and Lord Calix lead the shaken, stumbling Yiannis from the room. He was broken, wounded, and humiliated in more ways than one. She dropped her gaze from his stricken face as a lump rose in her throat. *Poor man. How will he survive this?*

Zeki stood up. "Kiral, if I may take the oikeios with me? I covet his assistance on the treaty."

Derya nodded her assent. "Please do. And be quick, before they change their minds." She waited for the door to close behind them. "Well, that's that. Now on to the next problem."

Nazif munched on a pastry. "You never stop, do you?"

"My father says it's a vital quality for a ruler. Are you saying it's too much for you?"

He grinned, merriment filling his blue eyes, and took another bite. "How may I assist the Heir of Cinar?"

The door opened and Kelebek returned. "I apologize, Kiral, but birds arrived from Cinar a few moments ago. Missives for you and Lord Nazif."

Derya stared at the thin rolls of parchment in Kelebek's long fingers. She'd only sent a brief message the night before, and this morning, a longer one. Kelebek, or Zeki, or even Nazif might have dispatched their own birds. That her father had answered so promptly could only mean one thing.

She smiled and held her hand out. "Thank you, oikeios. Would you stay? You can catch up with Oikeios Zeki later. I'm sure we'll have a lot to discuss."

Nazif was already frowning over his own letter, muttering. The only words she caught were "why expect more?"

Derya raised an eyebrow, wondering what her father had written to provoke that response. She fingered the fine parchment in her hand, remembering the last time her father wrote to her when she was in Nafplio. When he sent her to find the scepter. His letter had left her feeling he didn't believe in her. This message should be full of praise for her accomplishment. *I hope.* And when he learned she and Nazif had solved the murders, he'd be even more impressed.

There were few formal greetings, which was no surprise, but only a single line expressing his joy that she hadn't perished as reported. She frowned. No affectionate words, just language he could have used when writing to any of his subjects.

Ignoring the sting of hurt feelings, she pressed on. Some of his news she knew, that some of the southern vassal nations were threatening rebellion. They'd always been reluctant members of the empire. Perhaps Cetus had approached the coastal territories as he had Nafplio. Maybe her father would send her there to placate them.

The tidings of Pasargadae were more troubling. Border skirmishes had increased, and the emperor feared an invasion. He'd put her cousin Yildiz in charge of the army and sent him east to repel the invaders and to protect some of the empire's grain-producing regions.

Derya's head drooped. If Yildiz turned back an invasion, her father might name him co-emperor. The threat of Cetus paled before the reality of Pasargadae's legions. Too many of

Cinar's border towns had been destroyed by Pasargadian forces, who preferred complete destruction of any who resisted rather than showing mercy to the conquered.

But as fearsome as the Pasargadians were, didn't her father understand Cetus was far worse?

Her eyes widened as she read on.

I am pleased you found the scepter and expect I will soon hear you have formalized a treaty with Nafplio. But we hear tales that Cetus made not just a scepter but a crown, and their power can only be wielded if the user possesses both. Since you've proven yourself so capable of locating lost artifacts, find the crown.

What? He was giving her another quest? A weight settled on her shoulders, a heaviness that dragged on all her limbs. Nazif had told her the rumors, but she hadn't let herself believe them. How could her father do this?

If the situation in Nafplio allows, take Nazif with you. Start in the western islands. Or ask the barbarian king who helped you before.

Derishka, if you can't find the crown, it won't change either your current status or Yildiz's.

She froze, staring at the code word *Derishka*, the use of which negated the next phrase. So he attached a lot of significance to her finding the crown, enough that if she found it, he'd name her co-emperor. Or was that the meaning she wanted to attach to his words? If she failed, did that mean she'd lose her title as Heir of Cinar? The mention of Yildiz in that context burned. Was he considering Yildiz as a potential heir?

She lowered her head and bit her lip to keep the pain from spilling from her eyes. The constant ache for her father's approval oozed through her. Was there nothing she could do to earn his praise? Her confidence drained away as from a barrel with a hole in the bottom. Her usual way of bolstering her courage seemed empty. *I am the Heir of Cinar.* But for how long? *I will not be shaken.* No, just discarded and tossed aside.

She reread the letter. The timing of the new quest didn't make sense. If the crown was so important, why hadn't he set her searching for both at once? She could have gotten all the information out of Stigandr Tyr before she antagonized him and destroyed any hopes of an alliance with him. If the barbarian king ever saw her again, he'd skewer her with one of his bespelled spears and feed her to a wyvern.

The princess racked her brain for all she knew about the crown. She didn't remember reading any mention of it when she was researching the scepter. Like the scepter, Cetus must have infused it with much of his magic.

She rubbed a hand over her pounding forehead. How many quests would her father send her on before she proved herself? He didn't know how powerful a mage she was. Every time she used her magic, she could summon her power faster and use the amplifiers more precisely. And the writing on water was a new use she was just beginning to explore. Her magical powers would help overcome any prejudice her father's court had against her for being a woman.

Nazif tossed his parchment on the table with a snort. "I presume you received the same commission I did."

She eyed the coiled paper, wondering how her father worded his orders to Nazif. "You don't seem thrilled to go to sea with me."

"Can you blame me?" He gave her a frustrated shake of his head, and a bitter smile twisted his lips. "Once again, the price of success is more work."

"Kiral," Kelebek asked, "is the emperor sending you on a new quest?

She nodded. "To the western islands in search of another magical item Cetus forged: a crown."

"No." Safiye's protest was feeble, as if she realized nothing she said would change the emperor's decree.

Bahadir remained stoically silent. But his jaw was tight, the scars in his cheek twitching.

Nazif shook his head. "Yildiz is behind this, I know it."

Derya stared at him. "Yes, he stands to gain the most if we're lost at sea or killed by Cetus. Clever of him to use this pretext. If it works, the only one in line before him would be Utku." She exchanged a wry smile with Nazif. Utku was weak and easily led. With one military victory, the strong and ambitious Yildiz would overshadow him as a full moon dims the stars. "Yildiz probably convinced my father that to fight Cetus, we need all the magical help we can get."

"In that, Yildiz is correct," Kelebek said.

"And is shoving Nazif and me out of his way," Derya said. "I need to return home. No one else will plead my case as the rightful Heir of Cinar."

"I'm with you," Nazif said. "Except the part about pleading your case. I'd speak for myself though."

"The whole point of finding the scepter was to keep it out of Cetus's hands. If I sail west, I may as well take it straight to him."

"What, you're not leaving it with the Nafplians?" Nazif asked.

Derya scoffed. "Of course not. If they ever get their paws on it, they'd run to Cetus and try to use it to bargain for mercy. Besides, I only promised to retrieve it. Nobody said anything about who would keep it."

Bahadir rubbed his chin. "Kiral, I think we should sail to Ptolemaida."

"Why?" Derya asked. "There's nothing left there."

"I know." Bahadir gave her a sad smile. "It might be worthwhile to have a look. I'm thinking of Cetus's curse, and that it must be part of a larger strategy. Perhaps he's planning to invade through the ruins of Ymittos or Malkh."

Nazif drummed his fingers on the table. "He might."

"Shouldn't we turn our attention to our vassal nations, to Terramare or Exine?" Derya asked. "My father speaks of unrest there. Cetus may be trying to undermine our authority, and we should go stop him."

"That's sound strategy," Kelebek said. "But your orders were clear. Find the crown, and your way to it goes through the northern barbarians."

"But I can't ask the barbarian king." Derya scowled. "Or the king of Veleti, for that matter. Neither of them has any reason to trust me or want to help me. And Stigandr Tyr is an oily pig who would be an unreliable ally at best."

"Kiral, there are no perfect allies," Bahadir said. "Especially in times of war. We need to join forces with those we have, not the ones we hope for."

"Perhaps we'd do better if we were a little more particular about choosing our friends." Derya crossed her arms. "No, that barbarian king made an enemy of me, and I will not work with him. Ever. Under any circumstances."

"Cousin," Nazif said, "I understand you. But let's not lose sight of our goals. I would take immense joy in helping you put our conniving cousins in their place. Disobeying your father won't help us do that."

"But what if the empire falls apart while we're gone?" Derya asked.

"That's a real possibility," Kelebek said. "If Pasargadae invades and the southern vassals secede, there might not be a throne of Cinar for anyone to claim."

"Perhaps your father is protecting you," Safiye said. "By not naming you co-emperor, you're less of a target for Pasargadian assassins. And if the empire falls to Pasargadae, you'd be a figurehead at best."

"Or the first one they'd hang," put in Nazif.

"And you'd be dangling right there next to me." Derya

tried to smile at her grim joke but couldn't force her lips to curve upward. "You all believe I should seek the crown."

Bahadir shrugged, Safiye nodded, and Kelebek tapped the emperor's letters with his finger.

Derya let out a long sigh. "If I must. But, cousin, I'm in command of this little pleasure trip. And when I find the crown, it's mine."

11

N AZIF'S LIPS CURLED UP in a sly grin. "Claiming the crown is one thing. Keeping it another."

Whether he meant Cetus's crown or Cinar's, he was right. A second worry bubbled up in Derya's mind. She sighed through gritted teeth. "There's more. When I returned from the bath last night, I discovered my room had been ransacked. Quite thoroughly. Someone, I'm certain, was after the scepter."

"Did they find it?" Nazif asked.

"Of course not." Derya patted the scepter at her side, hidden under her turquoise and black tunic. She tipped her head toward her advisors. "We have a plan to protect it. But we need a metal mage. A very discreet one."

"I know just the person," Nazif said. "My new slave."

"You bought a slave?" Derya's eyes widened in horror, and she stared at her cousin. Safiye jerked and dropped her wax tablet, her stylus clattering onto the table. Kelebek stiffened, and Bahadir muttered something that sounded like a curse.

Cinar had outlawed slavery two centuries ago. Despite the emperor's efforts, the vassal nations still tolerated it. The eastern empires—Pasargadae and Tinaxia—allowed the barbaric practice, and she'd heard the northern barbarians weren't above it. Apparently, the Nafplians weren't either. "Raging waters, what possessed you to do that?"

"Well, I didn't plan on it. I was strolling along the docks one afternoon—"

"You? Out for a stroll?"

"If you must know, I enjoy all sorts of exercise. Not just the kind you accuse me of."

Safiye flinched, and Kelebek frowned. Bahadir grinned and leaned back in his seat.

"Please, cousin, you are embarrassing my danisman and offending the oikeios. What were you doing at the docks? Searching for a game of chance?"

He scoffed. "If you must know, I went to inquire of the last ships that arrived if they'd seen any sign of you. I was quite concerned."

He seemed sincere and genuinely hurt. She supposed he didn't want her dead, just not standing between him and the throne. "Thank you."

He gave her a look that suggested he wasn't completely mollified and continued. "A ship had arrived from the east, having left Khezer before stopping in Tulgutalp on its way here."

She nodded. Khezer was on the eastern shore of the Ishdeniz Sea, the sprawling inland sea that filled much of the center of Cinar. The port held a reputation for smuggling goods from Tinaxia in exchange for slaves, most of them kidnapped from rural areas of Cinar or territories of the northern barbarians.

"Anyway," Nazif said, "the captain was beating a slave girl. She had this look about her that reminded me of you."

"She looked like me?"

"Not exactly. Olive skin, like yours, but huge green eyes. It was the defiance in her expression, the way she stared at the man and didn't wince when he hit her that reminded me of you."

Derya chose to accept that as a compliment. "Go on."

"I asked the man what she'd done. He didn't come out and say so, but I gathered that rather than accepting his advances, she'd stabbed him with his own knife. Apparently when he held it to her throat, she used magic to twist the blade and cut his hand. Then she bolted off the ship, and he caught her on the dock. It sounded like a pretty piece of metal magic to me, so I bought her on the spot."

Derya's lip curled, and a sour taste filled her mouth. "What have you done with her?"

"Nothing, I swear. I wasn't about to play with a girl who can manipulate metal. I had her cleaned up and confined to a room until I decided what to do with her. Then you arrived, and that pushed this minor matter out of my mind."

"You could have set her free."

"Maybe. But I suspect she's Pasargadian, although she claims to be Isedonnian."

"Why do you think that?"

"Something in the way she talks. Her speech is melodic, and the consonants are softer." He shrugged. "Subtle differences, but they reminded me of a Pasargadian officer's wife I once—"

"That does complicate matters." Derya interrupted his reminiscing with a scowl. Pasargadae and Cinar had been enemies for centuries, and travel from one empire to the other was illegal for all but diplomats. A lone Pasargadian female was suspicious, and most likely a spy. "Are you sure she's a talented metal mage?"

"I had her demonstrate. She can bend metal and fling blades quite accurately."

"I'm surprised she didn't impale you with one of them."

Nazif chuckled. "I thought of that later. But her display was impressive. What do you want her to do?"

Derya leaned forward. "Safiye commissioned a metalsmith to make two copies of the scepter. Oh, don't worry. She gave him a sketch with the exact dimensions. She told him some story of it being a common item in Cinar, and that all the royalty carried one."

"But with that giant ruby as the finial, he'd be silly to believe her."

"She didn't include the ruby in the sketch."

"So you have two copies, minus the finial. Then what?"

"That's where the metal mage comes in. I have two extra rubies, which can serve as finials. After the mage attaches them, she'll infuse the fakes with a little magic, so a mage will think they are magical artifacts."

"What good is that?" Creases formed in between Nazif's eyebrows, and he shook his head.

"Bahadir, Safiye and I will each have one, and we'll trade several times a day. That way, no one but me will know who has the real one. If, as we suspect, the culprit is part of our entourage, this will make it harder for them to try again. They would have to steal all three to be sure of getting the original. Since we'll be alert for any attempt, we'll be more likely to catch him."

"I like it," Nazif said. "So. Do you want to use my slave?"

Derya wrinkled her face. "I don't think so. For many reasons."

"Such as?"

"Such as she should be set free. Oh, I know you think she's Pasargadian and therefore a spy. Interrogate her and find out. If she is, ship her back to Tulgutalp for questioning. But don't keep her enslaved."

"But she's a metal mage. And has reason to be loyal to me. After all, I saved her from that brute of a captain."

"Oikeios? Danisman? What do you think?"

"You of all people can't have anything to do with slavery," Safiye said.

Kelebek interjected. "Many in Cinar long to revive the slave trade, and this would be a prime excuse for them to flout the law."

Derya gave Nazif a triumphant look. "See? I'm right."

"But your cousin has a point, Kiral," Bahadir said. "If she's a spy, we must find out who sent her and why."

Nazif scoffed. "Where else are you going to find a metal mage who won't talk about what we ask of them?"

"We don't have any?" Derya asked.

Bahadir shook his head. "Our strongest ones died fighting the sea monsters. We have a few, but of limited ability."

"Besides, isn't the point to hide what we're doing from anyone who could be the thief?" Nazif said. "This girl is the perfect person. We know she's not the culprit. She's a powerful mage with no connection to anyone in your entourage. And she owes me." He crossed his arms. "Besides, if she's a slave, we can control where she goes and who she talks to. That ensures she can't tell anyone about the scepters."

"Perhaps we could ask her," Safiye said. "Offer her payment for both the magic and her silence."

"She probably wants freedom more than money," Derya said.

"A lack of money might be how she ended up a slave," Bahadir pointed out.

Derya sighed and nibbled her lower lip. They all made valid points. But it felt so wrong. She could ask the girl to help and even offer payment. But as a slave, the girl could hardly refuse.

"We have to pay her," Derya said slowly. "And grant her freedom."

"And if she's a spy?" Nazif asked.

Bahadir stroked his chin. "She says she's from Isedonnes?" At Nazif's nod, he continued. "Then we offer to take her home once our mission is complete. If she's telling the truth, that would be an incentive for her."

"Yes," Derya said. "Maybe we employ her until we can send her home. I'm sure she'd rather have us as an escort rather than travel alone and risk another run-in with slave traders." She paused. "But we offer freedom in any case, whether or not she helps." Derya eyed Nazif. "Do you agree?"

He shook his head. "We should hold out freedom in exchange for her cooperation and silence."

That is a logical move. Derya scowled and shook her head. The idea of owning another human was repugnant. "No. We free her now."

Nazif's stare hardened. "Strong rulers use all the tools at their hand."

"And wise ones don't allow expediency to corrupt them." She locked her gaze on his.

He was the first to blink. "I paid good money for her," he said.

She narrowed her eyes. What would it take to get him to agree? "I'll pay you back."

"Double."

She waved a finger at him. "Oh no. You're not making a profit out of slave trading. That's despicable."

"Is that what you call it? Very well. My scribe will prepare the bill of sale."

"And if she's a spy?" Bahadir asked.

"Why don't you have a chat with her?" suggested Derya. "If she's a spy, watch her closely until she's worked her magic on the fake scepters. Then arrest her."

"As you say, Kiral." Bahadir stood up. "But that leaves another question. We still don't know who tried to kill you."

Derya shivered. Her fingers turned to ice, and she buried them in the long sleeves of her tunic. Bahadir was right.

Three attempts on her life, two in Nafplio and one in Ethkarpia. She dragged air into her lungs, her tight chest fighting her ability to breathe. Her legs twitched, as if her feet wanted to carry her far away. Were the schemes against her the work of one person, or more? The problem was she had no idea. Her enemy, or enemies, could be anywhere.

12

Eighty days after the winter solstice in the 29th year of Emperor Vural Tzimiskes

TARJA TOOK EIGHT QUICK paces, covering the length of the room. She halted when she came face to face with the oaks and flowers of the ornately carved wooden door. Stealthily, she rested her ear against the wood. The corridor was silent other than a few jingles, creaking leather, and heavy footsteps. She scowled. The guards were still there, living, breathing barriers to her freedom.

She spun on her heel, paced to the window, and glared at the courtyard three stories below. Scarlet-clad soldiers flanked the iron gates. Smoke rose from a brazier where a guard was warming his hands.

Tarja pressed her hands against the uneven glass. Her metal magic could bend the iron holding it in place, allowing her to jump. With a shake of her head, she turned her back on the outdoors. Jumping wouldn't give her freedom, only a painful death on the stones below.

She ran her hands through her hair. How long was that oaf of a Cinarrian prince going to keep her captive? When he bought her, she had expected he would add her to his harem. To her surprise, she learned he had no harem, and he'd left her alone.

Alone in a small room fitted with a narrow but comfortable bed, a tiny table that held a basin and ewer, and a coarse woven mat covering the wooden floor. The walls were rough, with off-white plaster sloppily daubed over wood, leaving raised irregular grooves and ridges curving like wild vines over a deserted field.

She frowned. Slaves slept on straw and used outdoor privies and washed in a corner of the laundry yard. Harem girls were housed together, under the vigilant eye of eunuchs. But this room? Fit for an upper servant of some sort. What was that fop planning on doing with her?

The day before, an officer questioned her about her origins. The only others she'd seen were the guards and the maid who brought water for washing, meals, and changed the chamber pot.

He wasn't a complete fool, that Cinarrian prince. Knowing she was a metal mage, he'd ordered the room stripped of every scrap of metal and had a mage cast spells on the iron lock to her door. Two moments' exploration with her magic told her she could overpower those spells and unlock the door while practicing sword drills and reciting an ancient poem. She snickered. They thought she was a lowly slave. So far, she'd concealed her true identity. Let Lord Nazif underestimate her. He wouldn't be the first. Nor the first to regret it.

But even if she used her metal magic to open the lock, she wouldn't get far. A steady tramp up and down the corridor reminded her the prince's guards were ever present.

Their number had increased over the past day or so following the arrival of a large party. No doubt some self-important person whose entourage filled the courtyard with seventy or more horses. The maid who brought her dinner refused to answer any questions about the newcomers, most likely following Nazif's orders.

Tarja pursed her lips. Metal wasn't her only power. Could she use her light magic to escape? No ideas came to mind. Besides, she wanted to keep that power a secret. Even donkey-brained Cinarrians knew that mages with two powers almost always possessed royal blood. Probing inquiries about which royal blood flowed in her veins could prove to be dangerous.

She paused at the narrow window and looked out over Ziyamet. The Nafplian capital was small, as she'd expected. Wood houses clung to the side of the steep hills opposite the diodochi's palace. The south wind brought faint sounds to her ears, the cries of street vendors and the flapping of flags on the palace's roof.

Diodochi. What an odd name for a ruler. It stemmed from the Nafplians' desire to be independent of all things Cinarrian, so they came up with their own title, something no other nation used. That was an attitude she could understand and respect.

But the Nafplians were not her primary concern. She'd risked much when she fled her father's palace. She blinked back tears, remembering what she'd sacrificed, only to be captured by slave traders. The first man who bought her was a brute. She shuddered, grateful that he'd been enamored with another slave during the voyage and ignored Tarja until they docked in Nafplio. Which was another lucky break—to arrive just in time to be bought by a Cinarrian prince.

Now if she could escape and carry out her plan. That would be the only way her father would forgive her for defying him, for choosing to flee rather than marrying the obscure desert chieftain he'd chosen for her. If she played this right, she might even marry into Cinar's royal family. And bring down their empire from within.

Maybe the dolt who bought her would suffice. He seemed vain enough to fall for flattery. Everyone knew of Cinar's history, of the numerous courtesans, dancers, and circus performers who'd married into the royal family. And the cleverer and more ambitious became the genuine ruling power rather than their husbands.

She'd have to be careful. It would be too easy for Nazif to use her and cast her aside. Bile rose in her throat. If that happened, there would be no triumphant return home. Her father would kill her with his own hands for shaming the family. She'd be better off finishing her days as a kitchen drudge for some Nafplian noble.

The courtyard below filled with a dozen turquoise-and-black clad Cinarrians. They set to sparring, their swords clanging, and rough laughter filled the air.

With a sigh, she pivoted from the window. Lord Nazif had told her she needed to work, even in captivity. So she'd asked for a loom, preferring weaving to needlework.

Tarja had suppressed a grin when they brought a small loom, fit only for making mats, and made solely of wood. Even the weaver's tools were wood or bone. They weren't taking any chances.

The repetition of tying knots helped calm her jitters and keep her sane. Four days already. She clenched her jaw, trying to suppress her fear of what future Nazif planned for her.

As she moved toward the loom, Tarja frowned. The sun was halfway to its zenith. Where was that maid with her breakfast? She wrinkled her nose. And it was high time the chamber pot was replaced.

The lock clicked and the door creaked open. Instead of the girl, a swarthy man with a sharp chin entered, holding a tray.

He wore the livery of Nafplio, a scarlet tunic with a twelve-pointed gold star dominating the center of his chest. He closed the door behind him and set the tray on the table next to her basin. "Excuse me." He leaned forward and whispered. "Should I call you Your Highness?"

She froze and stared, her eyes wide. With an effort, she responded in what she hoped was a puzzled tone. "No. Why would you?" *Surely he doesn't know. He can't know.* She clenched her trembling hands into fists, hiding them behind her back.

He paused, studying her with piercing hazel eyes. "You resemble the Princess Tarja. If you were her, I'd be yours to command."

Tarja swallowed, trying to arrange her features into an expression of mild confusion. This had to be a trap. If the Cinarrians discovered who she was . . . She didn't want to consider that horrible possibility. "And not your Nafplian overlords?"

The man shook his head. "You have the emperor's eyes. And your mother's . . ." He stepped back, his spine ramrod straight. "Lady, may I offer you a pomegranate?"

Tarja stiffened. That was one of the code phrases used by her mother's spies. His use of the words couldn't be a coincidence. Pomegranates weren't in season. Had the Cinarrians— or Nafplians—discovered the code? If she acknowledged her identity to the wrong person, death would be her kindest end.

But to find an ally, someone who could inform her of events outside the four walls of this chamber . . . And to not feel so totally, completely alone. Unsure if she was sounding her death knell, she repeated the countersign. "Only if you have a sword to cut it."

The man knelt. "Princess Tarja. There's been such an uproar since you went missing. Your mother's vizier ordered all of us in her service to find you."

That could be true. "Which vizier?"

"Lord Senejan."

The tension in Tarja's chest and neck relaxed. Senejan had been in her mother's household for decades but was never publicly recognized as a vizier. He viewed obscurity as a shield against assassination attempts. Tarja's mother thought it ensured he didn't get caught up in plots. Either way, only a genuine spy would know Senejan was the mastermind behind her mother's network of spies and assassins.

Her breath hitched and she lifted her chin, forcing her shoulders into a straight line. It wouldn't be prudent for this man to see how exhilarated she was to have an ally. That display of weakness might sow doubt in his mind, causing him to question whether risking himself for her was wise. With an effort, she suppressed a grin of relief.

"How may I serve you?"

"First, stand up. If someone saw you, we'd be in trouble." She sat by her loom in the room's only chair, glad to be off her shaking knees. "How did you know I was here?"

The man rose to his feet. "When your father sent his spies after you, your mother dispatched hers." He held up his hands, beseeching. "Please forgive us. Your mother was imprisoned, and it was many days before she got word to Senejan to send someone after you. It was only by chance one of Senejan's agents spotted you in Tulgutalp. He sent a bird here, telling us to look out for you." His jaw hardened. "It's fortunate for that brute of a captain the Cinarrian prince bought you."

Fortunate indeed. Had a Pasargadian killed the captain for beating her . . . She couldn't bear to imagine the uproar that would have caused.

"It took several days to find the right maid and persuade her to accept a bribe."

Tarja nodded. "I'm glad you were persistent."

"I am the dust under your feet, highness."

She clenched her hands in her lap and forced herself to speak calmly. "Do you have tidings of my mother?"

The man hesitated. "Far be it from me to bring news that would cloud your days."

Tarja scowled. "Let me make it clearer than daylight. I want to know everything, no matter how dreadful." Her pulse throbbed in her temple, a rapid beat like a racing camel's feet.

The man bowed his head. "She is to remain in the dungeons until you return. Unless news of your death comes first."

Tarja swallowed the lump in her throat. She'd begged her mother to come with her, to flee when there was a chance. But her mother had insisted it was to Tarja's benefit if she remained. How a stay in the emperor's dungeons would help, Tarja couldn't imagine.

How best to use this man? "I'm weaving a carpet and need you to send it to my father. Can you do that?"

"I won't be able to go myself, highness. But one of your father's people will be leaving the day after tomorrow. He can be trusted with it."

"Come back that morning, then." Two days wouldn't give her much time. If she worked late every night and made the mat a narrow rectangle, suitable only as a decoration, she might finish in time. She glanced at the breakfast tray. "Did bribing the maid include performing her duties?"

"Yes." He strode to the corner and picked up the chamber pot. He carried it to the corridor and set it down, returning with an empty one. "If there is nothing else, highness . . ."

Tarja waved a hand in dismissal. "No. You may go."

As soon as the door closed behind him, she let herself sag in her seat. *Memjoon is in prison. I have to help her.*

Should she return home? She hated the idea of her mother languishing in a cell, at the mercy of the brutal guards. But her mother would be furious if she threw away her chance to escape. And her father's ire . . . If she returned without some triumph her father would value, without anything to show for herself, she'd be lucky to live long enough to see the inside of a cell.

No, she'd have to finish what she traveled west to do. Only then could she go home. Hopefully, her mother would still be alive.

Tarja regarded the small carpet she started weaving three

days earlier. She could weave a hidden message into the pattern, one that her father could read. The message would disturb the symmetry of the pattern, cuing her father to look for it within the colored swirls and shapes. What to communicate was the problem.

Eventually she hit on the idea of saying she was spying on one of the Cinarrian princes and would report more later. If only she had something more concrete to tell him. That might ease a little of her father's wrath. If he believed her mother knew nothing of her plans, he might be a little more forgiving. Refrain from torturing her, perhaps. Or even release her from prison.

For the next few hours, she wove the complicated pattern, fingers mechanically tying knot after knot. The rhythm soothed her, lulling her into thinking she'd be able to save her mother. That the rest of the day would be quiet, even if a bit dull.

The door swung open and crashed against the wall. Tarja jumped.

Lord Nazif stood on the threshold, leering.

Tarja stiffened. Was she about to learn his intentions toward her? Or had the spy been a trap? Her heart raced like a gazelle fleeing a lion. Only she had no place to run.

13

Lord Nazif sauntered into the room, his predator's gaze sweeping over Tarja. "Garzuli."

Tarja almost didn't respond. For half a breath, she didn't recognize the false name she'd told him. "Yes, my lord?" Heart pounding in her ears, she turned slowly from her loom and stood up. "What do you desire?" He loomed over her, the tiny chamber seeming to shrink as if the walls were rushing toward Tarja like an inexorable trap.

A smirk crossed his lips. "I'm not certain you want to know. But I'm not the one who wants something. It's my cousin."

Cousin? Which one could it be? The last Tarja heard, the heir, Derya, was in Ethkarpia, most likely flirting with every man in sight. If one of Nazif's male cousins wanted a little entertainment, she'd show him just what she could do with metal. "How may I serve?"

"I'll let her tell you." He stepped aside and a young woman of about Tarja's age entered the room as if she owned it.

She was tall and willowy, her black hair twisted into a complicated braid, its golden highlights glimmering as she moved. Her large hazel eyes seemed to laugh at everything and everyone. Her long tunic and trousers weren't much finer than Tarja's, the same sturdy material, the same unflattering straight cut.

But the girl's clothing was a vivid turquoise rather than the color of dead leaves, and a narrow line of gold embroidery embellished the tunic's hem. She carried herself as if she wore jewels and silks, and her air proclaimed that no matter how simply dressed, this olive-skinned girl was heir to an empire.

Her cheekbones stuck out as if she hadn't eaten well for some weeks. But that, Tarja reluctantly admitted, only enhanced the firm lines of her jaw. Tarja fixed her face in a bland expression, trying to conceal the resentment she felt toward this princess who had everything. Beauty. Acclaim. Power.

Perhaps worse was her arrogance. She strode across the room as if she was doing the floor a favor by walking on it.

Nazif gestured at the girl. "My cousin, Princess Derya."

His words confirmed what Tarja already guessed. She bowed her head. *So now I've seen her.* The odious, loathsome, insufferable Princess Derya. The girl she had vowed to kill. "Your Highness."

"This is your metal mage? She looks rather young."

Tarja wanted to spit on Derya for her patronizing, doubtful tone. *I'm only a few weeks younger than you. And not a flighty, brainless moth.*

"Just watch," Nazif said. He pulled the chair from the loom and thumped it down in front of his cousin.

The princess thanked him with a nod and sat. "Please, show me what you can do with metal."

Nazif produced a fork from the leather bag slung over his shoulder. "Start with this."

"What do you want me to do?" Tarja's stomach turned over. Demonstrating her magic to these strangers, these Cinarrians, was indecent. *Should I pretend to be unable? But they already know I have powers.*

"Just anything," Derya said.

Tarja twirled the fork in her fingers. She didn't have a choice. Refusing could prompt Nazif to use her for other purposes. Or send her back to the slavers.

She summoned her magic until the familiar prickly sensation grew almost painful and pushed the power into the metal. The prongs of the fork crumpled and twisted, forming the petals of a rose.

"See?" Nazif said.

"It's pretty," Derya replied. "Can you infuse metal objects with a trace of magic so they appear to be spelled, even if they aren't?"

A trick any child could do. Tarja stroked the metal flower, sending tiny bits of power into it. "Will this do?" With a deprecating shrug, she handed the fork to Nazif.

A slow smile crossed his face. "I feel the magic," he said.

Derya extended her hand, and Nazif placed the twisted fork in her fingers. She held it in both hands, rubbing her palms together. "Very nice work. This is exactly what we need." She turned to Tarja. "Garzuli, we have a request of you. Mind you, it's a request. You are free to refuse and we won't hold it against you. But you must promise you won't speak of this to anyone. It's just between the three of us."

Tarja opened her mouth to reply, but Nazif interrupted. "It's nothing illegal or immoral, if that's what concerns you. We're preparing a surprise for the emperor."

So far, Derya had worn a bland, pleasant expression. Insipid, Tarja had thought. But now the princess shot a sharp look at her cousin, a fleeting glance lasting less than a heartbeat. Tarja had nearly missed it.

Hmm. A surprise for the emperor? No. I wonder what they're up to.

They had to be plotting something important to Cinar. Using her magic to help them would be treasonous. The thought made Tarja's skin crawl. *Not to mention scandalous. What was wrong with these Cinarrians that they saw nothing unseemly in publicly wielding magic?*

My father would love to know what the Heir of Cinar is up to. Thwarting her scheme might be the one reason for him to forgive me and my mother.

"Very well," Tarja said. "I'll do what I can."

"Wonderful." Nazif dug in his bag, rattling its contents. He extracted a gold scepter adorned with turquoise, lapis lazuli, emeralds, and onyx and placed it on the table. Then he produced a second, identical to the first.

Tarja stared, gritting her teeth to keep from gasping. Was that Cetus's scepter, lost for a millennium? And what was the second one? She stared at the pattern of the gemstones on the shaft. One had an extra lapis lazuli, the other, an extra piece of onyx. They'd made a copy, with just a subtle variation, probably to help identify the original from the fake.

"Yes, they're stunning," Derya said. "I thought so too the first time I saw them."

"Excuse me, highness," Tarja said. "Where are the finials?" Cetus's scepter was capped with a large ruby. The tops of both scepters were empty prongs.

"I have them," Derya said. "We need them replaced, and the scepters infused. Will you do that? We'll pay you."

Tarja blinked. They were going to pay a slave? No, this wasn't kindness. It was a bribe to ensure her silence. "Thank you, but that's not necessary." It wasn't. They could simply kill her instead.

"Oh, but it is." Derya pulled a ruby from the bag that hung at her waist. "Can you start now?"

She should say no. Never would she aid a Cinarrian. But if she gained their trust, she'd discover what they were planning. And be alive long enough to find a chance to slay Derya.

Tarja bit the inside of her cheek. Derya and Nazif were

staring at her, waiting for her reply. "Of course, if you so desire, highness. But amplifiers would be useful."

"Which ones?" Derya asked.

"Pepper and wine, if it's not too much trouble."

Derya raised her eyebrows at Nazif. He huffed and left, banging the door behind him.

The princess shifted in her seat, making the flimsy chair creak. "Where are you from, Garzuli?"

"Isedonnes, highness."

"Oh, Skikda? I haven't been there for years. Has the governor's palace been rebuilt since the fire last year?"

Curse her. Tarja had no idea. She'd never been to Isedonnes, let alone its capital. "It's been two years, highness, since I . . ." Silence settled on the room like a menacing fog.

"Oh, how dreadful for you."

Was that genuine sympathy in Derya's tone? Or a pat dismissal of a slave's misfortunes? Tarja let her shoulders slump and her head droop. Let Derya think she was overcome with grief over her plight. She'd certainly despaired after the slave trader captured her. Her mind spun as she tried to guess how Derya found Cetus's scepter and what she planned to do with it.

Nazif returned, panting as if he'd sprinted to the kitchens and back. He held a small pepper grinder, a bottle of wine, and three glasses.

"We aren't planning a party, Nazif," Derya said.

"But scheming is thirsty work." He pulled the cork out with a pop and filled three glasses. "To the Rider."

Derya repeated his toast, while Tarja mumbled it. *Cinarrians and their superstitions.*

Tarja twisted the top of the pepper grinder, shaking a few grains of pepper into her hand. She put one on her tongue and sipped the wine. *By the desert sun.* Even mixed with the pepper's heat, she knew from the velvety undertones of spices under the fruit Nazif had chosen an expensive Isedonnian wine.

Keeping her eyes lowered to avoid revealing her surprise, she accepted the scepter and ruby Derya handed her. She wanted to turn her back, to sidestep using her magic under the Cinarrians' eyes. That was the proper thing to do. But it would expose her as a Pasargadian, one who believed using magic in public was shameful except in battle. The tiny room felt hot and crowded. She sucked in a breath. No matter how naked it made her feel, she had to do this.

Tarja's stomach writhed, and she held her lower lip between her teeth to still its trembling. Holding her breath, she placed the jewel within the prongs and magically bent the metal, securing the finial in place.

Nazif took the scepter and handed her the second one. When her fingers grasped the cool metal, she nearly dropped it. This one wasn't magical either. They'd made two copies.

She tapped her fingernail against the gold, listening to the faint clink as she considered. Did two copies mean they didn't possess the original? Frowning, she secured the ruby in the second scepter.

"Do you need to rest?" Derya asked.

Tarja repressed a snort. She'd barely tapped into her magic and was in no danger of overusing her power. But no point in letting Derya know that. "No, highness, I can finish." She infused the first scepter and handed it to Derya. "Is this enough?"

She hoped so. While easy, infusing objects held hidden challenges. Once in an object, the power was lost to the mage. Over time, the mage's power would refresh. No one wanted to diminish their power, even temporarily. Unless, like Cetus, they kept the object to store their magic. Once their power refreshed, they could access the stored magic and add it to their natural power.

Derya handed the scepter to Nazif. "What do you think?"

"It's perfect."

Tarja took a breath and infused the second scepter with a sliver of her power. Extending the artifact to Nazif, she asked, "Will that be all?"

Nazif slid both scepters into his bag and dropped the fork onto them, making a shrill clinking sound. "Yes, for now. But be ready. We'll be leaving in two days."

"For where?" Tarja asked.

Nazif grinned. "My cousin and I have an errand to the west to retrieve a long-lost treasure. You're coming with us. Always helpful to have a metal mage."

Who does he think he's fooling? Tarja fought to keep the grin from her face. *Go away already.*

He strode to the door. "Oh, I almost forgot." He pulled a coin from his money pouch and tossed it to Tarja.

She caught it and nearly scowled. This coin wouldn't buy a loaf of bread. "How generous of you, my lord," she said and gave herself a mental nod of approval for keeping any trace of sarcasm from her tone.

He waved and strode out. Derya stood. "Thank you for your assistance. I hope you don't mind coming with us, but we didn't know what else to do to insure your silence." She spread her hands out in an almost apologetic gesture.

Tarja rested a hand on her fluttering stomach. She didn't believe the other girl was truly sorry. Pasargadians kill slaves they want to silence. *Why doesn't Derya order my death?* "Yes, highness." Tarja made sure her voice held the proper tone of humble subservience. She'd had plenty of practice at it in her father's court. If a little groveling would keep her alive, she'd do it.

She gripped her hands, squeezing them to contain her impatience as she waited until Derya left the room and the door locked behind her. Then she whirled about in an ecstatic dance. Derya and Nazif had the scepter of Cetus. They'd made these two replicas, clearly to deter thieves.

And the long-lost treasure? That had to be Cetus's crown. Traveling with the Cinarrians was a boon. They'd take her to the crown, then she could steal both treasures.

What they didn't have was the band that combined them into one powerful object. Even Cetus needed all three to wield the power they contained. Too bad for Derya, the scepter and the crown were worthless without the band. Even though being near Derya made Tarja's stomach sour, she needed to stick close to her for now. She'd have plenty of time to plan her escape once she possessed both the scepter and the crown.

With a smile tugging at her lips, she resumed her seat by her loom. At last, she had consequential news to share with her father.

Perhaps this would be enough to secure her mother's release. A flutter of hope eased the tight worry in Tarja's shoulders.

Finally, her father would realize a daughter, even a defiant one, could be more valuable than seven sons. And to hammer the point into his skull, she wouldn't return home until Derya was dead.

14

Pasargadae

Forty-six days after the winter solstice in the 17th year of Emperor Cambyses III and in the 29th year of Vural Tzimiskes of Cinar

VEILED IN SHADOWS, TARJA crouched against the wooden wall, her heart thumping loudly in her ears. The heat in the airless hidden closet adjoining her bedchamber caused a bead of sweat to trickle down her neck. She peeked through a thumbnail-sized hole in the wall. From her vantage point, she had a clear view of her father's private workroom, where he met with his most trusted advisors. Her father, the emperor of the Pasargadian empire. A man who'd be apoplectic if he caught his least-favored daughter spying on him.

Tarja shivered, knowing what the penalty for annoying her father could be. He'd locked her oldest brother Samsher in the dungeons for a month simply because he allowed his gaze to linger too long on the emperor's newest concubine. Spying, no doubt, would merit a harsher punishment. Would he cut off one of her fingers? Or gouge out an eye? He'd never been that brutal with his children. But his temper was short these days, and slaves who failed to please bore the brunt of the emperor's wrath on their lashed and bloody backs.

Nonetheless, she had to risk discovery. Knowing what her father discussed in secret was her best way to survive.

It wasn't as if she held any real importance at court. She snorted at that thought. With half a dozen brothers, it was unlikely she'd ever take the throne. In other lands, like Ymittos and Cinar, it would be possible. Not in Pasargadae. If illness or accident or mishap in battle took her older brothers, she had plenty of younger ones to assume their places.

And even among the daughters, she wasn't first. Oldest, yes. But her mother had fallen from favor for having failed to produce no more children than one girl. Tarja's half sisters all had full brothers, which assured them favors and position Tarja could only envy. At nearly eighteen, her sole value to the emperor was as a pawn to be married off for the greatest gain to the empire.

But something was stirring. She could sense it in the viziers' tense posture and her father's deepening scowl. A steady stream of messengers had been coming and going for days. Dust-covered couriers who rode in from the north and west, bearing tidings from lands where winter still ruled.

Tarja wiped the sweat from her face with her long silk scarf. Maybe trying to learn anything by eavesdropping was pointless. For the last hour, her father had silently read message after message, handing them to his viziers after finishing each one. While the emperor made no comments, the viziers remained silent. *If only I could see those papers.*

The emperor frowned. "Who would be the better choice?"

Tarja stiffened. *At last.*

The first vizier, a man with gray-streaked hair and wide, flaring nostrils, tapped his fingers on the table. "Your Splendor, if I may, your son Samsher appears to have learned his place."

"Bah." The emperor's scowl deepened. "He's learned nothing. That one thinks he's the quickest wit from here to Tinaxia."

The second vizier, a stocky man whose left eye constantly twitched, leaned forward. "Your Splendor, Dastgir seems restless."

Dastgir, the second son. Not as clever as Samsher, in Tarja's opinion, and crueler as well.

The emperor nodded. "His antics are making me bald. It's time for him to be taught a lesson."

Tarja's eyes widened. How severe of a lesson was her father considering? And should she warn Dastgir? She would if she'd derive some benefit from sharing the information.

The emperor turned to the third advisor. "Your opinion?"

The man's beady, dark eyes darted from the emperor to the other viziers. "Your Splendor, you could send them both, along with a few trusted men, loyal only to you. If one oversteps his bounds and his brother doesn't deal with him first, he can have an unfortunate accident. It's not as though you don't have many other sons. Let them jockey for power. The one who prevails will have an interest in keeping his siblings in check. And you will have your eye on him."

The emperor rubbed his chin, then smiled.

Tarja's heart skipped a beat, and she pressed a hand against her mouth to suppress her gasp. Would her father plot to kill his own sons? Or set her brothers up so that one killed the other?

Stomach heaving, she clenched her jaw, swallowing the bile that surged up her throat. She'd known her father saw them all as tools. She hadn't realized how expendable they were. Whatever this mission was, it was likely one of her brothers wouldn't return.

She'd wanted to learn something by spying on her father,

and she had. That if he was willing to kill one son to keep the others in line, he'd have no scruples about disposing of her. As a lowly girl, she was worth less than an olive pit. The depth of her father's callousness was important to know, but the knowledge did nothing to ease the anxiety that was her constant companion.

The emperor tipped his head back and stared at the wall over his viziers' heads, the wall Tarja crouched behind. Tarja cringed. Had he spotted her spy hole?

The emperor banged the gong that stood on the table. Tarja jumped. The deep, vibrating chime was the signal summoning the emperor's children who were over the age of fifteen to an audience. Immediately.

Tarja bolted from the closet, twitching the tapestry that concealed the hidden door into place. Then she scurried to her washbasin and rinsed her face and hands in jasmine-scented water. She needed to appear perfectly attired and fresh when in her father's presence, not smelling like a musty closet.

A knock at her door, while no surprise, made Tarja start. A high-pitched voice called through the door. "Highness, your father requests your presence."

"I'm coming." *Requests.* She snorted. *As if I could refuse.* Her oldest brother, Samsher, once ignored the summons, too busy dallying with one of the slave girls. The disobedience provoked her father more than anything else. The emperor banished Samsher to patrol duty on the empire's borders. In the winter, the freezing north. In summer, the sweltering south. Five long years, and the emperor had just recalled Samsher. After Samsher's banishment, none of the rest of them had dared to even consider not running when the gong chimed.

Tarja brushed her long, black hair with shaking hands, praying to all the gods that her father hadn't spotted her spying. She straightened the layers of sheer, bright emerald fabric that formed her bell-shaped tunic, stooping to brush the knees of the trousers cut to hug her legs. Even though the tunic extended well past her knees, she didn't want to leave any trace of her time in the secret closet. She peered into the polished bronze mirror. Her olive skin was clean, but she could do nothing about the worried expression in her green eyes. She didn't look her best, but it would have to do. Straightening her shoulders, she opened the door and nodded to the eunuch. "I'm ready."

The princess followed the eunuch along marble halls lined with doorways topped with pointed arches, some leading to rooms, others to courtyards filled with greenery or fountains. The faint sweet scent of roses and lilies drifted in the air. As she walked, the gauzy layers of her tunic billowed around her, and she thought of the siblings who would be in attendance. Of the nine over the age of fifteen, only five were in the capital. One of her sisters and three brothers were at their mother's country estate. Too bad for them. They were going to miss something important.

But the others. The oldest brother, Samsher, who'd been so harshly reprimanded. Dastgir, the second oldest, who'd made no secret that with Samsher out of favor, he should inherit the throne when their father passed. Tarja wondered if Dastgir was scheming how to make that passing occur sooner rather than later.

Making a quick move would be the smart one, Tarja thought. That would shatter the others' schemes. If their disappointed ambitions festered into simmering resentment, the new emperor might have to help them cool off with a stint in the dungeons. Or remove the heads that might entertain thoughts of a coup.

Whoever ruled, she was still the daughter of the unfavored wife, vulnerable to anyone who wanted to use her for their own ends. Tarja hardened her face. She would not settle for that. She'd prove her value to her father and be rewarded with a position of her own. Not empress. That was as impossible as catching a tiger with a butterfly net. But something safe and protected. If such a condition was possible in turbulent Pasargadae.

Gaining the favor of whoever inherited the throne was always her best strategy. So could she use what she'd just learned? If she warned her brothers about the emperor's plan, they might mock her. Worse, they'd tell their father. Sweat beaded on Tarja's forehead. If she was caught helping her brothers at her father's expense, the consequences would be dire. Her best hope would be marriage to some obscure provincial landholder. If she lived that long. No, she'd keep her father's plot to herself. More than anything, she needed to survive.

The eunuch led her to a gold-plated bronze door. The gold was embossed with the imperial sigil of a pair of griffins facing outward, with a vertical staff between them, topped with a small, winged disc. Tarja's pulse sped up. *If my father saw me spying, what will I say?*

Her mouth went dry. For a few heartbeats, she fantasized about fleeing the palace and losing herself in the throngs of vendors, craftsmen, and vagabonds in the streets of Qidar.

That was foolish. She'd be found and flogged. She took a deep breath. *If he caught me eavesdropping, all I can do is say I live to serve him. If that fails to satisfy, whatever the consequences, I will show no fear in front of my siblings.*

The eunuch pushed the door open, his bracelets jingling. He inclined his head, the feathers on his turban waving with the motion. Tarja gulped and lifted her chin, determined to face her father's ire boldly. Even if this was her final day alive, she'd die a brave Pasargadian. *If I don't throw up first.*

15

Eighty-one days after the winter solstice in the 29th year of Emperor Vural Tzimiskes

"I CAN'T THANK YOU enough," Derya said to Lady Aspasia. "Really, you've been more than kind."

Lady Aspasia laughed. "I didn't expect you to consider a night in the cells a kindness."

"It was rather novel . . ." Derya cast her glance at her companions, her lips twitching into a smirk.

Bahadir, like any disciplined soldier, had embraced their temporary quarters stoically. In contrast, Nazif had been at turns offended, outraged, and petulant. The worst, he'd said, was being deprived of wine with his dinner. That they'd been served anything at all, Derya pointed out, had risked exposing their ruse.

The past two days had passed in a storm of devising schemes and debating their merits, trying to agree on a plan. Most ranged from what Bahadir called impractical to what Kelebek branded idiotic. The one thing they agreed upon was the need to shroud their hasty departure from Nafplio in secrecy.

Cetus's monsters had witnessed their return from the north. Those who'd slaughtered the wyvern and the frost giants had surely discovered the dead dragon and knew someone had retrieved the scepter. Derya didn't want Cetus's suspicion to fall upon her. Let him focus his attention on the king of Rorvik. Just what that lying king deserved. Their only chance of getting anywhere near the crown was if Cetus didn't know they were seeking it.

After a conference that stretched well past midnight, Derya and her advisors had agreed on a scheme. They would announce that one hundred of their soldiers would sail south on two ships to provide reinforcements to the emperor's forces in settling unrest in a Terramarian port.

Nazif, naturally, wanted a plan for the remaining two hundred soldiers, most of whom had arrived with him. Safiye, backed by Kelebek, argued for sending them all home.

At that point, Nazif's raised voice and reddened face revealed how unnerving he found that proposal. He pointed out that if one of their scheming cousins succeeded in being named co-emperor, having a small army on hand might mean the difference between survival and death for the newly deposed heir of Cinar. Not to mention one of the other principal contenders for the throne.

Derya, shuddering as she considered how Yildiz or Utku would hunt Nazif and her down if they came to the throne, had to agree with him. That Bahadir supported Nazif only confirmed her decision.

Under their facade of courtesy, it was obvious the Nafplian nobles wanted the Cinarrians gone. They were busy preparing for Nuura's trial and the election of a new diodochi. As more nobles arrived at the castle, it became clear the Cinarrians weren't welcome. Nobody wanted a Cinarrian puppet installed, and the three hundred Cinarrian soldiers in and around the castle made the Nafplians more fractious than they already were.

Lady Aspasia, the only person they took into their confidence, resolved the dilemma by offering one of her estates. She publicly invited Derya, her advisors, and their entourage to her remote mountain fortress to await the return of the others from Terramare.

But in reality, Derya and her advisors would slip away with the Cinarrian soldiers assigned to sail for Terramare. Only they'd journey north, rather than south, once they crossed the Vasiden Strait.

The stumbling block had been how the Heir of Cinar would leave Nafplio without anyone knowing. Kelebek proposed an elaborate deception. Derya, after some hesitation, had consented, simply because no one had devised anything better. *I hope I don't regret this.*

"Truly, I am grateful," Derya told Aspasia. "I'm just worried Cetus will make good on his threats."

Aspasia snorted. "If there's one thing we as a small nation stuck between greater powers know how to do, it's dissemble, negotiate, and grovel. We'll pretend ignorance and swear we knew nothing of the scepter. We'll lie for you as long as we can." She grimaced. "But if it looks like Cetus will act, we'll tell him the truth. You understand."

Derya and Aspasia exchanged knowing nods. Ancient tales told how Cetus rarely wasted time on vengeance, not until he'd achieved his main goals. Once he realized the Nafplians didn't have the scepter, the sorcerer would probably kill a few as a warning. Then he'd pursue his missing artifact like a hyena stalks prey. After he recovered his scepter, he'd return to avenge himself on those who had been less than cooperative.

Aspasia went on. "We've always prided ourselves that we'd die rather than submit to another power. And we nearly surrendered, just because the assassinations had unnerved us. No, you restored us to ourselves. Let Cetus bluster. He can destroy our harbors, murder our children, and slaughter our goats. We will not bend to him."

Derya's throat tightened, and tears pricked her eyes. *Any Nafplian deaths will be my fault.* "I won't let it come to that if I can help it."

"Do that, highness, and you will always have friends in Nafplio."

Derya picked up her rough rucksack and followed Aspasia through cold stone corridors, accompanied by Bahadir and Nazif. Aspasia led them up a narrow, winding staircase lit only by the flickering taper in her hand.

Lady Aspasia stopped at a small wooden door. "This leads to the courtyard behind the stables, and it's a short distance to the traders' gate. No one should pay you any attention."

Derya grinned as she glanced at her companions, amused by the sight of the chiliarch and her cousin with unshaven faces, wearing workmen's clothing, rough dun-colored tunics, trousers, and cloaks, much the same as her own garb. She wrapped a woolen scarf around her head, obscuring her face. Bahadir and Nazif pulled up their hoods, shrouding their own features. The three of them should resemble servants or stable hands and pass unnoticed to the gates.

She pressed Aspasia's hand in farewell and followed Bahadir into the courtyard. Around them, the Cinarrians destined for Aspasia's castle were assembling. Horseshoes clattered on the cobblestones, harnesses jangled, and the low rumble of a deep voice singing a Cinarrian war song filled the air.

"You!" one of Nazif's kentarchs shouted. "Yes, you," he repeated when Bahadir glanced in his direction. "Come here."

Derya's heart skipped a beat. If the Nafplians uncovered their ruse, all the goodwill she and Nazif had built up would shrivel like paper in a fire. And be humiliating for themselves and the Cinarrian empire. That was an outcome her father would not be pleased with. For a moment, she considered returning the way she'd come. No, it was too late to second-guess her decision. She stiffened, trying not to let her trembling knees betray her fear.

"Bring the steps for the kiral."

She lowered her chin to hide her confusion. What did she need steps for? Then she recovered. *He must mean the fake kiral, so she can mount her horse.*

Bahadir took an uncertain step toward the man. Derya's maid, Rasheda, rushed over to the kentarch. "No, no, I can do it." She seized the step stool and placed it next to Derya's chestnut mare.

"Let's go," Bahadir murmured. Derya and Nazif followed him around the crowd and slipped out of the castle gate. Once on the street, her breathing steadied. *Rider bless Rasheda for thinking quickly. Good thing we decided to leave her behind to attend the false Derya.*

They crept through quiet side streets to the docks where their ships waited, bobbing on the rosy-streaked sea reflecting the dawn sky. Hiding in an alley, they exchanged their brown Nafplian cloaks for sand-colored Isedonnian burnooses. Bahadir and Nazif wrapped their heads in white turbans, while Derya twisted a pale tan scarf around her head, veiling her face. The early morning wind tugged at the edge of her burnoose, making her shiver. *My life is one long, frozen journey. Land or sea, I'm doomed to frostbitten toes and chapped lips.*

She wrapped her arms around herself and stamped her freezing feet as the last of her soldiers boarded the ship. The tramp of their steps on the gangplank blended with the ships' flags snapping in the wind. Kentarchs Sezgin and Farooq had done a stellar job organizing their departure, hiring two ships with crews and getting them provisioned for their supposed journey south.

But the real genius of the plan was Kelebek's. One of the thorniest problems had been how to leave Nafplio and pass the Vasiden Strait before anyone knew they had gone.

Kelebek's idea required Derya, Safiye, and Nazif to pose

as artisans and servants of a trader. Bahadir would pretend to be a servant until they set sail. Then he'd resume his role as chiliarch. No one thought he'd be able to hide his identity from the men who served under him.

The oikeios strode down the gangplank, garbed in the sand-colored, flowing robes of a Terramarian trader, the long, pointed hood hanging down his back. Fully six inches of intricate embroidery embellished the hem of his garments. A small, scarlet, cylindrical hat perched on his head, its black tassel swaying as it dangled near his face.

Kelebek pointed at Derya. "You. Girl." He pointed to a small chest near the foot of the gangplank. "Bring that and get on board."

Irritation stabbed Derya, which was chased away by her amusement over the situation. *Oh, he's enjoying this.*

16

M AYBE I SHOULDN'T HAVE let Kelebek cast himself in the role of master trader. Derya had never witnessed such animated glee in him as when he was ordering them all about.

He pointed at two rucksacks at his feet. "Take these onboard." His voice took on an imperious tone. "And don't think you can slack on your quota today. Two tunics, no less."

Since embroidery was the only craft she was remotely proficient at, it was her assigned task. She picked up the chest and rucksacks and gave him a mocking bow. "Yes, sir."

Safiye scuttled in Kelebek's wake, clutching a wax tablet to her chest, playing the part of the trader's accountant and scribe. She wore a vivid yellow caftan and dark green burnoose, her face veiled by a matching green scarf.

Bahadir had already gone aboard, lugging a sack full of extra clothing for all of them, clothes that fit their true identities. Nazif had boarded with him, carrying a small satchel of tailoring supplies and a large bundle of fabric. He claimed he'd learned in the army, saying sometimes it was necessary to do your own mending. Who, Derya mused, would have thought that her pleasure-loving cousin could sew?

Garzuli, Nazif's slave, was to continue as a carpet maker. Derya pursed her lips. They'd sent the girl on board the night before, under heavy guard, to be locked in a cabin until they set sail. Guilt stabbed Derya's heart, making her wince. She wanted to offer Garzuli freedom before they left but conceded they couldn't risk even a rumor of their plans slipping out. Once freed, Garzuli would have had the choice to stay behind, which they couldn't afford to give her.

Derya shoved her regrets aside and let a fresh worry fill her mind. *Will this ruse fool anyone?* It wasn't a great plan, Derya knew, but all they had. Bahadir had hired ships newly arrived from Isedonnes, so there'd be less chance of the crew hearing about the Heir of Cinar visiting Nafplio. And Kelebek had outdone himself selecting the proper clothing for their new stations.

Derya twitched her shoulders, the rough shift she wore under the stained tunic scratching her skin. Perhaps this was taking the deception too far. Although Kelebek had a point that if anyone saw them laundering silk undergarments, it might give away their ploy. Just in case they managed to arrive in Veleti before Cetus discovered what they were up to, they didn't want the crew spreading gossip about them among the Veletians.

Derya clambered down a ladder to the lower deck and found the tiny cabin she was to share with Safiye and Garzuli. The girl's eyes had widened and her face flushed when informed of the arrangements, but she didn't protest. She sat docilely at her loom, sorting colored silk threads.

With a relieved sigh, Derya yanked the veil from her face. She sat and pulled out her embroidery. Her mother would have laughed to see her meekly bent over her work. But inside, she was chafing at the task. *Good thing this is all a farce.*

A sudden thought made her stop, her needle raised in the air. She'd always assumed her servants were tractable and content. Had they been masking inner frustration and resentment?

"Highness," Garzuli said. "If I may ask. How long is our voyage?"

A fair question, but Derya was loath to answer, at least not until they'd sailed far out to sea. "It's hard to say. Storms could delay us." With luck, nine days to Veleti. With even more luck, the king of Veleti wouldn't put up any difficulties, and Stigandr Tyr of Rorvik wouldn't try to kill Derya on sight.

Garzuli separated a crimson spool from a vermilion one. "It would be lovely if we encountered warmer weather."

That felt to Derya like she was fishing for the destination. "It's warmer in Terramare this time of year."

Garzuli bent her head, frowning as she tied a series of crimson knots. Derya pursed her lips. She suspected Garzuli didn't believe Terramare was their destination. Well, let her think what she wanted. While Derya felt she could trust the girl, she couldn't ignore Nazif's and Kelebek's warnings that she could be a Pasargadian spy. Bahadir had interrogated her and wasn't sure either way. Usually people from Isedonnes had darker skin and coarser hair than Garzuli's dusky olive complexion and sleek, black hair, but there'd been so much intermarriage that she could be who she said she was. Still, that accent . . .

Maybe I should try to find out. The princess threaded her needle with turquoise thread and took a few stitches. "This weather must feel freezing to you after Isedonnes."

"Oh, very."

"How long does the summer last?"

A pause. "Not as long as I'd like."

Derya finished stitching a bird's wing in blue. She cut off her thread and moved to the eye of a wolf. Garzuli was giving her vague answers. Did she prefer to avoid conversation? These were the responses a spy or assassin would offer. Her skin prickled. Derya narrowed her eyes and studied the other girl whose head was bent over her weaving. She could be a slave who didn't care to be friendly with her owner. *If someone bought me, I wouldn't want to be friends with them.*

Nazif flung open the door and slammed it behind himself. "This is the last time we adopt any of Kelebek's plans. He's having way too much fun."

"Oh?" Derya grinned. "What did he order you to do? Mend his undergarments?"

Nazif scoffed and dropped onto Derya's bed, its flimsy wood groaning under his weight. "Nothing like that. He offered my services to make the captain a set of trousers if he got us to"—he looked at Garzuli—"Terramare in a week."

Garzuli was eyeing Nazif, her eyelids drooping, but her interest in his words was obvious. Perhaps she really was from Isedonnes and wondered if after Terramare they'd sail further south. Only natural she'd want to see her homeland again.

And very unnatural that Nazif owned her. Just the thought of possessing another human left a sour taste in Derya's mouth. "Cousin. There is a matter I would discuss with you."

He glanced at Garzuli, eyebrows raised.

"It concerns her, so she should stay."

Garzuli stiffened.

Nazif glared at Derya. "Are you going to bring this up again?"

"You need to free her."

He huffed and flopped onto his back. "And what of the money I paid for her?"

"What of it? Raging waters, it was less than what you spend on wine or horses or women in a week." Out of the corner of her eye, Derya noticed an angry scowl cross Garzuli's taut face. The girl pressed her lips together, not completely masking her resentment.

"True. But who are you to judge how I entertain myself?"

"I am the Heir of Cinar."

"You think that. Who knows what's happened in Tulgutalp

since we last heard from your father. He could have died and
Yildiz seized the throne." Nazif propped himself up on one
elbow. "Then you and I, like so many before us, will be hunted
down as potential threats. Maybe having a slave will bolster
my disguise as a mercenary trader, allowing me to disappear
into the Isedonnian countryside."

Derya's stomach heaved. Nazif was right. They could be
in a precarious position. Perhaps she should wait to free
Garzuli. If the girl let slip a single word about the scepter, all
their scheming would unravel like a ball of yarn tossed to a
playful cat. Cetus would seize the loose strand and spin it into
a victory of his own.

And freeing a spy or assassin could destroy all their plans.
She had been too quick to trust in the past. She rubbed the
spot on her head where Stigandr had whacked it.

But no. She'd let her need for a metal mage warp her
judgement. Garzuli needed to be freed. Nazif's cold, prag-
matic reasoning didn't justify bending his morals. How else
could his reasoning be suspect? "Until we receive a formal
announcement with the official seal of the emperor, I remain
the Heir of Cinar. And I say neither of us have any business
owning a slave. You promised to write a bill of sale. Where
is it?"

Garzuli had stopped pretending to have little interest in
their conversation. She was staring at Derya as if the princess
had sprouted wings from her ears and tusks from her nose.

Nazif sat up. "My scribe wrote one. I concede your point
that it is distasteful to own another human being. But I won't
part with her without compensation."

"What?" Derya sighed wearily.

He spoke deliberately, choosing his words with care. "You
embarked on a quest and obtained something of great value.
Now we commence a second quest."

"Yes." Derya studied him from the corner of her eye,
unsure where he was taking the conversation.

"You control the first treasure. When we locate the second, I want the first try at taking it."

She didn't like that, not one bit. Nazif would surely attempt to use the crown against her to convince her father he deserved to be co-emperor, ousting Derya. She nibbled her lip. It had taken King Stigandr and her more than one attempt to get the scepter from the dragon. Retrieving the crown should be equally perilous, if not more. If Nazif tried and failed, she'd learn from his attempt.

And if they had to involve Stigandr, Nazif could be an effective buffer between her and the crafty king. *I might be able to use him to my advantage.*

"Very well. Go fetch your bill of sale, and Safiye and Kelebek to witness the transfer of ownership. Oh, and have Safiye write up the writ of freedom."

Nazif bounced off the bed, thumping his shabby boots on the floor. He bowed, adding a mocking flourish. "As you wish, Heir of Cinar. I only hope your charity doesn't come back to haunt you."

Derya eyed the door as it closed behind him. Freeing Garzuli was the just and moral course of action. But she'd caught too many odd flickers in Garzuli's eyes. There was something off about the girl. Nazif's words settled in her stomach in an icy knot. *Rider, let him be mistaken.*

17

T HE AIR RUSHED FROM the room, making spots dance in front of Tarja's eyes. Her jaw went slack. What had she witnessed? Had Derya convinced her cousin to give up ownership of her and intended to set her free? This was inconceivable.

The floor tilted and the walls of the tiny cabin whirled around her. She clutched the loom for support and struggled to breathe.

All her life, she'd heard stories of the lying Cinarrians, who pretended to be morally superior to other empires by not owning slaves. Everyone in Pasargadae saw through that farce. How else were the crops harvested, the ships built, and the roads maintained?

Tarja frowned and glanced at her companion. The princess was humming as she stitched, apparently not interested in conversation. Tarja rubbed her eyes. Had she misunderstood what Derya said? Maybe her Cinarrian wasn't as fluent as she thought.

Work. She needed to work, to occupy her shaking hands and collect her scattered thoughts. A lock of black hair tumbled over her face as she referred to her sketch. *Blue. Sky blue is next.* With trembling fingers, she sorted through the spools of silk and found the azure shade. She tied three knots. *Sepia next. Two knots.*

Maybe this was a trap, some kind of game Derya was playing. That would fit the Cinarrians. They'd stolen the secret of the fire that burned on water from the Ymittosians under the guise of promising lasting friendship. They'd convinced Isedonnes and Exine that Pasargadian trade ships from Kisiwenga, Var pan Chaata, and Adzope were pirates. Cinarrian warships destroyed the supposed pirates. Grateful for the protection, the two southern nations became vassal states of Cinar, further isolating Pasargadae. *Ninety generations of liars and thieves, that's what Cinarrians are.*

Added to the scandalous behavior of the royal family itself. Emperors and princes cavorting with dancers, actresses, and circus performers, and even making them empresses. So much for keeping royal bloodlines pure.

No wonder Derya was such a flighty flirt. So unworthy of the advantages she had. Did she understand the immense privilege of being named heir to the throne and not passed over for being a girl? Clearly not. It appeared to Tarja that Derya took her position as Heir of Cinar as a birthright and never considered she might not be empress one day. *How fortunate for her.*

Tarja frowned, casting a quick glance at the diligently sewing Derya. She hadn't observed much flirting from Derya, even when her cousin gave her obvious openings. Had that rumor been false? Or was Derya not interested in Nazif? He was, after all, a rival to the throne, and since he was married, Derya couldn't wed him to form a joint rule. Tarja curled her lip. The foolish Cinarrians only allowed one wife.

Pity the poor royal consort who failed to produce an heir. More often than not, childless wives of Cinarrian emperors conveniently died, paving the way for nubile replacements who would hopefully prove to be fertile. In Pasargadae, men shunted their barren wives aside for others, but at least the women would live.

Tarja mechanically tied knots to the end of the row, barely conscious of the symmetrical geometric shapes and stylized flowers forming under her hands. Focusing on the individual knots helped slow her racing thoughts.

It didn't matter if the rumors about Derya were true or false. Naïve or cynical, whatever she was, she was the Heir of Cinar, an enemy of the Pasargadian empire. Tarja swallowed the thought that she should be grateful to Derya for freeing her. *No. If slavery appalled Derya as much as she claimed, then she should have freed me immediately. Such a hypocrite.* Derya deserved to die. But how?

Perhaps if they encountered a storm at sea, she could shove Derya overboard. That would be the easiest. But if Derya was rescued, then the princess would demand an explanation. *Could I make it look like an accident? Or pin the blame on someone else?*

Tarja pursed her lips. Derya's soldiers on board were well armed but left the horses behind. So they weren't planning an overland journey. But they were expecting danger, some form of attack. *That might be my opportunity.*

She continued weaving, wondering why Derya was so placidly embroidering. The princess had made no secret of her hatred of the art. But here she was. *Is she watching me? Or waiting for something?*

Tarja got her answer before she'd knotted another half a row. Nazif returned with the woman Derya called her danis-man, which Tarja took to mean a combined counselor and chaperone. With them was the fussy, supercilious diplomat Kelebek who reminded Tarja of low-ranking viziers who preened when given a smidgen of power.

Nazif slapped a parchment on the table in front of Derya. "The bill of sale. You owe me one nummas."

Tarja suppressed a choke. He was selling her for the price

of half a loaf of day-old bread? Really, if he intended to sell her as chattel, at least he could ask a reasonable price.

"So you give up your claim to the other treasure?" Derya asked.

Nazif snorted. "Hilarious. I had to name an amount to make it legal and wasn't about to say 'treasure to be specified' or any such nonsense. No need to have scribes asking nosy questions."

Derya nodded. "Thank you, Nazif." She looked at Safiye and Kelebek. "What?"

Kelebek sniffed. "You are right to set the slave free, Kiral. But your cousin extracts a high price."

Tarja kept her eyes on her weaving. Did they know just how valuable Cetus's crown was? And how worthless, even though they had the scepter? Without the band, they'd never exploit the power in the two artifacts.

Safiye handed Derya another document. "I agree with the oikeios."

Such a silly title for a diplomat, Tarja thought. *Fits him, though. Like the squeaking of a pig.*

"What's this?" Derya asked.

Safiye tipped her head toward Tarja. "The writ of freedom."

"Oh, right." Derya perused the document.

Tarja's heart sped up. Was the princess really granting her freedom? This had to be a ruse. No Cinarrian would free a slave without some financial gain. And in making the bargain with her cousin, Derya stood to lose any leverage the scepter gave her.

"Safiye, where's my seal?" Derya asked.

Tarja stared, and her jaw drifted open as Safiye inked Derya's seal. Nazif signed the bill of sale, the princess signed the writ of freedom, and Nazif, Kelebek, and Safiye signed as witnesses. Then the princess pressed her seal over the signatures.

Safiye handed Derya two additional documents. "The copies."

After all signed the copies, Derya thumped her seal on them. She leaned back with a smile. "I feel better. My skin was crawling just thinking we had a slave in our midst."

Ever wonder what I felt?

"If you require nothing else, Kiral," said Kelebek, "we'll be off. This one"—he pointed at Nazif—"is behind in his tailoring. And your danisman has accounts to prepare."

"Since we have no sales, no inventory, and no debts, that will be an intriguing work of fiction," Derya said. "I look forward to reading it."

After they left, Tarja gazed at the closed door with a vacant stare. She rubbed her eyes and tried to focus her thoughts. She sagged against the wall, her shoulders slumped.

"Garzuli."

Tarja jerked to look at Derya, who laughed. "You didn't expect to be freed?"

"No, highness, I didn't." That was the truth.

"Well, from the minute Nazif told me he'd bought a slave, I determined to make this right. As soon as the ink dries, you can have the original writ of freedom."

Tarja flicked her gaze to the document lying on the table. Maybe Derya was still toying with her. "Yes, highness."

"Now, even though you're free, you're stuck with us, at least while we're at sea. So I propose to take you into my entourage. You're a skilled weaver; perhaps there's something else you can do. And I may need your skills as a metal mage. Would thirty bronze coins a month be acceptable?"

"Thirty . . ."

"As your salary. Too little? We'll, of course, cover your living expenses and provide two sets of clothing and footwear each year."

Tarja shifted in her seat and stared at Derya. The floor appeared to rock, a motion independent of the ocean's waves.

The princess seemed sincere. But this generosity couldn't be true. To cover her confusion, she pulled the knotted headband from her hair, smoothed a few stray strands back from her face, and replaced the band. *What game is Derya playing?*

"Think about it. I'm afraid that while we're traveling, I won't be able to do much for you in the way of clothing. But we'll dig up something better for you."

Tarja glanced down. Nazif had given her slave's clothes, a rough tunic and leggings cut straight like a sack, embellished with nothing more than rough bone buttons. A far cry from the flowing silks and gauzy linens she'd worn as a Pasargadian princess. "Thank you, highness."

Derya nodded. "I'd better finish this before Kelebek comes back and makes a scene." She shook her head and flashed Tarja a rueful smile. "He's enjoying this charade entirely too much."

Tarja resumed her own work, frowning. This version of Derya had to be an act. This Derya was thoughtful, compassionate, and even humorous. The kind of person who could become a good friend. Based on what Tarja had learned of Nazif and his ambitions, Derya could relate to Tarja's battles with her own siblings. Was this the real Derya? Or was the awful, spoiled flirt rumor told of the real one? Maybe Derya was playing a part, just the way Tarja often had.

The ship crested a wave and its timbers creaked, as if reluctant to continue on course. A whisper of uncertainty flickered in Tarja's mind. Did she truly want to kill Derya? For half a moment, she wanted to ally with her, to help her fight off Cetus.

Tarja's stomach quivered, and she shivered. She battled within herself, longing for a friend, to confess everything to Derya, to have someone see her for who she really was. Her fingers tightened around a scarlet strand, the silk cutting into her flesh as she surveyed the other princess. Maybe Derya could be trusted . . .

Tarja bit her lip hard. The Heir of Cinar was an enemy of Pasargadae. If she knew Tarja's true identity, Derya would lock her up. Or have her killed. No matter how parallel their circumstances, they were enemies and always would be. Tarja could never forget that. She only had one way forward. Derya had to die.

18

Pasargadae

Forty-six days after the winter solstice in the 17th year of Emperor Cambyses III and the 29th year of Vural Tzimiskes of Cinar

TARJA'S STEPS WHISPERED over the tiled corridor floors, a hushed counterpoint to the tinkle of fountains and the harsh drawl of a noble berating a servant. Weariness slowed her pace as she fought the fatigue. The audience with her father had been fraught with tension, made worse when she was the only one who elicited any praise from him. How he hated that his least favorite child was the most capable. And her siblings detested it even more.

Afterward, she'd sought refuge with her mother. Rather than offering sympathy, her mother set her to practicing magic.

Today's task involved opening locks. After hours of practice, she'd won a partial victory. In a matter of minutes, she could take the lock apart with her fingers and rebuild it.

But when using her magic for the task, she was utterly defeated. The strain of concentration sent throbbing pulses through her head. She longed to lie down in the silence and solitude of her own room. And she couldn't fathom how magically opening locks would help her in her ongoing war with her siblings, much less gain ground in the emperor's esteem.

As she passed the open door of her brother Samsher's apartments, a hand yanked her inside. Her pulse sped up, and she jerked her arm free. "What are you doing?"

"Keep your voice down," Samsher said. "I only want to talk." He closed the door and leaned against it.

Tarja crossed her arms and tried to convince her racing heart to slow. "You could have found a less startling way to get my attention." She glanced around his opulent sitting room. Piles of embroidered cushions rested on overstuffed divans covered with crimson silk. An intricate carpet in a complicated symmetrical design formed of black, gold, and green sprawled over a large section of the tiled floor. As far as she could tell, she and her brother were alone. But someone could hide in the sleeping chamber, or behind the silk wall hangings.

"Oh, but that would be boring." His dark olive face grew serious, and his pale blue eyes bored into her own. "Dastgir appears to be our father's favorite these days."

Oh, so it was to be that kind of a talk. The dangerous kind. The kind that could get you banished or tortured or killed, even though the emperor's blood ran in your veins. Tarja's stomach still heaved whenever she thought of the older sister who'd been hung on the ramparts for plotting against their father. Her mouth felt as if she'd eaten dust. "Yes, it appears so."

"But he isn't the worthiest."

For once, she could agree with Samsher wholeheartedly. "That's not for me to judge."

"He also doesn't seem to like you very much."

Then it's mutual, she almost blurted. "I'll have to try to change that."

"I've always liked you," he said. "You're clever."

Oh, no. It was a fine line she'd been walking, to get her father to perceive her intelligence, but for her brothers to overlook her abilities. "Thank you." She inclined her head in a small bow. "You are very kind."

"Clever people prize the admiration of the powerful."

Was he speaking truth, partial truth, or trying to flatter her? She tipped her head to the side and used her most innocent-sounding voice, high-pitched and girlish. "How does one gain the esteem of the powerful?"

"By sharing what they have."

She gave him a small smile. If he was probing for information, he was going to be disappointed. "Brother, you have more of everything than I do. *Everything.*" She emphasized the last word, gesturing at the room's luxurious decor.

His lips twitched into a smirk. "If that ever changes, remember me." He opened the door and gestured to the corridor. "I'll see you at dinner."

Tarja tipped her head and stalked away, clenching her fists. She dug her nails into her palms, punishing herself for not playing the role of innocent younger sister better. Samsher had seen through her facade of simpleminded docility. It would be perilous if anyone else had.

Dastgir, she thought, hadn't. He was too enamored of his own superiority. But his full sister, Fariba, might be more perceptive and dangerous. She'd always envied Tarja. In a rare moment of honesty, she'd spit out that she hated tall, thin women with green eyes.

Tarja still resented that. What did Fariba want her to do? Cut her legs off at the knees and spend her days lounging on cushions, nibbling pastries and dates until she was as round as she was tall? Fariba was jealous Tarja was the only one who had inherited their father's large green eyes. There was nothing she could do about her eyes, short of gouging them out. And that Tarja was not prepared to do to placate her half-sister.

She was still brooding over Fariba's animosity when she turned a corner and a sack shrouded her head. Suddenly blinded, she gasped and stumbled. Her heart raced, and sweat moistened her forehead. She scratched at the hands holding her. Her fingernails slid harmlessly over leather gloves.

A blow to her ribs took her breath away. "Quiet," growled a deep voice.

Her assailants dragged her down the corridor. One seized her under her arms. The other gripped her legs and lifted. Together, they lugged her down what Tarja assumed to be the servant's stairs.

Two of them, she thought. Fighting would be pointless. *We'd all end up tumbling down the stairs.* This was most likely some prank of her siblings. They'd done worse before. The worst outcome would be to disturb their father. No, she'd wait and let matters play out.

She smelled roasting lamb and frying garlic. Yes, they were on the servant's stairs by the kitchens.

Her assailants didn't pause. The air cooled as they descended. Were they taking her to the dungeons? Tarja's breath hitched, and she felt as if she was choking. She clamped her lips together to stifle a whimper.

The odors of cooking food were replaced by the stench of unwashed prisoners and their rotting waste. She'd thought her heart had been racing when Samsher grabbed her. That was a crawl compared to the frantic thumping now, faster than a trapped hummingbird's.

Without warning, her legs were dropped, and she staggered to gain her footing. "What are you doing?" Tarja asked.

A punch in the stomach was the answer. Pain shot through her core. Air whooshed from her lungs. She doubled over, arms wrapped around her cramping abdomen. Blows rained down on her back and legs. She lashed out, but blinded by the hood, failed to connect with either of her attackers.

A fist pounded her chest, and she grabbed it. She stretched her fingers to reach beyond the heavy glove and raked her fingernails over her attacker's wrist. A muttered curse confirmed her suspicions. Dastgir was one of the two. She guessed Fariba was the smaller one, whose blows weren't as painful. And they'd both been careful not to hit her arms, neck, or face. Her clothing would hide any bruises.

A final punch to her stomach sent her dropping to her knees. Then her attackers dragged her across the floor, and an iron door clanged shut. Rapid footsteps thudded up the stairs.

With a moan, she tugged at the sack covering her head. Her fingers fumbled at the string, cursing as she failed to untie the knot. She grabbed the string with both hands and broke it. With a quick motion, she yanked the sack off. She lay gasping for breath, retching as the foul stench filled her nose.

When her head stopped spinning, Tarja staggered to her feet, hissing and wincing. She peered through the barred door. A long, cell-lined corridor stretched before her, illuminated by a single torch fixed to the wall. Two men in a nearby cell were talking about her, their voices echoing in the darkness. From their accents, she guessed they were the Cinarrian spies who had been arrested a week ago.

The princess leaned her head against the cold metal bars. It took several minutes to steady her breath. She swallowed hard, commanding her heaving stomach to still. Panicking would be foolish. Eventually, the jailer would bring the prisoners' supper. She'd tell him one of her siblings had played a prank on her and be freed.

But she would miss dinner, which would earn her father's disapproval. Any favor she'd gained from the meeting earlier would fade like ink on ancient parchment. Which was most likely Dastgir's intent.

Anger flared up over her cheeks. No, she would not wait.

I'm a metal mage, by the gods. Tarja swore under her breath. Should she risk using her magic? Maybe not. If any of her siblings realized the extent of her power, they'd attack with more than just fists.

Biting her lip, she considered her options. She could melt the metal and bend the bars to create an opening. But it would leave a clear sign of her powers. Unless she bent the bars back into shape. Which would demand time she didn't have.

Tarja grabbed the bars and shook them, a repressed scream burning the back of her throat. If only she'd worked harder on the lock.

She curled her lip. Her mother wanted her to practice. Well, this was an opportunity. She ran her fingers over the cold metal. Reaching through the bars, she found the large keyhole. This lock was flat. A simple turn of a key would open it.

She summoned her magic and imagined the lock's inner workings. She sensed the tumblers—two, maybe three—and the piece that the key would press against.

Since she didn't know how many tumblers the lock had, it would be next to impossible to magically shift them all. There had to be a better way. *A key would move all the tumblers at once.* She imagined her power as a key and mentally inserted it into the lock. She let the magic spread, filling the space, seeking obstructions. When she thought she'd found them all, she turned her magical key.

Nothing.

She released her magic. *What am I doing wrong?* She huffed and glared at the lock. *So much for having a gift for metal magic.*

Tarja made a second attempt, then another. Then thirty more. Every time she gained a clearer picture of the tumblers' locations and the dimensions of their pins and edges. But each time, she felt wearier. Her toes were growing numb, a sure sign of overusing her magic. She stamped her feet, trying to warm them.

The princess rested her aching head against the bars. *One more try.* She pushed her magic into the lock, forming her key. Then she turned it.

There was a faint click, and the door swung open. Tarja darted out and slammed it shut. Then she bolted for the stairs, stumbling over her numb toes.

The two prisoners gaped at her. "How'd you get out?"

"They didn't lock the door," she answered.

Then she scampered up the steps, ignoring the aches in her ribs, abdomen, and legs. She had a dinner to prepare for, and the cost of tardiness was too awful to consider.

19

Eighty-seven days after the winter solstice in the 29th year of Emperor Vural Tzimiskes

WIND WHIPPED OVER Sundsvall Bay, tossing dinghies and rowboats over the white-topped waves like so many toys. The king of Veleti's gray stone castle glared over the bay, as if scowling at Derya and her ships. She tugged her sea cloak tighter. In Cinar, spring would have coaxed flowers into bloom. Here in the north, snow still covered the roofs of the town.

The ship's captain coughed, a harsh rasp that blended with the creaking of the ship and the snapping of Cinar's flag. Derya jerked her head from her contemplation of Veleti's rocky shoreline. After a week of sailing with him, Derya knew the cough meant he was nervous.

So was she. Unlike their trip to Nafplio, they'd had fair weather, only a few squalls interrupting the steady south wind. They'd made the usual nine-day trip in only six. Once past the Axum Strait, much to Derya's relief and Kelebek's annoyance, Bahadir advised they give up their pretense. The crew, Derya thought with a smile, got over their shock days ago.

The captain coughed again and spat over the rail. "Unnatural for this time of year," he growled. "South winds in spring bring trouble, same as bringing women on board." He paused. "No offense, highness."

Derya pressed her lips together to suppress her flicker of amusement. "None taken." Her mirth faded as she considered the captain's worry. It wouldn't be hard to believe that Cetus was manipulating the wind and waves, lulling them into complacency, believing they'd fooled him. When they least expected it, he'd conjure up a hurricane and smash them against the rocky coast. The closer they got to Veleti, the more uneasy she grew. Why did she feel like a mouse waiting for the cat to pounce?

"Kiral, we have a situation."

The edge in Bahadir's voice lacerated Derya's taut nerves. She spun to face him. "What is it? Is there plague in Veleti?"

"No. Look." The three scars in his face twitched as he pointed across the bay.

Now that they'd sailed closer, she could see the small boats she'd noticed more clearly. Hundreds dotted the bay, some no more than rafts. Most bore people, some motionless, others thrashing the air with frantically waving arms. Three Veletian longboats hovered over the far side of the flotilla, their sides rimmed with shields and dragon heads carved into their prows. The largest one flew the king's banner, a scarlet falcon on a black background. Even with hundreds of feet of water separating them, Derya could see bowmen lined up on the deck of the king's ship, all with nocked arrows on their bowstrings.

The princess frowned. "What is this?"

The ship's stocky mate bustled to her side. "My apologies, highness. The king's signaler sent a message." He held a wax tablet to her.

Derya of Cinar:

For grave offenses committed the last time you were on our shores, I order you banned from Veleti, its territories, and its waters. Leave at once.

Derya stared at the tablet. "Is this a joke?" Or was King Ollen that furious? She had placed him in an awkward position with the king of Rorvik. It seemed he hadn't forgiven her for that. He'd omitted her title, and the tone of the message was insulting.

"Three longboats of warriors say it's not," Bahadir said.

Derya's mouth went dry. *We need Ollen's help.* "Can we negotiate?"

Safiye shook her head. "We could ask the oikeios. But I wouldn't be too hopeful. Even his best efforts might provoke King Ollen further."

"Chiliarch?"

"We don't want war with Veleti, that's certain. Are you sure approaching the king of Rorvik won't work?"

"After what I did? Stigandr might forgive me for stealing the scepter, but using my magic to make him vomit? Never." If Ollen spurned her with thinly veiled insults, Stigandr would do so with blades and spells.

But she had to get past their anger. She surveyed the harbor and frowned. "What are all these little boats?"

Bahadir let out a long sigh. "A man we fished from the water told us. Cetus conquered the western islands, and these are refugees."

Her mouth, already dry, became a desert. Cetus's threats were now a painful, horrifying reality. "Surely this isn't the closest place for them to land?" Derya asked.

"With Ymittos gone, it is." The captain shuddered. "They barely made it here. Maybe some tried for Axum, but that's a long way south."

Derya scanned the flotilla of rafts. She turned her gaze to the longboats and eyed the bowmen. "Perhaps if we take some refugees on board the archers won't shoot. Then we can try negotiating with the king."

"Captain," said Bahadir, "how many could we take on?"

The burly man spat over the side. "We've only got food for three days."

"But we can't leave them on those rafts," Derya said. Those poor people had endured at least a week at sea, maybe longer. They had to be close to death. "Can we pick up twenty-five, maybe children or wounded, and hope that thaws the king a little?"

"And in two days when we run out of food, then what?" The captain shook his head. "I have to think of my crew."

"Someone has to help those people," Derya said, "and it doesn't look like King Ollen intends to. Maybe if we do, that will shame him into letting them land on shore."

With a sniff and a shake of his head, the captain said, "You better hope that barbarian king takes these people off your hands. Otherwise, we'll all starve." He ordered one boat lowered, which prompted the longboat crews to clang their swords against their shields.

Derya forced her spine straight as she glared across the water at the longboats. *At least they aren't shooting. Rider knows how many innocents the crossfire would kill.*

The Cinarrian soldiers rowed to the nearest group of rafts and returned with a boat full of sunburned, hollow-eyed refugees.

Derya, Safiye, and Garzuli sorted them into groups and seated them on the ship's deck. Sailors passed around water-skins. The refugees drank thirstily, gasping and moaning. Derya did a quick count. Six women with twelve children between them. Along with seven men, all of whom had missing limbs.

Derya knelt by one man and unwrapped the bandage around the stump of his leg. She froze. The limb ended with jagged, torn skin where teeth had cut and mangled the flesh.

Black scabs covered the stump, oozing pus. "What happened?" she asked gently.

The man squeezed his eyes shut. "They came at us, the mutant water fae did. Teeth like needles. Hooked tentacles." He shuddered. "They destroyed our towns and ports. We retreated to the boats, and more monsters emerged from the sea. Men with shark heads. They bit through the hulls of the boats and ate those who fell into the water. The lucky ones got their heads bit off. The others drowned, if they didn't bleed out first."

Derya gulped. As horrible as it would be to fall into the ocean, how much worse to be deprived of any ability to swim and sink helplessly beneath the icy waves. Death would be a mercy.

"Then we got here. The king won't allow us to land. Not until his men interrogate every one of us. Supposedly to make sure no one is Cetus's spy." He cursed. "Does he believe we'd chew off our own limbs? Half of us will die before he decides we're not lying."

She used her magic to dull the man's pain. "One of our healers will work on your leg. I'm sorry I can't do more." Not for the first time did she regret her magic wouldn't allow her to regrow a limb.

Garzuli appeared at her side. "What can I do to help you, highness?"

"Make sure they've all had something to drink. And get more water. We need to clean these wounds."

Garzuli scuttled off, a puzzled look in her eyes. Derya didn't have time to wonder what confused the other girl. She turned to the next injured man, this one missing his left hand.

Derya had just finished easing the second man's pain when a healer relieved her. She stood up, wiping her hands on a rag.

Kelebek beckoned to her. "Kiral, they're signaling again."

"The king?"

"I assume so."

"Any guesses what he wants?"

Kelebek shrugged. "This could go either way."

Derya nodded and strode to the rail where the captain and Bahadir waited. A sailor held signal flags, while another pressed a spyglass to his eye and called out the letters to the captain, who recorded them on a wax tablet. When the signals concluded, the captain handed the tablet to Derya.

Derya, Heir of Cinar:

That, Derya thought, was at least polite.

I see what you are doing, and I won't allow you to manipulate me into allowing you on my shores. Know that Kharan-Khuag is seeking what you stole and killed many of my subjects before he realized it was gone. For bringing that evil on my people, I beseech the gods to make it descend sevenfold on Cinar.

Kharan-Khuag. The name the northern barbarians used for Cetus. Whatever he was called, he was evil. And the king wanted something seven times worse to afflict Cinar? Derya huddled in her cloak. Ollen's wrath was implacable, and she was the one who stirred it up.

Her own ire flared. Who told Kharan-Khuag she possessed the scepter? Stigandr Tyr? He'd been enraged enough to betray her. Or someone in her entourage, the person who'd tried to steal the scepter, or worse, attempted to kill her? She shuffled back, tugging at the neck of her tunic. An enemy lurked nearby, she was sure of it. Glumly, she read the rest of the message.

But the refugees are blameless of your crimes. I will send you supplies for their care until we bring them to shore. Then purchase what you need for your voyage and leave. Don't come back.

Her breath came in quick gasps as she struggled to formulate her response. What would a worthy leader do? Nazif would dispatch a placating explanation with a veiled threat. Her father would never tolerate this insolence. King Ollen thought she was hapless and weak. Her shoulders slumped. Maybe he was right.

Safiye took the tablet from Derya and perused it. "Well, Kiral, this is a little better. We can restock and move on."

Move on. Safiye's words broke into the tumbling chaos of Derya's thoughts. *She's right. But to where?*

She returned to the second man she'd healed. He wore a silk tunic with mother-of-pearl buttons, and he had a look of authority about him.

Garzuli was holding a mug of broth to the man's sunburnt lips. He sipped it, the bound stump of his arm resting on his lap.

"Garzuli, do you need help?" Derya asked.

The girl looked up with a startled, surprised expression. "No, thank you, highness."

"What's your name?" Derya asked the man.

"Duke Cebrian de Jable. Although I suppose I'm Duke of Nowhere and Nothing anymore."

"I'm sorry," Derya said, and she meant it. She couldn't imagine being chased from her home, to be a wandering refugee holding an empty title and having bitter regrets for what was lost. The princess sat beside him. "Do you know what happened to your king?"

"He was murdered a week ago." His breath hitched, and he shuddered. "The mutant fae tore him limb from limb and tossed the pieces of his body to the shark-men in the water." He took a long breath. "Lanzare fell three months ago, Guanches and Cofeta were overrun two weeks ago. Jable fell soon after. My people took to the boats. Some headed here, others north to the smaller islands, hoping Cetus wouldn't bother with them."

Derya's throat tightened, and she blinked away tears. Those poor people. "Forgive me," Derya said, "but I'm not as familiar with the western islands as I should be. Can you explain why Cetus conquered the ones he did?"

"Guanches and Cofeta are farther west, and larger. Taking them would give Cetus a firm foothold. Jable is farther east and north, and poorer. I hoped Cetus would overlook us as not worth the effort of conquest." He cursed. "What a vain hope. We should have evacuated after Guanches fell. Then we might have salvaged some of our possessions." He held up his stump. "Or our limbs."

"You couldn't have foreseen what would happen," Derya said. "Are there any people still on the islands?"

"Oh, yes, Rider have mercy on them." The duke's voice hitched. "Many were captured and enslaved. And others"—he gulped—"were transformed."

"Transformed?"

"Turned into monsters. Men with sharks' heads. It was awful. I could even recognize some of them, who they used to be. All of them were compelled to fight us. From the way some threw themselves in the path of our blades, I presume they longed to die, just to end their agony."

Derya pressed her lips together and swallowed a painful lump in her throat. She sat silently for a few heartbeats, holding the duke's remaining hand and wiped a tear from his face, struggling to control her shaking hands. "Other than the obvious strategic reason," she said, "can you guess why Cetus conquered the islands?"

"None. At first, Cetus said he only desired our islands to stage his land armies, and as a rallying point for his sea army. When our king refused to grant him access, Cetus invaded. And vowed to take everything." The duke closed his eyes and leaned his head against the galley's wall. "When his monsters stormed the beaches of Jable, they screamed that Cetus's treasure would be returned. That sounded like they were after more than just a foothold on the land."

I can guess what that treasure is. But how can I get it? "I'm so sorry," Derya said. She had no words that could ease the duke's obvious suffering. "I wish there was something I could do to help you."

Duke Cebrian opened his bloodshot eyes and met her gaze. "Highness, you can. Commit Cinar to liberating the western islands."

Her first thought was to refuse. But she needed to go to the western islands anyway. The monsters' boast about Cetus's treasure convinced her the crown was on the islands. Having some Cinarrian warships would make the attempt to retrieve it less perilous. But she had to depart before Cetus found it first.

Her father would disown her if she committed the empire to a battle with Cetus without consulting him. Her mouth went dry, wondering whose wrath would be worse: her father's or Cetus's. "I'll talk with my advisors."

"Don't delay, highness. Cetus is bringing his war to Cinar, and I think you'd rather fight the battles on someone else's land."

20

Pasargadae

Forty-six days after the winter solstice in the 17th year of Emperor Cambyses III and the 29th year of Vural Tzimiskes of Cinar

F*IGHT YOUR BATTLES ON the enemy's land.* Tarja mused over her mother's earlier advice as she darted into her room and pulled the door closed behind her, locking it with a sharp click. She leaned against it with a sigh of relief, pressing a shaking hand to her bruised ribs. Her pulse throbbed in her aching head. *Dastgir wants a fight? I'll give him one.*

A ferret-faced maid bustled over, her eyebrows raised and inquiring. "High One, you—"

"Is my bath ready?" Tarja asked.

"Yes, High One."

"Good. I'll wear rubies tonight. I'm not sure which ones. Clean them all while I'm bathing. I'll dress myself."

Tarja ignored the girl's gasp of dismay. Her collection of

ruby necklaces, earrings, ankle bracelets, tiaras, and rings was extensive. Cleaning it, Tarja knew, would take the girl hours. The princess wanted no witnesses to her injuries, at least not before dinner. She also wanted to prevent any prospect of word getting to Dastgir that she had escaped from the dungeons, which meant her maid had to stay close by. Setting the girl an impossible task would ensure it.

Tarja stalked into her bathing room and shut the door, silencing the maid's offers to help. She shed her clothing and dropped it on the tiled floor. With a wince and a hiss, she climbed into the rose and lemon-scented bath.

The warm water soothed the aches and washed away the stink of the dungeons. Ice was what she needed to keep the swelling down. But she'd have to wait until after dinner for that.

Despite the water's warmth, she shivered. Her heart sped up and she wrapped her arms around herself. Dastgir had pulled nasty pranks before, but never this violent. She'd even feared he might lose control and kill her.

How dare he? Tarja slapped her hands on the water, wishing its surface was her brother's face. The smacking sound and splash did little to ease her ire. *Stupid Tarja. Of course, he dared.* Painful experience had taught her the emperor would take any of her siblings' words over hers, especially the boys'.

She dunked her sponge in the water. *Someday, brother, someday.* She raised the sponge and squeezed it hard. Water trickled and splashed into the bath. *Someday you'll be the terrified fish thrashing on* my *hook.*

She scowled and ran the sponge over her limbs. Gingerly, she washed her abdomen, stifling a moan when the sponge brushed a sore spot. *Thank the gods no ribs were broken.* But regrettably, she lacked sufficient time to wash her hair. Perfume would have to cover any lingering scent of the dungeon.

Reluctantly, she pulled herself from the water's soothing

embrace. Moving like a snail through honey, she climbed from the tub and wrapped herself in two towels, taking care to conceal every bruise under the thick cotton.

When she opened the door to her sitting room, her maid was cleaning an earring's dangling stones, her birdlike eyes darting from hook to rubies and back.

The girl started when Tarja approached. "High One, may I—"

"No, finish the earrings." The last thing she needed was the nosy girl spreading tales about her bruised back.

Tarja went to her wardrobe and chose loose, filmy trousers embroidered in gold and white and three layers of gauzy scarlet tunics, the hems embroidered with gold. Shielding herself from the maid's view behind the wardrobe's lacquered door, she dressed quickly, lips clamped together to stifle any hiss of pain. Ruby-crusted slippers finished her ensemble.

She sat at the table where her maid had laid out the cleaned jewelry. *Good. The girl had the sense to start with my favorite pieces.* The princess draped rubies around her neck and hung long, dangling strands from her ears. "Put the ankle bracelets on me." Between the pain in her ribs and her pounding head, she didn't want to try bending over.

The maid scurried to obey. Tarja watched the girl clasp the jeweled ankle bracelets as their tiny bells tingled, high-pitched and delicate.

"Bring me the bangles." She chose nine worked of gold that were studded with tiny scarlet rubies and shoved them onto her left wrist.

Scarlet. Pasargadae's military color. Let Dastgir puzzle over whether she chose the hue to reflect the emperor's war plans against Cinar or her own private war with the favorite for the crown.

"Now do my hair." She sat motionless as her maid brushed scents of rose and jasmine through her black hair. The maid formed an elaborate arrangement of braids and wove strands of rubies and diamonds throughout, forming a glittering crown. A cascade of ebony curls tumbled down Tarja's back.

Glancing in the mirror, Tarja nodded. She didn't look like someone who'd been beaten and tossed in a putrid cell. The high necks of the tunics hid the bruise on her collarbone. At least the nausea had passed. She might be able to eat without throwing up.

Tarja clenched her jaw and stiffened her spine. *Time to do battle.*

She stood and left her room. With a curt wave, she ordered one of the guards at the end of the corridor to follow her. Ordinarily, she wasn't important enough to merit a guard, but she was taking no chances. While she only had to traverse one corridor and a few courtyards, assailants could lurk in the numerous niches and alcoves along the way.

The guard's heavy tread on the tiled floor helped steady her fluttering heart. When they reached the dining room, she dismissed the guard with a jerk of her chin. Taking a deep breath, she pasted a bland smile on her face, nodded to the footman who opened the door, and entered.

Her father and all her siblings from the earlier meeting had already gathered, seated around the long table covered with gold plates heaped with grilled fish, roasted meats, mounds of fruit, and flatbread. Dastgir was waving a fig in the air as he spoke. "She said she didn't care to dine with us, not after the way she'd been humiliated earlier."

"Who are you talking about, brother?" Tarja asked sweetly.

Dastgir choked. He jerked to face her, his jaw hanging open.

She dug her nails into her palm, hoping the pain would help repress her grin. She strode to her place, ignoring the stiffness in her right leg that screamed for her to limp. The room had gone so quiet, the tinkling of her ankle bracelets was the only sound.

The emperor raised an eyebrow. "I heard you didn't want to come tonight."

Tarja broadened her smile. "Your Splendor, my brother must have confused me with someone else." She slid into her chair, her ribs and back protesting, clenching her teeth to repress a groan. *Later.* She'd see a healer later. "Thank you for doing me the honor of seeing you well. I apologize for my lateness."

The emperor grunted and picked up his glass of ruby-red wine.

Tarja flicked her gaze around the table. Usually, when the family dined alone, the emperor would include his wives, or at least the ones who were in favor. At the moment, that only included the three women who'd borne him sons, and three younger women who were in varying stages of pregnancy.

It was cruel of her father to invite his wives. They knew he would decide during the meal who he'd summon to his bed. The women would do their best to attract his attention and incite his desire. Sometimes he'd go for the young ones; other times, he'd seek comfort in the arms of a woman who'd belonged to him for many years. And sometimes he'd choose none of them, commanding a eunuch to fetch a girl, any girl, from the harem. The unchosen women would be publicly rejected and forced to pretend they were pleased the emperor had selected entertainment for the night.

Perhaps they had mixed feelings, Tarja thought. Was her mother better off forgotten and cast off, spared having to bed that brute? Rumors of his cruelty to his wives had reached even her ears.

But tonight, it was just the five royal children who were of age and in the palace. That meant her father's mind was consumed with something other than his own pleasures.

Tarja tore a piece of bread from a flat loaf. *The other four will gnash their teeth when they learn what they missed.*

Whatever her father planned to discuss, he clearly wanted to eat first. His attention was fixed on the grilled fish. Samsher conversed with his full sister, Nadereh, in low tones, while Dastgir and Fariba glared at Tarja.

She contented herself with ignoring their stares. Placidly, she ate roast lamb, saffron rice, and dates. The throbbing aches in her torso urged her to gulp down her wine, the tart, crimson liquid promising relief from all her pain. Tarja sipped the wine, holding each mouthful a few heartbeats before swallowing it, fighting the temptation to down the entire glass.

Under her outward serenity, she seethed. Life was unfair. Had she been born in Cinar, like the odious Derya, she'd be in line for the throne. Cinar believed none of this foolishness about males being the only ones worthy of ruling. It was all Tarja could do to keep from flinging her glass against the wall.

Why were her brothers favored? Dastgir spent most of his days writing obscene poems, harassing the maids, and sampling every cask of wine he could find. Samsher was only a shade better, cleverer and diligent in his studies. But he'd also learned their father's ruthlessness and considered it worth imitation. As for the other brothers, it was too soon to tell, or they didn't rival Samsher's talents, either for good or ill.

Her father finished his honey-drenched pastry and licked his fingers. He rested his arms on the table, his rings clinking on the wood. "Now is the time to strike Cinar. We'll head southwest with the goal of seizing their territory as far as Isedonnes."

Tarja took a sip of wine to mask her surprise. Her father's plan was ambitious. But empires didn't grow from lack of ambition.

The emperor nodded to his cupbearer to refill his wineglass. "But first, we must secure our southern border."

"Do you want one of us to wipe out the Ma'arikh tribe?" Dastgir asked.

Tarja tipped her face to look at her plate while studying her father's expression from under her eyelashes. His curled lip signaled he thought that was as stupid an idea as she did. If Dastgir kept this up, he'd replace Samsher as the most disappointing son.

"I was thinking of something that wouldn't involve risking any of our warriors just before invading our biggest enemy," her father said drily. His eyes drifted from Fariba, to Nadereh, to her.

No. Oh no, no, no. Tarja's mouth went dry. He was about to say the words she'd long dreaded, had begged the gods, if any existed, to never be uttered. *May his throat close before he says it . . .*

"I'm going to offer one daughter to Ghalib and another to Farees."

Her heart dropped below her knees. Ghalib and Farees were powerful chieftains of large desert tribes. Whoever married either would have a hard life in a nomadic tribe, living in tents and traveling from oasis to oasis on camels. And far removed from hot baths, books, or fresh cucumbers. The lingering taste of honey in her mouth turned to chalk, and she took a quick sip of wine. *Let it not be me.*

The emperor stabbed an apricot with a jeweled knife. "The gods know I have plenty of girls to spare."

"Have you decided who you will send?" Samsher asked, his voice steady in spite of the tremor of the hand holding his wine glass. Nadereh and Fariba had gone as still as leaves covered by an early frost.

"Azuzah will go to Ghalib."

An icy hand twisted Tarja's stomach. Her shy half-sister was only just fifteen. Ghalib was the more powerful of the two chieftains, and more palatable, having less of a reputation for cruelty and, at twenty-five, in possession of only two wives.

"Tarja will do for Farees."

His words battered her soul worse than her brother had beaten her body. Tarja willed a smile to her face and for the lamb to stay in her stomach. *No, no, no.* She pressed a hand to her abdomen. *This can't be happening. He's sending me to a fiend.* "Thank you, Your Splendor." The words scraped over her dry tongue. "I am the dust under your feet and thank you for honoring me with your trust."

"Honor me by following orders. You know your duty. I expect that you will fulfill it. Farees, they say, likes his women young. I hope you're not too old for him."

I'm barely eighteen. "Of course, Your Splendor."

He must despise her if he'd throw her to Farees, lord of a wild tribe that survived by raiding its neighbors. *He's sentencing me to life as a nomad, married to a savage.* Disappointment shriveled any hope she had of gaining her father's favor. She'd been a fool to even dream.

Her ribs refused to expand as she struggled to breathe. At least Ghalib's territory extended to the coast. Her sister wouldn't be living in squalor. Farees had nothing but desert, a few scattered oases and newly discovered salt deposits. Those mines bought him wealth, for whatever good that did the savage nomad. And at fifty, he already had seven wives, none of whom had borne him any children, not even an early stillborn. Tarja narrowed her eyes. She harbored no illusions that she'd succeed where they had failed.

Her father was speaking to her. "Keep Farees satisfied so he doesn't even think of raiding our southern satrapies."

The lamb she'd eaten tried to flee her stomach. Tarja clenched her jaw, willing it to stay down.

"Bear a son. Seal the alliance. And inform me of everything." The emperor's harsh, commanding tone lashed her soul. "Do you think you can do that?"

Surely he knew about Farees and his lack of children. Why was he demanding she do the impossible? She ground her teeth, suppressing her rage at the unfairness of it all. Heat flushed her body. Her hand twitched, longing to magically fling a knife at her father.

Tarja took a tiny sip of wine to moisten her dry tongue. "I am deeply honored to be the instrument of your desires. My zeal to increase the glory of Pasargadae will inspire me to do more than you expect, Your Splendor."

The emperor eyed her like a jackal surveys a rabbit. He nodded, then drained his glass. "See that you do."

Was he commanding her to have a son by any man? Tarja tore a piece of bread in two, concentrating on the falling crumbs to keep the shock from her face. Did the emperor seriously expect her to foist a bastard off on Farees as his heir? She pursed her lips. If Farees caught wind of such a scheme, her death would soon follow. Her throat tightened. Whatever means Farees used to kill her would be less gruesome than what her father would do if her cuckolded husband sent her home in disgrace. A quick death at the hands of an outraged consort would be her best end.

The emperor waved for more wine. "You and Azuzah will leave in a week."

Tarja inclined her head. "As you will, Your Splendor." She ripped a piece from the flatbread and stared at it, as if she contemplated no greater question than choosing which sauce to dip it in.

There's no honey-coating this. He's sending me to obscurity, to be an eighth wife who'll be at the mercy of the others. One glance at her father's iron face told her to abandon any hope of dissuading him or even getting him to delay. She would have been better off in the dungeons.

Think. After marrying Farees, then what? Make the best of it, become friends with the other wives, and pray Farees lost interest in her and found another. That was the safe option.

But she'd still have to endure the man's caresses until he

gave up hoping she'd produce an heir. That was a worse torment than her father's dungeons. She stifled a moan.

Could she wait for a suitable time and then poison her husband? Maybe the new chieftain would value the daughter of the Pasargadian emperor. Or find someone to overthrow Farees?

No. Those were ridiculous plans for the weak and the desperate. For someone who was giving up, accepting her fate and settling for a miserable life.

Perhaps it was time to put the plan into motion, the scheme she and her mother had concocted long ago, anticipating this very day. Just the thought of it eased her ragged breathing.

She'd flee. Not north to her mother's family estate, where everyone would expect her to go. But west. To Cinar.

But instead of seeking a distant cousin of her mother's in Isedonnes, she'd carry out her own secret plan. Tarja tightened her jaw and rubbed her sweaty palms on her thighs. She'd find Princess Derya. And kill her. She'd succeed where all her father's agents had failed. That would show her father he'd been mistaken to overlook her value. When she returned home, she'd demand a husband worthy of her.

And if she failed . . . Whatever happened couldn't be worse than marriage to Farees.

When she raised her head, she noticed Dastgir and Fariba openly rejoicing, their white teeth glinting in the candlelight. Nadereh was staring at her with a mixture of pity and relief. Samsher held up his wine glass in a silent toast, a wry smile tinged with sadness curving his full lips. *If only you knew, brother. If only you knew.*

21

Eighty-seven days after the winter solstice in the 29th year of Emperor Vural Tzimiskes

Derya tightened her grip on the duke's hand. Her breath hitched, and a shiver fluttered down her spine. *Cetus is bringing his war to Cinar.* And if no one stopped him, he'd plunder and slaughter his way through Cinar and beyond. Goose bumps prickled her arms.

The princess stood up, forcing her shaking knees to support her weight. "Can you walk?" She called Bahadir over, and together they helped the duke stagger to his feet.

She sent the chiliarch to find Kelebek, Nazif, and Safiye and escorted the tottering duke to her cabin.

Once there, she settled the duke into the cabin's sole chair next to Garzuli's loom and paced the tiny space. The groaning of the ship's timbers echoed her own impatience. What was keeping her advisors? They couldn't afford to waste a heartbeat.

When the others arrived, she barely waited for the door to shut behind them before she burst into recounting her conversation with the duke. "What do you think?"

"What does 'Cetus's treasure will be returned' mean?" Safiye asked. She squeezed past Kelebek and perched on the edge of her narrow bunk.

Derya raised her eyebrows and looked at Duke Cebrian.

He shrugged. "I thought it meant Cetus treasures the western islands and was reclaiming ownership of them."

"His first step in conquering the continent," Bahadir said.

"Couldn't that mean a treasure is hidden in the islands, an artifact that belongs to Cetus?" Nazif asked.

Derya rubbed the back of her neck. *It has to.* She looked at Duke Cebrian. "Does your people's lore contain tales of such treasures?"

"Do you mean the children's fables about the sorcerer losing something of value on the islands?" He pressed his lips together and wrinkled his forehead. "If the tales ever said what it was, I don't remember. One version said that a magical artifact was stolen and taken to Ardebil."

Fabulous. The crown could be anywhere on the continent. Unless the story's talking about the scepter.

Nazif drummed his fingers on his elbow. "Is there anyone who might remember?"

The duke shrugged. "You could ask the survivors."

"Are there any scholars among them?" Kelebek asked. "Learned people whose knowledge might be worth delving into?"

Derya frowned. Was he saying chasing rumors was ill-advised? But that's what they did when they sought the scepter. And found it.

"Perhaps," the duke said. His eyes widened. "There's a colony of scholars on Quenyo. If anyone is an expert in ancient tales, it would be them." He shifted his weight, groaning along with the flimsy chair he sat on.

Derya's heart lifted, and she raised her chin. *I've got to talk with them.* She tapped a finger against her lips, her slight frame rocking with the motion of the ship. "Oikeios?" She tipped her head toward Kelebek and met his gaze.

"Quenyo," he said, "is the smallest and most northern of the western islands. Very remote." His tone implied it lay farther away than the stars. He fixed his eyes on the duke. "As far as you know, Cetus hasn't invaded it yet?"

"That's right. He started with the bigger islands."

"Maybe he won't bother with it," Derya said.

"Kiral," Kelebek said, "that is a possibility. From what the duke tells us, Cetus himself attaches no significance to the western islands other than as a place to stage his armies. So it seems unlikely to me that what you seek is there."

She ground her teeth, and heat flared up her neck. A memory of a mutant fae cracking the bone of one of her soldiers merged into a sudden impulse to hit Kelebek's supercilious face. She held herself immobile until the urge passed. Violent attacks were not the way wise rulers handled dissent.

But what was she to do? Even after all they'd been through, Kelebek questioned all her decisions, while Bahadir and Safiye sometimes treated her as an impulsive child needing direction. Persuading them to support her on a risky venture would take time, time Cetus was probably using to find his crown. Nazif wouldn't have the same problem. He'd either issue orders in a commanding tone or use his seductive voice to win them over.

The duke glanced from Kelebek to Derya, his gaze beseeching. He clasped his hands together. "Please, highness, rescue my people. Hundreds set out on boats for Quenyo. If Cetus attacks it, they'll be dead. I beg you. Spare them what so many have suffered." He held up his stump, scarlet bloodstains dark against the white bandage.

Horror, pity, and anger warred within her. Visions of shark-headed monsters gnawing the limbs of screaming children raced through her mind. Heat flushed her veins, and she ground her teeth. She had to stop the carnage, to deny Cetus any more victims of his evil plans.

"We scarcely survived one encounter with his abominations," Safiye said. "What if Cetus himself shows up?"

Derya opened her mouth to snap a rebuttal, but the duke spoke faster. "He hasn't so far."

Kelebek nodded. "History tells us Cetus prefers to let his monsters and slaves do the fighting."

"We can defeat them when we use our magic," Derya said. "And we have several powerful mages."

"But," Bahadir said, "we don't know how many water fae we'll be fighting. Will our mages be enough?"

Derya gritted her teeth. Didn't they understand they needed to move now to find the crown before Cetus did?

"Kiral, if I may," Safiye said. "We should consider the consequences. If we rescue some islanders, or turn back the invasion of Quenyo, will that provoke Cetus to more aggressive action?"

The duke rubbed the end of his bandaged stump. "Does that matter? He's coming after you sooner than later. You may as well test your mages against his monsters. Then you can send word to Veleti, Rorvik, and Cinar and warn them what they are up against." His shoulders slumped, and he fixed his teary gaze on Derya. "Please, highness, save my people."

Derya nodded. "We could rescue the surviving islanders. And locate those scholars who might know about Cetus's treasures."

"Kiral, we shouldn't go alone," Bahadir said. "If King Ollen sends a few longboats filled with warriors, then perhaps we'd have a chance."

"I agree," Nazif said.

A vein in her head thrummed like a drum. *But it will take days to persuade Ollen to help, if he ever agrees.* "Maybe."

"It's a shame, Kiral, that we cannot ask King Stigandr as well," Kelebek said.

"The oikeios is right," Safiye said. "We're better off allying with both of them."

"Well, we can't." Derya spoke more sharply than she'd intended. But they were being obtuse. Didn't they understand Stigandr considered her an enemy?

"You surely don't plan to go alone," Bahadir said.

She shot him a glare. "We have to do something."

"Perhaps," Kelebek said carefully, "Duke Cebrian can persuade King Ollen to lend some aid. Refugees have filled the bay and will soon overrun his capital. Within a day, everyone will know the brutality of Cetus's invasion of the islands. The king's people will demand that he protect them from the same fate."

Rider bless you for that, oikeios. At least one of them is helping me. Derya took a breath. "Stigandr would as soon wed a wyvern as help me. At worst, he'd send his own longboats to attack us. The best we can hope for is he'll persuade Ollen to help us."

"Why would he do that?" Nazif asked.

Bahadir narrowed his eyes. "Stigandr knows if we succeed, we'll have reduced the threat against his realm."

"Regardless of the battle's outcome," Derya said, "Veleti will be weakened." She drilled her gaze into the chiliarch's. *He has to agree.* "That leaves Stigandr well placed to seize more of Veleti's territory and possibly even take it all. Which might not be all bad."

Safiye pressed her lips together, doubt wrinkling her forehead. "Why?"

"A combined Veleti and Rorvik would threaten the Kassians and Tarhuntassians. That threat would occupy them, leaving our northern border quiet." She paused. "On the other hand, if we fail . . ."

"Then Stigandr will be ready with a motivated navy." Kelebek nodded. "Good thinking, Kiral."

Did he actually approve of something I said? Derya nodded. "Thank you, oikeios." She puffed out a long breath. "But it makes no difference what Stigandr does. We don't have time to send messengers to him. We should leave in the morning."

"Not so fast," said Nazif. "We shouldn't sail anywhere without at least ten ships. From what you said, you barely survived the trip to Nafplio. Cetus could wipe us out with a single storm."

Kelebek, Bahadir, and Safiye nodded their agreement. Her stomach turned to stone, and her jaw ached from clenching it. *Raging waters. They were about to agree, and Nazif had to spoil it.*

A cold knot of suspicion formed in her belly. *Is Nazif right, or is he trying to trick me into making a weak move?* Ever since she learned he bought a slave, she'd been questioning his judgement. "Stop making camels out of fleas, Nazif," she snapped. "We're not planning on defeating Cetus, just rescuing whoever we can and finding the crown."

She ignored Safiye's sharp intake of breath, Kelebek's frown, and the flare of interest in the duke's eyes. That was a blunder to mention the crown. But if they didn't take the duke into their confidence, he might not share vital information. And she needed that crown. *Before Cetus arrives to slaughter us all.* Derya clenched her fists. "If we don't follow the only lead we have, how else will I find it? Call for it and expect it to fly to my hand like a trained bird?"

"And if Cetus captures you?" Nazif crossed his arms. "That would be a prize."

She raked her eyes over his face. *He doesn't just mean me. He's thinking of the scepter.* "We've taken precautions," Derya said. "That won't happen."

Nazif shook his head. "Your father won't be pleased with this."

His words sliced through her like a speeding arrow, a poison arrow that lodged in her liver. Her father, most likely, wouldn't approve risking herself on a rescue mission that could prove to be a detour from her main quest. And he wouldn't want her leading a military operation. He'd prefer a bold man like Nazif to lead the force.

Her confidence shriveled as Nazif's words seeped through her mind. If she didn't prove herself a worthy commander of armies, her father might name a new Heir of Cinar. All she'd done to prove herself worthy of her birthright would be in vain. And the new heir—probably Yildiz—would have no qualms about hunting her down to remove any threat she might pose to his status.

Sweat beaded on her forehead. She narrowed her eyes and scowled. Rage bubbled in her veins. Her father had betrayed her by not naming her co-emperor as he promised. Nazif was working against her, trying to manipulate her into a weak decision. "The emperor won't know if no one tells him. I'll send word once we've completed the task he gave us." *That victory will make him proud to name me co-emperor.*

Kelebek leaned forward. "If we are a rescue mission, then we must make haste. But your cousin is right. More ships mean at least some of us have a greater chance of surviving."

"I agree, Kiral," Bahadir said. "Ten ships at a minimum."

"Highness, please," the duke said. "My people are desperate. And if what you seek is in the western islands, you'd better go now, before Cetus solidifies his hold." He looked down at the table, then at a spot over Derya's head. "I'm beginning to recall more of those stories now that I think about it. There was some powerful magical item hidden on our shores."

Derya regarded him thoughtfully before scanning the faces of her advisors. Safiye's face wore a puzzled frown, and Kelebek, ever the diplomat, was unreadable. Bahadir was shaking his head as if he didn't believe the duke's last statement. She rubbed her hands together. Her father thought the crown was in the western islands. The duke's words confirmed it.

Nazif crossed his arms. "We shouldn't go after Cetus without help from both kings. And from what you say,

Stigandr is a powerful wood mage. That could be useful when sailing in wooden boats."

He made a valid point. But he was mistaken to consider going into battle with that deceitful Stigandr. The king would use any alliance to steal the scepter back or seize the crown for his own use. If he didn't hand her over to Cetus himself.

And Nazif. He aspired to rule Cinar as much as she did. She couldn't trust his judgement as much as the ice covering a pond in spring.

No, any new allies had to be trustworthy. That was what Stigandr taught her when he bashed her over the head and stole the scepter. "We can't trust Stigandr. Any chance to bring me down, he'd seize it."

"He wouldn't do that if it risked losing a battle," Bahadir said. "That one wants to win."

"Perhaps," Derya said. "But if he saw a way to punish me and still win, he'd grab it." *With great pleasure.* "No Stigandr. But as you pointed out, oikeios, King Ollen might help. Could you and the duke draft a request of King Ollen for warriors and ships?"

Nazif glared and Bahadir frowned. Derya spoke before either could voice their objections. "We don't need Stigandr." She spit out the words, trying to mask her irritation. Persuading them to see reason was like swimming up a raging, implacable river. "If Ollen helps us, fine. Regardless, we're going to the western islands."

Derya straightened her spine and lifted her chin. "I am the Heir of Cinar. This is my word." Delaying would gain them nothing. Her father might interpret her hesitation as incompetence and name another heir. Then she'd be caught between Cetus and whoever stole her throne. She had to act swiftly before she lost control of her followers. And recover Cetus's crown before she lost her own.

22

Ninety days after the winter solstice in the 29th year of Emperor Vural Tzimiskes

ERYA SQUINTED TOWARD the western horizon, staring over the frothing waves that rolled toward the ship and slapped its hull. Still no land in sight. They'd sailed for two days under a stiff southeasterly wind, and now, on the morning of the third, nothing. No birds, no floating vegetation, no clouds looming in one spot. Nothing.

She drummed her fingers on the ship's rail. The islanders could have perished by now. She leaned over and studied the waves crashing into the ship's hull. How much faster would they go if she used her magic? She raised her hand as if to push her power against the sea but dropped it. They'd all agreed that confronting Cetus with depleted mages would be as pointless as throwing stones into the sea.

At least King Ollen had committed five ships to the venture. Fewer than the ten Nazif and Bahadir wanted, but enough to convince them to quit grumbling about sailing into certain doom.

Garzuli joined her at the rail. "Is there any sign of land, highness?"

Derya shook her head. "If the rising sun wasn't behind us, I'd think we were sailing the wrong way."

"Voyages into the unknown always seem longer."

"Is that why you insisted on coming with us? To venture into the unknown?" Derya partly understood why the other girl had refused to remain behind in the barbarian city. But she'd given up a chance to return to her homeland. Garzuli had even teared up when Derya insisted she could trust her to keep secret her work on the scepters and offered a full year's wages to her. Derya found the girl's reactions baffling.

"I will keep my word," Garzuli said. "I promised to accompany you on this expedition, and to assist if I can. We'll go our separate ways once this is over."

Freeing her had been a wise move, Derya thought. *It was the moral thing to do, and I gained a loyal ally.*

The ship's prow dipped into a trough, and a wave of frigid salt water sprayed over the bow. The slate-gray waves grew higher, the swells rocking the deck under Derya's feet. The ship groaned as if protesting their course.

She clutched the rail for balance, ignoring the icy fear that ran down her spine. The captain had warned of rough seas near the islands. *Turbulent waters are nothing to worry about.* Derya checked that her bags of supplies were securely fastened to her belt. Along with magical amplifiers, she had water and dried beef to refresh herself if she used too much magic. Her amplifiers were one weapon she'd never be without, together with her jeweled dagger.

The lookout shouted, his words caught by the wind. The captain bellowed a response. Bahadir yelled a command and raced across the deck. The thumping of his footsteps set Derya's heart racing.

The commotion could only mean one thing. Cetus's

monsters had found them. But so far from the islands? Derya let out a long breath. "Well, Garzuli, are you ready?" *I'm not sure I am.*

"No, highness. But I'll help you anyway."

Derya gave her a grim smile. "Then shall we start with those?" She pointed at a quartet of fish-headed water fae climbing up the side of one of the Veletian longboats. The thought of facing the mutant fae and shark-headed men in battle made her heart gallop and her knees tremble. But she would not, could not show her fear. *I am the Heir of Cinar. I will not be shaken.*

The princess raised her hand and pulled at her power. She slammed a wave against the water fae. Two of the four fell into the surging waves.

The remaining two clung to the ship's hull using their hooked tentacles as extra hands. They chopped the wood with axes, digging holes and ripping out chunks of planking. Garzuli lifted her hand, frowning in concentration. A heartbeat later, the axes jerked from the faes' hands and slammed into their faces. One slid into the sea with a skull split in two. The other seemed to have only been stunned. It clasped the ship, shrieking.

The ship lurched over a wave. Derya grabbed the rail with one hand. With the other, she shielded her eyes from the sun and squinted. More fae were swarming the other vessel.

"Highness!"

Garzuli's shout seized Derya's attention. She glanced to where the other girl was pointing. Shark-headed men and mutant fae were climbing up the side of their ship.

Several other mages joined them at the rail. One raised her hand and pointed. A blast of air slammed three fae into the water. A second air mage followed suit, knocking a pair of shark-men into the heaving waves.

Derya prepared her own magic, savoring the liquid feel of

power that coursed through her veins. The instant the shark-men hit the water, she summoned a wave and drove them deep under the sea.

Behind her, Bahadir was shouting orders. The only words she caught were "protect the Kiral."

Raging waters. She didn't need protecting. *He needs to fight monsters, not worry about me.* She created a wave and drove it down the throats of a pair of fae climbing the sides of the ship. While they were choking, Garzuli used her metal magic to twist the blades in their hands and shoved them into their throats. Gray blood spurted, and they splashed into the sea.

There are so many of them. On the deck of the nearest ship, Derya spied a pair of barrel-chested Veletians dueling with two of the mutant fae. Though the fae were tall, the Veletian fighters towered over them and were twice as broad. They swung their battle axes as easily as if they were embroidery needles. Three quick strokes and the fae were lying on deck, a puddle of gray blood forming. The Veletians scooped them up and tossed them overboard.

Derya tore her eyes from the scene and shifted to her own ship. Below her, mutant fae were climbing up the hull. The first air mage sent a gust of wind down, snapping one fae's neck. The second mage copied her action, killing the second fae. Derya boiled the fluid in the third's eyes. Garzuli stabbed the fourth with its own sword.

"This is working!" Derya said to her fellow mages. "How is everyone feeling?"

The two air mages winced. "Not much feeling in my toes," one said.

The other nodded. "One foot's fine. My right foot, though."

"Take a rest and eat," Derya said. A glance confirmed the mages were equipped with waterskins and food pouches. "What about you, Garzuli?"

Garzuli looked at the deck. "I'm fine for now, highness."

"Good. We have more visitors to attend to."

Bahadir stepped from his position near Nazif and the archers and beckoned for Derya to come to him.

She scurried over, followed by Garzuli. Seven more water fae were clinging to the side of one of the Veletians' ships, hacking the hull. Under them, half a dozen shark-men were biting chunks of wood from the ship below the waterline. Derya frowned. "Can't the archers take care of them?"

"No," Nazif said. "Notice they're hiding in the waves, only surfacing long enough to strike another blow."

Derya looked at Garzuli. "Shall we?"

Garzuli nodded.

Derya summoned her power. She waited until two fae surfaced and gave them time to switch from breathing water to air. Derya shoved her magic at them, driving water down their throats into their lungs. They choked and went still. Garzuli drove the axes of two others into their owners' necks.

Suddenly, the remaining three water fae dove under the surface. Derya leaned over the rail, her heart pounding. She searched the water, seeking any trace of her enemies.

A curse made her jerk upright. Bahadir was shouting, pointing at another of the king's longboats. The craft's prow rose from the water, towering over the crashing waves. Soldiers and sailors leaped overboard. The ruined ship sank into the sea.

Swarms of shark-headed men pounced on the swimming warriors, seizing limbs in their jaws. With their teeth digging into their prey, they thrashed frantically, twisting their heads back and forth to saw through muscle and bone. One tore off a man's head, another a leg. A third clamped its massive jaw over a woman's head and bit. Derya watched in horror as scarlet fountains of blood sprayed into the air, spread by the north wind. Moments later, the swimmers were dead.

"That could have been us," murmured Garzuli.

"It could have been," said Derya. "But it won't be."

"Are you sure?" Garzuli asked.

Derya couldn't blame her for the question. She pulled a column of water from the ocean and slammed it into a fae climbing over the rail.

Garzuli hurled a knife into its eye. With a flick of her wrist, she twisted the blade. The fae jerked and tumbled off the rail. Another flick of the wrist and she summoned the knife back to her hand. Gray blood covered the shining metal.

Another Veletian longboat rolled, making a slow descent below the waves. This time, no one jumped into the water. Instead, the archers shot rapid volleys at the shark-men and fae who circled the dying ship.

Derya stared at the sinking vessel as they let down a boat. *What are they doing? Leaving their fellows to die?*

The tiny boat had no sooner reached the water when the shark-men swarmed them. The Veletian warriors parried and stabbed, killing monster after monster. But in the end, the beasts tore the boat apart and the sailors toppled into the water. The shark-men advanced with open jaws, biting off arms, legs, and heads.

Garzuli touched Derya's arm and pointed. Now she understood. Those in the boat sacrificed themselves so their comrades could swim for another ship while the shark-men were occupied. The water fae, it seemed, preferred to allow the shark-men to chase down survivors in the water. Or perhaps they didn't want to fight them for the prey.

A third ship slid under the roiling waves. Derya's stomach heaved. Only four of their seven ships remained. It appeared their enemies were leaving her ship for last, as if to make sure she witnessed the death of those she'd led into battle.

She swallowed the sour guilt in her mouth. Another group of shark-men were swimming toward her ship. An air mage blasted one with a mighty gust of wind, blowing the creature out of the water.

Derya's eyes flew open, and her breath caught. The shark-man wore loose trousers under a tunic. But their clothing was the distinctive white and black of the western islands. "Chiliarch," she said, her voice strained.

With a few long strides, he reached her and stared at the shark-man floating on the waves. "I see it, Kiral." He paused. "I don't think those beasts stole the clothes."

"Then . . ." She couldn't say the words.

"Those monsters are western islanders, bespelled into these horrible forms."

She shuddered and put a shaking hand on her throat. "Can the spells be reversed?"

"I don't know." A muscle twitched in his jaw. "If it were me, I'd want someone to kill me. End my agony and no longer be Cetus's slave."

Derya studied his grim face. "Now what?"

He waved a hand at the wreckage bobbing on the waves, broken boards floating next to barrels and a piece of the broken mast. "Nearly half our ships are lost."

"Are you saying we should turn back?"

"We could. Return with a bigger fleet. And more mages."

"By then, the islanders will have perished. Or been turned into . . ."

He nodded. "And those monsters could follow us back to Veleti."

She gave him a wry smile. "King Ollen wouldn't thank us for that." She shook her head. "No, we fight on until they retreat." *That's what my father would want.*

"Whatever we do, those creatures need to die. If they capture us, we'll end up like them." He shuddered.

Derya's throat tightened. "I led everyone here. My duty is to lead them home. But somehow, I don't think Cetus's monsters intend to kill me." With an effort, she continued in a steady voice. "Otherwise, they would have tried to sink our ship like they did the others." She gripped the rail. "They'll probably take me to him as a trophy."

Bahadir spoke gently. "I'm afraid you're right."

"Then we fight on." Sweat beaded on her upper lip and her chin trembled. "To the death." She squared her shoulders and faced him. Locking her eyes on his, she made the Cinarrian salute.

He returned the gesture. "To the death."

23

TARJA WENT RIGID WITH surprise, her feet rooted to the deck. The flighty Derya should be cowering in fear. Or ordering a retreat at the first sign the battle was turning against her. Instead, the princess vowed to fight to the death. That defied everything she'd believed about Derya.

Tarja flexed her toes. A few had gone numb, but she'd endured worse before. Her mother had often forced her to train until the paralysis crept to her waist.

More concerning was losing her sense of touch, the hazard of overusing metal magic. Not as bad as the deafness water mages suffered, but it made throwing knives accurately much more difficult.

She cast a glance at Derya. The princess employed as much magic as she had, yet didn't seem affected. Was she putting on an act? Or was she that powerful a mage? This last thought sent shivers through Tarja. If Derya sensed Tarja's actual intent, it didn't bear thinking about what Derya would do to her. Hurling boiling water at her would be just the start.

Would she exact severe punishment? Derya's last words with the chiliarch were valiant and self-sacrificing, the words of someone with a strong sense of duty. She sounded almost noble. Not at all like the spoiled, entitled girl Tarja believed her to be. Would she understand Tarja's obligations to her own empire? Or would Derya consider any Pasargadian worthy only of a quick death?

That didn't matter. Derya had to die. Tarja pulled her dagger from her boot. From what the princess said, killing her might be a mercy. As much as she resented Derya, allowing her to become a slave of Cetus was not a fate Tarja wished for her.

And she suspected that Derya was right. The fae and shark-men were after her, not the entire fleet. If she died, the monsters would leave the rest of them alone. Maybe.

Three mutant water fae leaped over the rail, long daggers clenched in their teeth. Tarja gasped as a sudden thought struck her mind like a gong. *They're looking for the scepter and think Derya has it.*

So they will take her to Cetus. If she has the scepter with her, he'll regain some of his power. But without the band and the crown, it won't do him much good. If she doesn't have it, he'll torture her until she tells him where it is. And if it sinks with her ship, he's got an army of water fae to find it.

The kindest thing I can do for her is kill her.

A long-nailed hand gripped Tarja's shoulder. A cold blade pressed against her throat.

Oh, no you don't. Tarja pulled at her magic and bent the blade, curving it into the hand that gripped it. The other hand released her shoulder with a curse. Tarja whirled and stabbed the horned water fae in the throat.

It gurgled and fell to the deck. Tarja frantically scanned the deck for Derya. She spotted the other princess between Bahadir and his kentarch, Sezgin. All three were wielding swords, fighting off five water fae. Bahadir dodged and parried with the dexterity of a master swordsman, but Derya and Sezgin displayed the skill of toddlers. *Derya would be better off using her magic. Had she depleted it?* Tarja edged toward them, skidding on the blood-spattered deck as the ship rocked and heaved.

A massive wave splashed over the deck, knocking her off her feet. She slipped on the uneven deck, fell, and slid toward the rail. Heart pounding, she dug her dagger into the wood. The hilt was slick with blood, and she nearly lost her grip on it. Her slide stopped as the ship rocked in the opposite direction. She clambered to her feet and crouched, assessing her next move.

Sezgin had his back to Derya and Bahadir. The mutant fae he was battling stumbled. Sezgin swung at its neck, but his stroke went wide.

Idiot. A five-year-old could fight better.

Sezgin swung again. Tarja frowned. It didn't look like he was putting much force behind his strokes. Was he wounded? Perhaps. Scarlet blood streaked his face and stained his shoulder.

Tarja shifted her attention to Derya and Bahadir, who were battling four water fae. A few feet away, Nazif was battling another two. He, at least, knew how to wield a sword.

She crept closer, trying to avoid getting caught up in the melee of fighting warriors and monsters. Several shark-men had climbed to the deck. One bit the head off an air mage with a crunch. Scarlet blood spurted, adding to the already slick wood.

Tarja winced. She waited for the nearest shark-man to lunge at a soldier wielding a sword in one hand, swinging a chain attached to a spiked ball in the other. The soldier swung the ball, sending the shark-man reeling backwards. Then he plunged forward, slashing at the shark-man's legs.

Tarja dashed past them. She skidded in a pool of blood and careened into Bahadir. He flailed and staggered and crashed against the ship's rail. It creaked but held.

Derya lunged to help him up. Tarja made a show of slipping on the blood. Her slide tangled her around Derya's legs. *Now if hapless Sezgin will do his part . . .*

Just as she'd hoped, his stroke went astray. The flat of his blade smacked Derya on the shoulder. "Sorry, Kiral," he shouted.

Heart racing, Tarja gripped her dagger as she pretended to struggle to regain her footing. *If Derya will just turn a little, I can stab her . . .*

Three more fae joined the fracas. Tarja spun to defend herself. She hurled her dagger at one whose pointed ears were twisted spirals. Behind her, Derya and Bahadir lurched to their feet. Clashing of swords rang through the air. Bahadir lopped off the head of a fae with a double row of spikes along its jaw.

Sezgin pushed in between Bahadir and Derya. Five mutant fae surrounded them. One gripped Derya around the throat. The princess's face turned red, and she clawed at the hands holding her. The fae dragged her a few steps toward the rail.

No. They're going to kidnap her. Tarja lunged for Derya, her dagger outstretched. *I have to kill her. I can't let them take her.*

One of the fae batted Tarja away as if she were a fly. She flew through the air and fell to a heap on the deck. Her knee thumped against the wood, sending a shock of pain through her. She groaned and gasped for breath. As she staggered to her feet, she saw two fae holding Derya's arms drag the thrashing, screaming princess to the rail.

Tarja took three running steps toward them. She slid on the blood-slicked deck and slammed into one of the water fae. Her dagger plunged into his side.

It screamed and lashed Tarja with its tentacle. Tarja raised an arm to block the blows of the clawed hook. She yanked her dagger from the hissing water fae, its malice audible over Derya's shrieks.

Tarja hesitated. *Should I use my light magic to distract them? No, I can't risk anyone knowing about that.*

Derya raked her fingernails over one of the fae's faces. It snarled. She dragged her nails down its neck and dug into its gills. It let out a piercing shriek as gray blood splattered Derya's face. The other fae stabbed Derya in the leg. She screamed.

"Derya!" Nazif shouted. He was battling three of the water fae. His sword flashed in the sunlight, clanging against the long knives of the fae and the clawed hooks of their tentacles.

Bahadir beheaded another fae, its head with bulging yellow eyes bouncing to the deck. Two more fae circled him, lashing him with their tentacles.

Tarja gripped her dagger. *If I crash into Derya, I can make it look like the fae killed her.* She lunged forward and launched herself into a slide.

She careened into Derya, knocking her into a water fae's arms. He vaulted up and over the rail, dragging the princess with him.

Derya's screech cut the air. It ended in a mighty splash.

The rest of the fae and shark-headed monsters retreated, sprinting for the rails and leaping into the sea. The moans of wounded and the groaning timbers replaced the clangs and yells of the battle.

"Derya!" Anguish filled Nazif's cry. He kicked off his sea boots and lurched for the rail.

Bahadir grabbed his arm. "Don't. You can't help her."

Nazif shoved the chiliarch, his eyes wide and frantic. "I have to save her!"

"How?" Bahadir's voice was grim. He jerked his head at the water. "She didn't just fall in. They dragged her under."

Were those tears shining in Nazif's eyes? Bahadir's face had gone gray, and the scars in his jaw twitched in a mad, staccato rhythm. Sezgin collapsed to the deck.

Safiye and Kelebek burst from belowdecks. "Where's the kiral?" Safiye's voice rose into a shriek.

Bahadir pointed to the angry gray surf.

"Go after her!" the woman demanded.

Kelebek dashed to the rail. He leaned over, staring at the waves. "Where are you, where are you?" he muttered.

Bahadir's head drooped. "I would go if I could breathe underwater."

"But the kiral can't!" Safiye wailed.

Bahadir shook his head. "You know the stories. Cetus's monsters use magic to keep their victims from drowning until they deliver them to their master."

"We can't allow her to suffer this alone," Safiye said. "I'm going with her."

"Danisman, they are long gone. All you'll do is drown yourself." Bahadir clamped his jaw shut. The only motion in his face was the twitching of his scars.

Kelebek turned from the rail. Tarja gaped. His drawn face looked as if he'd aged ten years. "This," he said, "is a catastrophe."

Tarja frowned. She'd thought Kelebek despised Derya, that he believed anyone would be a more worthy heir to the empire. But now grief bent his arrogant head, and he seemed lost.

After a moment, Kelebek blew out a long breath and straightened his spine. "The kiral often told me she had a duty to see we all returned safely. Let's do as she commanded. We should sail for Nafplio."

Bahadir sucked in a deep breath. "I don't agree. The kiral's last command was fight to the death. She also felt an obligation to the western islanders. And Lord Nazif still has a mission. We continue east."

"But those monsters . . ." Safiye said.

"Probably got what they wanted. While Cetus is distracted . . ."

Bahadir paused, and Tarja's stomach clenched. What horrors would Cetus inflict on Derya?

The ship groaned, echoing Tarja's feelings.

Bahadir continued. "While Cetus is distracted, we might find the crown. Or even the kiral. East is where we'll find her, not west."

Tarja sagged against the rail, mutely observing. Nazif had lost his biggest rival for the throne. But after his attempt to rescue her was thwarted, he slumped to the deck and put his head on his knees. His shoulders shook, and he clutched his hair in his fists.

Derya's danisman was making no effort to hold back sobs. And the chiliarch was clearly trying to be stoic, to be the proper military leader. He turned to Nazif, who was still clutching his hair. "Lord Nazif, your orders."

Nazif didn't even raise his head. "West."

Bahadir gave him the Cinarrian salute. He conferred with the captain, pointing west. Then he set crews to dumping the dead fae overboard, to seeing to their own dead and wounded and signaling to their three remaining ships. But Tarja thought she saw the tracks of tears glistening on his face, marks of sorrow he didn't bother to wipe away.

Tarja watched numbly. Derya was as good as dead. *I got what I wanted and removed her.*

She felt strangely hollow. *Where is the joy, the sense of accomplishment I should be feeling?* Tarja rubbed her hands together and shook her head. *Derya's dead and it doesn't even look like I had anything to do with it. A touch my father would appreciate.* Tarja stared at the ash-colored clouds swirling overhead, their motion mirroring the churning in her stomach and the tumbling of her thoughts.

This is the fulfillment of the plan I've nursed for years. She buried her face in her hands. *So what is this dirty feeling that makes me writhe and despise myself?*

24

D ERYA PLUMMETED TOWARD the sea, screaming. She clamped her lips shut as she plunged into the frigid water. The cold penetrated her limbs as she sank, weighed down by her sea boots. The light dimmed as she shot into the murky depths. Salt stung her eyes, and she screwed them shut. She held her breath, wondering how long she'd have to wait before the fae killed her.

Pressure built in her chest and throat as her lungs demanded air. She writhed and thrashed, fighting not only her captors' grip but the water's resistance. One of the fae clamped a webbed hand over her mouth and nose. After an instant, it jerked away. The bite of cold water against her face vanished. Her eyes flew open. A bubble had formed around her head. She took a tiny breath, then gasped. Her aching lungs filled with damp air.

The fae's nails dug into Derya's arm as if to pierce the flesh to the bone. She flinched but didn't fight him. Whatever magic they were using to form the air bubble, she didn't want to disturb it. Not while they swam twenty feet below the surface of the water.

The dim shape of a second fae swam underneath her. It

yanked the sea boots from her feet. Freed from their dragging weight, she felt a surge of buoyancy. Each of the fae grabbed one of her arms and dragged her with them as they swam.

Icy water rushed over Derya's limbs. The cold penetrated her bones, burning and stinging like the frost of a winter night in Rorvik. She glanced up. Small circles of light flickered on the surface. At this depth, the light was dim like a dusky evening, the water a murky blue-green. She couldn't see more than the fae gripping her on either side and an occasional silvery fish. Muffled squeaks and squeals teased her ears. Were those the calls of sea predators? *Don't lose the goats,* she told herself. *The fae don't seem worried. I just need to worry about them.* She pressed her trembling lips together. *Are they taking me to Cetus?* Blood whooshed in her ears in a frantic rhythm, and her chest tightened. She was breathing faster but felt as if she was smothering.

Derya bit her lip. *I am the Heir of Cinar. I will not be shaken.* She drew a shuddering breath. *But I'm close.*

Hours passed, or so it seemed, and the fae showed no sign of tiring. She didn't know how long they'd dragged her when the fae swam toward the surface. Her knees scraped against jagged rocks. Salt water stung an open cut. The fae jerked her to stand.

Rocks dug into her feet as she stood waist deep in the surf, shivering in the cutting wind. A wave splashed over her, and she staggered under its anger. The fae dug their nails into her arms as they held her upright. They shoved her toward the shore and hissed through their pointed teeth. Their tentacles waved at her, the hooks on the ends looking like accusing, pointing fingers.

One jabbed her in the back. She stumbled on the rocks, wincing as the sharp edges bit the soles of her bare feet. Her leg throbbed where the fae had stabbed it, and blood trickled down her calf. Hissing with each step, she hobbled to the beach. When she reached it, she turned. The fae were gone.

Derya stared blankly at the open sea. No fish-headed fae bobbing on the waves. No waving tentacles threatening pain. They'd abandoned her. Tossed her on shore like jetsam. Discarded her like a shattered jar.

Where am I? Derya wrapped her arms around herself and hunched her shoulders, trembling with cold. Rocky hills that blocked her view of the rest of the island hemmed the tiny beach.

Slate-gray clouds covered the sky in an endless, oppressive sheet, obscuring the sun. *Lovely.* Even that clue to her whereabouts was denied her.

Stinging pain in her calf claimed her attention. Through the rip in her trousers, the oozing gash was visible, not much longer than her forefinger. She tore a strip from her tunic and pressed it against the wound. When the bleeding stopped, she tied the fabric around her leg.

As the pain ebbed, fear rose. Her hands were shaking by the time she finished tying the knots. Panic twisted her stomach. She shoved it down. After a few slow breaths, she lifted her chin. "Alright, Derya," she said aloud. "Time to explore the paradise Cetus invited you to." The sound of her own voice restored a sliver of her courage.

She climbed the closest hill, picking her way among the stones, wincing as sharp rocks stabbed her bare feet. A gust of wind knocked her off balance and she stepped on a rock. The sudden pain drove a curse from her lips. She repeated the words, screaming them at the impassive, indifferent clouds. How dare that sorcerer kidnap her? And that was the least of his crimes. *If I ever get out of here . . .* She spent the rest of the climb imagining Cetus's demise.

She was winded by the time she reached the summit. While the exercise had warmed her, the sweat on her face chilled her cheeks under a puff of wind. Derya stood still, panting, and gazed forlornly at the restless gray waves. Her heart plummeted to her feet, all her bravado vanishing like a rock hurled into the sea.

The island was a desolate, crescent-shaped rock about two longboats in length, its rocky arms framing the tiny beach where the fae abandoned her. She squinted at the horizon, searching in all directions. Her mouth went dry as she realized no other land was in sight.

Derya let out a whimper.

No boats sailed on the horizon, no birds called overhead. The rushing of the wind and the roar and hiss of the surf taunted her, intensifying her sense of isolation.

She clenched her jaw, trying to keep hysteria at bay. Cetus's monsters marooned her on a remote island with no food or shelter or fire, soaked to the skin. From the wind's icy bite, she assumed she was somewhere far to the north, where nights around the spring equinox brought frost and snow rather than gentle rain or warm breezes.

Her lips trembled as she studied the tufts of seagrass dotting the slope. A few twisted, gnarled shrubs hugged the ground. No other plants grew, and she saw no signs of birds or animals. The only sounds were the rumbling waves and her own thumping heart. *How long can I survive here?* She didn't think Cetus would leave her alone for many days. Just long enough for panic to set in.

She stuck out her chin. *If the sorcerer wants a sniveling coward, I'm going to disappoint him.*

Derya grasped her waterskin. Half empty. *Rider bless Bahadir for insisting I always have water with me.* She took a mouthful and held the water, letting the fluid ease her dry tongue. Then she checked her bag of amplifiers. Her vial of vinegar was full. One drop, along with her magic, would purify water. Would the vinegar or her strength give out first? Shivering in the wind wouldn't help. Carefully, she picked her way back down to the beach.

Food was a problem, but perhaps she could do some fish-

ing. Were any of these shrubs edible? Shaking limbs and chattering teeth convinced her to make a fire first. Too bad none
of her tutors thought teaching her how to survive a shipwreck
was an important topic. She'd have to rebuke Safiye next time
she saw her.

If she ever did.

Derya gulped, then shook herself. She would meet Safiye,
and Bahadir, and Kelebek again. Rider knew she'd be elated
to see even Nazif again.

But first, she needed to find a sheltered area to build a fire.
She picked her way down the slope to the beach and surveyed
the sand. The high tide mark lay only a few feet from the
furthest part of the rock walls. She frowned at the sky. *If a
storm rolls in . . . No. I can't worry about that now.*

The rock walls loomed over the beach, providing scant
relief from the wind. She strolled along them, seeking
anything that could resemble shelter. As she walked, she
collected every piece of driftwood she spotted.

A cleft in the wall made her step faster. On investigating,
she discovered it led to a narrow alcove wide enough for her to
crouch inside, and its floor was about a foot higher than the
sand. She dropped her armful of driftwood and huddled into
the cleft, dizzyingly grateful to have escaped the worst of the
wind. And for the overhang that offered protection from what
rain or snow might fall.

Derya rubbed her frozen fingers and massaged her blue
toes. *Fire. I need fire.* She pulled her dagger from its hilt and
stared at it. Over the past few months, she'd seen the soldiers
start fires hundreds of times. Most had a flint, but on occa-
sion, they used a blade and a rock.

She made a small pile of seagrass on a flat rock. Gripping
a stone with a sharp edge, she struck it with the blade. All she
produced was a high-pitched clink.

With a sigh, she tried again. And again. Her first spark
flew into the air and vanished. She was nearly sobbing with

frustration by the time she'd made a spark that caught a tuft of dry seagrass on fire. Then the driftwood ignited. She held her hands to the flames, wincing in pain as the warmth returned to her fingers. Rumbling hunger pains made her ignore the anxious thoughts predicting her death in all kinds of ways. Freezing to death was the most pleasant.

The next morning, Derya crouched over the flames, staring out to sea. She'd survived the frosty night, sleeping only in fits and starts. Fear kept her alert, fear of her fire going out or a vicious high tide sweeping her away alternating with her terror of the fae—or Cetus—appearing.

As the first streaks of pink tinted the baleful clouds, she dug a few clams. She slurped them down right out of the shell, grimacing at the slimy feel. It took several gulps of water to get the salty grit from her mouth. At least she wasn't starving.

But how long would she rot on this cursed rock? And what happened to the rest of her fleet? She hoped no one had been so foolish as to jump into the sea after her.

If Cetus is trying to unnerve me, it's working. He'd threatened Eliana that he had personal and intimate plans for her. Now that Eliana was dead, had Cetus chosen Derya to fulfill those plans?

Never. I'll cut my own heart out first. That beast will never lay a hand on me.

The waves began to froth and writhe, as if attempting to flee something below the surface. Derya pulled herself to her feet. Something was emerging from the water. Not another of those shark-men. Or fish-headed fae. *Please.*

She stood to face whatever was coming, willing her chin to lift and her shaking knees to still. *What if it's Cetus himself?* The clams in her stomach lurched as if they sensed approaching danger and wanted to flee.

Three forms surfaced, moving with reptilian grace. They were water fae, with the tentacles of the mutants. Like the others, they had gill slits on their necks. But these had the heads of human-like fae with oval, expressionless faces. Their dead, pale-blue eyes fixed on her. Somehow, their more human appearance made them more terrifying.

The fae stalked across the sand, their tentacles waving above their heads, as threatening as if they were brandishing swords.

Derya squared her shoulders, her heart racing. One fae grabbed her and threw her onto the sand. Her head hit a rock. Pain burst through her skull, and she cried out. She curled up, her arms wrapped around her head.

The three fae pounced on her like buzzards to their prey. They tore Derya's clothing, fingers groping and seeking, seizing her few possessions. Every move she made to resist was answered with a slap or kick in the face.

One found her bag of coins and scattered them on the sand. He turned and kicked her fire, sending sparks flying. *No! Not my fire!* A few stamps of his feet and the flames died out.

Tears pricked her eyes as she tried to pull at her magic. A fae smacked her head. Black spots floated before her eyes, and the beach rocked like the deck of a ship in stormy seas.

Another dumped out her waterskin and tossed her bag of amplifiers to the side. The third yanked her dagger from its sheath on her belt and flung it out to sea. Derya watched it splash into the waves, feeling as if she was losing her last friend.

One of them jerked the scepter from its hiding place along her thigh. "It's here." He held it up, grinning, his pointed teeth shining bone white in the sunlight.

A slow smile crossed the tallest fae's scaly face, intensifying his malevolent aura. Fear skittered up Derya's spine as he spoke. "Foolish princess. Why would you bring such a treasure on a dangerous mission?"

She was still gasping after the rough search that was more

like an assault and didn't bother to reply. With an effort, she forced herself to sit upright.

The tall one chortled and yanked her off the ground, forcing her to stand. Her clothing, now little more than rags, waved in the icy breeze. He grabbed her chin. "You are fortunate His Magnificence ordered us to leave you unmolested and to bring his property to him. He wants you for his own games." He leered and brought his face so close to her, the horn in his forehead nearly poked her in the eye. "My name is Txartomal."

"Why do I care?" Derya wanted to spit, but her mouth was too dry. It had taken every shred of her will to speak without whimpering.

"Because I'm the one who will own you when His Magnificence tires of you."

He released her so abruptly she lost her balance and toppled over. His companions made a few ribald jokes. Laughing, they strode into the waves, leaving a sobbing Derya alone on the sandy beach.

25

Ninety-one days after the winter solstice in the 29th year of Emperor Vural Tzimiskes

ERYA LAY IN A HEAP, quivering on the damp sand. She tucked her head to her knees and wrapped her arms around her shins. Sobs wracked her willowy frame, her gasps mixing with the murmuring surf. Her stomach heaved, and sour bile filled her mouth. She gagged on it, then choked it back.

As her fear receded, the pain of her wounds demanded attention. The scratches and scrapes left by the fae stung and burned, and the bump on her scalp throbbed. The roar and hiss of the waves hitting the sand sounded like a crowd of derisive mockers intruding into her misery.

Now what? The lingering sourness on her tongue was unbearable. Derya stumbled to her feet and crept to the water. She scooped up some seawater and used it to rinse out her mouth. "Uggh." She spat it out, finding the salty taste to be a scant improvement.

With a sigh, she scanned the beach for her scattered possessions. The empty waterskin perched in a clump of seagrass. She lifted it high and drained the last few drops into her mouth, moaning with relief. After appraising the wispy clouds in the sullen sky, she shook her head. Nothing to give her the slightest hope of rain.

Derya continued her search. She found the bag of amplifiers near a tidal pool and frantically searched the contents. A sob burst from her lips when she discovered all the little vials were intact. She hurried to the shore and filled the waterskin with seawater. Then she tasted the vinegar and pushed her magic against the waterskin. Without a pause, she gulped down pure, fresh water. When she'd drunk the entire waterskin, she refilled it and purified the water.

Her thirst eased, she retrieved her coins that littered the dry sand. Not that she expected any vendors hawking their wares to come sailing by. But if she ever escaped the island, coins could come in handy. Preserve your resources, her father had taught her.

But she didn't have many. She sat on the beach, staring out to sea where she thought the fae had thrown her dagger. From the marks on the sand, she decided it was high tide. Maybe in the low, she could find her weapon.

She rubbed her throbbing scalp, grimacing when she felt sticky blood. *What good is being a water mage if you can't heal yourself?*

Use your resources. What did she have? Nothing. The fae had destroyed her fire and smashed the remaining driftwood. Without her dagger, she couldn't cut more from the stunted bushes, let alone start a new fire. Even thinking about standing up was taking more energy than she had.

And why bother? It would take Cetus half a heartbeat to realize he had a counterfeit scepter. Terror gripped her bowels in an icy grasp. His wrath would be horrifying. And that odious Txartomal. She clapped a hand over her mouth, suppressing the urge to vomit.

How did she get into this mess? She'd done what her

father ordered. Why had it all gone so wrong? Her head drooped, and her shoulders slumped.

Nazif's words flooded her mind. About their need for additional ships and mages. How could she have been so stupid to refuse Nazif's obviously sage advice?

Because of her pride and reluctance to ally with Stigandr. She knew he wasn't to be trusted. But knowing the stakes, Stigandr would have more than likely done his part to defeat Cetus's monsters.

Instead, three of the king of Veleti's longboats sank. Their crews drowned or skewered by the mutant water fae, their limbs chewed off by the shark-men.

King Ollen would never forgive that. The deaths of his warriors and the loss of his ships were all her fault. Instead of forging an alliance with Veleti, she'd made one impossible.

Desolation crept through her soul. Her isolation on the island was complete. She'd have no company, not until Cetus descended upon her. Her lower lip trembled. She clamped her jaw shut. *I'd rather die and let the birds eat my carcass than submit to him.*

She scoffed at herself. It was one thing to keep up a defiant front when she was alone. Faced with that ancient, menacing evil, would she be able to hold out?

If I had my dagger, I could end myself. My parting apologetic gift to the others. Nazif could take the scepter, and Cetus would be none the wiser. Nazif would persuade Stigandr and Ollen to collaborate with him, and together, they could defeat Cetus.

Her cousin, at least, had the sense to understand the folly of scorning all but perfect allies. That if someone made a mistake it didn't mean they should be discarded like yesterday's trash. That allying with imperfect people could be the path to victory.

Raging waters, I have less sense than a cucumber. Her own past mistakes and foibles surged through her mind. Even when she'd scandalized the Pasargadian ambassador and offended the Ethkarpian queen, her advisors hadn't abandoned her. Kelebek, she thought with a wry smile, probably wanted to. But they stuck with her. The queen, when appealed to, forgave her.

Then there was her reputation. Growing up, she'd cultivated a frivolous persona. With three older brothers, she'd entertained no expectation of taking the throne. But many younger children of emperors came to power through disease, coups, or assassinations. She'd pretended to be shallow and simple for the sole reason of preventing anyone from forming a coup on her behalf. She shook her head, thinking of the ways she'd been capricious and flirty, so fickle no one would dare trust her word from one day to the next.

Then her brothers died, one by one, and suddenly she was the heir. It was hard to shed the persona that had become second nature to her. A smile twitched her lips as she recalled shocking people who'd written her off as simple with her fluency in languages and grasp of international affairs. But many still thought of her as flighty, Nazif among them.

She pounded the heels of her hands against the sides of her skull. Her guilt went deeper than just making a bad tactical decision. It permeated the core of who she was.

When she ascended to being Heir of Cinar, many of her father's viziers suggested that any of her male cousins would be far better suited for the role. She determined to prove them wrong.

The problem was she was uncertain how to navigate the tricky waters of her new position. She'd long observed how the court deferred to her father, brothers, and male cousins. So she imitated them. Imperious when she needed to command. Frivolous or even shocking when she was bored.

But the cataclysm that destroyed Ymittos had shattered the defensive walls she'd built to hide her true self. Ever since that day, she'd been forced to lead in ways she'd not anticipated. She'd made decisions on instinct and guessing what her father would do.

And tried to be the warrior she knew her people expected from their emperors. She didn't look the part, not like Nazif or Yildiz. Their height, muscular builds, and deep voices commanded obedience and respect. The best she could do was wheedle and persuade.

She clapped a hand to her forehead. *I was so bent on proving Nazif wrong, I mistook anyone else's valid concerns for opposition. Instead of displaying superior judgement, I let the duke's pitiful condition sway my reasoning.*

And it all ended in ruin. Half her fleet sunk, the rest probably battling for their lives. If they still survived. All of them, most likely, glad to be rid of her.

Nazif is rejoicing that I'm out of his way, which leaves him free to vie with Yildiz for the throne. Utku, the cousin who was next in line, was weak and would easily be shoved aside like a doddering old man. Between Yildiz and Nazif, Utku didn't stand a chance.

Kelebek, well, he'd always despised her. He'd attach himself to the next Heir of Cinar as soon as one was named. Maybe he'd consider her replacement worthy of him.

Safiye might grieve for me, and maybe Bahadir. Even though I recklessly endangered their lives because I had to be in control. I should have known better.

She slammed her fist on the sand. *My brain is smaller than a newborn flea. I should have made peace with Stigandr.* Nazif understood that. Maybe he was the one deserving of the throne of Cinar.

Derya groaned and scrubbed her face with her hands. She tugged at her hair, grateful for the pain. If only she'd figured this out sooner, before they sailed west. *I'm not worthy. Who was I fooling to think I could ever rule an empire?*

The missteps of the past few months rose in her mind,

thundering over her like the waves roaring onto shore. The hissing surf derided her shame. She deserved no better.

So many blunders. Using magic in front of the Pasargadian ambassador. Angering the Ethkarpian queen. Trusting Stigandr Tyr. And now this.

Kelebek and Nazif could have approached Stigandr. *Even though he betrayed me, attacked me, and tried to steal the scepter, I should have made the attempt.*

She curled her lip, sneering at herself. *But I had to be fastidious.* Genuine leaders understand the only path to victory is to set aside differences and gather as many allies as possible. *Not me. I'm just a scared girl. Not a worthy Heir of Cinar. The one thing I did right was free Garzuli.*

She sat, running her fingers through the cold sand, watching the tide recede. *And I retrieved the scepter.*

Two waves rolled toward her in quick succession and hissed as they retreated, leaving tiny bubbles of sea foam behind.

I healed Hebeci. And rescued the kidnapped girls. So I accomplished a few things I'm not ashamed of.

Derya watched a wave rise and tumble over itself with a roar. *There's always another wave.*

And another day. She sat up straighter.

I can't let Cetus win. That's the only way to atone for the deaths I caused. She gathered a handful of sand and let it trickle through her fingers.

But how? I'm no warrior, and I have no weapons.

A wave ran up the shore and splashed her feet.

I'm just a water mage.

Derya froze. *I'm a water mage with an unlimited supply of water.*

She pressed her lips together. Water was a resource. What else did she have? Sand. Wind. Sun. None of those seemed like they'd be of much use. She let out a long sigh.

I'm also good at shocking people. And have a talent for deception.

She twisted her mouth into a sneer. Not qualities that

anyone would value in a ruler. *But my only subjects are the bushes and rocks, and I don't believe they care. This is who I am, and it's going to have to suffice.*

Derya stared at the tumbling waves. *So. How can I use my magic to shock Cetus by escaping?*

Derya nibbled her lower lip, forming a plan. The chill north wind freshened as the sun began its descent in the west. She stood up. Time to find something to eat. And flee the island.

She turned her face to the east. *And then I'll defend Ardebil. Whether I'm still Heir of Cinar or not. Cetus can't be allowed to destroy any more realms.*

A lump rose in her throat. Malkh and Ymittos were gone, victims of Cetus's evil ambitions. Eliana died in the cataclysm, trying to break Cetus's curse. *Now it's my turn. For Eliana, for Ymittos, and Malkh, and Cetus's victims everywhere. No matter the cost, I will not let Cetus prevail.*

26

Chorokha

50 days after the winter solstice in the Year 999 (Chorokhese reckoning) and the 29th year of Emperor Vural Tzimiskes of Cinar

ELIANA SAT IMMOBILIZED, as if she had turned into a stalagmite, her eyes wide and unblinking. Adakizh's companions, Tigran and Bednieri, had insisted he perished at sea fighting mutant water fae.

But he was here.

The dim light of the glowing mushrooms cast shadows on his face, making it hard for her to read his expression. Were his large eyes angry or eager? Was that glimmer in them ire or joy?

His blue eyes locked on hers as he took a slow step toward her. Sweat dampened her hands, and her heart beat an erratic cadence. She rose from her chair and moved around the table, clutching it for support. Her mouth opened, but she couldn't get enough breath to speak. She mouthed his name. *Adakizh.*

Her soundless word seemed to break something in him. In two quick strides, he rushed to her side. He swept her into his arms and crushed her to his chest, lifting her so her toes left the ground. He smelled of seawater and sweat, fish, and beer. She grabbed fistfuls of the back of his tunic, clutching him, never wanting him to let her go.

He cradled her head in one of his large, powerful hands and murmured into her hair, "I didn't think I'd see you again."

She'd thought the same and wondered if she was imagining the warm pressure of his embrace. The steady thump of his heart reassured her. Adakizh really had returned.

A few coughs and shuffling feet returned her to reality. Heat spread across her face. She'd forgotten about Batraz and the others in the room.

Apparently, Adakizh had as well. He released her and stepped back. With a tip of his head, he said, "Lady Queen, I am relieved to see you are in good health."

Startled by his formal tone, Eliana stiffened. *What was he doing?* After straightening her spine and lifting her chin, she responded in kind. "I am relieved on your account. Rumors reached us claiming you were lost at sea."

He lifted an eyebrow. "The rumors lied less than they usually do." He gestured to the teapot and dried fruit on her writing table. "Do you have more tea? And some food?"

"I'll go," Bednieri said. He darted for the steps, the thud of his footsteps diminishing as he ran downstairs.

Tigran made a move as to embrace Adakizh but stopped when the tagavoi snapped a frosty glare at him. "Adakizh, we were distraught when we couldn't find you. I am truly overjoyed to see you."

Adakizh gave him a curt nod.

Batraz stepped forward. "Tagavoi, I, too, am relieved. I was on the point of leaving to search for you."

Adakizh raised his eyebrows.

Eliana spoke up. "Yes, we agreed that he should comb the coast on either side of the river. Then you turned up, unharmed." Her heart wrenched as she noted the dark circles under his eyes. "You—you are unharmed?"

"Yes." He strode around the writing table and dropped into the chair Eliana had occupied.

She allowed a tiny frown to crease her forehead, then pulled a chair to his side and sat. "Are you going to explain how you are here? The last we heard, you'd been battling mutant water fae and disappeared in the sea." She glanced at the two Saumarotas. "Please sit. I sense this won't be a short story."

Adakizh chuckled. "Actually, it is. You know about the chest that we found buried in the ocean floor, the chest belonging to Kharan-Khuag?"

Eliana nodded.

"We couldn't lift it so decided magic fixed it in place. I used my magic to raise it. Somehow, in breaking that spell, I overused my power."

"We guessed that's what happened," said Tigran. "Why you didn't respond when we called."

"That came later. When the mutant fae attacked, I used my magic to repel them. But I didn't realize how much I had drained myself. Suddenly I couldn't feel my feet or hear anything, not even the water rushing past my ears."

Eliana's breath hitched. Sound traveled well under water, far better than light. Without his hearing to guide him, he must have swum in the wrong direction.

"We called and called," Tigran said. "We lost our voices trying to find you."

Adakizh nodded. "My legs went numb, and I got caught in a current that swept me far out to sea."

"How far out were you?" Tigran asked.

"I don't know." Adakizh shook his head. "I was barely conscious for some time. When I recovered enough to escape the current, I tumbled into a pod of whales." He shuddered. "Thank the Rider none of them swallowed me by accident. Or there were no hungry predators around. I broke away from the whales and surfaced."

Eliana cast a glance at Tigran. His olive skin was faintly flushed, and he was staring at his feet. *The fools should have searched the surface.* Batraz was glaring at his cousin, shaking his head.

Adakizh continued. "By the sun's position, I guessed an hour or more had passed. I spotted the cliffs of the shore, about five miles away. So I started to swim."

He picked up a piece of dried fruit and tossed it in his mouth. "Halfway there, four of the mutant fae popped out of a wave. Four more converged from behind."

Eliana gasped.

He gave her a twisted smile. "That was my reaction. I had my dagger but didn't think it would be enough to fend off eight fae wielding spears."

Eliana inclined toward him, unable to breathe. *How did he get away?*

"Just as I resolved to end as many of them as I could before they killed me, I realized I wasn't completely alone in that fight."

"But none of us were there," Tigran said.

"You weren't. My unexpected ally was of a different sort." Adakizh leaned back in the chair. "Over the shoulder of the biggest and ugliest of the fae, I spotted something silver and pale pink floating on the water."

Eliana shrugged. "So?"

"You've not swum much in the sea," Adakizh said. "Or you would know." The corners of his lips twitched up. "I lunged for the biggest water fae. He recoiled and swam back. Right into a school of pink and silver stinging jellyfish. He died shrieking before his companions could react. The jellyfish stung the three nearest to him, and that was the end of them."

"What about the others?" Tigran asked.

"Naturally, they were hesitant about swarming me, since that would bring them closer to the venomous floaters. I dove deep, swam under the jellyfish, and made my way to shore. The fae didn't follow me."

A shiver ran through Eliana. Adakizh was making light of his narrow escape. He could easily have ended up dead.

Adakizh gave Tigran a cool stare. "Imagine my surprise when I found Narek and learned I'd only been missing for a few hours. But you and Bednieri had already left with news of my death."

Tigran's throat bobbed. "We didn't want the lady queen to hear from anyone else."

Adakizh's stare was frostbitten stone. "Yes. I see." He didn't seem to think that was a valid reason for stopping the search. "You made good time coming back. We hardly stopped to eat or sleep for four days and weren't able to overtake you."

Eliana narrowed her eyes. Were Tigran and Bednieri trustworthy? Or had they panicked?

"And what of Kharan-Khuag's chest?" Batraz asked.

"The Zhilakhurs have it under guard."

Eliana waited for Adakizh to reveal its contents, but he didn't continue.

A brooding silence settled on the room, broken when Bednieri returned. He brought a teapot, cups, roasted mushrooms, and dried figs. With a faint clatter, he placed the tray on the writing table.

Adakizh flicked his gaze at him. "Thank you. Now, if you would excuse me, I am tired and hungry. We'll talk later."

The Saumarotas and Bednieri murmured their farewells and headed for the stairs. For half a heartbeat, Eliana thought of leaving with them. She stopped herself. Her muddled, confused thoughts needed resolution. Was Adakizh happy to see her? Or had that fierce hug been an act?

But should she wait until he'd rested? She'd seen him in cranky and pessimistic moods. Perhaps the wise course would be to delay. She'd lived with this quivering anxiety that disturbed her sleep and churned her stomach for weeks. She could persevere a little longer.

As the thump of footsteps on the steps receded, Adakizh poured himself a cup of tea. When it was full, he looked up and frowned. "Oh, you're still here."

Eliana gaped at him. Her throat tightened and tears stung her eyes. *What happened to "I didn't think I'd see you again?"* Anger stilled her quivering lips. She stood up. "Other matters require my attention." Her father couldn't have infused more outraged dignity into his tone.

Adakizh set down his teacup with a clatter. "I'm sorry. I didn't intend for you to go."

She crossed her arms. "What did you intend?"

He let out a long breath. "I don't know. I'm—I'm glad you didn't leave with the others."

Slowly, she lowered herself back into her chair. She bit her lip. They had much to say to each other, but she would not be the first one to speak. She wasn't sure she had the courage to break through the barriers between them, not when exhaustion was making him irritable.

He drained his teacup and refilled it. "Have you made progress on the javelins?"

Her heart contracted. This wasn't the conversation she yearned to have. But if he preferred to be all business, she could oblige. "We've built several models. Some of thin tubes for distance. Some thicker to send larger projectiles." She tipped her head to the side. *Should I tell him my latest idea?*

"Good." He spooned a pile of mushrooms into his mouth and talked around them. "We found several sites near the mouth of the river that would be suitable places to mount the javelins. And a few above water, just in case Kharan-Khuag tries to attack by land."

"I'm glad you were successful," she said flatly.

"So am I. Narek went to scout the other rivers to see if we could put some defenses there."

"It's always good to look ahead."

He met her icy stare with a puzzled frown, his black eyebrows meeting over his nose. After a pause, he continued. "I didn't want to speak in front of the others, but I'll tell you."

At last. Maybe an apology, perhaps an explanation. Her heart beat a little faster. And maybe . . .

He leaned closer to her, so close that his dark curls stroked her face. "That chest of Kharan-Khuag's? It contained magical weapons. Spears with tips sharper than a shark's tooth that could cut through stone as easily as air."

Her eyes widened, and she repressed a sigh. While interesting, that was not the romantic declaration she was hoping for. She rebuked herself for being a fool. He clearly hadn't forgiven her yet. Still, he was confiding in her, sharing knowledge he hadn't told the others. Maybe she should reciprocate. "Some of our engineers are trying to imitate Cinarrian fire." When his frown deepened, she added, "Cinar uses it in battle. It burns even on water."

His eyes widened. "That would be useful. Tell me more." He shoved another forkful of mushrooms into his mouth.

As she explained what she knew of Cinarrian fire, she watched him eat and studied his face. He was grimy and unshaven, several days' dark growth covering his jaw. Drooping eyelids and slumping shoulders betrayed his fatigue. A lump formed in her throat. His last week had been grueling. He needed sleep.

But she was more than ready to shatter this wall between them. She'd barely kept her composure when she thought he'd died and didn't think she could endure that again without having spoken. Desperation to learn his true feelings tightened her chest. Did he dread or welcome their proposed marriage? Should she anticipate years of loving joy or resolute duty?

He leaned forward, propping his head on one hand. How she wanted to wrap her arms around him again, to feel the comforting reassurance of his presence. To regain those few glorious moments of believing that he still cared for her.

Instead, she twisted her shaking fingers together. She didn't dare touch him. She wasn't about to risk a rebuff. But she could use speech to push for answers. Her heart raced and her mouth went dry. With an effort, she forced the words from her lips. "Adakizh, we need to talk."

27

THE ONLY SOUND WAS Eliana's thumping heart. She held her breath and clamped her gaze on Adakizh's rigid face. This was it. He was going to tell her he regretted the pretty things he said before they broke the dark. That their marriage, if it took place, would be one of political convenience. She clenched her jaw and steeled herself for the hurt his words would inflict.

"We do need to talk." He paused. "I don't know where to start." His eyes flicked to the ceiling, and he spoke to the shadows beyond the blue glow of the mushrooms. "When I left for the coast, I was angry. I'd escaped one curse only to bring down a catastrophe on myself and my kingdom. And ended up trapped in a political marriage. Rather than a new life, bright as steel, all I had was rusty rubbish."

Eliana's vision blurred, and her heart shrank to the size of an inchworm. She pressed a hand against her chest and blinked away her tears, resolved to hide her pain.

"I was relieved to escape our peoples' squabbling and the problems between us, which felt like pebbles in my shoe." A wistful tone crept into his voice. "It'd been a century since I last swam in the sea, and I looked forward to plunging under the waves, as if I could lose my troubles in the depths." His lips twitched into a wry smile. "Little did I think I'd almost lose myself."

She clamped her jaw to repress her scream. *Get on with it. Tell me the worst.*

"I hadn't realized how fast I'd depleted my magic raising the chest."

"It's easy to do," she said coolly.

"Then the current yanked me out to sea. By then, I was nearly unconscious. Burning in my lungs jerked me awake. Donkey that I am, I'd forgotten to blow all the air from my lungs when I dove and switched to my gills. In the shallows, it didn't matter. But in the depths, the pressure inside could've killed me. I blew out the air but was still helpless against the current's force."

He had nearly died. Eliana stared at him, horror-struck. She'd only known him a month and a half, but losing him would be like chopping off half her soul. Which was a dismal reality she needed to brace herself against.

"After I escaped the fae and found my bearings, I took my time swimming for shore. I wasn't sure how to apologize to the others."

They're not the only ones who deserve an apology. Eliana bit back her retort. "What do you mean?"

"I was the leader of the mission. I insisted on taking the crate. The Zhilakhurs had been reluctant. We could have retreated, made a plan, and gotten more help. Taking the crate was the right decision, but I should've been smarter about how I retrieved it."

He studied his long-fingered hands. "When that revelation penetrated my mind, it felt like a wave slapping me into the sand."

"Why?" She was growing impatient with his story and clamped her lips together to imprison her thoughts in her throat. *What does this have to do with us?*

"Don't you see? That was what you did when you promised Shirdona to marry me. Yes, you could've handled her more effectively. But distracted and weary, blind and shaken, you made a snap decision."

Eliana flushed and scowled. Was he going to hold that against her forever?

"You drew the right conclusion but executed it wrong. Just as I did with the chest."

Eliana narrowed her eyes. Was he working up to an apology? *It better be brilliant.*

"How could I have misunderstood you so completely? I had just grasped the fact that I have withered mushrooms for brains when the water fae surrounded me." He grimaced. "The largest one had pink-gray skin and five horns on its head. Beady eyes like a lizard's over a mouth filled with spiked teeth. He waved his tentacles and flared his gills.

"For a moment, I considered flaring my own gills. Perhaps that was the mutant fae's way of expressing contempt. Or it could have been a come-on." He snorted. "I decided not to risk it."

She frowned, unsure of how to respond. "That must have been frightening."

"Terrifying. The big one flared his gills again. 'Surrender,' he said." He shuddered. "He dragged the 's' out in a long hiss. Gave me the shivers."

"What did you say?"

"I refused using rather salty language. All the while wondering if I could lose them underwater. But if there were more of them . . ." Adakizh shook his head. "The fae informed me their master had need of me. 'I have no need of him,' I answered."

His face hardened. "Then he added, 'And your promised bride.' That's when my heart about stopped."

Eliana's stomach lurched and she struggled to breathe.

Kharan-Khuag hadn't abandoned his personal and intimate intentions for her.

He looked at her with a stricken expression. "I couldn't let them even think of taking you. But at the time, I didn't have strength for much more than staying afloat. So I tried to deflect. 'What bride?' I asked."

"The fae said, 'The princess of Ymittos.' All the water fae were flapping their gills and letting out cackling snorts I took to be their version of laughter."

He rubbed a hand over his forehead. "I informed them you make your own decisions about marriage."

Unless a wily tavkatseen outmaneuvers me.

"The fae answered, 'Not if our master rules over all.'"

Eliana shuddered. "Which is what he's always wanted," she whispered.

"The fae smirked at me and said, 'Once our master's done with her, she's my reward. Bride or slave. I haven't decided.'"

Eliana's shoulders twitched as a frigid shiver ran down her spine. She stared at him, her icy fear turning to soul-numbing horror.

A muscle rippled in Adakizh's jaw. "The thought of that ugly fae breathing the same air as you made my stomach churn. I wanted to strangle him with his own tentacles. Rip the horns from his head and shove them into his gills. I would die before I let anything threaten the sole of your boot." He took a long breath. "That's when I saw the jellyfish, and you know the rest."

Eliana rubbed her chest where her pounding heart beat against her ribs, rivaling the thumps of the workers' hammers outside. *So, Kharan-Khuag still entertains vile plans for me.* She'd have to ensure they never came to fruition. Even though she almost died breaking the dark, she'd gladly sacrifice her life now if it saved the continent—and kept her out of Kharan-Khuag's grasp.

After all, what hope for happiness did she have? She

wearied of the uncertain state between Adakizh and her, back and forth, cold and hot, always feeling like an intruder in his life, an unwelcome tag-a-long, with only tiny glimpses of the warm person she'd grown to love in the days they worked together to break Kharan-Khuag's curse. She had no kingdom, only a remnant of her people, all of them refugees in a strange, dark underground realm. *I just want to belong. To some place. To someone.*

Adakizh's voice rose. "When that monster claimed you, something snapped within me. I couldn't let them kill me. Not until I saw you again."

"For what?" The question burst from her, sounding more annoyed than she felt.

"You're angry? You should be," he said. Words came tumbling out of his mouth. "I am so sorry, Eliana. For how I treated you the past few weeks. I was an ox, a fool, a worm. When I regained my hearing and I learned you had promised that we would marry, I didn't know what to believe."

"I—"

He held up a hand. "Please, let me finish. During the time I was chasing you in the tunnels, drawn by the curse that impelled me to kill you, I felt another compulsion. To be with you, to protect you. I think that's why I was able to avoid killing you. The desire to not harm you battled the curse, and won."

Eliana stared into his eyes, eyes that she now noticed were the color of star sapphires.

"But when I wasn't chasing you, I was wondering how I was going to claim my kingdom. All my friends and relatives were dead. I had no living soul I could call a friend, only the hope of meeting descendants of my relatives who still held loyalty to my family." He gulped. "I didn't know if the royal storehouses remained untouched, or if the contents had been looted decades ago. Had I inherited my family's wealth, or was I a pauper?"

His face drooped, and a reluctant empathy tugged at her. He was as alone as she was.

He glanced down at his hands. "I started to hope I'd found an ally in you. A friend. And possibly even more. But then I learned of the promises you'd made, and I was angry. Because it felt like the one person I could trust had betrayed me."

"In a way I had," she said.

"You were tired and hungry, not to mention blind. That you gave in to Shirdona's manipulation in a weak moment was hardly a deliberate betrayal. Although fool that I was, I interpreted it that way. It shook me to the core, and I took it out on you." His wistful eyes moved over her face. "I was so wrong. Can you forgive me?"

Eliana pinned her gaze on his face. *He admitted he'd been wrong!* Tears stung her eyes. "Of course. If you forgive me."

"I think your offense is much less than mine, but if you choose to be generous, I forgive you."

She breathed out, allowing a smile to spread across her face. "It's no sacrifice on my part."

"Sacrifice," he said. "Is that what marrying me is? An unpleasant duty?"

Oh, no. If he planned to cast her off, she was not about to speak first and do his dirty work for him. "Is that how you view it?"

He leaned back in his chair, cradling the teacup in his hands. "When I was young, I had all sorts of romantic dreams. Wooing a beautiful and valiant girl."

He paused and his face darkened. Eliana's stomach dropped. She'd heard tales of the girl he loved before he was cursed.

Adakizh stared off into the distance. "A girl whose intellect matched mine. And possessed a kind and generous heart. I thought I had found her."

Eliana's chest tightened, and she crossed her arms. *I don't want to hear this.*

His head drooped, and he sucked in a ragged breath. "Then Kharan-Khuag pronounced his curse, giving me three days' warning of what would befall me. In an instant, all my hopes and dreams were shattered." He set the cup down with a thump. "My parents and I raged together, cried together. Then we discussed what they would do to ensure the people would recognize me as tagavoi when I woke up. What I would do to gain the trust and respect of my people. Possible marriage alliances were part of the conversation." He stared into his teacup, as if he was finding the next words written in the tea leaves. "I told you my final waking thought was to not kill the one who broke the curse."

"Yes," she said gently. "I honor you for that vow. You were willing to sacrifice your kingdom for me."

"That was before I knew you."

Eliana tightened her arms around her ribs, chills running down her spine. *Does that mean now that he knows me, he wouldn't make such a sacrifice?*

"Then you woke me. The first thing I beheld after a century of terrifying nightmares was your beautiful face."

She raised her eyebrows. "Pretty, in a disheveled sort of way, were your exact words."

Adakizh stole a glance at her, a sheepish smile tugging at the corners of his mouth. "Did I say that?"

"You did."

He shrugged. "If you say so. What I remember is the smudge on your forehead, right over your lovely eyes. Dark eyes that held fear restrained by curiosity and what I've since learned is an unflinching sense of duty and resolve. When you ran, it was like watching a long-desired treasure flee from me. I knew you were brave; anyone who ventured to break Kharan-Khuag's curse had to be. The next few days revealed your clever mind and compassionate heart."

Eliana thought she'd lost the ability to breathe.

"The curse drew me to you, but as I fought it, I realized I was fighting my own heart."

His head drooped and he rubbed a hand over his mouth. "Every tunnel I ran through brought back memories. Here my father and I battled a vishapion. There was the shaft I climbed for my first cattle raid. And the waterfall where I met Tamazi."

Adakizh raised his head. His red-rimmed gaze skittered over Eliana's face, then slid away. "Everyone I'd known had been dead for decades. But it felt like they'd passed only yesterday. In the midst of mourning, I was wrestling with guilt. How could I think about a girl other than Tamazi?"

28

E LIANA STARED AT HIM, gritting her teeth. Adakizh's words raked her heart. Was he casting her off for a dead girl?

He didn't seem to notice her turmoil. "But Tamazi, my parents, everyone, all begged me to not grieve for them. While that made logical sense, when I woke up, I couldn't help yearning for them. How could I face the future alone?"

"How horrible for you." A lump formed in her throat as memories of her own struggles with the ache of loss broke from the place in her mind she'd hidden them. She'd mourned Evander for many months. *Adakizh's had only one.*

He slumped, his eyes taking on a forlorn expression. "I'm not sure I've got it all sorted out yet."

A melancholy hush settled over them. *Here we are. Both hurting and lonely. And we can't find our way to each other. Does he even want to?*

Adakizh broke the silence. "It's been rather bewildering. I don't like it. It makes me cranky."

"Oh? I hadn't noticed."

"Liar."

She snickered. Suddenly, both of them were laughing.

"Oh, Eliana, this is what you do for me." Astonishment brightened his tone. "Even in our bleakest moments, your optimism lit up my soul in a way that the darkest magic could not extinguish. Somehow I knew that if the Rider gave me a future, it had to be with you."

"Are you sure you want me, not Tamazi?" Eliana blurted.

Adakizh recoiled. "You. I made my farewells to her. She'll always have a place in my heart."

Just as Evander lives in mine.

"Now that I know you, I'd sacrifice a hundred kingdoms for you."

Her breath caught, and the weight she'd carried for weeks eased. "You would?"

"Yes." Beaming, he gazed into her face, then drew back. His countenance took on a stony expression. "But perhaps you don't feel the same." He sighed. "I hoped there was something growing between us, something that could last a lifetime. Maybe I deluded myself. Or killed whatever affection you had for me by my stupidity. So be it. I will save you from Kharan-Khuag and his monsters or die in the attempt. The least I can give you is a chance to find your own happiness." A tear rolled down his cheek, marking a trail through the dirt and grime.

Tears spilled from her eyes. The intensity of his emotion robbed her of any capability to form words.

He searched her face, his eyes pleading. "Maybe you don't feel the same, and maybe you can't believe me, but my love for you grows every day. It will grow into a love stronger than that for air or mushrooms."

She snorted. "Mushrooms?"

"What's so funny? Without air or mushrooms, we die."

"I don't know. It just sounds odd to me." She frowned. "If you love me more every day, why have you been so cold?" *Or do you love Tamazi more than you care to admit?*

He winced. "I deserve that." He hung his head. "I wondered if I was doomed to die for my people. It would be unfair to entangle you in what remained of my life."

Eliana scoffed. "If telling the realm you're going to marry me isn't entangling, what is?"

He studied her face for a long moment. "Duty brought us together. I intend to fulfill it. But—" His voice cracked. "But the feelings I have for you are transforming that duty into joy."

She stilled herself, scrambling to sort out the tangle of emotions. They both had prior loves. But they both felt a pull toward each other. Maybe it could grow into love. That sparks flickered between them was more than most royal brides could hope for. "Perhaps for us, duty and desire demand the same thing."

He took a deep breath. "Know that whatever happens, you have my heart. If you choose to hurl it into the sea or feed it to a vishapion, I'll accept your decision."

"I don't think it will come to that." She tipped her face up and smiled.

His eyes widened, and a smile spread over his features. He took her face in his warm hands. Her heart sped up, and she held her breath. He pressed his lips to hers for a heartbeat before pulling back. He gazed at her in wonder. "Oh, Eliana." He moved closer and kissed her with the desire of a hundred years burning through his lips.

Warmth gushed through Eliana, tingles shooting to her toes. She wrapped her arms around his neck. He deepened the kiss, and she returned it, feeling an urgency that drove her to cling to him.

Too soon, he pulled away. "Eliana Xanthia Vassilika Kastellanos, will you marry me?"

She gasped out her reply. "Yes."

Adakizh smirked. "I was pretty sure you'd accept."

"Seeing as I'd told Shirdona, and she informed all of Chorokha, I can see why you'd think that."

"It would have been mortifying if you changed your mind."

She ran her fingers over the stubble on his chin. "Imagine how I felt when you were angry with me."

He flushed. "I'm so sorry."

"Let's promise. Ask first, then get mad."

"I agree." He kissed the top of her head. "Now let's make this official. Please, come with me."

Grasping her hand, he stood up and strode for the stairs. But instead of going down, as Eliana expected, he climbed up to the seventh floor, to the chamber where he spent a century in the cursed sleep.

"Doesn't it bother you to come here?" she asked.

"No. I was on the seashore when the curse claimed me. My father must have moved me here later." He waved a hand. "This was the tagavoi's chamber for centuries. My parents used this room, as will I." He smiled at her. "And you." He peered into her face. "Unless you mind terribly. About the curse and all."

"No, it's fine." *But why are we here?* Surely "making it official" didn't mean consummating the marriage on the spot. Although the urgent heat surging through her suggested that part of her didn't object to that idea.

He dropped to his knees by the bed and pushed the draping edge of the coverlet onto the top of the bed. The thick mattress rested on a raised platform. The sides of the platform were solid stone, intricately carved with goats and fish leaping over winding vines. Gemstones of crimson, blue, green, purple, and white studded the carvings.

Eliana gasped. "I can't believe no one stole those stones while you slept." She knelt beside him to get a better look at the jewels.

He chuckled. "My parents laid protective spells intended to deter any would-be thieves."

Adakizh ran his fingers over an emerald set in a square onyx tile. "I'm going to show you a closely guarded secret. You can tell no one. The spells allow only the tagavoi and tagavli to open it. But we don't want anyone to know it's here in case someone would be foolish enough to try."

He muttered a few words, and Eliana heard a few clicks. Adakizh pressed the emerald and released it. The onyx tile lurched forward as if propelled by a spring.

Adakizh pulled it out and laid it on the floor. Then he reached inside and extracted a small stone box, its cover so encrusted with gems the stone underneath wasn't visible. "These are the tagavli's jewels."

She held her breath as he opened the lid. Diamonds, rubies, sapphires, emeralds, and amethysts twinkled in the dim light. "These are more beautiful than the treasures of Ymittos." She reached in and picked up an enormous ruby, her fingers tingling as she grasped it.

"Are you surprised? We have huge lodes of gems, gems of all kinds, and crystals as well."

She replaced the ruby. "So you're rich."

"No. Pretty rocks are so plentiful they hold little value here. The only thing special about these is the workmanship of their settings and their history. Some are infused with magic. But food has always been our most valued commodity."

"But we could trade these for food from Cinar."

He sat back on his heels and gave her an approving glance. "You're right. Once this war is ended, we could use our jewels for trade." He gave her a half-serious frown. "But that's not why we're here." He dug around in the box. "Do you like sapphires? Or blue topaz?" He held up a dangling earring, its cascading tiers a blend of dark-blue sapphires and aquamarine-tinted topaz.

"That's beautiful."

He held it close to her face. "I think it suits you." He found the earring's twin along with a matching bracelet. "The earrings I give you now to seal our betrothal. The bracelet I will bestow when we marry, as a sign of fidelity."

"We usually exchange rings."

"You can't see the ring I choose for you until the day."

"I don't have a ring for you."

"You don't give me one. Our custom is we marry the girl, not any riches she brings."

"But what of my customs?"

He pursed his lips and nodded. "If you want to give me a ring, I'll accept it."

"How much time do I have to find one?"

He ran a hand over his hair. "Eliana, Kharan-Khuag could attack any day. I think in the interests of unifying our people, and for, as you say, our own joy . . ." He paused and raised his eyebrows suggestively. "We should marry as soon as possible."

"You mean before any more cataclysms or curses?"

"Exactly."

The floor seemed to tip under her feet in a silent earthquake. He was serious. Not casting her off. "When—" She had to pause to catch her breath. "When do you suggest?"

"I'd rather not rush things." He let out a slow breath. "To have the joy of courting you. Of getting to know you, to understand you. And I think we both need a little time."

Eliana released her own sigh. He was right. She'd love some time to solidify the growing trust between them. For both to work through the grief and loss that had assaulted them through the curse and the cataclysm. To move beyond the specters of past entanglements.

A sudden image of Adakizh in the court of Ymittos made her snort. "Yes. Time. You want to understand me? You'll need to study our philosophers and poets."

He stared at her with wide eyes until she grinned. With a knowing wink, he chuckled. "And you have yet to develop the proper appreciation for mushrooms and their uses."

She snickered. "When you cultivate an understanding of the seven rules of debate."

"Oh, I can show you rules of debate you've never imagined." He stroked her cheek.

She repressed the desire to fling her arms around him and wrestle him to the floor. "I would welcome such lessons. We are called to make sacrifices for our people." She said the words primly and finished with a smirk.

He laughed. "If only all sacrifices offered such rewards." He drummed his fingers on the jewel box's lid. "But we don't have time to wait. Would a fortnight be too soon?"

Would it? She'd known him a scant six weeks. But somehow he seemed to understand her more than Evander had, and far better than Istvan ever did. And waiting could mean another disaster could separate them. Their people needed this alliance. *Forget the people.* She needed him.

Her heart hammered in her chest. "No. That's perfect."

He buried his hands in her hair, pulled her to him, and kissed her hungrily. Her arms wrapped around his broad shoulders. The rest of the world evaporated, and he was all that remained. She'd die if he stopped kissing her.

He pulled back with a groan.

"We need to stop." He shifted to sit on the floor and pulled her next to him. He chuckled. "That answers one question."

"What?"

"That ours will be much more than a political union."

Her breath hitched, and she struggled to speak over the lump in her throat. "Much more."

Whatever was between them, they'd make it work. Her mind raced with colliding emotions. Relief. Joy. Trepidation. This was all too much.

She snuggled into his side and rested her head on his

shoulder. As she leaned against him, his arm around her was a refuge in the midst of a raging battle. Her heart slowed. She savored the peaceful moment listening to Adakizh breathe.

Through the open windows the faint sounds of the workers drifted in, the pounding of their hammers and indistinct shouts forming a comforting background. The noises of rebuilding, of normal life. The hope of life after Kharan-Khuag's defeat. And—dare she let herself believe it—a marriage of love?

Adakizh's breathing deepened, and his head jerked forward. He gave her a wry grin and rubbed his eyes. "I'm sorry."

She brushed his tangled curls from his face. "You're exhausted."

"I was in such a rush to get back, we stopped only when fatigue took over." He replaced the jewel box and tile, and tugged the coverlet into place. "I don't want to leave you . . ."

"Go." She wrinkled her nose and smiled. "Get a bath. Then sleep."

"Do you mind?"

"Go. I'll be fine."

"Maybe over dinner we can hash out our plans. You should have a chat with that tricky Shirdona. She'll love planning a wedding, I'm sure. And I need to find a kavor." After a final, lingering kiss, he staggered to his feet and disappeared down the stairs.

Eliana remained on the floor and leaned back against the bed. She studied the earrings in her hand. A smile spread across her face, pulling at her cheeks. She closed her fist around the jewelry and squeezed her eyes shut.

She wanted to shout, to dance. A weight like one hundred stalagmites had lifted from her chest. The glowing mushrooms that lit the room seemed to shine brighter. Adakizh loved her.

They might be rushing into marriage, but surely almost dying together draws out the truth of who someone was.

Better than stilted conversation at a formal banquet and a handful of letters. Although this started as a political union, it had the potential to be more.

Her smile widened. *Much, much more. Let's hope this betrothal turns out better than the last.* She frowned. *But what's a kavor?*

29

Ninety-one days after the winter solstice in the 29th year of Emperor Vural Tzimiskes

ERYA LICKED HER FINGERS. Raw clams were not her idea of a delicacy, but now she savored the flavor as if it had been succulent roast lamb. She took a mouthful of water and rinsed a few grains of sand from her mouth.

The food lifted her spirits. *There must be a way to escape. Maybe a passing ship?*

She shook her head, staring into the horizon. Cetus had chosen this prison well. No one would ever travel past this remote isle unless a refugee from the western islands floated by.

She scanned the waves but saw only foamy lines racing toward her island, ripples that rose and crashed against the beach. The setting sun illuminated a dark spot on the eastern horizon. Could that be land? If only she could fly like the seagulls that squawked overhead.

Fly. Habeci. Derya smacked her forehead. Habeci, the winged horse she'd healed. He'd flown Stigandr and her to the frost giants and the dragon, and he helped her escape after the king betrayed her. Would he rescue her again? Hope fluttered in her chest. She called to the magical animal, pushing her magic behind her thought.

Nothing. *Am I too far away and he cannot hear?* Or will Habeci refuse to fly over the sea? She called again.

Nothing.

She slumped, shaking her head. *What did I expect?* He gave me three trips for healing him. *He owes me no more.*

Derya clambered to her feet and brushed the sand from her clothes. *I need a boat.* She spent the remaining light searching the beach, seeking driftwood or anything that would float.

Nothing. She returned to her shelter and huddled in her rags, beseeching the Rider for help.

No signs from the heavens or flashes of inspiration. Nothing.

She woke in the chilly dawn with a rumbling stomach and a stiff neck. A gulp of water and raw clams served as breakfast. Eating was the best way to add stamina to her magic. Even food that made her retch. She swallowed the clams with a grimace, forcing them down past her nausea.

With a glare at the baleful clouds that blocked the sun's warmth, she set out to search the island.

Her own beach held nothing larger than a seashell. She climbed over the rocky hills, wincing as her bare feet encountered sharp pebbles. Cautiously, she descended the far side, making her way to the narrow strip of sand revealed by the low tide.

Nothing. I'm finding a whole lot of nothing. Bits of broken glass and pottery lay at the foot of the hills, a silent testimony of ships lost at sea and their contents hurled against this forsaken shore.

A large, lumpy object half-buried in the sand caught her attention. She poked it with a long stick, half-expecting it to be a sleeping marine creature. When it didn't budge, she inched closer.

"Oh, yes!" The words burst from her lips. It was a heavy sea cloak. Useless for getting her off the island, but priceless for providing warmth.

After a last glance around, she slung the cloak over her shoulder and returned to her beach. She rinsed the cloak in the ocean and spread it on the sand to dry.

So nothing to build a raft with. Maybe my magic? She tapped a finger against her lips. Salt was an amplifier that would intensify waves. Perhaps she could create a wave she could ride to the nearest land?

Derya stifled the voice in her head that pointed out she didn't know where the nearest land lay. She tasted some of the salt she'd brought with her. Pushing with her magic, she created a wave that sped from the shore.

Then she tried again with salt from the sea. This time, the wave rose twice as high, signifying its greater power. *Interesting. I wonder how I can use that.*

The returning waves crashed against the shore. A long piece of wood bobbed on the surface, something shining stuck in it.

Derya plunged into the surf and retrieved the wood. It was two long planks fastened together. Could she use it as a raft? She wrinkled her nose at that idea. She'd have to float with her legs dangling in the sea. That would be too tempting for a shark to ignore.

Only after returning to the beach did she investigate the shiny object. Stuck in the crack between the boards, tangled in seaweed that wrapped around the wood, was a jeweled dagger, caught under some kind of latch. Tears pricked her eyes when she spotted the letters DVOT etched into the center of the crest of the Heir of Cinar, an eagle with flared wings. Her initials, her dagger, the one snatched from her two days ago.

Thank the Rider. Now she had a weapon and a rudimentary raft.

She rubbed her mouth, wondering. *If I made more waves, would I find more wood?* She was about to make the attempt when she spotted a raft approaching. Her heart leapt. *This is just what I need.*

Then she noticed three figures seated on it. She stiffened, squinting, desperately trying to discern if they were potential allies or a new set of enemies. The raft crested a wave and she recognized Txartomal and his cronies. Gulping down her fear, she hid the dagger in her belt.

The fae bounded from the raft, splashing in the waves. They dragged it to shore and flipped it over.

Derya gaped. Now she noticed the raft was part of a ship's hull, with runes carved into the wood. This was from one of King Ollen's ships, the *Dreki,* she guessed, from the length of the word. Bitter testimony of her failure.

Txartomal chortled, his tentacles waving over his head. "We sank all your ships."

Derya's heart stuttered. She clenched her lips to silence her dismay. *He's lying, he has to be. They can't all be dead.* The princess fixed what she hoped was a disdainful stare on the water fae.

Txartomal gestured to his companions. They smashed the boards and tore them apart. Using the hooked ends of their tentacles, they fractured the wood into splinters.

The crunch of the wood sounded like breaking bones. Derya watched the fae turn what had been a makeshift raft into a pile of fragments, mourning the destruction of her slim hopes for escape.

"That is His Magnificence's intentions for Cinar. Because you angered him."

Derya stiffened her shaking knees and stuck out her chin. "I'm not happy with him either."

The water fae sneered. "He thought you'd play games."

He stalked toward Derya. "You have something that belongs to His Magnificence. Tell us where it is. You might as well, you know. He'll find it eventually. The longer you delay, the more annoyed he'll be with you. He'll have to think up some special games to play with you."

Derya's stomach twisted, and her throat tightened. "And if I don't care to play?" Would she be able to use the dagger to kill herself before that happened? Death would be preferable to whatever loathsome acts Cetus would force her to perform.

The second fae slapped the leader on the back. "You owe me two slaves. I told you she wouldn't give in quickly." The third fae snickered.

Txartomal scowled. "You think you can hold out. But for what? You'll never get off this island. Our karcharia will make sure of that."

She wrinkled her forehead. "Your what?"

"Karcharia. The men with sharks' heads."

Derya rubbed a hand over her mouth, trying to hide her dismay. Now, for whatever good it did her, she knew what those monsters were called. Maybe letting one of them bite her head off would be preferable to revealing what Cetus demanded she tell.

The second fae snickered. "The karcharia had fun with your friends. They haven't had a feast like that for a while."

The third nudged him with an elbow. "Not all of them were her friends."

She frowned. Was he talking about King Ollen's men?

Txartomal gave her a condescending sneer. "The clever Heir of Cinar didn't know she harbored an assassin in her midst?"

Derya froze. The assassination attempts. The first one on the road across Ymittos, was that their man? Not unless they'd hired the other mercenaries. But the attempts in Nafplio, where someone tried to drown her in the bath and stab her on a staircase. And the falling icicle in Ethkarpia. That was one of Cetus's agents?

Txartomal shook his head. "His Magnificence is going to be disappointed. He overestimated you. And your guards." He turned to the others. "Taking over will be easier than we thought."

She crossed her arms. "I don't believe you."

That provoked another guffaw. "About the assassin? Want to know who it is? He's got—" Txartomal broke off. "No, better His Magnificence tells you. He'll enjoy the game."

So, a man then. Who had been nearby for all the attempts? This was maddening. She felt she should know who the culprit was. She pressed her lips together. Maybe if she remained silent, the sneering fae would reveal more.

Txartomal grabbed Derya's chin with his long, spindly fingers and dug his pointed nails into her skin. He pulled her toward him. "His Magnificence wants his property. Where is it?"

Her eyes flared wide, and her lips trembled. Her entourage was gone, her friends dead. The scepter lay at the bottom of the sea. Cetus could easily retrieve it. If he'd had an assassin in her ranks, that meant his fingers were everywhere. Resisting him was hopeless.

The fae dug his nails in deeper. A single tear leaked from her eye and rolled down her face.

Txartomal laughed. "Not so brave as you'd like us to think, are you? You'll break. They all do."

He turned, smirking. Followed by the others, he strode into the water and dove under the ash-gray waves.

Derya collapsed to the sand in a heap. Her breath came in ragged pants, and her heart raced faster than a rabbit from a fox.

Thank the Rider he gave up. Another instant and she might have broken.

She pulled in a few deep breaths. *I promised Bahadir I'd fight to the death. To the death it is.*

Taking a deep breath, she eyed the pile of wood from the ruined raft. By some miracle, the fae hadn't bothered with the boards she'd found earlier. Perhaps she could salvage enough from the fae's raft to attach to the intact boards to make a suitable craft. But she'd have to hurry. She had no intention of being on the island when the vile fae returned.

She picked through the pile of wood and laid out the biggest sections, arranging them like the pieces of a puzzle. Fortunately, the fae hadn't shredded all the boards. A few of the longer ones might bear her weight. If only she could find something to bind them with.

Stigandr's wood magic would sure be useful right now. But he's not here. She'd have to figure it out on her own. The sudden reminder of her isolation brought the sting of tears to her eyes.

She clenched her jaw. *Enough. Time to get to work.*

DERYA SHIVERED in the bitter cold, waiting for dawn. The sea cloak had been a boon, sheltering her from the worst of the night wind. She tugged the cloak tighter around herself, grateful for its protection. Hunching to shield her face from the freezing gusts, she tucked her icy fingers under her armpits.

The moon cast enough light to allow her to appraise the crude raft she'd constructed. The only thing she'd found to bind the wood together was a gnarled, thorny vine.

At first she'd cursed the thorns, wincing every time one of them drew blood from her stiff fingers. Then she realized they were a blessing. She used them to tack the vine to the boards, gratified they worked almost as well as nails.

She'd labored far into the night with only the moonlight to see by. But her tiny raft was done. The moment the eastern sky shifted from black to rosy, she would set sail. She needed to disappear before the water fae returned.

What she'd do about the karcharia, the shark-headed men, she wasn't sure. Her only hope was to use her magic to propel her faster than they could swim, or to shove them away with waves. If that didn't work, she'd most likely end the day missing an arm or leg. But at least she wouldn't wind up as Cetus's toy.

She jiggled one of her feet up and down. Would the sun never rise? Every splash made her jump, every wave brought the possibility of the mutant fae's return. She checked that her waterskin was full and choked down a handful of raw clams. Her stomach protested, sending burning sourness surging up her throat. She swallowed it, grimacing. *I will never be able to even think about eating shellfish again.*

At last, a bluish glow spread across the eastern sky, and the first streaks of mauve appeared. She tugged her raft to the shore and waded into the icy surf, gasping as the water chilled her legs. When she was waist deep, she threw herself on the raft. The next wave tossed her back to shore.

With a huff of annoyance, she dashed a few drops of seawater into her mouth, working the salty taste over her tongue. That would intensify the waves she created. Then she dug in her bag of amplifiers. After a drop of citrus to amplify her ability to pull water toward her, she summoned her magic. It pooled within her, its liquid force like water pressing against a dam. She released a tiny bit, pulling on the seawater.

The raft shot from the shore, skimming over the breakers, hurling toward the east. Curtains of spray rose on either side of her craft. Derya grinned. Using salt from the sea amplified her magic more than she'd ever done before. *This just might work.*

She directed the raft toward the rising sun. Since the spring equinox had been a day or two ago, she reasoned the sun would rise due east. She didn't know if that course would take her to Rorvik, Veleti, or the ruined coast of Ymittos. But anywhere was better than the deserted island. Rider willing, it would be warmer.

She clung to her craft, propelling it with her magic. Once the island was out of sight, she could slow her pace and save her strength. She couldn't even guess how far she'd have to sail to make landfall.

If she made it that long. The raft sailed up the side of one wave, then crashed into a trough. Then up the other side. On board ship, this rocking motion was calming. On an open, tiny raft, it was terrifying. And she was already drenched, chilled to the bone.

The sun had risen over the horizon before she decided it was safe to slow up. She'd use her magic without amplifiers for a while. If only she wasn't so hungry. All she had were dried berries, and they needed to be saved to use as amplifiers.

Hours passed with no sight of shore. Derya stared at the place the sea met the sky, the sun now high overhead. Midday would be trickier for navigation. And she was tired. The sleepless night and early morning escape were wearing on her.

The princess took a mouthful of water and pressed on. At least the sea was calm. A dolphin surfaced, fixed a limpid eye on her, then dove out of sight. No sign of birds or plants floating on the waves. *That must mean I'm still far from land.*

After another glance at the sun, she decided she'd veered a little to the north. She corrected her course. Soon, soon, she'd have to see signs of land.

A jolt of fear took her breath away. What were those dark shapes in the water? *Please, oh, please, let them be dolphins. Or big fish. Or even normal sharks.*

Five triangular fins cut through the water. They circled her raft. Squinting, she spotted their human legs. *No. Not the karcharia.* Taking a taste of salt and citrus, she thrust her magic against the sea.

The raft leapt ahead with such force she nearly slid off it, scraping her elbow. Ignoring the stinging pain, she dug her fingernails into the rough boards. She shoved harder with her magic, willing herself to escape the karcharia.

When her toes went numb, she released most of her magic, pulling just enough at the water to keep the raft moving. Her reserves of power dwindled, flowing more like a small stream than a gushing river. She looked behind her. No sign of life broke the ocean's surface.

With a frown, she faced forward. To her dismay, three mutant fae swam lazily toward her, their tentacles waving in the air.

When they reached her, they assumed positions on either side of her raft, effortlessly keeping up. "Where do you think you're going?" Txartomal asked.

"You forgot to bring me breakfast," Derya said. "So I'm going to find some."

"Breakfast, she says. And were you planning to return? His Magnificence is quite hurt you left without so much as a thank-you for his hospitality."

"Is that what he calls it?" Derya took a sip of water, hoping to gain some strength. Then she slipped salt and citrus into her mouth. "Tell him I found the accommodations lacking."

The princess rammed her magic against the waves. This time, she had a firm grip on the raft. She shot forward. A smirk crossed her face at the startled curses of the fae.

Her legs felt cold and numb. She tried to wiggle her toes and failed. *This is not good. The side effects are getting worse, and I'm almost depleted.*

She strained to see in front of her. The sun sparkling on the water made it hard to look into the distance. Was she imagining it, or was that a dark line on the horizon? She pushed more at her magic, hoping to find help before the mutant fae captured her.

Derya shot a glance over her shoulder. Three shapes were swimming after her, keeping pace with her. She heaved her magic, giving the raft another burst of speed. It jolted over the waves, bouncing her against the planks. Pain shot through her elbows and forearms. That she felt nothing in her legs and knees made her mouth go dry. The numbness was spreading.

And the sound of sloshing waves was diminishing. But the dark line had thickened. She had found land.

Her elation was short-lived. She was losing feeling in her arms. Every breath was a struggle. Txartomal popped up in the water to her right. His mouth moved as if he was shouting. She couldn't hear a word.

The princess gritted her teeth. She had to make it to shore. A large ship was sailing on the horizon. If she could reach it, maybe someone would help her. Or the fae would give up.

Dark spots floated in front of her eyes. Her eyelids grew heavy. She fought to keep them open. *No. I can't stop. Even if I never walk again or lose my hearing forever.*

She was so close. Seagulls circled overhead. Just a little longer and she'd be there.

A scaled arm grabbed her raft. She wanted to bat it away but couldn't lift her hand. She bit down hard on her lip and pulled on her magic. The torrent of power that had gushed from her earlier dwindled to a trickle. Her raft slowed, bobbing with the waves. Another fae drove the hooked end of his tentacle into her raft's wood. Her heart sank. The last things she saw were Txartomal's mocking face and long, sharp teeth. Then blackness overtook her. Her final thought was that she had failed.

31

S HARP PAIN IN DERYA'S wrists wrenched her into
consciousness. She was seated on cold, damp stone,
leaning against a rocky wall. *What's holding my arms up?*
She tried to lower her hands, but something hard and cold
dug into her wrists. With an effort, she opened her sleep-
crusted eyes, blinking in the rays of the setting sun. *Raging
waters, how long was I out?* It had been late morning when the
fae caught her.

A slap on the face made her gasp. She snapped her gaze
toward her assailant. Txartomal. His jaw was moving up and
down, but she heard no words. Then she noticed the foamy
waves heaving silently against the rock.

"I can't hear you." She didn't even hear her own words,
just felt the vibration in her throat.

The fae's mouth opened and his tentacles waved. Was he
laughing at her? He yanked her to her feet. Now standing, she
could lower her hands to waist level. The relief in her stiff
shoulders was immediate. They'd at least allowed her to keep
the sea cloak, but her bare toes were blue against the icy stone.
She shuffled her feet, clanking the fetters that tethered her
ankles to the rock. *Lovely. Maybe escaping wasn't such a wise plan.*

Before her, the rock extended about six feet, then dropped off into gray, surly waves. The view to her left was the same. And the right. "Where am I?"

Txartomal smirked.

Why bother asking? Even if the fiend answered, I couldn't hear him.

Her mouth was dry, so dry. And she was ravenous. The cure for overused magic was sleep and food. She'd slept for hours, but it didn't appear the fae had any plans to feed her. She shuddered, wondering if they'd chained her to the rock to provide dinner for some monster of the deep.

The fae leered at her and leaped into the ocean, leaving Derya alone.

The setting sun painted the sea blood red. She watched the colors change from scarlet to fuchsia, then darken into purple and finally black. A few stars twinkled in the frosty sky.

The moon hadn't risen when the wind freshened from the north. Water splashed Derya's feet. If they weren't still numb from overusing her magic, they'd be achingly cold. Another wave drenched her to the waist. She tugged at the chains, but to no avail.

Drowning, she decided, might be preferable to being chained up. *It would serve Cetus right that punishing her meant the demise of his plaything before he had the chance to enjoy it.*

Bile surged up her throat.

She choked it down. Isolation on the island had been grim, but at least she'd had shelter, water, and the use of her limbs. She'd never escape this. Her sole consolation was knowing she wouldn't live long enough to witness Cetus's ultimate victory or the deaths of all she cared about.

Another wave poured frigid water over her feet, splashing her to her shoulders. Salt water stung the half-healed cuts and scrapes on her arms. She was going to drown on this rock, chained and helpless.

A tear trickled down her cheek.

The wind rose, and clouds obscured the stars. The waves

grew higher, sometimes surging over her head. Now in total darkness, Derya couldn't see their approach. Still deaf, her only warning of a fresh onslaught was the rising motion of luminous spots riding the waves, which gave her just enough time to hold her breath. Soon she was hanging from the chains, sobbing and dripping, shivering from the cold. She no longer cared what Cetus planned for her, as long as this protracted death would end. *I am the Heir of Cinar. And I have been shaken.* She closed her eyes, begging the Rider to grant her a quick end.

Some time later, Derya opened her eyes to a pale-gray sky. She'd slipped down to sit on the rock, her arms held up over her head by the chains. Her salt-crusted, drenched cloak blocked the wind but did nothing to ease the aching cold that penetrated her bones. But instead of silence, her ears filled with dull roaring. Her hearing was returning, but slowly.

And her gnawing hunger was a ravenous beast. If Cetus offered her a piece of stale bread, she might just throw herself at his feet for it. *No. Better to starve. Rider, help me stay resolute.*

She let her eyelids close, as squinting into the sparkling sun on the waves sent stabbing pain into her eyes. Her head throbbed, and her nose was dripping. She wiped it on her shoulder and sneezed. Despite the frigid wind, she was sweating. She sneezed again. Hot soup and a warm bed. That's what she needed. She leaned against the wall and closed her eyes, hoping to doze off.

"Oh, the princess has a runny nose, does she? His Magnificence doesn't want that."

Derya jerked. Txartomal and another fae stood on her left not two feet from her. When had they shown up? She could scarcely hear his words through the roaring in her ears. Maybe he was shouting to be heard.

"Stand up. His Magnificence has a gift for you."

Derya's heart thumped in a wild cadence. Her stomach fluttered, and sweat trickled from her forehead. Sick, starving, and cold, she was not ready to face Cetus. "I'm sorry. I have no need for sea slugs or whatever creature he considers a pet."

"Sea slugs!" The fae snickered. "He won't like that."

Txartomal shook his head. "Oh, the little princess overused her magic. Such a pity." His lips contorted into a mocking sneer. "Lost her kingdom, too, from what I hear. The title of Heir of Cinar has passed to another."

Derya's heart plummeted to her feet. She struggled to breathe and forced herself to keep from breaking. *No. He must be lying.* Or even if he was telling the truth, once she returned with the scepter and the crown, her father would reinstate her. She had to believe that.

Txartomal ran a finger down her cheek, pressing his pointed fingernail into her skin.

A repulsed shudder wracked her frame, chafing her sore wrists against the manacles.

"Lucky for you His Magnificence prefers his toys to be healthy."

She wanted to scream, to shove him from her, to do anything to escape him and his fishy-smelling breath.

He uncorked a small glass flask filled with a mud-brown liquid. "Drink."

Derya stared at it. "No."

"You will." He grabbed her chin in his fingers and forced her jaw open. The second fae pinched her nose shut. Then Txartomal poured the potion down her throat.

She gagged and retched as the noxious brew surged into her stomach. The fae released her, and she gasped for air. She spat in a futile attempt to clear her mouth of the lingering taste of decay.

Her hearing returned so acutely that she could hear not only the crash of the waves but Txartomal's breathing. The heavy, tired feeling that went with illness disappeared. She felt refreshed, as if from a peaceful night's sleep.

Txartomal dug his nails into her chin. One of his tentacles

hit the top of her head with its hooked end. "The proper response is 'thank you.' Perhaps being alone has made you forget your manners."

"What else do you expect when my only company has been beasts and monsters?"

"Listen to her," Txartomal said. "She's insulting us."

His companion snarled. "Perhaps she'll do better with other company."

Derya's heart clenched. Had Cetus captured one of her friends?

The two fae chortled and dove into the sea.

She stared after them. Now what? The potion had cured her deafness and whatever illness had been brewing and restored the feeling in her legs and feet. Which wasn't all good. The relentless cold made her toes ache and burn.

She released a sigh, pursing her lips. *Now I'm back to "where am I?" and "for how long?"* She tugged at the chains, but the bolts fastened to the rock refused to move. She narrowed her eyes. *He's not going to kill me. He wants me alive.* She refused to let her imagination linger on what his plans for her were.

Instead, she spent the day seated with her arms held overhead by the chains, watching the waves roll up to her rock, wincing when spray spattered her face. She scrambled to her feet when a whitecap surged near, gasping when it doused her. She called out to the Rider of the Ancient Skies. Thought of her father, her friends. And vowed no matter what sacrifices she'd make, privations she'd endure, or terrors she'd face, she'd defeat Cetus.

The sun meandered across the cloud-streaked sky and made its descent in the west. The clouds massing on the horizon turned a brilliant orange, fading to peach and pink until indigo overtook them. The dark was nearly complete, only a handful of scattered stars shining through breaks in the clouds.

Derya drifted in and out of slumber, only to be yanked

from it by the icy spray and splash of the waves. At some point, the sea calmed, so she sank to sit and rested her head against one of her upraised arms. In spite of the cold, an uneasy sleep settled on her like a rough blanket.

Loud grunting awakened her. Her eyes flared open, and fear trickled down her spine. What kind of monster had slithered onto her rock? Under the cloudy, moonless sky, she couldn't see anything other than stray luminescence on the seething surf.

Cautiously, she pulled her feet under her and stood, careful to avoid clanking the chains. Holding her breath, she strained to listen. The heaving waves hissed and splashed. Cold spray doused her, and she bit her lip to restrain a gasp.

Whatever was on her right groaned, a deep moan of profound pain. It was wounded, whatever it was. *A walrus? Shark? Karcharia?*

A wave surged against the rock, drenching her to the knees. The thing groaned.

Derya stared in the direction of the moaning. Hopefully the beast was too badly injured to attack her. And maybe the Rider would send a gigantic wave that would wash it back out to sea.

Hours passed as Derya listened to the beast groan and grunt. Was it growing weaker? Or had its pain driven it into unconsciousness? Would Txartomal return before the creature roused enough to eat her?

A sick feeling twisted her insides. Was this what the fae had meant about giving her company?

Feeling the night would never end, she glared at the still-dark western sky. To her left, the southern sky was pinkish gray. *Finally.*

Derya swiveled to look right. A dim form was there, chained to the rock like she was. Now she could make out arms and legs. Was the thing human? It let out another groan.

As the light grew, she noted more details about her

companion. He was propped against the wall with legs outstretched, his muscular arms held aloft by the chains. Tattered trousers covered his long legs, and he wore scuffed boots. Other chains bound his ankles to the rock. His head slumped over his broad chest, his face obscured by long, damp hair.

Derya frowned. His hair was darkened by the water, but it wasn't black. That ruled out most Cinarrians or Pasargadians. He could be Ethkarpian or Tavrosian. Or one of the northern barbarians.

That last made the most sense. Maybe he was one of King Ollen's men, captured from the wreckage of a sinking barbarian ship. A flicker of hope stirred in her. Perhaps together they could find a way out. If he survived.

She waited until the sun rose to rouse her companion. "Hey. Wake up."

For answer, he growled a curse. Then slowly, he raised his head and lashed her face with a furious glare.

She stared wide-eyed, her breath wrenched from her lungs. It couldn't be. Not a potential ally but a foe.

Stigandr Tyr.

32

S TIGANDR'S GRAY EYES HELD Derya's startled gaze captive. After a long moment, he spoke. "Who are you?"

"What?"

"Who are you?" His voice was low and raspy, as if he'd been shouting.

"You know who I am."

"No, I don't."

Her eyes widened in disbelief. Maybe being chained up had made him lose his reason. "When did Cetus capture you?"

"You mean Kharan-Khuag?" He wrinkled his brow. "It's all blurring together. What is this, last month of winter?"

"No, the equinox was six days ago."

He stared at her. "You're saying I've been captive for what . . . forty-one days?"

Derya screwed up her face as she counted backwards in time. "Not that long." She tipped her head to the side. "I met you thirty-eight days ago."

"Met you? No. I don't know you."

"Are you saying you've forgotten the night we spent

together?" He could lie all he wanted, but his Ar-Debish, spoken with a faint, lilting accent, gave him away. He was the king of Rorvik.

His eyes flickered over her. "I'm sure when you're not drenched like a drowned rat you'd make a memorable partner, but I've never enjoyed a night with you."

"That's not what I meant." She jerked at her chains. "You remember, when we fought the dragon . . ."

He scoffed. "I'm not such a fool as to go chasing dragons with every pretty girl who comes along."

"So you deny it."

"Of course."

"And you deny stealing from me."

"What do you take me for? I have no need of whatever paltry coins you have."

Derya snorted. Any ten pairs of her shoes were worth more than Stigandr's entire stockade. "Liar."

"I'd say the same of you."

She huffed. "When did I ever lie to you? If you've never seen me before, I couldn't have told you anything, true or false."

"Claiming you know me is a lie."

This was getting her nowhere. "Why did you do it?"

"Do what?"

"Whack me over the head."

"Whack you?" He snorted. "Write this behind your ear. I don't know you."

Derya ground her teeth. Stigandr had lost his mind. Or, perhaps, was using his well-honed skills at deceit. She wasn't going to waste her breath talking with him. Her tongue felt cracked, like mud dried under a summer sun. She had no strength or desire to converse with either a madman or a liar. She turned her head to the side and glared at the seething gray waves.

A whooshing sound jostled her from a doze. Thirty feet

away, a whale had surfaced. Another whale launched itself from the sea and crashed back onto the waves with a splash. The cold water surged against Derya, soaking her to the shoulders. She let out a gasp and shivered.

"What's your name?"

Stigandr's question, the only words he'd spoken for several hours, disrupted Derya's musings like a pig running through a market.

"My what?"

He responded slowly, speaking as if to a child. "I asked you your name."

"You know what it is."

"Humor me."

"Derya Vashi Oyunbaz Tzimiskes."

Stigandr stared, then laughed. "And Derya Vashi Oyunbaz Tzimiskes, where are you from?"

She scoffed. "Your efforts to keep up this facade are quite impressive. But I'm not fooled. Surely you aren't the ignorant barbarian you are pretending to be."

"Ignorant?" He sounded truly perplexed

"Anyone could guess from my family name where I'm from."

"Tzimiskes." He chuckled. "Cinarrian, right?"

She rolled her eyes. "How clever of you." She infused her words with as much sarcasm as she could. "But my name isn't important. Do you know what Cetus, or Kharan-Khuag as you call him, wants?"

"He seems to think one of us has something he values."

"Do you have it?" She posed the question casually, wondering how long he'd continue to lie.

"No. Do you?"

You know I do. "No."

"That's unfortunate."

She stared, wondering. He seemed to believe that she didn't have the scepter. Was he bespelled? She'd never heard of magic that would rob someone of their memories. But that didn't mean it was impossible.

Or had Cetus tortured him into insanity? Half-healed wounds littered Stigandr's arms, visible through his ripped, blood-stained clothing. A purple bruise ringed one eye. The king's lower face, covered with several weeks' growth of beard, had bare, raw spots where it looked like chunks of hair had been torn out. That must be it. The king had gone mad.

Stigandr cursed.

Txartomal was clambering out of the thrashing waves onto the rock. Derya echoed the king's oath, the angry words a feeble effort to mask her alarm.

The fae leered at Derya. "Oh, you're awake." He grinned, exposing his sharp teeth. "His Magnificence approaches." He dove back into the sea.

Derya sagged against the rock, her knees suddenly unable to support her weight. She gritted her teeth in a vain attempt to still her quivering lips.

Long before she saw the sorcerer, she felt his presence. An aura of heavy, ancient malice surrounded her, so palpable that she could almost smell it. Oily, noxious waves of magic seeped through the air. It held a power she knew her magic could no more subdue than a raindrop could water the desert.

Then the sorcerer leaped from the sea and landed on the rock.

Transfixed by fear, her eyes were riveted on him. She wasn't sure what she'd been expecting. A monster with six heads. Or scaled skin and a long, spiked tail. But he resembled an ordinary man and could pass for a Cinarrian: average height, olive skin, wiry, muscular arms, black hair held back by a jeweled circlet that crossed his forehead. He wore a plain tunic and trousers tinted the gray of an angry, stormy sea.

Nothing human remained in him. His eyes were the color of an overcast sky, white with a cold tinge of gray. Derya gazed into those eyes that had beheld a thousand atrocities and reveled in the sight and thought she would vomit.

The princess gripped her chains in her shaking hands. She tipped her chin up, pressing her lips together to contain a whimper. Whatever horror he'd prepared for her, he was about to unleash it. She'd show him what steel Cinarrians carried in their spines. *I am the Heir of Cinar. I will not be shaken.* Somehow face to face with pure evil, the words didn't stiffen her resolve as they normally did.

"So, little water mage. Have you decided?"

Derya jumped at the sound of Cetus's purring voice, making her chains rattle and clank. Sweat beaded on her forehead, and she stuck her chin in the air. "The pit you call home grew lonely, so you had to seek company in our current residence? I regret we have no refreshments to offer you."

Cetus ignored Stigandr's snort and advanced upon Derya. "Oh, lovely princess, you don't understand. You *are* the refreshments."

She gritted her teeth, struggling to contain the dry heaves. Although spewing vomit in Cetus's face would be a gratifying act of defiance. Probably her last one but satisfying none the less.

"Princess?" Stigandr asked. "She's a princess?"

Cetus whirled and slapped him across the face. "As if you didn't know. Or are you that foolish you'd give a treasure to just any water mage who strolled through your kingdom?" He tapped the end of Stigandr's nose as if he was a toddler. "You will tell me what I want to know."

He waved a hand at Stigandr's chains. The man's eyes widened, then he shrieked. He flailed his arms, tugging at the clanking chains.

The smell of burnt flesh stung Derya's nose. She felt as though she couldn't breathe, that she, too, was burning. She sagged against the rock, held up by the shackles on her wrists.

Stigandr's head drooped. The skin around his manacles

was scarlet and black, and a white slash of bone peeked through the burned flesh.

"Why did you give her the scepter?"

"I never had it," Stigandr ground out through clenched teeth.

"Oh? Then you told her where to find it. Why would Rorvik be so foolish as to help Cinar?"

A flick of Cetus's fingers and a wave splashed over Stigandr. He let out a bellow.

Derya winced. Salt water on his wrists must have punished his burned flesh terribly.

Cetus waved his hand again. The man's face turned red, then purple. His eyes rolled up into his head.

Cetus released the magical bonds around the king's throat. Stigandr fell to his knees, taking deep, gasping breaths. The sorcerer grabbed one chain and tugged it. Stigandr shrieked as the manacles dug into his burned wrists. Cetus seized the blond hair on the top of Stigandr's head and jerked his face up. "Where. Is. It."

"I don't know."

Cetus slammed Stigandr's head against the rock. "You've made me angry, barbarian."

The sorcerer pierced the man's cheek with a jagged blade. Blood spilled down Stigandr's chin and dripped to the rock, mixing with the salt water. The king went still, kept from falling to his face only by the chains around his mangled, burned wrists, shackles that held his arms over his head.

Derya's mouth fell open, and her heart thudded in her chest. What a mercy the king passed out. But she was next.

Cetus stood staring out to sea for several long moments. Derya's hands trembled, and terrified sweat dampened the back of her neck. She was about to beg him to begin the torture. Anything would be better than this horrible waiting, the fear, the anticipation that was worse than the reality. And after Cetus finished, she might lapse into blessed unconsciousness like Stigandr.

The sorcerer turned. "Oh, little water mage, princess of a dying empire," he said in a mocking, sing-song tone, "you could end this now. Just tell me what you did with my scepter."

Derya lifted her chin but couldn't bear to look into those dead eyes. She stared over his head at the cloudy sky. *Rider help me.* After a long moment, she choked out a single word. "No."

"Perhaps you don't think I deserve to wield it? It was mine to begin with. I created it and infused it with my power."

"To use for great evil." As soon as she spoke, she regretted the words.

But Cetus only laughed. "Evil? What do you mean?"

"To conquer and enslave." She was trembling, terrified of enraging the sorcerer but unable to contain her outrage.

"I only want what is mine. I ruled the land you call Cinar until it was wrested from me. Under me, the people's labor and resources were properly used for production and the creation of wealth. Is that any different from how the emperors of Cinar reign?"

She gawked at him, stunned into silence. "Yes."

Cetus chortled. "Oh, you want to debate the matter? This will be fun. How is it different?"

"We don't enslave anyone."

"No, you don't call it that. But the peasants who work your lands don't have much choice about their destiny."

"But they aren't chained to the land. Because of us, they live in peace. We offer protection and stability."

"Do those who live on the border with Pasargadae feel safe or protected? Or the ones on any of your borders?"

She opened her mouth to protest, but he cut her off. "That's not the point. I offer true protection and stability instead of your illusions. One ruler over the continent. There will be no more of these petty wars for land or livestock or riches. Under my rule, I will ensure a lasting peace. Everyone will live in security, knowing their place and receiving their portion."

"But—"

"You object because you would no longer rule. Would your subjects have the same opinion?"

Something was terribly wrong with his argument, but something was terribly right. The hammering of her heart and the bile stinging her throat made it impossible to think, to sort out the truth from his devious lies and distortions.

"Little princess, you claim to desire the best for the people, but what you crave is the power."

"Without power, we couldn't protect them."

He shook his head sadly, as if she was a child who'd made a mistake. "Who says you are worthy to wield the power?" His face contorted into a sneer. "I alone am worthy to rule."

"What about the Rider of the Ancient Skies?"

He turned on her with an expression of loathing and rage, full of fury like the sea during a hurricane. She cringed against the rock, her racing heart slamming against her ribs like an animal desperate to escape its cage.

The sorcerer stalked nearer and snapped his fingers. Five heads bobbed up out of the waves, five of his mutant water fae, including Txartomal. "Do you see them? I've decided that if you don't tell me what I want to know, I'll give you to them once I've finished with you. Oh, at first I was going to keep you for myself. While your defiance is appealing, I fear it will get old." He gave her a smile that made her skin crawl. "Come, little mage, talk to me. Where is my scepter?"

Derya swallowed hard and studied a writhing cloud.

"You are a fool, little mage. You had my scepter and gave it to another to hold." Cetus ran a long finger down her cheek and under her chin. He traced a line down her neck. "Oh, I will enjoy subduing you, little mage." He slashed Derya's cheek with a talon-like fingernail, scraping open a wound.

A sharp cry escaped her throat, and a tear spilled from her eye.

"My water fae will find it and torture whoever has it. But if you tell me now, I'll have them killed quickly."

Derya screwed her eyes shut.

"Still stubborn? I can wait. I'll enjoy watching the emperors scramble and fight each other. Once the empires have slaughtered each other and destroyed the lands, the survivors will welcome me." His mouth contorted into a mocking sneer. "I've waited a millennium to regain power. By this time next year, all the pieces will have fallen in place and I'll rule Ardebil. No one will be able to withstand me, no matter what they do. You can languish here or watch from my side."

Derya pulled in a long breath. She was tired, so tired. She'd give anything to end this terror. Maybe she could bargain with Cetus, have him heal the king. She could tell him the scepter had sailed south and hope her father's armies could fight the sorcerer off.

A faint clanking noise drew her attention to Stigandr. He raised his bloody, battered face, and his intense gray gaze caught hers. He mouthed the word "no."

I am the Heir of Cinar. I will not be shaken. Her hands were trembling so badly they rattled the chains restraining her. "I don't know."

"I'll be back when I have time to enjoy it. Answer me, or I'll cut up your accomplice and make you eat him, piece by piece." He grinned, exposing his sharklike teeth, and leered. With a sudden move, he grabbed Derya's left breast and twisted it. "Then you and I will play."

He gave her a rough shove that banged her head against the rock before diving into the sea, leaving a whimpering, cowering Derya huddled near the rock.

33

Chorokha

Fifty-seven days after the winter solstice in the Year 999 (Chorokhese reckoning) and the 29th year of Emperor Vural Tzimiskes of Cinar

"THEY KILLED THEM ALL, that's what they did." The grizzle-haired man's gills flared, and he spat.

Eliana stared, dumbfounded, and pressed a hand to her mouth. The Alaf-Shilams couldn't have slaughtered all her people. That had to be a rumor.

"Are you certain?" Adakizh asked.

"As sure as there's stone overhead. Every overworlder who fell into their territory was put to the sword."

Her chest tightened. "Why didn't you stop them?"

He shrugged. "We only learned of it a week ago. We caught one raiding our mushrooms. He said if we didn't let him go, we'd end up like the overworlders, missing our heads and lying at the bottom of a crevasse."

Eliana clenched her fists, anger heating her face. Now she

understood why she'd never heard of any Ymittosians living among the Alaf-Shilams. She froze. They'd only found a fraction of her people. Search parties came back empty-handed, if they returned at all.

Her innocent people. They survived the cataclysm, only to be butchered by savages.

Adakizh put an arm around her shoulders. "We'll look into it. And thank you for doing your part to help the Ymittosians."

"We haven't eaten our brains with our mushrooms. Kharan-Khuag is coming, and we need every hand we can muster to fight him off."

Eliana didn't hear Adakizh's reply. Mechanically, she murmured her farewells and let Adakizh lead her on their way. She blinked the tears from her eyes. "Those savages. How could they?"

He gave her fingers a squeeze. "We don't know if he spoke the truth. The Minarilis and Alaf-Shilams have been feuding for centuries. He could be trying to force us to take sides."

Eliana grabbed his words like a rock climber clings to a rope. She took a few deep breaths. "If they live so close together, why are they quarreling?"

"They say one of the Alaf-Shilams—they weren't called Alaf-Shilam then, I forget what their name was—was bathing, and a Minarili threw his clothes into the river. The tagavoi of the time considered it a wonderful joke and refused to decree any punishment. The Alaf-Shilams never got over it."

"Seems like a stupid reason for a feud."

"The reasons for most of them are." He chuckled. "Years later, the Minarilis came up with the name Alaf-Shilam, meaning arrogant son of a giant, father of dogs. Out of defiance, the Alaf-Shilams claimed the name. So it stuck."

She rested a hand on the hilt of her sword. "If they killed even one Ymittosian, I'll stick them with worse than a name."

"And I'll help you." He kicked a rock, and it clattered

against the side of the tunnel. "The Alaf-Shilams thrive on lies and deceit like fish in water. You could start fighting back-to-back with one of them, fending off mutual foes. But when a sword pierces your liver, the Alaf-Shilam probably wielded the blade. Which is why I brought reinforcements." He jerked his chin to the hundred Ymittosian and Chorokhese warriors who tramped behind them.

Eliana ground her teeth. She fought the urge to rush ahead, to throttle the first Alaf-Shilam she encountered and force a confession out of him. Adakizh was right. Soon enough, she'd learn the truth. All she could do was wait.

She'd had ample opportunity to practice patience. The initial two days after Adakizh's return had been crammed with meetings with Shirdona over planning the wedding, in between conferences with complaining Ymittosians and squabbling Chorokhese. Rallying allies was harder than scrounging for food.

Then they started a five-day trek to the coast where the Tekhuri River plunged into the sea. They paused at every tower they came to, spending time with the scattered members of the Kambadas and smaller clans, reassuring them that unifying with the Ymittosians was their best defense against Kharan-Khuag. Nearly everyone pledged their support.

It all seemed to be going so well. And now this.

The corridor bent and widened into a brightly lit space. Eliana blinked, wincing in the sunlight. They stood at the bottom of an immense rift that opened to a sunny sky. She strolled into the sunshine, almost in a daze.

Shafts of sunlight poured into the chasm, glinting off the river and making the crystal walls shine and sparkle. Squinting, Eliana could see dark spots on the upper walls. *Moss, maybe? Or bushes?* She sucked in a breath, catching a fleeting scent of fresh air. She'd forgotten how much she missed the sun and open air. Memories of riding on the high mountains of Ymittos surged through her mind, and she smiled, remembering the feel of wind in her hair.

Like twin swords, grief and rage stabbed her heart. Ymittos was destroyed and many died. If any of her people had been slaughtered, she'd personally see to it the Alaf-Shilams suffered.

The clang of metal against metal jerked Eliana from her smoldering thoughts. She froze, trying to make sense of the faint echoes that drifted to her ears.

A shrill shriek echoed through the caverns, followed by screams and the clash of weapons. Jitters shot along Eliana's nerves. She *had* heard something earlier. Were the Alaf-Shilams fighting the Minarilis? Or had Kharan-Khuag launched an attack?

Adakizh sprinted ahead, Narek, Bednieri, Tigran, and Krikor on his heels. She broke into a trot, clutching her bag of magical amplifiers. While she was skilled with the sword, she knew her greater contribution to the fight would come through her magic.

Sound traveled far in the tunnels and was deceiving. At times, Eliana thought they were about to burst into a battle of one thousand warriors. At others, the fray seemed far off. A stitch stabbed her side, and she pressed her hand to it, hoping Alessia stayed back behind the warriors.

The cave walls parted, and they reached a massive cavern, its ceiling too high to see in the shadowy darkness. Glowing blue mushrooms and a few stray rays of sunlight that snuck through sinkholes on the surface illuminated the battle.

On either side of the river stood two towers, Qala Alaf-Shilam on the near side, Qala Minarili on the opposite bank. Fighters wielding swords and spears filled the area around both towers. Under the mushrooms' dim light, the combatants were dusky shadows, and it took her several moments to make sense of what she was seeing. Lithe Chorokhese were battling what looked like water fae, tall and willowy, but their heads were fish, and long tentacles that ended in barbed hooks waved from their shoulders.

A poisonous blue octopus slithered among the fighters. It wrapped a sucker-lined arm around the leg of an Alaf-Shilam and yanked.

Krikor yelled and darted forward. He slashed the monster's arm. With a guttural bellow, he drove his sword into the beast's bulbous head. Blue blood shot into the air.

"Eliana!"

She jerked her attention from the octopus's feebly waving arms. Adakizh jumped onto a large rock. "Light, we need more light," he said.

Heart racing, she summoned her magic. When the familiar gentle warmth pooled within her, she cast seven balls of light overhead.

Now the battlefield was obvious. A score of Chorokhese and Ymittosians lay dead. But what were they fighting? Dozens of mutant water fae, along with blue octopi and tsovuls, slug-like creatures who prowled on tiger's legs and wielded poisonous barbs. A ragged line of Alaf-Shilams defended Qala Alaf-Shilam, while a thinner line fought along the river, meeting the attackers as they crawled out of the water. The same scenario played out on the opposite shore.

She sprinted to Adakizh, who pulled her up on the rock next to him. He was scanning the battlefield.

"Narek, take thirty men to defend Qala Alaf-Shilam. Get Krikor to help you. Bednieri, lead another thirty and fight the ones coming out of the river. I'll take ten up the middle. Eliana, you keep the rest."

He drew his sword and looked into Eliana's eyes. "I want to tell you to get away from here, to be safe."

She opened her mouth to protest, but he laid a finger on her lips. "I won't. All I'll say is be wise." He spun, raised his sword, and with a mighty yell, leapt from the rock and lopped a tentacle from a water fae's shoulder.

"You too," she murmured after him.

General Alecto climbed to stand beside her, his broad shoulders and towering frame making her feel like a tiny child. "What are your orders, highness?" His bass voice came from deep in his barrel chest, steady and calm.

"Wait to see who needs the most help."

Her eyes followed Adakizh, who slashed his way through a clump of mutant fae who were beating a downed woman with their hooked tentacles. Eliana cast her gaze over the battlefield.

The defenders of Qala Alaf-Shilam, aided by Narek's brigade, were pushing back the fae. The Minarilis on the opposite bank were holding their own, but that didn't seem like it would last. She narrowed her eyes and sent up another ball of light.

On the near side of the river, a dozen water fae emerged from the water, overwhelming the fighters. Where were Bednieri and his brigade? She scanned the combatants, looking for any sign of him.

Merciful winds. Bednieri had led his men to Qala Alaf-Shilam, not the river. Had he misunderstood? She pointed at the river where scores of water fae were climbing onto the stony bank. "There, General."

He nodded grimly.

"Leave me three guards. You take the rest."

He shouted a few orders but stayed by her side. "I won't leave you."

"Well, then, you can help me." She glanced at the two warriors who remained by the rock. "Can you two keep the monsters away?"

After they nodded, she turned to Alecto. "You're an air mage, right? I think we need some wind."

"What do you have in mind?"

She fished in her bag of amplifiers and found the dried berries. She placed one in her mouth and pulled at her air magic. When the airy feeling inside intensified, she released it, directing it at a pair of water fae with orange spikes on the sides of their faces who were scrambling out of the water. She used the magic to hurl them across the river, cracking their heads on the opposite shore. They went limp and slipped into the dark water.

"Good plan," Alecto said. He accepted a berry. "I'll work upstream."

Eliana nodded. Blowing gusts of wind at groups of three or four water fae, they sent the enemies flying, smashing their heads on the rocky far bank. Soon the river was full of floating dead bodies mixed with the ash-gray blood of the dead and dying fae.

Eliana surveyed the battlefield. She and Alecto had given Adakizh enough time to mow down the fae who'd already climbed on shore.

Screams from the opposite side of the river yanked at her attention. Two score water fae were storming Qala Minarili.

"Adakizh!" she yelled.

He beheaded a water fae, ducked to avoid the fountain of blood from spattering his eyes, and sprinted to her side. He vaulted onto the rock.

"Look."

He let out a curse. "I'd take some warriors over, but we can't swim the river. The water fae would kill us from underneath."

Eliana grinned. "The general and I can help. Do you want to go first?"

He frowned. "What? You're going to use your air magic tricks?"

"On my signal, jump as high as you can."

He flicked his gaze across the river's expanse, then nodded. "If I hadn't seen you do this before—"

"Jump."

He leapt into the air. Eliana pushed her air magic under him, creating a wind that bore him across the river.

"General?"

"That's some magic, highness. I've never tried that."

She gave him a few pointers and had a warrior join her on the rock. She flew him across on a gust of air. "We've got to hurry," she said. She could scarcely see Adakizh in the crush of mutant fae.

Together, she and the general sent twenty warriors across the river. Ten lined up along the riverbank, repelling the fae who were climbing out. The others joined Adakizh in the defense of Qala Minarili.

General Alecto shouted a warning. A blue octopus slithered toward them. Alecto jumped from the rock and slashed it. He hacked off four arms and lunged closer. His sword sliced off a fifth arm. The creature recoiled under a spray of blue blood.

The general drew his blade back, readying his next strike. His face contorted, and his whole body twitched. He shrieked and crumpled to the ground.

Directly in the path of a tsovul's poisonous spike.

34

THE TSOVUL CROUCHED on its tiger-like legs, one of its long facial spikes dripping with scarlet blood. It lunged and thrust its spike into the general's neck. Alecto writhed and moaned. The tsovul stabbed him again and the general went limp.

Eliana gasped. Pain bored into her chest as if she'd been pierced herself. She drew her sword and leaped from the rock. The octopus was gnawing on Alecto's arm. She drove her blade into its head, jumping back to avoid the spurt of blue blood. Then she whirled and sliced the tsovul's throat.

Her breath hitched as she sank to her knees next to the general's limp body. "General—"

A rough hand grabbed her arm. "Get up."

It was her cousin Ormolai, streaked with crimson and indigo blood and breathing hard. He spun and engaged a water fae that lurched toward them.

Surprisingly, he was a competent swordsman. Three quick strokes and he'd slain his opponent.

Two fae brandishing spears converged on them. She had no time to ready her magic.

She stood back-to-back with Ormolai as they fought off

the fae. Her adversary loomed over her, a foot taller than she. It lashed a hooked tentacle at her. She batted it away, ducked, and swung her sword, slicing through the fae's lower leg. It howled and toppled over. She slew him with a stab to the heart.

The sounds of battle were diminishing. A few clangs, a few shouts. No more water fae climbed from the water. The handful of survivors dove into the river.

She darted to the bank and peered frantically to the other side at the remaining fighters. There. She let out a gasp of relief. Adakizh was sparring with a water fae. He looked unharmed, but the dim light and distance made it hard to tell.

Once the fae were defeated, Eliana and a pair of air mages summoned winds to fly Adakizh, his warriors, and three of the Minarilis across the river. Blue and gray blood stained the tagavoi's tunic. She sighed, relieved the blood wasn't his. Their gazes locked, and she answered his reassuring nod with one of her own.

The Minarilis and Alaf-Shilams began shouting at each other. A tall, willowy Minarili marched up to a man Eliana thought was Hakob Alaf-Shilam, the tavkatsi, and waved his fist in his face. "What did I tell you?" he shouted. "Where are your warriors? Hiding among the mushrooms?"

"One of mine is worth thirty of yours," Hakob spat. "You don't know which mushroom to eat, let alone which end of the sword to hold."

Adakizh caught Eliana's eye and rolled his own. When the argument seemed to wear down, he interrupted. "Have the fae attacked before?"

"Yep. It started a few weeks ago," Hakob said.

A Minarili piped up. "They might attack three days in a row, then nothing for several days. But this was the worst. They just kept coming and coming."

Adakizh frowned. "Bednieri," he said, doubt lacing his tone, "why didn't you stay by the river?"

"To fight the fae climbing out? I wondered why you sent me to defend the tower. I could have been more help at the river."

A few mutters greeted his words. Eliana understood only a few of them, all critical of Adakizh and his leadership.

Adakizh scowled. "That's what I did."

"Oh, is that what you said? All I heard was 'help the Alaf-Shilams.' I must have missed the other part." Bednieri shook his head. "I truly am sorry. I misunderstood." He winced. "Don't tell my mother about this."

Eliana's lips twitched. Shirdona's wrath at her son's mistake would be fearsome to behold.

"I wondered that too," Ormolai said. "And why the queen stayed on the rock. What a coward."

The mutters increased. Eliana was too stunned to reply.

"She's always been that way," Ormolai continued. "Weak. Scared of the dark. Got lost in the wine cellars once and wet herself."

Eliana's face heated. How dare he dredge up that old story? She was pulling her thoughts together when another voice broke through the murmurs.

"You want to bring up childhood stories?" Alessia asked. "I seem to recall you squealing like a cornered mouse when a hunting dog barked at you. When you were twelve."

Ormolai flushed. "That's not true." He curled his lip. "Your word means nothing, commoner."

"Since our fathers were cousins, you share that common blood." Alessia shook her head. "To everyone in the family's undying shame."

Eliana decided it was the moment to intervene. "As heart-warming as these childhood memories are, we have bigger prey to stalk." She cast her gaze around the hard faces of the Alaf-Shilams and Minarilis. "And whatever tales my cousin has to tell, remember this one. Along with your tagavoi, I broke the dark. I faced death that you might have time to fight on to preserve your freedom."

"If that's not courage," Adakizh said, "I don't know what is." His gaze traveled over the seething crowd. "What is it you want? Freedom? Or servitude?" He paused. "You can keep your old enmities and continue sneering at the Ymittosians. Cling to your feuds and weaken yourselves. Do that and you might as well invite Kharan-Khuag to enslave us all tomorrow."

"But—" A deep voice roared from the back of the crowd.

"But nothing." Adakizh faced in the speaker's direction. "We lose our prejudices and relinquish our feuds and together make a stand against our ancient foe. That's our one chance."

"Maybe not," said a lanky Minarili, a woman with an elongated oval head. "We can always retreat into the upper tunnels. No one will come after us there."

"You forget the meaning of Kharan-Khuag's name," Adakizh said. "Insatiable greed. He won't stop while one free soul breathes."

Hakob laughed. "That may be true. But our honor won't allow us to help the Minarilis. We'll be fine on our own."

"You would have been overrun had we not come along," Adakizh said.

"And you've shown them how strong we are. Most likely, they'll attack up the Qvirila next time." Hakob waved a dismissive hand. "Don't expect our help when that happens."

"But our only chance of defeating Kharan-Khuag is together," Adakizh said.

"For a millennium, we've known if Kharan-Khuag invaded the continent, we'd be the first to go. You want us to help? What do those overworlders do besides eat our food?"

"Even if we defeat Kharan-Khuag, what then?" the Minarili asked. "The food from Ymittos will be gone. We teetered on the edge of poverty when we could raid them.

Now we have twice the people to feed. We'd win the war only to starve in peace."

Eliana held her face rigid. A sudden thought illuminated her mind like sunlight piercing a cloud. "Just upriver there's a rift. The walls are steep, but not too steep for olive trees and berry bushes. If you plant blackberries now, you'll have a crop next year."

"So we're to live on berries?"

"And other things that will grow on the slopes of the rifts. That would be one way to augment our food supply. Ymittosian farmers would know how to get the best yields."

"And how will we climb up there?" Hakob scoffed.

Eliana tapped her upper lip. "I seem to remember you had sophisticated pulley systems that helped you steal our cattle. Use them. And I'm sure air and stone mages could help as well."

Adakizh beamed at her. "Wonderful idea."

"Fine," Hakob said. "But it doesn't answer the bigger question. How do we know you'll look after the interests of every Chorokhese, not just the Kambadas and Zhilakhurs?"

"What do you want?" Adakizh asked blandly.

"Maybe an alliance of a different sort. Put aside the overworlder queen who's as useless as a spoon without a handle and marry one of ours," Hakob said. "I've got four daughters of age. Pick one. Then we'll know you'll look after our interests."

Eliana tried to catch Adakizh's eye. What was he thinking? Was he considering Hakob's proposal?

Many of the Alaf-Shilams were muttering, and it sounded to Eliana like they agreed with Hakob.

Adakizh stared at the ground, rubbing his chin. An icy hand twisted Eliana's heart. He was considering it. Thinking about sacrificing their relationship for the good of their peoples. Spurning her to gain the support of an ally they couldn't afford to antagonize.

Should she speak up? Volunteer to step aside? Doing so would shred her soul. But should she count her own happiness above the safety of her people?

A vein throbbed in her temple. The muttering of the throng grew louder. Ymittosians yelled at the Alaf-Shilams. The Minarilis inched away, moving toward the river. Shirdona's warriors were arguing among themselves.

"Enough." Adakizh spoke softly.

The murmuring continued.

"Enough," he said louder, the word echoing in the cavern.

When the bickering continued, he raised a hand. With his magic, he pulled a stalactite from the roof of the cavern and smashed it into the river. Water sprayed those nearest the banks.

"Do I need to do that again?" Adakizh shouted. "Or will you all listen?"

The voices ceased. The only sounds were shuffling feet and the gurgle of the river.

"I took the curse for all of you," Adakizh said. "So you could prepare to defend yourselves. From what I can tell, you abandoned the defenses my father put into place. You've all gone your own ways rather than remaining unified against our ancient foe."

He drilled his gaze into the crowd. "Then the Queen of Ymittos woke me from the curse. And we broke the second dark curse. Yes, it came with a cost. Was that too high of a price to pay? We may labor for years rebuilding. But is that worse than a lifetime of slavery?" He drew a deep breath. "I tell you, our one chance is to unite. To that end, the Queen of Ymittos and I plan to wed. I cannot marry everyone, so I can only forge one alliance that way."

Eliana's heart sank. Was the political alliance the real reason he was marrying her? Were his loving words his means of making the best of the situation? Given an opportunity, would he reconsider?

"You want me to cast her aside? I will not. Ignoring the great dishonor to her and her people, I don't want to. I have grown to love Eliana Kastellanos and would sooner cut out my gills than forsake her."

He sucked in a deep breath. "If a marriage with one of your own is the only way you'll ally with me, then say so. I know you've suffered in the past. But that was then. All I can promise is to treat you fairly. For now, the choice is obvious." He took Eliana's hand. "Ally with us, and we will protect your territory as if it were our own. Stand against us, and we won't send as much as a single blade to help you."

Adakizh ran his gaze over the crowd. "You don't have to tell me today. If your tavkatsi and tavkatseen attend our wedding, we'll take that as your pledge to stand with us. If you decide against us, don't bother coming."

Eliana surveyed the faces of the crowd. The Minarilis seemed to be receptive to Adakizh's words. The Alaf-Shilams' stony expressions told her nothing.

But she didn't care. Adakizh chose her, even if it meant losing his kingdom. And that, she decided, should put all her doubts to rest. For now. Forever.

35

Chorokha

Sixty-five days after the winter solstice in the Year 999 (Chorokhese reckoning) and in the 29th year of Emperor Vural Tzimiskes of Cinar

E liana shifted from foot to foot, waiting in a room on the third floor of a tower belonging to one of Shirdona's cousins. Or niece. She couldn't remember. They had chosen that tower as the place for her to dress for the wedding because it was the closest to Adakizh's.

That was one wedding custom her people shared with the Chorokhese, keeping the bride and groom separate until the ceremony. She'd already had the nuptial bath, assisted by Alessia, and now it was time to dress. Time to become a wife. And the tagavli.

Wall sconces piled with glowing mushrooms cast a dim blue light over the room. The room's only furnishings were a few wooden chairs with seats woven from salvaged palm fronds and bark—remnants of the fallen realm of Ymittos. Another painful reminder of how much they'd all lost.

Eliana sighed and raised her arms, allowing Alessia to slide a scarlet dress over her head. The soft fabric whispered over her skin. Eliana tugged the end of one long sleeve into place, running her hands over the intricate embroidery on the fore-arm, wondering from whom the Chorokhese had stolen the material. And how it had survived the cataclysm.

Alessia gave the full skirt a few tweaks. "Is it heavy?"

"Yes, very." Floral designs made of tiny crystals sewn onto the fabric covered the bodice and ran down the skirt and around the hem.

"Glad it's you and not me." Alessia chuckled while she fastened a jeweled belt around Eliana's waist. Then she added another, one with strands of gold coins draping down. She stood back to admire her work. "It is pretty. Good thing Shir-dona's sister is your size. But I still think red is an odd color for a bride."

Eliana suppressed a huff. They'd had this conversation over and over. Red was the traditional color for Chorokhese brides, the most fitting for the woman who would become tagavli. And she wasn't about to insist on wearing white, as Ymittosian brides did. No one owned anything white as every garment was now irrevocably stained tan or rust from the dust of the rocks. "Where's the jacket?"

Her maid plucked the short jacket from a chair and held it up. Eliana slipped her arms into the sleeves. They were tight from shoulder to elbow, then flared out and draped to her knees. As Eliana moved, the sleeves swayed and the tiny jewels sewn into the fabric twinkled, pale reflections of the mushrooms' soft blue light.

Alessia slid a jeweled hairpin into place and set a circlet of feathers on the crown of braids piled on Eliana's head. Last, she slid the hooked ends of the earrings in place. "How do they feel?"

"Unexpectedly light."

"That's a relief. What's the point of jewelry if it hurts to wear it?"

Quick footsteps on the stairs cut off Eliana's reply. "Are you ready, my sunshine?" Shirdona's voice was surprisingly tender, void of her usual mocking tone.

Eliana turned to her. "I am. Thank you for all you've done."

"It was the least I could do." She pointed down the stairs. "The kovar awaits."

Eliana's breath caught. The kovar, Eliana had learned, was chosen by the groom as someone trustworthy. His role was to escort the bride to the groom's tower, making sure no one tried to steal her.

The princess smirked to herself. Theft seemed to feature prominently in Chorokhese culture, whether it was stealing cattle, brides, or mushrooms. She'd never thought to lump herself with cows or fungi. *They do treasure their mushrooms. I hope it extends to their wives.*

Arm and arm with Alessia, she followed Shirdona down the stairs. Alessia tipped her head toward Eliana. "If someone tries to steal you, what will you do?"

"I could stab him. Or blind him with light."

"Use the light," Alessia advised. "Not so messy. You don't want blood on your dress."

Eliana snorted and her maid giggled. *Thank the Rider for Alessia.* The walk down the steps would have been far too daunting to do alone.

A gray-haired man wearing an ornately embroidered red tunic stood at the bottom of the stairs. Adakizh's kovar. He turned to her and nodded. "You look beautiful, highness."

Tears pricked Eliana's eyes. Corban. Adakizh had chosen Corban. *What a lovely, generous thing to do.* He could have chosen any of the tavkatsis to bestow a public gesture of favor.

Instead, he selected the one person who could take the place of her father on such a day.

"Thank you." She tucked her hand under her old tutor's elbow.

"Are you ready?" he asked.

"Yes." She met his inquiring gaze and answered the question behind his question. "Keerios Corban, I want you to understand. The days Adakizh and I spent leading up to breaking the dark told me all I need to know about his character. Despite everything, I grew to love him."

He squeezed her hand. "He impresses me as honorable, if nothing else. You complement each other well."

"What do we want?" shouted a man from outside.

"We want a wedding!" roared a crowd. High-pitched bells rang, and tambourines jingled.

"Your attendants are here," Corban said. "Shall we?"

In answer, she took a step towards the door. They stepped out of the tower into the cavern. Scores of people waited outside.

Everyone wore their everyday tunics and trousers, but they were all draped with necklaces and bracelets of gemstones, rubies, sapphires, emeralds, diamonds, and amethysts that twinkled under the dim light of the mushrooms and the few shafts of sunlight that pierced the dark realm.

Corban led her to a dozen of Shirdona's warriors, who carried swords and spears. They nodded to Eliana. Half of them set off walking toward Adakizh's tower. The others would follow as a rear guard.

Shirdona strode next to Eliana, with Alessia just behind. The maid was accompanied by three carefully selected young women—a Saumarota, a Zhilakhur, and Ardashil Khatavian. Usually, the principal attendants would be friends of the bride. But as the queen, she had to choose for political, not personal, reasons. Even if she'd wanted to include a childhood friend, it was impossible. So far, none of the girls she'd known well in Ymittos had been found alive.

She shook off that gloomy thought and lifted her chin. This was, after all, supposed to be a happy day. The crowd formed a procession behind her, singing raucous songs about love and marriage.

Shirdona was chattering about something, but Eliana couldn't comprehend her words. The entire scene appeared to her like she was watching a play. If not for Corban's steadying arm, she might have stumbled over every stray stone. They rounded a corner, and a shaft of sunlight illuminated a yellow stalagmite, the light dancing off the crystal surface.

By the day's end, she'd be tagavli, ruler not only of her Ymittosians but over Adakizh's Chorokhese. They'd rule united as one, sharing the power and the responsibility. Whatever came, they'd face it together. Somehow, she'd grow into this new role and be the wife Adakizh deserved and the sovereign her people needed.

Footsteps echoed in the cavern, along with the singing behind her. The accompanying bells and tambourines sent their echoes skittering, sounding like a parade of thousands. The song was about fish and flowers and pouring water, chaotic rhymes that made no sense. She wished the warriors ahead of her would walk faster.

They rounded a bend. Now they trod on the mosaic pavement that led to Adakizh's tower. She caught a whiff of roasting fish and heard scattered laughter, accompanied by the wispy piping of flutes and jingling tambourines. She craned her neck, trying to see past the men marching in front of her.

There. Her eyes locked on Adakizh. He stood in front of the entrance of his tower. Intricate carvings of images of the Rider of the Ancient Skies flanked the double door, which was painted a blue so dark it appeared nearly black. A scarlet tunic hugged his broad shoulders and chest. Sand-colored trousers extended to his braided leather shoes. Every move he made set off twinkling lights from the sparkling gemstones that covered his clothes, a twinkling contrast to the night-dark door. A crown of feathers perched on his sable hair, his long curls braided in rows over his head, the ends left free to cascade past his shoulders.

Was that the prince she'd run from in the dark tunnels? The one she broke the dark with? She felt she was gazing at a stranger. In some ways, she barely knew him. But ever since they'd reconciled, he'd been wooing her as if she was an uncertain prize to be won, as if he couldn't believe her feelings for him were as ardent as his for her.

And they were passionate, these feelings they shared. At times, she could hardly believe that he could love her so much. It was terrifying to love someone so intensely. And to let herself go and give in to it? To be disappointed in love again would carve terrible wounds in her soul. All the more because she loved him so fiercely. It was like jumping off a ledge. If the other didn't catch you, you'd be broken into bits.

But he seemed to have no doubts. His eyes were shackled to her, as if she was the sole source of light in a dark room.

She pulled her gaze from his, unable to bear the profound look of love in his eyes. He was flanked by Tigran, Bednieri, Narek, and Ormolai. A brilliant diplomatic move on Adak-izh's part to include her cousin.

Adakizh took a few steps to meet her. Corban squeezed her hand and stepped back. Adakizh grasped her hand in his, sending a wave of tingling warmth to her toes. His eyes glittered as if they were many-faceted diamonds.

She tipped her head and offered him a smile, studying the man she was about to marry. He was handsome, exotically so, with his golden tan skin and long, bouncing black curls. How she longed to stretch one out just to watch it spring back. Or run a finger over his determined jaw.

The gill slits on either side of his neck still seemed odd to her. *Would it hurt him if I touched one? Will our children inherit them and the ability to breathe underwater?* A smile tugged at her mouth, and her heartbeat quickened at the idea of making children with him.

She turned to face Batraz and Shirdona, who both wore scarlet clothing and the cylindrical hats that marked them as tavkatsi and tavkatseen, heads of their respective clans. Since neither Adakizh nor she had living parents, they chose surrogates. Hopefully, her choice of Shirdona would go far to keep the woman's loyalty.

Shirdona recited the traditional words of the Chorokhese marriage ceremony. Eliana, of course, had heard them during the mad rush of wedding preparations and knew they spoke of duty and honor and love. But now they washed over her like a passing breeze. The only reality was Adakizh's warm fingers caressing her own.

Batraz continued uttering the formal words, binding her and Adakizh to each other, sworn by the Rider of the Ancient Skies to be loyal and faithful, respectful, and loving.

Bednieri handed Adakizh the sapphire and blue topaz bracelet, and Adakizh fastened it on Eliana's wrist.

Then Shirdona dropped two gold rings into an earthenware goblet and held it to Eliana. "Drink, Eliana Xanthia Vasiliki Kastellanos."

Eliana took a sip, eyes widening at the citrusy taste that finished with a sharp sweetness. Was this from one of her father's prize bottles of wine? She handed the goblet to Adakizh.

He sipped as Batraz pronounced his names. "Adakizh Bonvarnon Alagata Bisen." Then Adakizh fished the rings out. One he placed on her finger, the other he passed to her. She slid it on his finger.

Alessia removed the crown of feathers from Eliana's head and replaced it with one of finely wrought silver, while Narek did the same for Adakizh.

Ormolai stepped forward, the one chosen to perform the

Ymittosian custom of anointing the bride and groom. He held a small vial of scented oil. When he uncorked it, Eliana caught a whiff of jasmine. He dabbed Eliana's forehead with the scent, then Adakizh's.

Batraz turned to the assembly. "What do you say? Are they wed?"

"They are wed!" the crowd responded.

"Then," said Shirdona, "we invite you to the feast."

Musicians began to play, the flutes, harps, bells, and tambourines trilling and chirping, filling the cavern with wild music that stirred Eliana's soul. Her heart thumped to the stirring rhythm created by men beating stalagmites with rubber mallets, the deep booming sound vibrating within her chest. Still feeling like a spectator at some event far away, she barely noticed Adakizh tug her hand.

He led her to a table set up near the door of his tower. It was decorated with flowers made of precious stones. He held the chair out for her and gestured for her to sit. "Eliana Xanthia Vasiliki Kastellanos Alagata Bisenti, will you dine with me?"

She burst into laughter. "Why so formal?"

He smirked. "You looked so serious. I thought that was what you wanted."

"If that's what you thought, you don't know me at all," Eliana scoffed. "Since when have I desired formality from you?"

He sat next to her. "Since never. I just wanted to see you smile." He leaned over and kissed her. "You're my wife."

"That's what all those people say."

"Don't you believe them?"

"I'm not sure I'm even here."

His gaze roamed downward before returning to meet hers. "I'll make sure you realize it later."

Her cheeks heated when she caught his meaning. She didn't have time to respond, because two of Shirdona's daughters brought over plates of roasted fish and mushrooms, and dried apples and pears. This was a far cry from the wedding feast she would have enjoyed if she'd married Istvan. There would have been seven kinds of fish, roasted venison, grilled skewers of beef and chicken, fresh tomatoes and cucumbers, towers of fruit, honey-drenched pastries, a feast presided over by her father . . .

Stop. Ymittos is gone. This is my life now. She tucked her arm under Adakizh's. *And it will be a happy one. It must.*

She took a bite, but it tasted like damp parchment. Maybe later, when her nerves calmed down, she'd eat more. She watched the people milling about, some eating, some toasting her and Adakizh, others dancing. Ten or so women gathered in a circle, weaving an intricate pattern of intersecting rings.

A group of men formed a circle, clapping to the music, leaping about in a way that reminded Eliana of goats on a mountainside. Other men jumped on their shoulders, forming a second tier. Bednieri motioned to Adakizh to join them.

Adakizh stood up and grinned. "Just for a while. I've got to save my strength, you know."

That prompted a bawdy reply that made Eliana laugh.

She watched Adakizh stride to the circle of dancing men. He leaped with agile grace onto the shoulders of a beefy Saumarota. The dancers cheered. The upper ring laced their arms over the shoulders of their neighbors, and the dancing men spun in a ring.

Eliana watched them dance, her eyes glued to Adakizh. He swayed on his perch, moving with the motion of the dancer under him and the throbbing rhythm of the music. Now he was facing her, his gaze entangling hers. He was so far away, separated from her by the reveling throngs.

The dancer under him stumbled, and Adakizh flailed for balance. Roars of laughter erupted from the other dancers. "Keep your mind on the dance," one shouted. "You'll ride another partner later."

Eliana blushed and put a hand over her mouth to hide her smile. They'd have their own dance, indeed. But for now, she had to ignore the heat in her core and the fingers that ached to caress her new husband.

She snapped her attention to the rest of the crowd. Lanky Zhilakhurs, led by a pair of Kambadas, danced with lithe Minarilis, while swaggering Saumarotas were playing some kind of drinking game with a trio of prim Ymittosians and a handful of Khatavians. The only ones missing were the Alaf-Shilams. *Is that my fault?*

"Where's the tagavli?" a woman shouted.

Eliana took another sip of wine, then started. *Tagavli. That's me.* She looked up, seeking the speaker.

Shirdona strolled over. "Tagavli, you're not eating. Is the food not fine enough for you?"

"It's wonderful," Eliana said. "I'm not hungry."

"Oh, but you have to eat, my sunshine. It's bad luck if you don't." Shirdona gestured at Eliana's plate.

Eliana picked up a mushroom and chewed. It held no more flavor than paste made of sawdust.

"Tagavli! Tagavli!" The women's chant echoed.

"Now what?" Eliana asked.

"They want you to dance," Shirdona said.

Eliana stared at her wide-eyed. Too often the Chorokhese had mocked her dancing, saying she was ox-footed. She'd never learned the traditional dance where a girl strung coins over her forehead and danced so smoothly not a single coin moved. She didn't want to humiliate herself publicly on her wedding day. If only she could concoct an excuse to leave.

"What, are you afraid?" Shirdona said. "Not dancing at your wedding means you're scared or unwilling. Are you telling us the tagavoi married either a coward or a cold fish?" She leaned over. "The tagavli, of all people, needs to prove herself. What else are you going to do?"

Eliana's desire to flee vanished like smoke under a furious

wind. These people demanded to see a vibrant, valiant tagavli. Even on her wedding day, she couldn't just savor the moment. Even now, they were testing her to see if she was worthy of being named tagavli.

Fine. She'd show them *what else.* She grabbed her wine goblet and drained it. "You want to see dancing?"

She stood and stalked to Alessia. "Dance with me." She led her maid in one of the languid dances of Ymittos, strangely at odds with the wild rhythms of Chorokhese music, but at the same time, creating a complementary sensual pattern of its own.

Ardashil joined them, laughing as she stumbled over the intricate steps and arm movements. A few Ymittosian women, including, Eliana noted with surprise, the odious Narcyzia, also joined the dance.

Eliana spun with her arms raised, letting the long sleeves of her dress swirl and sparkle. As she danced, her eyes were drawn to Adakizh. His blue eyes looked black in the dim light, but the desire in them made her shiver in anticipation.

As she whirled past the watchers, Eliana pulled more women into the dance: a Saumarota, a Minarili, a Zhilakhur. All of them protested, laughed, and tottered in lurching attempts to follow the steps. Eliana tipped her head and snickered. *Now who are the ox-footed?* She caught Alessia's eye and traded a grin.

Still chuckling, she led her line of dancers around the double ring of dancing men, letting the surging rhythms move her arms and feet. She'd never noticed just how erotic this dance could be. Her face heated when she realized she couldn't rip her eyes from Adakizh, still perched atop the Saumarota. He threw his head back, laughing at something one of the other dancers said, his eyes never leaving Eliana's face. Was he wishing all these people would leave as much as she did?

After a few circuits, Eliana grabbed Shirdona's hands and dragged her into the circle.

The woman shook her head. "Ymittosian dances aren't for me."

"Don't tell me you're scared," Eliana said. "You have to dance with me. I'm the bride. What else are you going to do?"

Shirdona burst into laughter and leaned closer. "Very good, my sunshine. If I ever had any doubts about you, they're gone."

Adakizh appeared at Eliana's side and draped an arm over her shoulders.

His face glistened with sweat, but his smile was broad. He offered a goblet of wine to her. Suddenly thirsty, she took a swallow and handed it back to him.

He drained it in a gulp. "If you're done dancing, we can leave. Whenever you like."

Was she ready to go? Like her people, the Chorokhese practiced the tradition that a newly married couple sequestered themselves for several days, some for as long as a week. Any fewer than three days was considered unlucky. Besides . . . "Adakizh, I think we're on borrowed time. We should start our three days as soon as we can."

A joyful smile bloomed on his face. "I was hoping you'd say that." He seized her hand. "Friends, enjoy the feast."

Alessia made a languid turn and spun into Eliana's arms, offering a quick hug. "You look like you're about to crawl into an eggshell. There's no need to be frightened."

Oh, she has no idea. Nervous, maybe a little. She shook her head and smiled. Breaking the dark and nearly dying together had forged an intimacy of its own. Tonight they'd create a different one. Her skin prickled at the thought. She was more than ready to leave the feast.

Bednieri, Tigran, and Narek crowded around, slapping Adakizh on the back and laughing.

He pulled away from them and took Eliana's arm. "If you'll excuse me, I'd like a word with my wife."

That was answered by hoots of laughter and more ribald jokes. Adakizh pulled Eliana into the tower and slammed the door shut. "Finally, alone with you."

Now that the jokes and guffaws were muffled by the door, she could draw breath more easily. It was a relief to not have to keep smiling at people she barely knew whom she didn't know were truly wishing her well or not.

She followed him in silence up the stairs, huffing a little from the exertion of climbing steps wearing the heavy dress. When they reached the seventh floor, he pulled her into his arms and held her close to him, cradling her against his chest.

His heartbeat thumped against her cheek, and she leaned into him. This was so right, like she'd been wandering in dark tunnels only to follow a light that led her to safety and joy.

She tipped her face up to search his eyes. The muffled sounds of the festivities faded, as if she and Adakizh were the only people in the world.

He smiled and tugged at her jacket. "You don't need this anymore."

She shrugged out of the garment and let it fall to the floor. "What do I need?"

"To know that if Adakizh the cattle thief had met Eliana the milkmaid he'd have given the world for a single kiss."

Her breath caught. He knew her oh so well. He knew just what she needed to hear. Warmth spread through her, heat fueled by love and something that demanded to be released. Now if he would only understand she'd die if he didn't touch her.

He shuffled closer. "No more tagavoi and tagavli. Can we just be Eliana and Adakizh for the next few days?"

Eliana wrapped her arms around his neck, savoring the warmth of his chest against hers. She tipped her face up and held her mouth close to his. "What are you waiting for?"

36

Chorokha

Sixty-seven days after the winter solstice in the Year 999 (Chorokhese reckoning) and in the 29th year of Emperor Vural Tzimiskes of Cinar

ELIANA STIRRED UNDER the sheet, drifting out of her contented sleep. Languidly, she opened her eyes. The tower room was dark and still, the only light a pot of glowing mushrooms, the only sound Adakizh's slow breathing.

She raised herself on one elbow and studied his face. This was how he looked the first time she'd seen him, deep in his enchanted slumber, his long eyelashes fanned over his lower eyelids. When she thought she'd break the curse and return to Ymittos, leaving Chorokha for good, never to see him again.

Instead, she fell in love with the sensitive prince whose bouncing black curls enthralled her as much as his sense of duty and wry humor.

Eliana settled back onto her pillow. Over the last two days they'd laughed and loved together. When hunger claimed them, they'd walked downstairs to the second floor kitchen. Shirdona's daughters had done their work well, leaving platters of dried fish, fruit, and mushrooms, along with plenty of water for tea, bathing, and washing the dirty plates. Eliana nearly giggled, thinking of the games Adakizh came up with when they were in the iron bathtub. Not all of them involved his water magic.

After they ate, they drank endless cups of tea, sharing childhood stories, hopes, and dreams. All about them. No politics. No invasions. Just revealing pieces of themselves they'd never shared with another.

Now, she pursed her lips. Part of her enjoyed watching Adakizh sleep. Another part wanted to snuggle down beside him and revel in holding him. And another part wanted the chamber pot.

"Ho! Tagavoi!"

Who was that? It hadn't been two days. Her breath caught. This could only mean one thing.

She jostled Adakizh. "My love . . ."

"What is it?" His words slurred, as if he was half conscious. "Ready for more?"

"No."

He opened one eye. "No? Tired of me already?" His eyes flared open. "Or are you sore?"

She felt a tinge of heat climb up her neck. "There's someone outside."

"Tagavoi!" The shout was more insistent.

Adakizh frowned. He slid out from between the sheets, the muscles of his back rippling as he stretched. He plucked a dressing gown from the floor and tossed it to Eliana. "Whatever they want, you'll need to hear it too." Then he strode to the window and leaned out. "Can you not count higher than one?"

"Apologies, tagavoi."

Eliana pulled the robe around herself and joined her

husband. Holding torches made of glowing mushrooms, Tigran, Bednieri, and Narek stood below.

Narek bowed his head. "My apologies, tagavoi, tagavli. But my clan sent word that they've spotted mutant water fae and karcharias. They think they're Kharan-Khuag's advance forces."

Eliana's heart skipped a beat. *No. Not already.*

"We wouldn't have disturbed you," said Tigran, "except—"

"I ordered you to tell me." Adakizh crossed his arms. "Thank you. Did they say how many?"

"No. Just that there are scores."

"If I may, tagavoi," Bednieri said, "you need to lead the defense. Immediately."

"He can't do that," said Tigran. "He needs to stay with her for three days. Otherwise, the marriage won't be valid."

Heat spread across Eliana's face, and she scowled. Kharan-Khuag's interrupting her nuptials was one more crime to add to the ledger.

"Exceptions have been made," Narek said. "After all, the three days are more tradition than law."

"But he is the tagavoi," Tigran said. "His duty is to continue the line. Which is why he can't leave yet."

Adakizh raised an eyebrow, and his lips twitched. "I can assure you the tagavli and I are well aware of our duty and have zealously endeavored to fulfill it." His face grew serious. "Find Batraz and Shirdona. And some of the Ymittosian leaders." He rattled off a few names before glancing at Eliana. "Did I get everyone?" After she nodded, he continued. "When you come back with them, we'll talk."

Eliana watched them leave before turning to Adakizh. "Are we sure this is the invasion?"

He wrapped his arms around her and pulled her close. "We're not. But can we take that risk?"

"No. You have to go." She gulped, loneliness filling her at

the thought of him leaving. "Do you want me to come with you?"

He let out a long breath. "Let's talk over breakfast, shall we?"

After dressing, they descended to the kitchen and prepared what she feared might be their last meal together for many days. While he poured water into a kettle, she filled two plates with dried fruit and roasted mushrooms. "At least the new javelins are ready," she said. "Or should we keep them secret until the real invasion comes?"

He frowned. "That's a good thought. But if this is the invasion and we don't use the javelins and lose, all that work will have been in vain."

She set two teacups on the table and spooned tea leaves into the teapot. Then she slid onto a chair. "At the least, the weapons need to be placed."

Adakizh pointed at the kettle. An instant later, steam rose from its spout.

So convenient to have a water mage for a husband. Good for so many things. She ducked her head, hoping he didn't see her face reddening as she thought of the many talents he'd demonstrated.

He carried the steaming kettle to the table and poured water over the tea leaves in the pot. "You're right about the javelins." They hashed out his plans, identifying which people to take and how many of the engineers he'd need to place the weapons.

"Don't forget a few armorers," Eliana said. "In case you need to make adjustments."

He leaned over and kissed her. "I'll miss you."

"Why? For my clever strategic advice?"

"That and a thousand other things."

She took one of his hands in hers. "Will you be alright on your own?"

"No. I leave half of me behind." He gripped her hand. "Eliana, we may never . . ."

"Don't say it." She pinned her gaze on his eyes.

Her fierceness must have startled him, because his eyebrows lifted. He smiled and tipped his head to the side. "What was that line you used to say? Think the unthinkable? What happened to that?"

"That's just for solving problems. For considering all the options. This is different."

"How so? We need to face it. We might not survive this."

"If you think that, we might not. But we will trust the Rider to help us." She pressed her lips together. "I should go with you."

"But—"

"I have four reasons."

"Only four?"

"Think about it." She held up a finger. "I am a powerful mage. If we use our magic to repel the invaders, we don't have to reveal the weapons we aren't quite ready to use."

"True."

"Also, it will help me see how you've been placing the javelins. That may give me some insights to share with the engineers here."

She extended two more fingers. "That was two. Third, our people just celebrated our wedding. It's not our happiness they care about. They want a unified rule. We need to show them that. Us going into battle together is one way to reinforce the message."

"What's the fourth?"

She pulled on one of his long curls, stretching it out and releasing it to bounce back. "You owe me another day. I don't care to let you out of my sight until I get it."

He chuckled and put a finger under her chin, lifting it. "That's your best argument, by far." He held her face in his hands and kissed her. "Believe me, I intend to claim it someday."

Eliana pulled back. *No. I have to go with you. Don't shove me into a corner to keep me safe.* She sipped her tea, her mouth too dry to even think of trying to chew something. "You think I should stay."

With a rueful sigh, he nodded. "Yes, and here's why. We don't know if this is the opening salvo or Kharan-Khuag's full invasion. In any case, given the time it takes word to arrive from Qala Zhilakhur, it started at least four days ago. If it was just a feint, then it's probably all over by now. If it's the invasion, you need to direct the women and children to safety. And lead the final defense of the united Ymittos and Chorokha."

Her heart stuttered, and she felt as though she'd lost the ability to breathe. *Merciful winds.* They'd talked about this after the battle at Qala Alaf-Shilam, starkly considering the worst possible outcome. Their last defense might involve a suicide pact rather than allow a single soul to fall into Kharan-Khuag's hands. Adakizh wasn't shoving her to the side. He was asking her to take on what could become the far harder task. It didn't matter what she wanted. She needed to accept her duty and do it well.

He refilled his teacup. "But, assuming this is just Kharan-Khuag's first move, then we need to repel it quickly and not be distracted in case other enemies decide to attack."

She stared at him, the food in her stomach hardening into stones. "Meaning the Alaf-Shilams." Even though they hadn't spoken of the Alaf-Shilams' absence from their wedding, she'd known it weighed on him. "Evil has many legs. Cutting one off won't slow it down."

His gaze hardened. "Exactly."

Eliana rubbed a hand over her mouth. "I'll also muster a small force to be ready for the Alaf-Shilams."

"I know it's a lot . . ."

She cut off his words with a kiss, not wanting him to see

the fear in her eyes. "Nothing your tagavli can't handle. Leave me Shirdona and Batraz, and I can manage."

Two hours later, Eliana stood in the open doorway of the tower. She and Adakizh had bathed. She'd packed him a change of clothes, a small kit of bandages, and extra food. They'd met with the Chorokhese and Ymittosian leaders, who, other than offering a few token objections and minor suggestions, agreed with the plan. Even, to Eliana's surprise, Ormolai. Was it fear or something else making him so agreeable?

Tigran, Narek, and Bednieri stood nearby, armed and ready, as were twenty other men and a squad of engineers led by a grey-haired woman in her sixties who Eliana knew only by reputation as the most gifted Ymittosian engineer of her generation.

Corban and Alessia would stay with Eliana, as would a few Ymittosian guards. Eliana sent word to Ardashil Khatavian, hoping she would join her. In Adakizh's absence, Eliana wanted a strong ally close at hand.

All too soon, Adakizh was ready to leave. He pulled her into a fierce hug and pressed his face into her hair.

Eliana wrapped her arms around him, running her hands over the taut muscles of his back, not wanting to let go. When the noise of shuffling feet grew louder, she tipped her face up and kissed his mouth, not caring who was watching. "You come back to me."

"Of course." He touched her cheek with one finger. "Rider keep you." Then he turned and strode away.

The tagavli stiffened her spine and forced her shoulders to straighten. She stood motionless as she watched the others follow him across the cavern and disappear into the gloomy shadows. Clenching her jaw, she ignored her palpitating heart and rising dismay. No one could see the panic that fought to rise within her. They had to see a valiant, confident tagavli. Adakizh would return, safe and victorious. He just had to.

37

Ninety-five days after the winter solstice in the 29th year of Emperor Vural Tzimiskes

ERYA CROUCHED AGAINST the rock wall, her breath coming faster than the thumps of her racing heart. She rubbed her injured cheek against her shoulder. The resulting pain did little to erase the oily, filthy feel of Cetus's fingers. She could scrape her skin off and she'd still sense the sorcerer's touch. A surge of revulsion made her jerk at her chains, and their rattling sent a flash of angry heat to her face. *That monster groped me. Nothing can stop him from doing it again.* Her head drooped, and sobs burst from her cracked lips.

A wave roared against the rock, drenching her half-dried cloak. Would this misery never end? Cold and terror made her whole body tremble, and her clanking chains gave voice to her fear.

A ray of sunlight pierced the dour clouds and glinted on the waves. *It's noon,* Derya thought, *or just past.* Stigandr was still unconscious, his head lolled forward, chin on his chest. Derya grimaced. Angry scarlet rings circled the blackened, charred skin around his manacles. Yellow pus oozed from the wounds and seeped over the exposed bone. The king shifted and moaned. Could she heal him?

She lifted a finger. *Or maybe not.* She might burn out her power and make herself deaf. Or Cetus would kill him anyway. Her stomach heaved. She wouldn't eat him, no matter what Cetus did. If he shoved pieces of the king down her throat, she'd vomit them all up.

But if the king woke up, he'd be in agony. She shuddered at the memory of his bestial screams that seared her eardrums and pierced her bones. As angry as she was with him for assaulting her and stealing the scepter, she couldn't abandon him to his suffering. Doing something about his pain gave her a tiny measure of control over her own. And would serve as a small act of defiance.

She narrowed her eyes, studying Stigandr's left wrist, the one closer to her. Cetus had burned it to the bone. She'd have to rebuild the skin and muscle under the charred area and restore the blood vessels and nerves. It would be tricky to heal the wounds concealed by the manacle, but not impossible. How much use he'd have of his hands was anyone's guess.

She pulled on her magic, letting it pool within her. Her hunger and fatigue were wearing on her, the power building much slower than normally. The princess nibbled on her lower lip. After a moment's hesitation, she decided to mend what injuries she could before her magic took its toll on her. The rest would have to wait.

Derya pointed at his wrist and let the magic flow in a gentle stream. Gradually, the noxious pus vanished, and the blackened skin turned red as she knit the muscles back together and weaved the edges of the skin into a seamless whole. Derya closed her eyes, sensing where the injury extended under the metal shackle, imagining healthy arteries and nerves under smooth, healthy skin.

When she thought she'd healed enough of the damage so he wouldn't be in ferocious pain, she stopped and leaned against the wall. That hadn't been as tiring as she'd feared. After a rest, she'd attempt the other wrist.

Derya watched the anxious waves toss droplets of seafoam into the air. A whale surfaced, water pouring from its gray body. A low, guttural tone boomed as the whale snorted spray into the air. *If only I could escape on its back.* She pursed her lips. No birds circled overhead or dove to catch fish. *Land must be far away.* Her throat thickened, and she slid to sit, the relentless chains pulling her arms uncomfortably above her head.

A wave broke over the rock, wetting her to her shoulders. Blue-gray water swirled around the unconscious king, tugging at his ragged clothing as it retreated. The princess frowned. If the waves grew as rough as they had the first night she'd spent here, the king would drown. *Time to get on with it.*

She reached out with her power, trying to sense where the burned skin of his right wrist met healthy flesh. It had been easier when she could see the wound. She closed her eyes, seeking the heat of infection and pain, and let the tendrils of her power seep into the charred skin. Her head ached when she finished, not from the use of magic but from the intense concentration.

When the heat dissipated, she decided she'd done enough. Not a neat job, she was afraid. If wounds like his weren't healed promptly, they'd leave scars no healer could remove. And he needed a more practiced healer to work on the nerves. Now if the king would hold up his head, she could heal the hole Cetus poked in his cheek.

Or perhaps she could without seeing it. After a moment's consideration, she directed a tendril of magic to the king's face. She found the gash; the injury pulsing warm against her cool power. She started with the inside of his mouth and finished by stroking his cheek with her magic to smooth the skin. An experienced healer would leave no echo of scars. *And I'm no skilled healer. Pity to mar such a handsome face.* She sent some magic into the raw spots where hair had been yanked from his chin and jaw.

Satisfied with her work, she leaned against the rock, letting the sunlight warm her face. She flexed her toes, relieved they hadn't gone numb from the intense use of her magic. That was one mercy. The sun was another, as was the barely perceptible breeze. Her cloak was drying, and while her bare feet still felt like blocks of ice, she no longer cowered before icy gusts.

The king's chains rattled, and he let out a low moan. "Rissa? Is that you?"

Derya raised her eyebrows. "Who's Rissa?"

He lifted his head, then dropped it. After a long pause, he shook it. "Who—" He rolled his shoulders. "Oh, it's you." One corner of his mouth turned up. "I must have been dreaming. Someone stroked my cheek."

"That might have been me."

He snorted. "Right. You freed yourself, caressed my face, and chained yourself up again."

"I used my magic to heal you."

His eyes widened, as if he'd forgotten the agony that drove him senseless. He glanced from wrist to wrist and gasped. "You *did* heal me. Thank you. And I mean it. That was the worst pain I've ever endured. All I could think of was how much I wanted to die."

"Can you move your fingers?"

The fingers on his left hand wiggled faintly. "A little. It feels like they don't belong to me."

"I'm sorry. I did the best I could."

"Don't apologize. I'm grateful to be out of pain." He shuddered and his chains clinked.

"Turn this way."

He did as she asked. "Why?"

"Not bad."

"Nobody looks their best after being tortured. You should see when I try."

Derya snorted. "I was talking about the job I did healing the hole in your face."

He shuddered. "I forgot about that." He opened his mouth wide and shut it a few times. "I don't feel it pulling like it would with a scar."

That's because I didn't leave one. "How grateful are you?"

"Immensely. Name your price, and I'll give it to you. Anything but my lands and my arm rings."

"Keep your dirt and trinkets. I'll settle for truth. Why didn't you answer Cetus? Why do you pretend you don't know me?"

"Cetus?" He frowned. "Oh, you mean Kharan-Khuag. The answer to your second question is because of a blood oath I swore." He chuckled. "You're confused. I was too. Why would a Cinarrian princess I've never met insist she knew me? When Kharan-Khuag mentioned his scepter, it all fell into place."

Derya jerked her hand as if to hit him and snorted. "Are you going to answer me today?"

He smirked. "In due time. Let me guess. You traveled to Rorvik intent on finding Kharan-Khuag's scepter. Right?"

"You know this."

"The king promised to help you. Where was it? With the wyvern, the frost giants, or the dragon?"

Derya scowled at him. "You were there."

"Humor me."

"Dragon."

Stigandr grimaced. "So the pair of you killed the dragon and found the scepter. Impressive."

"Yes, I was. You helped."

He chuckled. "Then the king tried to steal the scepter

from you, and you stole it back. Which is what I would have done."

She rolled her eyes. *Why wouldn't this fool admit his guilt?* "Which? Steal it, or steal it back?"

"Both."

"But you were there."

"No, not me. If I'm not mistaken, my brother Arlan was."

Derya gaped at him. "He said he was Stigandr."

Stigandr nodded. "That's not surprising. Arlan is just ten months younger than me. Even growing up, we could pass for twins."

She studied his face. Other than his injuries, he was an exact replica of the man she'd met in the far north.

He sighed. "For centuries, the Rorvikian kings held the secret of Kharan-Khuag's scepter. Knowledge of its three possible locations was passed down from father to son. In the past few years, my father grew concerned about Kharan-Khuag rising, so he revealed the secret to both of his sons. His caution turned out to be wise, because he was killed in Kharan-Khuag's attack on our capital." A muscle twitched in his jaw, and he dropped his gaze.

After a few heartbeats, he continued. "What the sorcerer didn't know was we had prepared a ruse. For years, Arlan and I have traded places, practicing being the other. That way, if we went to battle against Kharan-Khuag and one of us was killed or captured, the other would profess to be Stigandr, the king. So my people would still have their king to lead them. And Kharan-Khuag couldn't use the king of Rorvik as a bargaining tool. We swore that if I was captured, we'd never reveal to anyone that Kharan-Khuag had the genuine king."

"So you claim the man who led me to the dragon is your brother Arlan?"

Stigandr nodded.

"He's a deceitful thief."

Stigandr chuckled. "Well, he can be. That is what we do, you know, raid and plunder. Stealing's in our blood."

"He knocked me out and stole the scepter. And left me there, helpless, knowing Kharan-Khuag's servants were on their way."

He frowned and rubbed the side of his face against his shoulder. "Please don't judge him too harshly. He was desperate, and most likely planned to either trade the scepter for my release or wield it against Kharan-Khuag. Either way, I'm glad you stole it."

Derya pursed her lips. "That's a ridiculous story. I don't see how that would help your people at all."

"This way, Arlan, as me, can rally the people to fight back or flee east as he sees fit. No one is throwing away their life in a futile attempt to rescue me. And while Kharan-Khuag has me, he's not trying to capture Arlan."

"But won't he find out that there is a King Stigandr ruling Rorvik?"

"He knows, because I told him. He believes I'm Arlan, and that I know where the scepter is."

"But he wouldn't think that. I had two counterfeits made, and he took one of them from me. He knows you don't have it."

Stigandr shook his head. "He probably thinks the king of Rorvik tricked you with a fake. It's the kind of skullduggery Kharan-Khuag would delight in. Most likely, he's wondering if he could ally with my brother, who seems like his sort of person."

Derya frowned, wondering if she should believe him. "Your brother has a thick accent when he speaks Ar-Debish."

Stigandr sucked a breath in between his teeth. "Many Cinarrian women came to live among us—"

"You mean were kidnapped," Derya spat.

He bowed his head. "Kidnapped. One was our nurse. She spoke to us in her mother tongue, told us tales of empires, heroes, and the Rider of the Ancient Skies. I worked hard to learn her speech. Arlen didn't."

Derya regarded him. That explained the lack of accent. She detected another subtle difference between the two men. The one chained to the rock seemed less callous, perhaps. But would he be as devious as his brother?

She was still debating with herself when the heads of two water fae broke the surface of the sea.

38

R*AGING WATERS, WILL THESE beasts not leave us alone?* Derya's heart thumped as she watched the water fae swim to the rock. They clambered onto it, water dripping from their lean bodies.

Txartomal swaggered to Derya. Four small leather bags dangled from his bony fingers. "His Magnificence was hurt that you think him a stingy host. He sent you the refreshments you requested."

The other fae snickered, his long tentacles waving over his head like serpents coiling to strike. "The karcharia crave well-fed prey. After we've had our fun, they'll divide you up."

Stigandr spat at Txartomal's feet. "Everyone wants a piece of me. You'll have to get in line."

His bravado ignited Derya's wavering defiance. "I'm sure his cooking isn't up to our standards."

Txartomal snarled. "You won't be laughing when the sun sets. If you're determined to remain silent, His Magnificence said we can have a turn coaxing you to cooperate." He motioned to the other fae.

The second fae opened a bag and extracted a lump of

something flabby and grayish. He advanced on Derya and held it to her lips. "Eat."

"How do we know it isn't poisoned?" Stigandr asked.

"We have easier ways of killing you," Txartomal replied. "Now eat, or do we have to force you?"

Derya clamped her jaw shut.

"Look, fish boy. You're wasting your time," Stigandr said. "Neither of us are hungry."

Derya's stomach rumbled.

Both fae burst into laughter. "I think she disagrees." Txartomal said. He drew out the 's' sound, making the hairs on the back of Derya's neck rise.

His companion shoved the cold mass against Derya's mouth. "Open up."

Derya compressed her lips together and scowled at him. The gray lump smelled of decayed clams. Whatever foul creature it had been in life, she wasn't eating it. She clenched her jaw and turned her head to stare into Stigandr's steady gray eyes.

Txartomal jabbed a pointed fingernail under her jaw and forced her to face him. "You might refuse to eat, but you will drink." He took a waterskin from his companion. "You won't last long without water, and His Magnificence wants you alive." He punched Derya in the chest. When she gasped, his companion seized her hair and jerked her head back. Txartomal poured water into her mouth.

Derya sputtered and choked as most of the water surged down her throat. It was warm, but not foul. She wiped her dripping face on her shoulder.

"You next," Txartomal said to Stigandr.

"Can't we wait a little?" he answered. "I want to see if she dies first."

"Are you a coward?" Txartomal jeered. "Afraid of a little water?" He frowned and grabbed Stigandr's wrist. "Oh, look, the water mage has been doing some healing." His voice took on a sing-song tone. "Naughty, naughty. His Magnificence will not be happy." He motioned to the other fae, who dumped water over the king's face.

The muscles of Stigandr's throat bobbed as he swallowed. He let out a long sigh. "Tell His Insignificance to send mead next time. And politer servants."

Txartomal snarled. His tentacle whirled, and its heavy hooked end whacked the side of Stigandr's head. "You'll be lucky if there isn't a next time. Far better for you to be savaged by a shark than face His Magnificence's wrath. If he wasn't busy dealing with some other human royals who play at being mages, he would have come himself. You'd better hope he's successful. Otherwise, he won't be in the mood to play."

He stabbed Derya in the chest with a long fingernail, poking the bruised spot where he'd punched her. She almost didn't hear his next words over her gasp. "And when he's out of sorts, his tastes turn to rougher games. I'll be looking forward to my turn with you." He gave Derya a parting leer, and the two fae dove into the sea.

Derya let out a shuddering breath. She sagged forward until the chains caught her. Her thumping heart vied with the roar of the waves.

When her breathing slowed, she lifted her head. "Are you alright?"

"I've been hurt worse."

Not really an answer. "Do you think the water will kill us?"

Stigandr shrugged, making his chains clink. "I don't know. But it's a relief to not be so thirsty. What did he mean about other human royals?"

"Was he talking about my father? My cousin?"

"Or my brother?"

She met his questioning look. In his furrowed brow and tense jaw, Derya noticed reflections of her own worry. "We have to escape."

"No." He snorted. "Why didn't I think of that?" He

tipped his head back, rolling his eyes. "Maybe because it's impossible."

"Perhaps if you help me, we could."

He regarded her with an appraising look. "Why would I help a Cinarrian?"

"For the same reason I'd help a Rorvikian?" She curled her lip. "The people who've raided our coasts for centuries?" She had sworn to oppose the northern barbarians at every turn. But now, faced with a common enemy, she wasn't so sure.

He tugged at his chains. "Anything to defeat Kharan-Khuag. Is that it?" When she nodded, he raised an eyebrow. "Are you sure you trust me? After all, I'm brother to the lying deceiver who stole from you."

Did she trust him? No. But he was an enemy of Kharan-Khuag.

"Trust has to be earned," she said slowly. "And it often begins with having common goals. We both want to escape. That's a start."

"And if we do manage to get off this accursed rock, what then?"

She stared at him for a long moment. "I want to find whatever's left of my fleet and sail for the western islands."

"What for? Kharan-Khuag overran them weeks ago."

"To rescue as many people as we can. Surely it's the least I can do." She tried to speak innocently, raising her inflection at the end of the sentence the way young girls did.

Stigandr rubbed his chin on his shoulder. "The least you can do? Does that mean you have another reason for pursuing such a hopeless goal?"

"You don't trust me." She pouted, trying to look like a spoiled girl.

Stigandr chuckled. "Oh, very good, Princess. I almost believed you. But sadly for you, I can guess your real motive."

"I doubt it." Derya assumed her most imperious face, one that even the Queen of Ethkarpia would quail under.

Stigandr's grin widened, and he laughed. "If you weren't a princess, you'd have a distinguished career in the theater." He shook his head. "The girl who killed a dragon, retrieved Kharan-Khuag's scepter, and got said scepter away from my cunning and devious brother can only have one goal. You're looking for the crown."

Derya opened her mouth to deny it. Stigandr's sparkling eyes and mocking grin made her sigh and slump against the rock. "It's that obvious?"

"Why else would you risk your life heading west? You are clearly a compassionate person"—he waved his wrist—"for which I am grateful. But I don't think your sentiments would lead you to sacrifice yourself in a hopeless quest."

"Is the crown in the western islands?" If he could confirm it, that would make going there more reasonable.

He shrugged. "Some of our lore tells us the crown remained in the west."

"Then it is on the islands."

"Maybe. But I don't think so. If it had been hidden there, Kharan-Khuag would have retrieved it by now and gloated over the fact."

"Then where is it?" A wave splashed over them, submerging Derya to the waist. Derya shivered as its retreat tugged her toward the sea, her chains preventing it from pulling her from the rock.

"That, I don't know." He spoke pensively. "If I had to guess, somewhere in Ardebil, maybe to the east. Anywhere away from Kharan-Khuag."

Derya went limp and let her head thump against the rock. If he was right, then she'd sailed west and been captured for no reason.

"You didn't ask what I would do," Stigandr said. "But I'll tell you anyway. I'd help you however I could. Using our magic together would be a powerful weapon against Kharan-Khuag."

"What do you mean?"

"We'd merge our powers, of course."

"What are you talking about?"

"Don't tell me you don't know when two mages merge their magic, it multiplies their power."

She narrowed her eyes. That was a use of magic she'd never heard of. But then, she'd only had elementary training. Had she progressed farther, she might have learned more advanced uses. "Do you know how to do that?"

"Of course."

She stifled a huff of irritation at his superior tone. "Then maybe we can free ourselves. If you'll deign to work with a Cinarrian."

"It's no more distasteful to you than for me, Princess."

She paused, a tiny gasp escaping her lips. He would find it distasteful to work with her, the Heir of Cinar? *I guess, from his perspective, I am the enemy.*

"But I have a duty to my people, so I'll do it." He spoke as if facing a repugnant task.

She ignored his disdainful tone. "Barbarians aren't known for doing their duty."

"Oh, Princess, we have many duties we gladly fulfill. Why do you think we have such large families?"

Warmth crept into her cheeks, and she ignored his leer. He seemed to enjoy shocking people as much as she did. That sword could cut both ways. "I thought it was because wyverns visit your camps when the men are at sea."

He frowned, then burst into a guffaw. "Oh, you are fun, Princess. I wouldn't have expected it of a Cinarrian. So. Do you have any objections to melding your magic with mine?"

Maybe. Would he try to control her power and use it against her? But the possibility of escape gave her a tiny surge of hope, like the tip of a root poking out of a seed.

Combining their powers could make her stronger. As long as she didn't lose control to him. "What magic do you have?"

"Wood and metal."

"Same as your brother." When he nodded, she tipped her head toward his manacled wrists. "Can't you use your magic to break the chains?"

"No." He shuddered. "Kharan-Khuag enchanted them to burn me if I tried."

"But would it burn me?"

"Maybe not. Let's say no. You're free. How would you leave?"

"You mean, after I free you?"

"I would hope so. But you might decide to leave me here."

"That's the most insulting thing you or your brother ever said to me. Even if you were Pasargadian, I wouldn't leave you to face Kharan-Khuag alone."

"How benevolent of you. But how would you escape?"

"Well, perhaps my henchman—"

"Henchman? Since when are you the captain of this ship?"

"Accomplice, then." She stifled a grin, pleased she'd annoyed him. He was fun to tease. "My accomplice, the wood mage, could use his power to pull some driftwood to us, enough for a raft. Or at least for flotation. Then I could use my water magic to propel us somewhere, anywhere."

"You're sure you can do that?"

"Of course. How do you think your brother and I got to the dragon's lair?"

"Fair point."

"The problem is finding wood on this rock."

"Maybe not." He raised a hand, his chains clanking faintly. Deep creases formed between his eyes. He stretched his fingers wide, then curled them into a fist. A grin spread across his face, his generous lips separating to reveal gleaming white teeth. "There's a shipwreck just below us. At least, there's a lot of wood, I guess, from a large ship. I shifted a piece easily. When we're ready, I'll lift some."

"Why not now?"

"Because, dear water mage, if our host shows up before we're ready to depart, I don't want him to know our plans. He might decide to remove all the wood. Or us. Then where would we be?"

"Fair point." Derya frowned. "And if he catches us in the attempt, then what?"

Stigandr gave her a wry grin. "I'll be dead. You'll eat a very gruesome dinner and be served to Kharan-Khuag as dessert."

39

Derya's mind raced over the possibilities, each worse than the last. Stay and wait for Cetus to torture them again. Try to escape, and if they failed, end up tortured anyway. Her chains clinked as she shuffled her feet. "Do you suppose we have a chance?"

He shrugged. "Rider willing, we do. Better to go down fighting, don't you think?"

Using so much magic could deplete her, leaving her at the mercy of this barbarian king. She tipped her head to the side, assessing him. His brother, Arlan, would exploit any opportunity to shove her off whatever raft they made. Stigandr? Maybe. Maybe not.

Everyone, from her father and tutors to the nursemaid who told her stories at bedtime, had declared that even newly born fleas knew better than to trust a barbarian, no matter the circumstances. A whack on the head had reinforced that lesson. While she'd much rather ally with an Ethkarpian or Tavrosian, this Rorvikian was her only choice.

She glanced at the sun, still high in the cloud-mottled sky but beginning its descent to the west. Txartomal had hinted that some awful event would occur at sunset. She didn't want to wait to discover what it was. "Then we agree. We use our combined powers to escape and defeat Kharan-Khuag."

"Or Cetus, as you call him. After that, I return to raiding, and you go back to your flirtations."

Oh, that's what you think of me? "I could try to unheal you, you know."

He gave her a mocking bow as far as his chains would permit. "I beg your forgiveness, oh clever and benevolent princess, powerful and skilled water mage."

She snorted, then paused. This was it. Once they started their escape attempt, they were committed. And once she allied with the barbarian, only success in defeating Cetus would make her father, and her countrymen, forgive her for such a travesty. It had been one thing to persuade Arlan to help her find the scepter. But to forge a wartime alliance was a much bigger matter. But there was no other way. She extended one chained foot toward him. "Go ahead. Try to free me."

"What about you freeing me?"

"I have an idea. First, let's see if you can remove the chains without scalding me."

Derya screwed up her face and closed her eyes, waiting for him to begin. Normal pain she could endure. But burns. That was a whole different kind of agony. She focused on the crash and hiss of the waves.

A faint click and clang seized her attention. The shackle that had bound her right ankle lay on the ground in two pieces. She kicked her foot up, smiling with relief.

Stigandr chuckled. "No burning. Good. Now show me what you can do."

Derya studied the chain attached to his left foot and shifted her gaze to the place where its metal spike was driven into the rock. She took a deep breath and pushed her power. A thin stream of water drilled against the stone, sending a fine spray into the air, accompanied by chips of rock and fine grains of sand.

Stigandr tugged on the chain with his foot, working the metal back and forth in the hole Derya was digging around it. With a final yank, he swung his foot free, the chain dragging on the ground. "That's better. Can you do the other three?"

"Yes, can you?"

"Why haven't you started already?"

Derya scrutinized his face. Once he was loose, he could leave her behind. She removed the shackles from his right ankle while he freed her left hand. She slumped against the rock, stunned by the relief she felt when she lowered her arm. Her fingers tingled, and she tucked her icy hand in her armpit.

Then she started on his right hand while he concentrated on her left foot.

His lips twitched. "What a dilemma. If you free me, I could summon enough wood for a raft and paddle away."

"Or I could demand you fetch me a raft before I free you completely."

"Then what? I free you, you leave. And I am fed to the fish."

Fear of trusting the wrong person again made her stomach churn like the waves beating against the rock. She stared into the distance, and her breath hitched. "Are those sharks?" She gulped and shoved that fear aside. No time for doubts. With a wave of her hand, she directed her magic to the rock holding Stigandr's remaining shackle.

By the time she freed him, all her chains lay on the rock and what looked like an oversized door bobbed in the surf nearby. In the distance, the fins of four sharks were cutting through the water straight toward them. Derya's chest tightened. *Please let them be sharks.*

Stigandr tucked the ends of his ankle chains into his belt

and swung the ends of his wrist chains over his shoulder. He pointed at the makeshift raft. "Get on."

Derya scrambled to the edge of the rock. She put one foot on the wood, and it tipped toward her.

"No, just throw yourself into the middle."

She glared at him. The sharks—or were they karcharia— were circling closer. She imagined one biting her hand off. *No. That's not going to happen.* Sucking in a breath, she cast herself onto the raft. She landed with a thump and a grunt, elbows and knees smarting from the impact.

A moment later, Stigandr fell beside her, chains clanking. "Let's go!"

Derya pulled at her power. Fear made her hasty. When she shoved her magic at the water, the raft shot forward with a jerk that nearly sent her tumbling into the sea. She dug her finger-nails into the waterlogged wood to keep from sliding off.

Stigandr rose to his knees. "Stay down."

"Why?"

"I don't want to hurt you." His chains rattled and clinked. He was gripping the chain attached to his wrist like a weapon, snapping it at the karcharia as they caught up. "If you could go faster, that would be helpful."

"Would this be of use?" She slid her dagger from a hidden sheath sewn into the lining of the sea cloak.

"You've been holding out on me." He yanked it from her without a word of thanks.

A karcharia grabbed the raft. A heartbeat later, the dagger buried itself in its eye. Stigandr curled his fingers in a beckoning motion, and the knife returned to his hand.

"Princess, I know you're in awe of my magical skills, but could you watch later? I'll demonstrate anytime you want. Just get us out of here."

Derya's cheeks burned. She *had* been impressed. "Oh, sorry." She pushed more of her magic at the water and the raft sliced through the waves, sending a trail of froth behind them. "I was amazed that a barbarian knew that sticking someone in the eye could kill them. Then again, that is something a savage would know."

"This savage"—he swung the chain, flinging the manacle so that it wrapped around the throat of a karcharia that was clambering aboard—"knows a few tricks."

The karcharia hissed and grabbed at the chain. Stigandr stabbed it under the ribs and jerked the knife upward. When the monster went limp, the king hurled it onto another of the monsters, unfurling the chain as it left his grasp.

Freed of the extra weight, the raft rocked violently. A wave rushed over one corner. Derya pulled at the water to right the craft. Then she pushed harder, sending the raft skimming over the waves.

"Not fast enough," Stigandr said.

She looked over her shoulder. The two remaining karcharia were keeping pace with them. "Are they trying to wear me out?"

"Or hoping more will show up?" Stigandr grunted. "Let them catch up so I can get rid of them."

"What if there are more?"

"Then I hope you will have found new strength watching me fight."

She scoffed. "Unless I've exhausted myself laughing. But if you insist . . ." She let her magic dwindle, and the raft slowed.

They floated up one side of a wave and crashed down the other as the two karcharia swam closer. Stigandr gestured with the dagger. "They'll come for you, because they think—"

"That I'm the easier prey. But they would be wrong."

He raised a dark blond eyebrow and grinned. "As you say, Princess. We'll see."

Derya eyed the approaching karcharia. As Stigandr predicted, they swam to her side, keeping away from the king and the chain he twirled in the air. She dug in her bag of amplifiers. *Where's the pepper?*

The two karcharia hurled themselves out of the water and landed on the raft. It tipped, threatening to dump them in the sea. The karcharia knelt, one brandishing a spear at Stigandr while the other clutched Derya's leg. She shrieked at the clammy touch on her skin and kicked it in the face. It opened its jaws, exposing its double row of sharp teeth. She kicked again, this time connecting with the beast's arm.

It snarled and tightened its grip on her ankle as it tugged her toward the frothing water. She writhed and thrashed, desperate to free herself from its grasp.

Stigandr threw himself at the monster. It opened its mouth wide and snapped its jaws shut. They closed on Stigandr's forearm, scraping over the metal shackle on his wrist before sliding off. The other karcharia stabbed him in the leg with its spear.

The king bellowed. To Derya's surprise, instead of defending himself, he hacked at the hand clutching her. He sliced it off, gray blood gushing over Derya. The beast grabbed its bleeding stump, gnashing its teeth.

The other karcharia lunged for Derya and pushed her toward the edge of the raft. She kicked and writhed, gasping in her panic, too rattled at first to use her magic.

Taking a deep breath, she pulled at the water with her power, raising a wave. The karcharia dug its fingers into her flesh and opened its jaws in a snarl. Derya heated the water to boiling and shoved her magical wave into the karcharia's gullet.

For a few heartbeats, she didn't think she'd succeeded. The karcharia tugged her again. Then it opened its mouth in a soundless roar. Steam poured from its throat, and the smell of scalded fish soured the air. The beast toppled into the churning waves.

Stigandr was still dueling the other karcharia. He sliced off its other arm, and gray blood spurted into the sky. The armless monster fell on the king, its ash-colored blood mixing with the scarlet seeping from Stigandr's wounds.

Stigandr ducked and drove the dagger into its abdomen. He twisted the blade, and the karcharia went limp. Stigandr shoved the beast over the side.

The king collapsed on the raft, panting, facing Derya. She forced herself to slow her gasping breaths and to ignore the dark spots that danced in front of her eyes.

A hand settled on her shoulder. "Are you hurt?"

Warm tingles spread through her at his touch. Was that concern she heard in his voice? *Stop it, Derya.* Why wouldn't he worry? He'd be marooned if it wasn't for her magic. None of these odd feelings meant anything.

Derya sat up. "I'm fine. I just needed a moment. Are they all gone?"

"Looks like it."

He shifted to a sitting position and tore a strip from his ragged shirt. He winced as he dabbed at the teeth marks on his arm.

"You're hurt!"

"Just a scratch. No, don't offer to heal me. Get us out of here before their friends come looking for them."

She'd already begun pooling her magic. He'd risked himself to save her. For that, she owed him a healing. And a bit more trust.

But he was right. Flight was their best option. "Which way?" Derya gestured to the open sea.

"Well, east, of course." He said it as if she was a slow child. "We'll hit land, eventually. But I think southeast might be best."

Derya ignored his condescending tone. "For the warmer weather?"

"That too. See those clouds? They're a little lower to the southeast."

She was about to argue, then clamped her lips shut. Of course the king of a seafaring nation knew how to read the signs of approaching land. "As you say." She pulled at her magic and pushed the raft forward. "As you say."

40

Chorokha

95 days after the winter solstice in the Year 999 (Chorokhese reckoning) and in the 29th year of Emperor Vural Tzimiskes of Cinar

THE ECHOES OF TRAMPING men pounded like the beat of a war drum against Eliana's ears. Instead of providing reassuring guidance, the glowing mushrooms' blue light offered a broody warning. Her skin crawled with the sense she was marching toward her doom.

She'd left Qala Bisen within an hour of receiving Adakizh's terse request for her to meet him at Qala Kambada. Forced marches, hurried meals, and catching a few hours' sleep on stony ground surrounded by fifty others wasn't what she'd expected from married life. But then much of what had happened during the past four weeks shattered her illusions like rock that tumbled from a cliff.

The tunnel widened, and they passed between a pair of crystal pillars that resembled braided tree trunks made of shiny yellow rocks, pillars that marked one entrance to Qala Kambada. Eliana's steps quickened. *Finally.* A single shaft of sunlight illuminated the space, revealing the six-story tower standing proud and tall.

A crowd of seated people, both Chorokhese and Ymittosian, surrounded the tower like spectators at a play. With a start, Eliana realized that many bore gashed faces and bloodstained limbs, and the muffled sounds they made weren't low conversations but moans and sobs. Eliana's heart lurched. What happened? She broke into a run, weaving through the throng, darting toward the tower. Where was Adakizh?

A lump formed in her throat when she spied him standing near the tower's entrance. Dark circles ringed his eyes, and his high cheekbones jutted out like cliffs. Weeks of racing from one underground river to another to battle mutant water fae and karcharia had drained him. No wonder he looked like a refugee himself, fleeing both famine and the horrors of war. She folded herself into his arms, shocked at how thin he was.

He crushed her in a tight embrace, pressing his face against her hair. "You don't know how much I've missed you."

"If it's anything like how I missed you . . ." They'd only met twice in the month since he'd been called away to defend Qala Zhilakhur.

The last time he told her bits and pieces of the battles he'd fought. Sometimes fighting broke out near where the underground rivers spilled into the sea, other times far upriver. Every assault felt like a test of their defenses, because whenever the battle swung in their favor, the enemy fled. Adakizh had been in agony over what trap Kharan-Khuag was preparing to spring, feeling always six steps behind the sorcerer's plot.

She tightened her grip on her husband. While his arms circled her, she could feel something other than corrosive fear.

After a long moment, he released her and tipped his head toward the tower's entrance. "You got here just in time. We need to talk." He led the way into the tower. But instead of ascending the stairs as she'd expected, he pulled her behind a row of casks and sat on the floor.

She settled beside him, leaning against his warmth rather than the cold stone wall. "Where is Shirdona? And Bednieri, and—"

"They can wait." He heaved a sigh. "Thank you for coming so quickly. I needed you."

"I need you too."

"Eliana." He paused and his shoulders slumped. After a few deep breaths, he continued. "Qala Zhilakhur is lost."

"Lost?" Eliana's mouth went dry, and she shook her head. *No.* "It couldn't be."

"It's all my fault." He pulled his knees up and rested his head on them. The sounds of the footfalls of people passing by and fleeting bits of Shirdona's shouted orders filled the long pause before he spoke again. "We thought we were so clever, making all those magically enhanced javelins. We found what we believed were the perfect placements, ready to repel any invaders."

"What happened?"

"Somehow, a squad of water fae found the javelins and killed the people who were ready to use them. Then the rest of them and their karcharia just swam up the river. Fools that we are, we never considered that possibility. The Zhilakhurs couldn't retrieve the javelins. So they were worthless. The best we can hope for is that the fae won't figure out how to use them."

Eliana stroked the back of his head, silently castigating herself. *How did I miss that?* Oh, she'd thought she'd been so clever, figuring out a way to use water propelled by magic and forced through a tube to extend the javelins' range. Placing the javelins near the sea provided an unlimited source of water. *I have rocks for brains. We should have used something like wineskins and prepared a supply of them, full of water, ready to use, so the javelins could be used anywhere and not stuck in a fixed position.*

"It gets worse. Remember the chest we pulled from the sea?"

"Kharan-Khuag's weapons?"

He nodded glumly. "That's lost, too." He let out a long sigh. "How goes it with you?"

"Well, the Minarilis found a huge cache of tubing. With it, we doubled our stockpile of javelins. That makes up for the loss of the ones at Qala Zhilakhur."

He straightened to sit upright. "That's the first hopeful news I've heard in a week," he said. "Anything else?"

She'd been dreading this. "I'm so sorry." Her throat tightened, and she nibbled the inside of her cheek. "I let you down."

"What do you mean?"

A coppery taste filled Eliana's mouth. *I deserve to hurt, to bleed.* "I sent scouts to explore the upper tunnels, closer to the surface. Based on their reports, I thought we'd found sanctuary for the aged and mothers of young children and started moving a few families."

Her mouth went dry. "Two boys died painful deaths from poison centipedes." Guilt tightened Eliana's throat as if she'd personally slain those innocents. "I forgot how dangerous the upper tunnels are."

"Seems everyone else did too," Adakizh said, his voice heavy and resigned. "Including me. Since the cataclysm wiped out most of the vishapions and bagalas, I'm not surprised we overlooked the other dangers."

A drop of her guilt ebbed away. "So . . ." She blinked to banish a tear. "Then we sent word to the Saumarotas and Khatavians. They agreed to welcome refugees if they would help build new tunnels. But that didn't ease the people's fears or silence their muttering that perhaps it would be better to take their chances with Kharan-Khuag."

"That poison is spreading, and we've got to stop it. But I don't know how." Defeat dulled his voice. "Yesterday we got word that Qala Minarili fell."

"Qala . . . Minarili?" She slumped against the wall.

He fastened his stricken gaze on hers. "The Alaf-Shilams turned on them. They used the javelins." His tone hardened. "And fought alongside the water fae and karcharia."

"That's horrible." The taste of sour milk filled Eliana's mouth, and she curled her lip. Sudden understanding broke through her shock. "That's who all those people are. The remnant of the Minarilis." Ice spread through Eliana's veins.

"Oh, there you are, my sunshine. Who are you hiding from?"

Eliana jerked her head up. "Just wanted a private word with my husband."

Shirdona tossed a long braid over her shoulder and squatted next to Eliana. "Have you told her yet?"

Eliana's heart skipped a beat. "Told me what?"

Adakizh pulled her closer to his side. "Remember that rumor about the Alaf-Shilams killing the Ymittosians?" He paused. "It's true."

Hot anger coursed through her, and blood pounded in her ears. "How do you know?"

"The Alaf-Shilams were bragging about it as they sacked Qala Minarili." Shirdona cursed. "Said they'd do the same to the Minarilis."

Eliana clenched her fists. *Those Alaf-Shilams are going to pay a high price for their treachery.* Images of her revenge flashed through her mind. Throw them in the path of a blue octopus. Impale them on a tsovul's spike. Throttle them, every one.

"That's not the only news the Minarilis brought."

From Shirdona's grim tone and the way Adakizh started rubbing her back, she knew she didn't want to hear it.

"My sunshine, as they promised you, the Minarilis sent scouts north to look for more of your people."

"Did they find any?"

"None alive."

Eliana put a hand to her mouth, unable to speak.

Shirdona's face hardened. "Many of the search parties never returned. So they sent others. When they found the dead scouts, they grew alarmed. A little farther on, they started seeing bodies. Some in piles, some in what looked like family groups. All dead."

Eliana's hot rage turned to icy dread. She shivered and gripped Adakizh tighter.

Shirdona let out a long breath. "When one scout began coughing up blood, they knew."

Eliana stared, wide-eyed. "Knew what?"

"Breathstealer blight. Caused by poison air. It's always fatal."

Every one of Shirdona's words was a stab to Eliana's heart. "There's no cure. The Minarilis retreated, of course, but a few of them died."

So many deaths. She could barely comprehend the enormity. "But my people . . ."

"Eliana," Adakizh said gently. "Any who fell into the poison air are dead."

"But what about farther north? What about the survivors there? We need to find them!"

"We can't," he said in a regretful tone. "All the tunnels have poisoned air."

"So, we just assume they're all dead." Eliana spoke flatly. "Hundreds of thousands of people." She stared unseeing before her, her breath coming faster as the enormity of the tragedy washed over her like a stormy wave. "We should have sent more search parties. Tried harder to find them . . ." The floor seemed to tilt under her. She put her face against Adakizh's shoulder, and her body shook with sobs.

He tightened his arms around her and kissed the top of her head. "We did all we could."

"But it wasn't enough." A fresh wave of sobs took her breath away.

"We don't know they're all dead. Maybe when this is all over, we can go overland and try to find another way."

Maybe. She scoffed. His words did little to ease the agony she felt for those who died of a painful disease in the darkness.

When her sobs ebbed, she lifted her face to his. "I killed them all."

"No, my sunshine," Shirdona said. "You saved the continent from immediate invasion. How many millions would be dead already if you hadn't?" She put a hand on Eliana's shoulder. "Consider the real villain in all this."

"Kharan-Khuag," Adakizh said.

"Yes, Kharan-Khuag. But we have a more pressing problem," Shirdona said.

Eliana closed her eyes and let her head droop. *I can't take any more. Not now.*

"The Alaf-Shilams are on the move," Shirdona said. "They're coming for Qala Kambada."

"They're coming for Qala Kambada?" Eliana struggled to keep from screaming.

"They are." Shirdona's voice cracked on the second word. "This is my hearth, my home. I'll not let those turncoats take it."

"If we leave," Adakizh said slowly, "we could rally the Saumarotas and Khatavians. Once the Alaf-Shilams grow complacent, we could retake your tower."

"Perhaps." Shirdona didn't sound convinced. "Or those sons of donkeys would invite more water fae to destroy us."

Eliana took a deep breath and rubbed the tears from her face. "Or we could set a trap."

He narrowed his eyes. "Trap?"

"Yes. Lure them into pursuing us into a cavern. Then have some of our warriors attack from behind."

"That would only work if they sent a smaller force after us than we have."

"But we have a vast supply of javelins." She explained her thought about using filled wineskins as a source of water. "Even after we run out of water, the weapons are still useful. The metal mages strengthened and sharpened the blades. A powerful warrior can cut through a tsovul's shell."

He regarded her, rubbing the stubble on his chin. "Bed-nieri showed me a cavern the other day. One that looks like a dead end but isn't. It connects to a tunnel leading to the Saumarotas' territory." He pursed his lips. "What about this? Send everyone but three hundred fighters to the south, to the Saumarotas and Khatavians. The rest of us will defend Qala Kambada. We'll pretend to retreat into the cavern. When a large force of Alaf-Shilams and water fae follow, we use the javelins. If we kill them all, we stay here. If not, we flee through the cavern and block the tunnel behind us."

They discussed the finer points of the plan for a few moments. Then Adakizh and Shirdona went to inform the other leaders. Eliana didn't envy them the task. Telling someone their home would soon be the front line of a war and might need to be abandoned would not be easy. But then, nothing ever seemed to be. She sighed and stood up. The work of preparing for battle wouldn't get done by itself.

After toiling late into the night, they'd sorted the refugees into groups, assigned leaders and guides, and supplied them with full waterskins, packs of food, and weapons. Maybe, Eliana thought, the supplies would ease any resentment on the part of the Saumarotas or Khatavians.

Among one of the first groups to depart, she spotted Narek Zhilakhur's mother. "Tavkatseen," she began.

The woman shook her head. "I'm tavkatseen of nothing," she said. "Those fiends overran us before we even knew they were there. It was all we could do to fight our way out."

Eliana asked, "How many——" Her voice hitched.

The tavkatseen sighed. "I'd say half the clan is dead."

The woman's grief scraped Eliana's soul. "I'm so sorry."

The tavkatseen gave her a grim smile. "I hope to see you again, tagavli. But those monsters . . ." She gave Eliana a nod, slipped her arm around a man with a bloody bandage on his head, and joined the line of refugees heading for the cavern that would take them to tunnels leading south.

Eliana let out a long breath. The people were on their way to safety. Her fingers curled. *I'd like to strangle every last Alaf-Shilam.* She strode to the cavern's edge near a formation of braided crystal that formed a towering pillar of yellow and red. The magical javelins were stacked high next to a mound of waterskins. Eliana joined in the work of filling waterskins, grateful to have something to occupy her hands. As she twisted the cork from a skin, she thought of doing the same to an Alaf-Shilam's neck. Rage pushed aside her nerves. The murderers of her people were approaching, and they were about to face her wrath.

Soon scouts arrived with word of an advancing force consisting of Alaf-Shilams and fish-headed water fae. "It's bad, tagavli," said their shuddering leader. "The only reason they aren't here already is the fae are eating the dead."

Bile rose in Eliana's throat. "Then we must make sure no one else is eaten today."

Adakizh sent Tigran, Narek, and Bednieri to lead brigades on the three sides of Qala Kambada, leaving the cavern's north side undefended. He secreted another group in the cavern selected as their escape route, all bearing the magically enhanced javelins. Eliana and Adakizh waited on the first floor of Qala Kambada, along with Shirdona and several of her fiercest warriors.

Too soon she heard the soft tramp of leather-shod Chorokhese, the slapping tread of barefoot water fae, and the slithering of whatever beasts accompanied them. Her heart pounded and she set her jaw. Never before had she anticipated a battle with anything other than dread. This time she was ready, eager even, her fingers itching to avenge her slaughtered people.

Her eyes widened and her tightening throat trapped the breath in her lungs when the vanguard appeared. Krikor Alaf-

Shilam, who'd once pledged undying friendship to Adakizh, strutted at the head of a column of warriors. He'd skipped their wedding. Eliana had assumed his absence was due to pressure from his family. Now she knew. All his promises of friendship were weaker than reeds in a marsh.

Behind Krikor marched scores of water fae, their fish heads shining blue in the dim light, their spiky teeth gleaming white. Tsovuls crept forward on tiger-like legs, their long spikes bobbing with each step. Behind them slithered poisonous blue octopi.

Eliana winced. She hated those octopi. The cavern filled with the sound of hundreds of tiny hammers hitting the stone. *What was that?*

Adakizh raised his sword. "For the Rider!" he yelled and sprinted straight for Krikor.

His warriors echoed the cry and charged. Swords clanged, echoing through the cavern. Shirdona eased forward, cracking her whip. It curled around the throat of a balding Alaf-Shilam and she yanked. The man toppled to the ground, his neck bent at an unnatural angle.

Eliana tore her attention from the tavkatseen and sought Adakizh. She pulled at her magic. With a throwing motion, she hurled a blast of air in the face of the water fae threatening to stab her husband. *No. Not good enough. Shirdona had the right idea. But I can do better.* Eliana used her power to form a band. She twisted it around the fae's throat and tightened it. The fae's head fell off in a shower of gray blood. Its death appeased a tiny fragment of her rage. She looked for Krikor but couldn't see him in the melee. *Any of the Alaf-Shilams will do.* She strangled a tall man with a spiky beard. *They all deserve death.*

The man to Adakizh's left collapsed with a gurgle, the spikes of a tsovul slicing his leg. A blue octopus slithered over and wrapped an arm around his face. The man died with an agonizing scream.

The echoes of his death wail hadn't faded when the clicking sound intensified. Around the corner crawled a massive crab, as large as a war horse and the gray-green hue of decaying seaweed. Its legs were the length of a man's, and when it reared up, its eyes were well above Adakizh's. Long tentacles like a squid's protruded from its shoulders. It scooped up the dead man with a pair of tentacles. With one of its claws, it snapped the man in two. Then it fixed its bulging black eyes on Adakizh.

"Behind you!" Tigran shouted.

Adakizh ducked. A sword sliced the air, skimming past his left ear. He crouched and lunged, hitting the attacking fae in the stomach with his shoulder. Then he shoved his opponent to the ground. It rolled into the blue octopus. The fae's high-pitched dying shriek assaulted Eliana's ears.

The monstrous crab clicked its way toward Adakizh. Eliana created a band of air and used it to bind two of the crab's legs together. It wobbled and fell on its side. Tigran slashed its belly. The beast's foul-smelling entrails spilled over him. He scrambled backwards, skidding on the now slick stone.

A tsovul crawled to Adakizh. He charged it, thrusting his sword into its throat. He whirled and parried a blow from a fae, his blade clanging against the fae's long knife. Eliana sent another band of air at the fae, strangling it with her invisible garrote. *Stay away from my husband.*

Adakizh was moving so quickly she lost sight of him. Her eyes darted over the fray, heart racing until she spotted him as he vaulted an octopus. He stabbed it in the head as he passed over it. Blue blood spurted into the air.

She scanned the cavern. Maybe half the fae were down, along with ten Alaf-Shilams and at least thirty of their own fighters. Limp octopi lay about. It didn't seem any of them had survived the initial encounter.

But the tsovuls. One stalked Tigran, who was battling two

of the water fae. Adakizh scooped up a chunk of rock and used his magic to hurl it at the tsovul. It thunked the beast's helmet-like head and shattered it into pieces.

Tigran cleaved the head of one of the fae and turned his attention to the other. It waved its hooked tentacle in Tigran's face, scraping his cheek. Tigran yelled and lopped the tentacle off.

Another tsovul slunk toward Adakizh, and he spun to face it. Eliana's heart raced. She couldn't help him. A pair of water fae were sprinting toward her. She used her air garrotes to circle their necks, and she yanked, slicing the heads from their bodies. They slammed to the ground in a widening pool of gray blood.

A wounded water fae staggered toward Adakizh, sword outthrust. Bednieri lunged for it and tripped over a tsovul. Tigran stabbed the water fae as Adakizh thrust his sword into the tsovul's throat.

Narek tugged at Eliana's arm. "Tagavli, we're losing." Drips of blue, scarlet, and gray blood stained his face.

She clamped her lips together to repress her shouted denial. Her own assessment told her as much. They'd underestimated how many water fae the Alaf-Shilams would bring, and how fiercely they'd fight. She flexed her fingers, preparing to strangle another foe, then let her hands drop and her shoulders slump. Even with her air magic, they were hopelessly outnumbered. Revenge would have to wait for another day.

The tagavoi was already shouting for the retreat. She and Narek ran to him and slowly backed around the tower. Shirdona's cracking whip sent the tsovuls skittering and kept the Alaf-Shilams at bay.

Adakizh used his magic to hurl stone at their foes, while Eliana used blasts of air to knock them over. She paused, panting. A quick glance confirmed all their warriors had fled to the escape route.

Adakizh shouted, "Go!"

Following their plan, Eliana darted after Tigran, with Narek on her heels. Shirdona and Adakizh brought up the rear. The sounds of crashing stone and the cracking whip echoed.

They sprinted for the far end of Qala Kambada's cavern, where an opening the size of a large city's gate led to the next cavern.

Shirdona halted. "Where are you going?" she asked. "The tunnel south is on the east side." Her eyes flared wide, the whites tinged blue from the mushrooms' glow.

"This one does, too," Adakizh said. "Bednieri said this was the best way."

"You must have misunderstood, my sunshine," Shirdona said. She cracked her whip at a charging water fae. "This is a dead end. We're stuck."

42

I CY FINGERS OF TERROR crawled through Eliana's veins. *Stuck. Trapped.* Helpless against the waves of water fae and karcharia. Two hundred warriors crammed in the dim cavern. Victims of Krikor's treachery. She pressed her quivering lips together, suppressing the moan that rose in her throat.

A pair of water fae surged toward the cavern's entrance, their elongated tentacles writhing in a sinuous dance, long spears with scarlet-stained tips clasped in their hands. An Alaf-Shilam roared, "Spear the tagavoi!"

Anger stormed through Eliana. She'd watch the last mushroom wither before she let those monsters touch Adakizh. If they wanted to play with spears, she'd show them how. She pooled her magic, allowing her rage to suggest weapons she'd never tried before. Unsure if this would work, doubt needled her. Holding her breath, she condensed air into two spears and thrust them at the advancing water fae.

Her magical spears dove into the fae's gaping mouths between their sharp white teeth. Gray blood spurted like spray from a whale. The fae toppled backwards and knocked over a karcharia and a thickset, bald Alaf-Shilam.

The remaining water fae and Alaf-Shilams lurched back-ward, tripping over each other in their alarm. Eliana's lips curved into a ferocious smile. *Those beasts never faced invisible weapons like mine before.*

She stole a glance at Adakizh. Her air spears had given him time to pile stone around the cavern's entrance. Behind her, Shirdona was yelling for stone mages, some to help Adak-izh, others to work on breaking an exit through the cavern's opposite end fifty yards away.

A man spattered with gray blood sauntered over, sheathing his sword. Eliana blinked. Her cousin Ormolai was actually helping Adakizh without complaint, heating stalagmites until they cracked. Then he tossed the pieces of broken rock and crystal to fill in cracks between boulders. Even more astounding was how powerful a mage he was. Not like Adak-izh, but more than most. Adakizh melted the crystal to seal the rocks together. As he worked, most of their remaining warriors slipped into the cavern. Ten stood nearby, holding magical javelins.

Heat billowed from the rock. Adakizh's face dripped sweat, and Eliana's was damp from the heat radiating from the stone. The tagavoi pulled another stalactite from the cave's ceiling, and it fell to the ground with an echoing crash.

Four water fae charged at Adakizh. Two toppled in a spray of gray blood, magical javelins in their throats. Two other javelins flew over their heads and disappeared into the next cavern. Corban limped to Eliana's side, waving a hand as if beckoning. The four javelins flew to his feet, their steel blades summoned by his metal magic.

Krikor swaggered to the front of his lines, yelling, "Look at the pretty tagavoi playing with rocks. He hides behind his wife and the ox-footed overworlders. Who wants to follow a cowardly son of a donkey like that?" Raucous echoes repeated his mocking words as he hurled a stone at Adakizh's feet. "Maybe you should wear this instead of a crown."

The stone bounced before it rolled to a stop. A blue tuft was tied to it—the Chorokhese symbol of cowardice and shame. Eliana ground her teeth and began creating another air spear.

"It's more fitting for you," Adakizh answered, staring up at the cave ceiling. "At least I didn't sell myself to our worst enemy."

"That's because you know he despises you as the worm you are," Krikor shouted. He opened his mouth to say more, but a cracking sound from above made him stop. With a yelp, he staggered back.

Adakizh had loosed a stalactite and dropped it right next to Krikor, its crystal shattering with a crash.

"Now who's the coward?" Adakizh snickered.

"You won't be laughing when you read this." Krikor hurled something that looked like a white tube. It bounced off Adakizh's leather armor and clattered to the stone floor.

Adakizh curled his lip. "You've eaten your brains with your mushrooms if you think a little stick will cow me." He raised a hand in the air and clenched his fist. A boulder rolled to the cavern's mouth, blocking about a quarter of the opening. He jerked his chin at his remaining warriors. "Go." Five of them slipped through the narrow gap to the cavern beyond.

Eliana nudged the tube with her foot. No hidden blades burst from its sides; no poisonous liquid oozed on its surface. Maybe it was just a message. She picked it up and nearly dropped it when she realized it was a bone, the forearm of a child. Words were etched on it, the letters of a language she didn't know.

Corban leaned over her shoulder. "That's Old Malkhian." He muttered to himself, then read aloud, shouting so Adakizh could hear.

Surrender. If you surrender to us, we'll ask Kharan-Khuag to be merciful to all. Except the tagavoi and tagavli, who dared to oppose His Magnificence.

"That's what he's calling himself?" Adakizh snorted. "I can think of more apt names." He shoved another boulder in place. "We're not surrendering. If you Alaf-Shilams think you will fare better under Kharan-Khuag than us, you're welcome to try. But we will not participate in such evil folly." His gaze fell on Eliana. "Do you agree?"

"Absolutely," Eliana replied. "I'll die defending my people. And I'd sooner fall on my sword than be captured." She hadn't forgotten about the personal and intimate plans Kharan-Khuag claimed he had for her, and a shiver ran down her spine. The idea of anyone but Adakizh touching her like that made her blood run cold.

"Clan Kambada is with you," Shirdona shouted.

"As is Clan Zhilakhur," Narek added.

"And Clan Saumarota," Tigran yelled.

"And Clan Minarili, both of us," shouted a woman.

Krikor waved his sword. "That's all who will remain of you. One to weep and the other to wail that you failed to accept His Magnificence's offer."

"This is what I think of his offer," Eliana said. She placed the bone on the ground and smashed it with a rock, venting her fury at the arrogant words. The bone shattered into two pieces.

"Krikor," Adakizh shouted. "You think you are walking on the sky by allying with Kharan-Khuag. Simpleton that you are, you're worth less to him than rain is to a fish."

"Is that your answer?" Krikor yelled.

"This is," Adakizh roared. He backed up several yards, motioning for Eliana and the others to follow. Once they'd all passed through the aperture, he turned and peered through the opening. He raised a hand over his head, then brought it down with a sharp, sweeping motion. The cracking sounds of shattering stone echoed through the cavern, ending with the roar and smash of dozens of stalactites crashing to the cavern's floor.

Eliana closed her eyes against the dust, holding her breath. When the pressure in her throat and chest was unbearable, and she could stand it no longer, she opened her eyes. Most of the dust had settled. She inhaled sharply and, with a flick of her hand, used her air magic to blow the remaining dust away. The pile of stalactites completely blocked the entrance.

Adakizh seized her hand and sprinted for the back of the cavern, followed by Shirdona, Narek, and Tigran. With a sense of relief, Eliana noted the stone mages making the final cuts through the cavern's back wall, forming two small doors.

A dust-covered woman whose gray hair was matted with sweat joined them. "The door on the left connects to a tunnel that goes due south, to the Saumarotas. The other winds to the southeast, to the Khatavians."

Adakizh nodded. "Where's Tigran?" The stocky man stepped forward, his goatskin cloak stained with scarlet and gray blood. Adakizh put a hand on his shoulder. "Can you lead half of these people to safety?"

"Of course. I'll go south to my clan."

"Shirdona, will you lead the others?" Adakizh asked.

"No, let me," Narek said. "Most of my clan went to the Khatavians anyway."

"Yes, let him," said Shirdona. "Leave me my fifty Kambadas, and we'll guard the rear. That pile you made won't hold them for long. And block these entrances when you leave."

"How will you get out?" Eliana asked.

"I have a few stone mages." Shirdona chuckled. "We're well experienced in changing the tunnels, just a bit slower than the tagavoi."

Adakizh frowned and huffed out a breath. He pointed at the doorways. "Tigran, Narek, get everyone moving."

He watched his friends sort the warriors by clan before turning to Shirdona. "Tavkatseen, are you sure you want to stay? I should lead the rear guard."

Shirdona shook her head. "I'm staying. If we can force them to retreat, we'll look for Bednieri."

Eliana's stomach clenched. "The last time I saw him, he'd tripped over a tsovul." She winced, imagining the painful death Shirdona's son had faced. "We'll help you find him."

"No, you need to rally the Khatavians and Saumarotas. This business of clans cooperating can't be taken for granted."

Eliana took a steeling breath. She exchanged a glance with Adakizh, knowing all too well how easily the clans could turn on each other. Or on the Ymittosians. Adakizh nodded his assent.

The sound of shuffling footsteps was already diminishing as most of the people filed through the far doors. The noise was replaced by the scraping and cracking of stone and Krikor's muffled commands to his mages to work faster.

"We can't leave you," Eliana said.

"What else are you going to do?" Shirdona spat. "Let that spawn of a centipede's mockery snow on your brain? Someone has to live to fight another day. It's best that it's you."

Adakizh wiped sweat from his forehead. "I can't argue with that. But first we'll block one tunnel so it looks as if nobody has passed that way. Then you'll only have one to worry about." He paused. "We'll go to the Khatavians and wait for you there."

Shirdona shook her head. "Only wait a few days. If we haven't made it by then, rally them and the Saumarotas and whoever's left and avenge my death."

Krikor's shout of triumph seized Eliana's attention. Large gaps in the pile of stalactites had appeared.

"Hurry up, you," Shirdona yelled at the remaining warriors.

The last of them scurried into the left-hand tunnel. Adakizh sprinted to it. He pulled down an avalanche over it, spreading the stone to look like it had lain there since the cataclysm. "Where's that cousin of yours?"

"Ormolai?" Eliana scoffed. "He was one of the first to leave."

More stone rattled from the entrance. Moving shapes of water fae were visible through large gaps between the fallen stalactites. "Go," Shirdona said.

"Rider be with you," Adakizh said. "Tavkatseen . . ."

"Go," she said and turned to face the foe, her fifty Kambada warriors arrayed behind her. A large section of rock crumbled and fell.

The tagavoi seized Eliana's hand and pulled her into the tunnel. Eliana took a final look at Shirdona, wondering if the woman who'd been so kind and so deceitful would survive.

Adakizh began pulling down stone. Over the crashing and crunching of rocks and crystals, all Eliana could hear were the Kambadas' war cries and the cracking of Shirdona's whip.

43

Ninety-six days after the winter solstice in the 29th year of Emperor Vural Tzimiskes

BRIGHT LIGHT SHINING in Derya's eyes woke her. She raised a hand to shield her face, then froze. *How can I move so freely?* The memories crashed over her like a surging wave. Escaping the rock. Arriving on land. She had a dim memory of her numb feet and muffled hearing, signs she'd overused her magic. And an even dimmer recollection of Stigandr carrying her and laying her down somewhere.

Derya sat up with a start. She was alone in a tiny cave, barely more than an alcove. With a groan, she staggered to her feet, wincing as the feeling returned to her lower limbs. She limped toward the open air. An icy breeze sliced through her damp, ragged clothes, and she tugged her cloak tighter. The sun was already high in the sky. About midmorning, Derya figured.

She stood in a little valley, surrounded by tall sand dunes on three sides, with a wall of cliffs to her back. Scruffy pine trees mixed with a few stunted birches filled most of the rest of the space under a serene azure sky. Faintly, she heard the roar and hiss of the sea. *Not the most beautiful spot, but a paradise compared to that barren rock.*

A sudden thought made her heart skip a beat. Had Stigandr abandoned her? She scrambled up a sandy dune, scraping her feet on the sharp seagrass. Upon reaching the top, she scanned the beach and let out a relieved gasp when she spotted their raft, pulled up on the sand well past the high tide mark. But where was the king? She'd try calling, but the muted sound of the surf made her realize with her still impaired hearing she might not hear his reply. Since he wasn't on the beach, she decided to try exploring.

An overgrown trail led between the pine trees, and she followed it. A faint yell hit her ears. Derya stiffened and her heart raced. Was Stigandr in danger? Or hurt? As she progressed, the yells intensified into roars. Even with her muffled hearing, Derya could feel the rage behind them.

She burst out of the pines and skidded to a stop. Stigandr stood naked under a waterfall facing the rocky cliff. He was beating the manacle on his right wrist against the rock, frustration and anger permeating his shouted curses.

For a moment, she considered joining him under the falling water. Anything to cleanse herself of Kharan-Khuag's touch. Stigandr must want to erase the haunting humiliation of captivity even more.

Abruptly, he stopped shouting and pressed his palms against the cliff. He leaned his head on the rock, and his shoulders shook.

Derya gaped. Was the king crying? She studied him, now noticing the sharp definition of work-hardened muscles over his broad shoulders. Her gaze traveled down his body, and her eyes widened. Marring his skin was a network of angry wounds. Some looked old and well-healed. Most were fresh gouges and infected tears. Purple, green, and yellow bruises mottled his pale skin. She counted back in time. Kharan-Khuag must have captured him at least six weeks ago. Her throat tightened. His raw wounds revealed what the sorcerer had done to him over that time.

She raised a hand to heal him, then paused. Maybe she should allow him his solitude. The Rider knew she wouldn't want to be caught in such a moment of weakness and vulnerability. As emotional as he was, how would he react?

The princess pursed her lips. She'd heal him later. Maybe use the promise of healing him to maintain some control over the situation and offset his far superior physical strength. And perhaps wait until she'd gotten a sense of who was more magically powerful.

Derya silently retreated the way she'd come, shivering in the breeze. The sun was warm, but this far north, just after the spring equinox, the air still held winter's bite. She spread her cloak out and weighted it with rocks. After taking a gulp from her waterskin, she set about collecting anything that might serve as firewood.

About an hour later, Stigandr ambled into view, accompanied by the jingle of his chains. The ends of his leg chains were tucked into his belt. He'd braided his long hair back from his face, and his tattered clothing clung to his muscled form, damp as if he'd attempted to wash out the bloodstains. Two small birds dangled from one hand, held by their feet. The chain attached to his left wrist was wrapped around a bundle of firewood. "Would you care for breakfast?"

He seemed, Derya thought, to have recovered his composure. "Absolutely. Do you know how to cook?"

"Yes. Better than you."

She scoffed. "You underestimate me." During the months she'd been traveling, she'd taken great pleasure shocking her servants by insisting on learning to cook game. Shocking the king would be even more satisfying.

He dropped the wood next to her pile of collected twigs and dried brush. "Are you waiting for the servants to start the fire?" He sat next to her and tossed her a bird. "Too bad they've all quit. You want to eat, you'll have to pluck that one."

She smiled sweetly and set to work.

"How do you feel?" he asked. "You weren't well last night."

"If you mean I was losing my hearing, it's coming back. The sleep helped a lot." *But how are you?* The memory of his agony made her reluctant to ask. "Where are we?"

"Kvimsoya Island, off the coast of Veleti."

"Does anyone live here?"

"Only a few birds."

Derya tugged at a clump of wing feathers. "How did you know about this cave?"

"There's a good harbor to the south."

She frowned as she yanked out another feather. "Why didn't you have me take us there?"

"Because that would be the first place Kharan-Khuag would look for us if he guessed we made it this far."

She ran her fingers over the bird's bumpy skin, seeking tiny feathers she'd missed. He wasn't exactly evading her question but wasn't giving her direct answers. "You've been here before."

He gave her a rueful nod. "The Ymittosian navy didn't take kindly to us confiscating their wine and goats. We'd leave one vessel in the harbor as a decoy, and the crew would hide here. The other ships would sail north, then would return. When the Ymittosians stopped to plunder our ship, they were in for a surprise. Made for a grand adventure." He chuckled, as if savoring the memory of a childish prank.

Derya curled her lip. "So raiding and looting is a game to you?"

He spread his hands out helplessly, waving his plucked bird. "What would you have us do? In the north, winter lasts eight months. Some years, all that stood between us and starvation was a sack or two of looted flour. If you had a houseful of whimpering children, wasting away for lack of food, you'd go raiding too."

"You couldn't trade for food?"

"Oh, perhaps." He laid the bird on a rock. "We do trade with Veleti, mostly wood and ore." He picked up a handful of small sticks and laid them on the sand. "But you don't understand. Every minute spent making something to sell, whether fine jewelry or leather shoes or carved wood, that was a minute not spent feeding our families or defending against attacks from the savages from Tarhuntassia and Kassia. And before you suggest making treaties with them, save your breath. Their gods demand sacrifices of blood, plunder, and fear."

While she didn't agree with his reasoning, she understood what drove the northerners to raid the more prosperous south. She lifted her gaze from the bloody bird in her hands. "You don't enjoy raiding."

"No." His tone became pensive. "Oh, we laugh and boast and sing songs in praise of the boldest raiders. But it's not a peaceful life, always wondering if your wife or sister or daughter will be the next one captured." He balled up a tuft of seagrass and tucked it under his pile of kindling.

"You did the same to Ymittos and our southern vassals."

He reached into his boot and pulled out Derya's dagger.

She stiffened. Was he about to show her what barbarians did to captive women? She reached inside and began pooling her magic. *If he so much as twitches a finger in my direction, I'll boil his eyeballs.*

44

"I DIDN'T." ANGER sharpened Stigandr's tone. He stuck the dagger through a loop of seagrass and sliced it, making a shorter length. His chains rattled. "Some did, yes. But I never permitted my crews to steal any of the women. Food, animals, anything of value . . . yes. But we left the girls alone."

He was so indignant, Derya almost believed him.

"Violating women, that's despicable," he went on in a harsher tone. He struck the dagger against a stone. A tiny spark flared and went out. "I saw what Kharan-Khuag did to you. For that one crime, I'll chop off his hands and fling them in a fire. After I do the same to his shriveled manhood. Or rip out his liver and feed it to the crows."

His unexpected protectiveness made tears prick her eyes. He struck the blade again, and this time the spark caught the seagrass alight. Within a few moments, he had a steady fire blazing.

Stigandr gestured with her dagger. "Those water fae didn't take this from you?"

"With my hands chained to a rock? Why would they bother?"

He smiled, and with one slice, cut open a bird. He scraped the entrails out, stabbed a hole in the bird's body, and stuck a long stick of birch through it. "Here," he said, handing it to Derya. "Show me your cooking skills."

"Prepare to be astounded." She held the carcass over the flames. "Do you have any spices?"

Stigandr snorted. "Not unless you call sea salt a spice." He finished cleaning the second bird and speared it. "This would be another fitting end for Kharan-Khuag. I'd love to hear him squeal."

She would too. The smell of roasting meat made her realize how hungry she was. She shoved aside thoughts of the sorcerer and put her attention to her steaming bird.

When she could wait no longer, Derya ripped meat from the bird's leg, singeing her fingers. She moaned as the warm meat filled her mouth. *Raging winds. It must have been three days since I've eaten.* They ate in silence, sucking the meat from the bones like animals.

Stigandr wiped his mouth. "Maybe feeding Kharan-Khuag to a dragon would be the best end for him."

"That's about the fourth way you've come up with to kill him."

The king hurled the stick his bird had cooked on, tossing it like a spear at a nearby rock. "I've had plenty of time to dwell on it." His face hardened. "Six long weeks," he said in a flat tone.

Derya's chest tightened. She'd been a captive for five days, and her spirit had nearly failed. "What did he do to you?"

Stigandr glared at her. "What didn't he do? Name a torture, a deviant act, he or his minions did it. The only thing they didn't do was carry out their threats to cut off valuable body parts. Just to keep that fear alive."

Now that he'd started speaking, it seemed he couldn't stop. "Worst was how they toyed with me. Cutting, slicing, groping, fondling, seeking to cause the most pain and humiliation.

When they found a torture they particularly enjoyed, they'd heal me so they could do it all over again." His mouth twisted into a snarl. "I decided I'd rather them kill me than answer their questions about the scepter." He took a long breath and hung his head. "It was getting harder and harder to not tell them where it might be. I had no idea you had it."

"I must have taken it about a week after your capture."

"That's when they started playing rough."

Guilt stabbed Derya's heart. Her success made the king's torment worse. "I'm sorry."

Stigandr didn't seem to hear her. "I begged the Rider to end my life." He took a shuddering breath. "I don't know what was worse. The pain. The taunting. The degradation." His voice cracked.

Tears rolled down Derya's face. Her gaze met his watering eyes. Suddenly she was in his arms, weeping out her terror and relief on his shoulder. He was sobbing as well, his grief pouring from him in deep gasps of agony.

When her emotions subsided, she became aware of his strong arms wrapped around her, lost in the embrace of a man she barely trusted. Embarrassed by her vulnerability, she scooted away from him.

His face flushed, and she guessed he was equally abashed. She ducked her head and began digging in the sand with a small stick.

"There was one night." He picked up his story as if there'd been no emotional interruption. She glanced up to see his face contort. He winced. "Brutal, even for them. I passed out watching my blood pool on the floor, thinking that was the end, they'd decided to kill me." He tipped his head to the side. "I woke up chained to a rock. With you."

His raw pain sent a surge of heavy grief over her, and she clutched the stick in her fingers, afraid that hearing more of his torment would shatter her. "I'm sorry I wasn't able to receive you more politely."

He chuckled. "You dragged me back from the edge. At least sparring with you took my mind off everything else. And if truth be told, your snide comments and bold opposition gave me new courage."

If only you knew. His insolent bravery had bolstered her strength. She wasn't sure she'd admit that to him, not quite yet. "Speaking of opposition, what should we do next?"

"Go to Rorvik."

"My fleet isn't there."

"But my home is."

"My people could be in danger." *And I led them into it, fool that I am. Are they even still alive?*

"If that's true, then you'll need reinforcements."

She snorted. "Your people won't help."

"They would if I commanded them. After all, you saved my life, proving that at least one Cinarrian isn't rotten like an egg left in the sun."

For the first moment in days, she felt she could control the course of her life instead of being tossed by the waves. "Going north would waste time."

"Blasted woman." His chuckle made her think he was enjoying the sparring as much as she was.

"I could abandon you here."

"Oh? How will you get the raft into the water without my help?"

He had a point. She couldn't lift the raft, let alone drag it to the sea. She narrowed her eyes. Was that the reason he moved it far from the shore?

He added a few sticks to the crackling flames. "No wonder the Pasargadians are trying to kill you."

She scoffed. "Of course they are. We've been enemies for centuries."

Stigandr clucked his tongue. "So you don't know."

"Know what?"

He smirked. "Maybe I shouldn't tell. Or only tell you if

you promise to take me to Rorvik." He dug in the sand, creating a small hole.

He was getting more annoying by the minute. "What could you know that would interest me?"

"Oh, quite a bit. Like how to annoy bossy princesses. And how to eavesdrop on conversations you're not meant to hear."

"Eavesdroppers never hear anything good." She spoke primly.

He swept the pile of bird entrails into the hole and covered them with sand. "I didn't say I overheard something good. I said it was useful."

"Who were you listening to?"

"Kharan-Khuag."

Derya's eyes widened. "What did he say?"

"Mind you, he'd already had me beaten to half-consciousness."

"You can drag this on all night if you enjoy hearing yourself talk so much."

Stigandr chortled. "A fae reported the last attempt on a woman's life—and I'm guessing that meant you—was unsuccessful. The Pasargadian agent in her entourage had failed again."

Derya froze, staring straight in front of her. Txartomal had said a man in her entourage was trying to kill her. But she'd never dreamed the assassin was in Pasargadae's employ. A seagull squawked overhead.

Stigandr spoke softly. "So there have been attempts on your life?"

"Several. Two in Nafplio, one in Ethkarpia."

"Any idea who?"

She shook her head. "No."

He cracked a stick into two pieces and tossed them on to the fire. "The fae said they'd hoped for better since the person was so close to you."

The meat in Derya's stomach hardened. She didn't want

to return to suspecting her advisors. It couldn't be Kelebek. He only joined her entourage by accident after catching wind of the plot to kill the Ymittosian royals. But Safiye and Bahadir?

"If it helps," Stigandr said, "the fae kept referring to the agent as 'he.' So you can rule out women."

Derya's shoulders lightened. Safiye, then, wasn't a suspect. And she refused to believe the assassin was Bahadir. That left her with about one hundred other candidates.

"Be reasonable, Derya. Let's go to Rorvik and raise a navy."

After her mistake last time, she should take his advice. But she couldn't help feeling that time was of the essence. "What about this?" she asked, weighing each word. "We head south. But if we see a ship headed north, you get on it. Once I've found my fleet, I'll sail to meet you."

"No," he said flatly. "You don't know where your fleet is. We head for Rorvik first."

She crossed her arms and glared at him. The insufferable man was a match for her in stubbornness. "Did your time as Kharan-Khuag's guest leave any wounds in need of healing?"

"Why, no, princess. I have a magic porpoise that heals my every ill."

She gave him as sickly-sweet of a smile as she could muster. "Since your porpoise seems to be lost, I could offer to heal you if you'd listen to reason."

"I don't need your help if you're going to be that way about it."

Her face heated. He was right. Those gouges on his back must send throbbing pain through him with every move. Dangling the prospect of relief over him to get her way was cruel. "Fine. I'll heal you. It's the least I can do after you freed me from those chains. Where are you wounded?"

He pulled his ragged tunic off and spread it on the sand. Then he lay down on it. Up close, Derya could see the extent of the damage. She sucked in a breath. *Oh, Stigandr.* She reached for her bag of amplifiers and found the bitter herbs. Once the taste filled her mouth, she began. Slowly, she pushed her magic and cleaned out the infection and knitted the torn muscles and skin back together. As she worked, she could see the tension ebb from him, and it almost appeared as if he was sleeping.

"That's the best I can do with your back," she said.

He flipped over to expose his muscled torso. More half-healed gouges and lash marks crisscrossed his chest, some extending to his arms and neck. She pushed her magic into the wounds, finishing with his black eye. She frowned at the result. "I'm not a very skilled healer," she began.

He looked at her from under his drooping eyelids. "Empress of healers in my mind."

She laughed. "And you are the king of cooks."

"Life would be simpler if that's who we really were. A healer and a cook."

Her breath hitched. A simple life with a man, just as a cook and a healer, untroubled by sorcerers and empires and assassins. Life with a man she could trust to not have designs on her throne. It held a tantalizing appeal. "There. That's as good as I can do."

He sat up. "Thank you a thousand times for each mended scratch and scrape."

"Did I get them all?"

He shook his head and smirked. "My modesty forbids me to show you any more."

She scoffed. "Right. Then let's leave. My fleet probably returned to Nafplio."

He shook the sand from his tunic and pulled it over his head. "We can go there after we obtain ships. And weapons. I don't want to be caught on that raft a—"

His gasp made her jerk to look at him. He froze, his eyes bulged and his mouth fell open, slack and wide.

Are you humans going to argue all day?

That voice in her head. It couldn't be. Derya started and scrambled to her feet. "Habeci?"

The gleaming white pegasus stood a few yards away, flaring its wings and tossing its mane.

She sprinted to it. "How did you find me?"

The Rider told me to help you.

"Why now? Why not when I was a prisoner?"

To help both of you. Together.

Scuffling noises told her Stigandr was cautiously approaching. "You do know winged horses are dangerous?"

"So they tell me." She stroked Habeci's long nose. "But this one's . . ." She almost said "a friend" but stopped herself. It felt presumptuous to call such a resplendent creature her friend.

Make haste. You have a task.

"We need to go," Derya told Stigandr.

"On the pegasus?"

"Of course. Unless you're scared." She scooped up her cloak and wrapped it around her shoulders.

He snorted and stamped out their fire. With a smooth motion, he boosted her onto Habeci's back. A moment later, he vaulted to sit behind her.

"Habeci," Derya said aloud. "Will you take us to my fleet?"

"No, to Rorvik," Stigandr said.

Foolish humans, we go where the Rider sends me. The pegasus leaped into the air, flapped his wings, and soared west.

45

CHILLY WIND BLEW Derya's hair around her face, and her heart lunged into her throat. Habeci was flying west toward the lands Kharan-Khuag had already conquered. "Habeci?"

The pegasus flapped its wings harder. The foamy tops of the gray waves grew smaller, and the roaring surf diminished, leaving only the wind in her ears and the beats of Habeci's wings telling her she hadn't gone deaf. A lone seagull flew underneath and dove to the water, soaring up with a fish in its hooked beak.

Derya tightened her knees on Habeci's withers and buried her fingers in his shining mane. A smile tugged at the corners of her mouth. This thrill of flight would never get old. It was all the more glorious since she'd never hoped to experience this joy again.

Habeci banked to turn slightly north. Derya leaned against the motion, trying to keep her balance. The muscular arms wrapped around her waist tightened. She stiffened as Stigandr pressed his chest against her back.

"I hope you don't mind, princess. But I'd rather not end up in the sea."

"Had enough swimming this week?"

He snorted. "For this year. And maybe the next. Where are we going?"

"All Habeci said is to wherever the Rider sends him." *This is like living in an ancient legend.* A sudden thought took her breath away. *The Rider rarely intervened, and only as a warning that matters were about to turn dire.*

"How do you know what he says?"

"I can't explain, but we read each other's thoughts. Sometimes. It's all very odd and unsettling."

"I can see why." He shifted his seat as Habeci banked to avoid a wispy cloud.

They flew without speaking for the better part of an hour, or so Derya guessed by the motion of the sun to her left. She tucked her freezing toes against Habeci's sides and shivered. Stigandr pulled her closer to him. *I shouldn't be enjoying this. That's how I got in trouble with his brother.*

The king nudged her. "There."

She looked down. Dark blotches sprawled on the sea like a gigantic map. As they neared, she could see mountain peaks covered with lush forests, surrounded by hilly fields. Gleaming white beaches edged the islands, ringed with turquoise water that darkened farther from shore.

But what should have been idyllic islands were no more. She spotted the largest island, Guanches, where the king's castle was a blackened ruin. Lanzare, the farthest east, was a faint shadow, its harbor town no more than a gaping wound on the beach. Closer were Cofeta, Jable, and Pirador, their devastated towns, cities, and ports ragged scars on what had been beautiful lands. Derya's vision blurred, and she blinked away the tears that stung her eyes, tears that had nothing to do with the icy wind in her face.

Habeci turned toward the tiny, northernmost island of Quenyo. As they descended, she spotted two ships near its harbor. A mob of several hundred people crowded the beach, surrounded by what looked like karcharia and mutant water fae.

"Is this why the Rider summoned us?" Derya asked. "To rescue the people?"

Habeci didn't answer. He circled the ships, sinking lower. No banners flew to announce whose ships they were. The people onboard stared upward. A few brandished swords. Derya strained to see if she recognized anyone.

Tell the humans to get out of my way.

She waved frantically at the people on deck. "Stand aside!"

At first, no one moved. As the pegasus descended, the people scrambled backward. Derya's hair whipped her eyes, and she shoved it back, trying to catch a glimpse of a familiar face.

The pegasus landed on deck, his hoofs making soft thuds. *Farewell, Heir of Cinar. The rest of this day is up to you.*

Stigandr slid from the horse. He put his hands around Derya's waist and swung her down. Her bare feet slapped the wooden deck.

She patted Habeci's neck. "Thank you, I think. Will I see you again?"

Only the Rider knows. Oh, and he said to tell you to not forget about Malkh. The horse spread his wings, leaped in the air, and flew away.

She had no time to puzzle over what his words meant. The people were cheering.

"Kiral! Kiral!"

Now she noticed them, a handful of people in Cinarrian black and turquoise, all with awestruck expressions on their faces. Her hands tingled, and a heavy weight lifted from her shoulders. At least some of her entourage had survived. A wide smile pulled her lips apart.

A pair of arms seized Derya into a hug and a woman murmured her name. "You're hurt."

"Safiye?" Derya returned the embrace, sinking into the familiar comfort of her danisman's arms. "I'm fine. You're alive." The worry she'd carried in her chest for days eased.

Safiye released Derya. "I'm so sorry."

Derya felt a pang as she studied the dark circles under Safiye's eyes. "Why, that you survived?"

"No, Kiral," said Bahadir. "We abandoned you."

Derya's heart skipped a beat as she peered into his face. "You what?"

"When you went overboard," Bahadir explained. "Nazif tried to go after you, but we wouldn't let him." He shook his head. "He would have died, and . . ."

Nazif wanted to come after her? That was surprising. She studied Bahadir's drooping eyelids and red-rimmed tired eyes. She grinned and gripped his arm. "Chiliarch, I am delighted to see you."

"And I you, Kiral."

"What's a kiral?" Stigandr said.

"What are you doing here?" Bahadir asked coldly. "I should kill you for what you did to the kiral." Steel rasped as he drew his sword.

Derya moved between him and the king. "Let me introduce you. Chiliarch Bahadir, commander of my entourage. Danisman Safiye, my counselor and advisor." She paused, anticipating their shocked reactions. "Stigandr Tyr, king of Rorvik."

Bahadir scowled. "We've met."

Derya grinned. "No, you haven't." She pushed her tangled hair from her face. "We've got a lot to catch up on. Can you arrange for some food? Healers? And fresh clothes for both of us?" She gestured at her tattered clothing and bare feet.

The scars on Bahadir's cheek twitched, and he dispatched a soldier on the errand.

"Shouldn't you be fighting the water fae?" Stigandr asked.

Bahadir glared at him. "We tried, but they pushed us back

and issued an ultimatum. Surrender or they kill all the islanders. They gave us three hours to decide."

Derya surveyed the crowd on the beach, most wearing the black tunics and dresses of the western islanders. Even at this distance, she could see their gold-embroidered clothing was ragged and torn. "How much time remains?" Derya asked.

"Two hours."

"Then we have time to prepare." Stigandr rubbed his scruffy jaw where chunks of his beard had been torn out.

The deck tilted and a sail snapped as the wind shifted. Derya staggered to regain her balance. "It's a long story. Do you mind if we sit while we talk?" She settled on the deck near the mast and leaned against it. Stigandr, Bahadir, and Safiye joined her.

"It's like this . . ." Derya told of her captivity, her meeting with the real Stigandr, and how they worked together to escape. "Chiliarch, is there someone who could remove those shackles?"

He eyed Stigandr with suspicion. "Are you sure?"

"Yes. If not for him, I'd still be chained to that rock." She shuddered.

Bahadir scrutinized Stigandr's face. "He's skinnier than the other one." The chiliarch let out a sigh. "I don't know. His story makes sense, but it's hard to believe."

"Look at his face," Safiye said. "See the eyes? This is a different man."

Derya wasn't sure what Safiye observed but was grateful for the support. "He is," she said.

"There's a blacksmith on board," Bahadir said.

"Good. Please fetch him." After the chiliarch sent a soldier for the smith, Derya continued. "What happened after I was captured?"

A shadow fell over her. She looked up to see her grinning food taster holding a tray with steaming tin mugs and hunks of dried meat and hard bread. Never had shipboard food looked so appealing.

The princess nodded her thanks for both the food and her taster's professions of joy at her return, took the tray, and set it on the deck between her and Stigandr. She grabbed a mug and sipped the hot tea, savoring the warmth as it flowed down her throat. Stigandr was already gnawing on a stick of dried beef.

Bahadir picked up the story. "We were down to four ships. Following your orders, Lord Nazif had us sail west. There was no pursuit, so we assumed that once Cetus had you, he lost interest in us."

"Four ships? I only see two."

"One of King Ollen's returned to Veleti with their wounded." Bahadir's lip curled. "As for the other, I regret to tell you, Kiral, your cousin abruptly changed his mind and insisted on returning to Cinar to inform your father personally of your demise."

Derya scowled. So much for wanting to rescue her. Nazif preferred to assert his right to be named Heir of Cinar. *Raging waters*. She'd deal with him later. "Why are you here?"

"Lord Nazif sailed off in the fastest vessel. We decided rather than obeying his command to return to Cinar, we'd follow your last orders and save the islanders. We sailed a day and a night before getting caught in a storm that blew us southeast for two days. After it passed, we set course for the east, planning to restock in Axum before continuing. But a strange current dragged us northwest. We ended up here only a few hours ago."

She chewed a piece of hard bread and washed it down with tea. Picking up a slice of dried meat, she gestured at the shore. "What's happening there?"

"With the survivors of the invasion?" He shrugged. "We intended to rescue as many as we could. Then the fae surrounded them and gave their ultimatum. We were debating what to do when you showed up."

Heavy footsteps made the deck creak. A man with huge sloping shoulders and bulging arms stood next to Stigandr. The man held a massive chisel and hammer in one hand. She winced. The hammer looked like it could crack a man's thigh bone.

Stigandr stretched out his right leg. The smith slid a board underneath the shackle and placed the chisel against the steel around his ankle. "This could take a while to break," he said, his deep voice rumbling like distant thunder.

The king waved a hand. "Take your time. Just don't break me."

The smith grunted. He pointed to his assistant. "Hold it still. You too," he added to Stigandr.

The assistant knelt next to Stigandr and took hold of the chisel. He held it upright with one hand and steadied the shackle with the other.

A muscle rippled in Stigandr's jaw. "Go ahead."

The smith struck a clanging blow, then another.

"Speaking of broken, where are the healers?" Derya asked, raising her voice to be heard over the bangs of the hammer.

"One is waiting for you in our cabin," Safiye said. She touched the half-healed scar where Cetus had gouged Derya's cheek. "Garzuli is seeing to some hot water. Are you hurt anywhere else?"

"Just a few scrapes. Stigandr is worse off."

The smith grunted and swung the hammer again. The shackle fell off with a clatter. While the smith wiped the sweat from his face, Stigandr flexed his foot and frowned at the raw wound that circled his ankle. At the smith's direction, he stretched out his other leg, placing his foot on the board. The clanging resumed.

Derya crossed her arms. "So, we have two hours. Why not fight the fae and save the islanders?

Bahadir scrubbed a hand over his face. "We can't."

Defeat weighed Bahadir's tone, and Derya looked at him in surprise. "Why not?"

"There's a monster. A vicious dragon that never sleeps."

"Well, I have killed a dragon . . ."

"But, Kiral, it was asleep when you attacked it. That's an advantage you won't have now."

Clanging chains hit the deck. Stigandr's left ankle was free. He grunted, leaned forward and rested his right arm on the board. The blacksmith's assistant placed the chisel. The smith struck the chisel with a clang.

"There's more," put in Safiye.

Derya let out a huff. "What else could go wrong?"

Safiye pointed to the shore. "The people are bound together with magical golden cords that can only be unlocked with a golden key."

Derya narrowed her eyes, noting Safiye's worry and Bahadir's resignation. She let her shoulders slump. "Don't tell me. The sleepless dragon is guarding the key."

Bahadir nodded and lifted his head. "Did you notice who else is on the beach?"

She walked to the rail and squinted, putting a hand over her eyes to shield them from the sun's glare. "Who are those people near the forest?"

Bahadir joined her. "If you thought the water fae were bad, meet the mutant forest fae." He shook his head. "Cetus outdid himself with these creatures. He attached the heads of wild boars on the fae, complete with long tusks. They've got tiger's claws on their hands and feet. One slash can cut your arm off."

A deep voice uttered a string of curses. Derya smiled to herself. Even though she didn't fully understand the

Rorvikian, it was obvious he was denigrating the forest fae, their parentage, and the sorcerer who spawned them. The smith muttered something, and the clanging resumed.

Safiye leaned on the rail on Derya's other side. "Really, Kiral, are you going to tolerate this barbarian's language?"

Derya shrugged. "He is King Stigandr Tyr of Rorvik. A valuable ally in our war with Cetus." She softened her tone. "After we win it, we can give him a lesson in courteous speech." She glanced at Stigandr, who sat as if frozen with his eyes closed. The hammer struck the chisel, and a muscle in the king's jaw twitched. *Impressive that he's so still when that hammer could shatter his wrist.*

Safiye put a hand on Derya's arm. "Did you hear the chiliarch? We can't defeat these monsters any more than the islanders could."

Derya hesitated. They'd barely escaped the water fae. The forest fae were far more formidable. And a sleepless dragon. Her head drooped, and she gazed at her scraped, dirty feet. It seemed impossible. Maybe Nazif had the right idea. Return to Cinar and plead with her father to muster his navy. She would have failed in her quest and might be deposed as heir. But Cinar's military was the best hope for defeating Cetus.

She took a deep breath, a sense of defeat weighing on her. A seagull's squawk made her glance up as it soared overhead. But this was where Habeci brought her. *If the Rider wills it . . .*

"I don't see any other course but to try," Derya said. She stiffened her shoulders. "If we don't, those people on the beach will die. Or worse, become Cetus's toys." She strode back to the king and waited for the smith to complete another clanging strike. "Now, King Stigandr, what do you think? We slay the dragon and as many of those forest fae as we can, retrieve the key, and rescue the survivors? Are you with me?"

Stigandr grinned. "You'd make a good raider, princess. I like that attitude. No foe is too big."

"May I remind you of how easily the water fae and shark-headed men ate through our fleet?" Safiye asked.

"I haven't forgotten." Derya shuddered, thinking of the fierce battle that ended up with her sliding overboard into the repulsive embrace of the water fae. "But Habeci said the Rider commanded him to bring us here. If not to fight these monsters, then why?"

Bahadir and Safiye exchanged long glances. Several more clangs filled the silence. Derya crossed her arms, waiting.

"I can't argue with that, Kiral," Bahadir said. "But we need a new strategy."

"Do you have spears?" Stigandr asked.

"Yes," Bahadir said. "But the shark-men bite through them."

"You mean the karcharia?" Stigandr smirked. "I wasn't the one wielding the spear."

Bahadir bristled

"Ignore him," Derya told the chiliarch. "But you might want to give him a spear."

Another series of clangs, and the shackle fell from Stigandr's wrist. He shook his hand and scowled at the twisting scars, ugly reminders of how Cetus burned him. He rested his left arm on the board. "Last one."

After a few clangs, Bahadir shouted to a soldier. "Bring me ten spears." He turned to Derya. "You can never have too many weapons."

"I like him," Stigandr said. "Princess, is there time for a bath? And those clean clothes you were talking about?"

"Absolutely. And healers."

He nodded. "If it's not too much trouble, I want to shave." He ran a hand over his inch-long ragged beard.

"What?" Bahadir asked. "You're about to fight a dragon, and you're worried about your looks?"

"Of course," Stigandr said. "You never know if this day is

your last. It's important to make sure you look your best when you go to the afterlife."

Of course. "How could I forget?" Derya ran a hand over her tangled, salt-crusted hair. *Maybe I need to look my best, too. Just in case this day is my last.*

46

DERYA GRIPPED THE ship's rail so tightly her knuckles ached. The waves below churned and slapped the ship, as if they, too, were anxious for the battle to begin. She tipped her face to the sun, letting the gentle breeze caress her still-damp, braided hair. In her haste, she'd allowed Safiye and Garzuli to assist her with only a quick sponge bath and a hurried rinse of her hair. The healer mended Derya's wounds and expressed the hope she'd gotten to them in time to prevent any scars.

Dressed in clean clothes, all Derya could do was wait. She wiggled her toes, reveling in the comfort of thick socks and soft boots. After a week barefoot in the cold, warm feet were a luxury she would never take for granted. She rested a hand on the hilt of her sword, Hrathung, the gift from the swans she'd saved from Cetus's curse. *Thank the Rider I didn't have it on me when I was captured. Hrathung is our best hope for killing the dragon. But we have to get past the fae first.*

Soft footsteps behind her heralded Garzuli. "As you commanded, I replenished your amplifiers." She held up two small pouches. "I've one for the king as well."

"Thank you," Derya said. She took one and fastened it to her belt.

"Where are the spears?" Stigandr's voice boomed.

Derya whirled to face him. Gone was the ragged captive with a wounded face and ragged beard. Now his clean-shaven, newly healed face stole the air from her lungs. She hadn't noticed how strong the planes of his jaw were. Dressed in Cinarrian black and turquoise, his gray eyes turned a sensual blue.

He ran his gaze over her and gave her a fleeting smile, so rapid she almost missed it. "Do you have a metal or wood mage?"

"Garzuli is a metal mage. What do you need her for?"

"Infusing the spears." He sat on the deck near the pile of spears Bahadir had collected, gesturing for the girl to join him. Soon, they were both at work. Garzuli infused the metal tips with her magic, and he did the same for the wooden shafts.

Heavy footsteps approached, and she felt Bahadir's steady presence before she turned to him. "Kiral, we're about ready. The Veletians will send six landing boats to the left. We'll take ours to the right."

"And at the first opportunity, the king and I go after the dragon." She pursed her lips. "Are we sure King Ollen's men will fight with us?"

"They signaled that they will." Bahadir ran a hand over his hair. "I hope they don't turn on us when this is over."

Derya hoped so too. "You're sure Farooq understands his part?"

Bahadir nodded. "He didn't like staying out of the battle but won't flout a direct order from you. If all goes badly, he sails to Cinar and informs your father." He gave her a wry smile. "The way he talks about you and that winged horse, you'll become a legend."

If any survive to remember me.

"And you understand your part?"

"Yes, chiliarch. I stay by the boats until the king and I can get past the forest fae." When he didn't look convinced, she put a hand on his arm. "I promise."

Stigandr stood up in a single fluid motion, the muscles in his thighs bulging under the black trousers. He swung the spears onto his shoulder. "Are we going to talk or fight?"

For answer, Derya climbed into one of the small landing boats and was joined by Bahadir, Stigandr, and nine warriors. The king sat and held the spears vertically between his knees, embracing them like a lover.

"You and your brother are the same," Derya said. "Fascinated with pointy objects."

"Kiral . . ." Bahadir said.

"I apologize, chiliarch," Derya said. "But it's true."

She was rewarded with a snort from the king and chuckles from the soldiers. She gave Bahadir a shrug.

His lips twitched. "And that, Kiral, is why so many are loyal to you. You never stop laughing. Even in grave danger."

If only you knew that my knees are shaking so hard I don't think I could walk. That I'm about to vomit. Or wet myself.

Once the boat had been lowered to the water, Stigandr handed spears to seven of the warriors, retaining three for himself. "See what you can do with these," he said. To Derya, his tone sounded like a weapons master handing practice swords to an inept group of students.

One soldier laughed. "You might learn something from us."

Stigandr snickered. "Are all Cinarrians this amusing?"

By the time the twelve boats reached shore, it was lined with scores of the mutant forest fae. The islanders huddled together farther up the beach, bound by the golden tether. The water fae and karcharia had vanished into the sea. *I hope that means they'll leave the forest fae to do the fighting.*

Bahadir jumped out of the boat, splashing in the tumbling

surf. Around them, warriors from the other boats followed. With a shout, Bahadir led a charge to the right. Stigandr leaped into the water. He extended a hand to Derya. "Coming, princess?"

She smiled. "You think of the most exotic entertainments." She took his hand and stepped into the cold, churning water.

Bahadir's sword split the face of a forest fae, loosing a torrent of mossy-green blood. A forest fae extended its long claws. It slashed and tore at the arms of the Cinarrian next to Bahadir, cutting through his leather armor as if it was silk. With a swipe of its claw, it severed the man's metal shield as if it were an overripe pear.

"Huh." Stigandr shifted two spears into his left hand. "Are you ready?"

"I've been waiting for you." *Can I go back to the ship?*

Stigandr let out a bellow and hurled a spear into the open jaws of a forest fae. The point protruded from the back of its skull. He summoned the weapon to return to his hand before the corpse hit the sand. He whirled and stabbed another in the eye, then sidestepped to allow Bahadir to chop off the fae's head.

Derya watched transfixed as Stigandr spun and thrust, ducked and blocked. He threw one spear and skewered two of the fae, allowing the soldiers to finish them off. He threw two more spears. They impaled another pair of fae. With a wave of his hand, he recalled his weapons.

Five of the mutant fae charged Bahadir. He slashed at them, removing the head of one. Green blood squirted into the air. Another leapt on him and bit his left shoulder. He jerked, his face contorted with pain. A second fae sliced his calf with a long, outstretched claw. The chiliarch toppled to the sand.

Four snarling fae loomed over him. They held up their extended claws. One kicked Bahadir, the talons of its foot slicing through the chiliarch's armor. Through the tattered leather, Derya saw scarlet gouges on his back.

Derya stifled a scream. No, she couldn't lose Bahadir. She pulled at her magic while anger pulsed through her veins. Those mutant fae were going to die.

With a mighty shout, Stigandr hurled a spear. It drove through two of the fae and they toppled on top of Bahadir. With a flick of his wrist, Stigandr yanked the spear out of the dead fae. The weapon soared back to his hand.

By the time he caught it, he'd already hurled a second. It gored the belly of another fae.

Four others massed on Stigandr. Derya watched with an open mouth. The way Stigandr battled with his spears was a complicated dance. He leapt, he spun, he stabbed. Muscles bulged under his sweat-soaked clothing. Determination hardened his face to resemble a warrior carved in stone. *How can such a big man move so gracefully?*

Nazif, famed for his skill at single combat, wasn't as lethal a fighter. More amazing were Stigandr's speed and stamina, even after his long captivity. What had he been like before? Or was an inner rage driving him to defeat the sorcerer who'd tortured him?

A roar from the last fae standing over Bahadir jerked Derya from her admiration of Stigandr. The chiliarch was struggling to squirm out from under the dead fae on top of him. Another with blood dripping from its tusks slashed Bahadir's legs with its claws. Hastily pooling her magic, she pulled water from the sea and heated it. Then she flung it at the fae.

Her rage ruined her aim, and the boiling mass soared past the fae's head, splashing one pointed tusk. The fae roared and opened its jaws. Then it bent toward Bahadir.

Derya took in a shaky breath, gathered more water, and tried again. This time, her watery projectile hit the fae's foot. *Concentrate.*

Judging by the bellows, all she'd done was enrage him. And distract him for half a moment.

Which was enough. Stigandr cut down a pair of fae. He whirled and flung a spear at the roaring fae. It lodged in its throat. A second spear pierced its heart. The beast fell onto the sand, writhing.

The fae retreated from Stigandr, and the combined Cinarrian and Veletian forces looked to be prevailing. Derya could wait no more. She darted up the beach, dodging the fighters until she reached Bahadir lying in a pool of scarlet blood mixed with the green blood of forest fae. Two of the monsters lay dead on top of him.

She grabbed an arm of one of the corpses and tugged, but it didn't budge. She braced her feet, yanked, and pulled. By the time she rolled it to the side, sweat dripped down her face.

A sharp burn in her calf made her shriek. One of the fae she'd assumed was dead had clawed her leg just below the knee. It staggered to its feet, snarling.

She grabbed Bahadir's sword. *Raging waters, it was heavy.* Even with both hands, she struggled to raise it higher than her waist. With a scream, she shoved it at the fae's throat, putting all her weight behind it.

The fae's roar turned into a gurgle. It tumbled over, Derya on top of it. She lost her grip on the blade and the sword fell from her grasp.

A rough hand seized her tunic and yanked her to her feet. "If you're going to play with corpses, princess, make sure they're dead first." Stigandr stooped over the scattered fae, slitting each one's throat with a long knife.

Then he hoisted the dead fae still lying on Bahadir as if it weighed no more than a leg of lamb. He tossed it aside. "Are you hurt?"

She grimaced and pointed to her leg. "One of them

scratched me. But it doesn't matter." She dropped to her knees. "Chiliarch?"

He didn't respond. Scarlet poured from his shoulder. *He lives.* She tugged the torn tunic away from the wound, the fae's teeth marks distinct triangular slashes, a flap of skin and muscle dangling. Bahadir's sticky blood coated her fingers. She closed her eyes and pulled at her magic. This kind of healing was beyond her abilities.

But she had to try.

"Princess? Not all the fae are dead." Stigandr's voice held a trace of impatience.

"Take care of them, will you? I can't let him die."

"As you say."

She let her magic flow through her hand into Bahadir's shoulder. The bone was intact, but the shredded muscles made her pause. How could she reattach what had been severed? She wasn't certain what tendons and ligaments were supposed to be there. And how to stop the bleeding?

The princess pushed her magic. All she could do was imagine Bahadir's shoulder functional, healthy, and whole. She thought of him swinging a sword, making a salute, calming his horse.

A soldier dropped beside her. "Kiral, I can take over."

"How did you know I needed help?"

The soldier pointed at Stigandr, who was dueling the last fighting fae. Kentarch Sezgin was already sorting out the wounded Cinarrians and Veletians from the dead, laying them out in rows on the beach. Soldiers were piling up the dead fae.

Derya, though reluctant to leave Bahadir, knew she and Stigandr must go. This young soldier could carry on. "I did the best I could with his shoulder but didn't finish. And I didn't even start his other wounds."

The young man nodded, concern in his tawny eyes. "I'll take care of him, Kiral."

Stigandr ambled over, his three spears resting on one

shoulder. He looked like a man who'd been sparring for pleasure, not one fresh from battling deadly foes. And by the
Rider, he was strong. Maybe they did stand a chance against
the dragon.

"Princess, how is Bahadir?"

"He'll live. After that, I don't know."

"And you?"

"I'm fine." She looked him up and down. The only blood
on him was the mossy green of the fae. "I don't have to ask
about you."

"I told you I can handle a spear." He stared at the forest.
"Hope all this racket hasn't riled up the dragon."

The sleepless dragon.

Her mouth tasted of ash, as if she'd been singed by a
dragon's flaming breath. She pulled her waterskin from where
it hung on her belt and drank, watching the soldier expertly
heal Bahadir's injuries. Healing the wounds so quickly might
mean he wouldn't end up with more scars.

"Soldier," she said, "will the chiliarch be able to use his
shoulder?"

The man shook his head. "That, Kiral, we won't know for
a while. This kind of healing takes time, you know. He'll have
to retrain the muscles. But you did a fine job." He frowned.
"You're wounded too. May I?"

She'd forgotten about the slash on her leg in her concern
for Bahadir. "Please." She extended her leg, pulling her
trouser leg up to reveal the shallow gash in her flesh.

The soldier nodded. "He only grazed you. But I'm sure it
stings." He waved a hand and the wound closed, leaving only
a scarlet line of blood.

Stigandr—the man seemed to have boundless energy, or
did the thrill of battle replenish him—was guzzling water,
collecting weapons from the fallen, and tossing dead fae into
piles.

He bounded over to Derya, Kentarch Sezgin in tow. "Are

you ready, princess?" The king sounded as if they were about to attend a feast after having fasted for forty days.

She held a hand to him, pleased her fingers didn't tremble and betray her fear. "I'd be delighted to have you assist me."

He let out a guffaw. "We'll see who assists who." He pulled her up to stand next to him as easily as if she was a small child.

She jerked her head at Sezgin. "The kentarch will oversee things here."

"Let's hope the fae take a while to plan their next move," Stigandr said. "I'm not sure what will happen if they attack before we return."

Derya followed his gaze from the dark, brooding inland woods to the writhing surf. Either could hide more blood-thirsty fae. And karcharia. Or something worse. She nodded curtly, impatient to start before dread froze her in place. "Then let's get to it." She took a gulp of water. "Which way to the dragon?"

47

S TIGANDR SHRUGGED. "Why don't you ask them?" He pointed a spear at the mob of cowering people.

A warm breeze wafted the stench of fear over Derya, stinging her nose and turning her stomach. Derya stared at the huddled mass. Hundreds herded together like cattle, or worse, like refuse. How many had wet or soiled themselves? And how long had the magical cords ensnared them? A few babies were crying, as were several men.

The princess took a few steps toward the survivors. Thin chains shimmered in the sunlight and wove among the people, binding them together, held in place by a large golden lock.

"Kiral, if I may." One of Bahadir's sub-kentarchs spoke up. He pointed with his sword. "The scouts say that way. About a quarter of a mile along the trail."

She shuddered. *So close.* "Thank you. And thank the chiliarch. Take him to the ship as soon as you can."

With a final glance at Bahadir, who was trying to sit up, she turned and stalked toward the forest. Her boots crunched on the white sand. Stigandr marched next to her, matching his pace to hers.

"Are you sure," she asked, "that no forest fae are preparing to jump us?"

"No. So be alert. But I don't think they'll attack. After that beating we gave them, my guess is they'll let the dragon take care of us."

It was generous of him to say "we." He'd been the unstoppable, magnificent force that beat back the forest fae. Without Stigandr, her soldiers might have won the day but suffered heavier losses. And she hadn't contributed much to the battle. It had been him, all him, with those graceful whirls and thrusts of the spear, the rapid use of magic to hurl and retrieve his weapons, and that awe-inspiring intrepid courage to face down monstrous foes.

His efficient slaying held a mesmerizing beauty, his arms wielding the spears in a blur of motion with lethal skill. Her thoughts slipped to the memory of those arms wrapped around her, offering consolation, sparking a yearning for more of his touch.

This man would be a valuable ally if she could trust him. *Or maybe he could be something else . . .* She shoved aside the reckless desire bubbling within her. *Stop. This is a battlefield. You've a dragon to kill.*

Stigandr paused about twenty feet from the woods, staring at a narrow trail that led between the pines. The forest was still, the branches of the conifers motionless, as if cast into stone.

"Are you sure this is the right path?" Derya asked.

He held a hand to his lips, gesturing for her to lower her voice, then pointed at a tree with a thick, gnarled trunk that stood apart from the forest. Overhead, its branches spread out like a parasol covered with dense, sword-shaped leaves.

"A dragon tree," she whispered.

He scooped up a fallen leaf from the ground and ripped it. Crimson sap dripped like blood from the dark green leaf. "It is."

Derya stared at the dripping sap. Healers prized it for its supposed medicinal properties. She picked up a handful of leaves and stuffed them in the pouch that held her amplifiers. "These might be useful." *If we live.*

He bent and put his mouth close to Derya's ear, his breath tickling her skin. "Be ready."

Easy for him to say. He was the one carrying magical spears. She had Hrathung, three full waterskins, and her magic. She hoped they would be enough.

Stigandr advanced between the trees, moving as silently as a mountain lion stalking prey. She followed in his footsteps, putting her feet where his had just left, trying to keep from crunching the dry twigs. No birds chirped, no buzzing of insects broke the silence. No small animals disturbed the underbrush. Fear of the dragon must have driven them away. *Smart animals.*

She breathed through her mouth, taking slow breaths, partly to be quiet, and partly to keep her rising fear at bay. It had been one thing to attack a sleeping dragon. This sleepless one couldn't be taken by surprise. They'd have one chance to kill it. If they got even that.

Far too soon, Stigandr slowed his pace. The trees ahead were thinning. *We must be close.* Her heart raced and sweat dampened her palms. She clamped her jaws together. *I will not whimper.*

Stigandr paused. She peeked around him. In the center of a clearing stood a massive dragon, its face turned away from them. The ground was sere and black, as if the beast had burned all life to cinders.

Gold and black scales covered its back, topped with spiky plates along its spine. Its long tail ended in six spikes, each the length of Derya's arm. The beast stood on legs like pillars, its claws gouging deep ruts into the ground.

Derya let her gaze travel to the beast's head. She could only see one angry vermilion eye, the pupil black like a night without moon or stars. She felt if she looked into its eyes, she'd dissolve into nothing.

I am the Heir of Cinar. I will not be shaken. She pulled at her magic. "Just say the word," she muttered.

"No time like the present."

He took a step into the clearing. "Ho! Dragon! Prepare to burn your last ember."

Derya frowned. Was he trying to insult the dragon? If he was, his taunt was rather lame. And perhaps not the best way to engage.

The dragon turned toward them and opened its maw, snarling. Two rows of yellowed, spiky teeth protruded. The beast tipped its head up and spewed fire and smoke into the sky.

"Fine," Stigandr said. "You don't want company." He hurled a spear at the dragon. It dug into the scales and stayed, dangling.

"You might need to throw harder," Derya said.

"Ha. Now you try. And hurry."

Was that a trace of worry in his voice? He was right to be concerned. The dragon was roaring, and smoke streamed from its nostrils. She opened the first waterskin and pulled at the water with her magic. Then she hurled it at the dragon's open throat. It sizzled against the dragon's fire and dissolved into hissing steam. The dragon jerked and stepped back a pace, shaking its head. It sucked in a breath and roared, smoke and flames pouring from its mouth.

So that didn't work.

Stigandr raced to the dragon's side. Derya grabbed the vial of peppercorns from her bag. She shook one out and placed it in her mouth, wincing as the hot pepper burned her tongue.

The king whipped his arm and let another spear fly. Shouting, he ran to a spot several yards from Derya. Their plan was to distract the dragon enough that it paid her no attention, but she had to be able to see its eye. Focusing her magic on a target she couldn't see would take time she didn't have.

She pulled at her power, concentrating on the dragon's right eye. She pushed, willing her magic to heat the fluid within. The dragon screeched, an agonized wail surging from its throat. Its eye burst in a shower of black blood.

The dragon bellowed and charged, its massive tail swinging. Stigandr shoved Derya to the side. She stumbled. The tiny vial flew from her hand, spraying peppercorns on the ground.

The king yelped. Flames licked the sleeve of his tunic. He threw himself to the ground and rolled in the ashy dirt as the dragon growled. In another heartbeat, Stigandr was on his feet, his left sleeve charred and smoking. The underbrush behind caught fire, the flames crackling as they gnawed through dried leaves and downed branches. The king roared, whether from rage or pain, Derya couldn't tell.

Where are my peppercorns? She scrabbled in the dirt. Without them, she couldn't boil the fluid in the dragon's other eye quickly enough.

A claw swiped over her head, and she scrambled back, avoiding the dragon's stomping feet by inches. It roared again and pawed at its ruined eye.

Stigandr hurled another spear into its belly. The dragon whirled on him, its pounding footsteps shaking the ground. The king darted to his left. The beast growled and shot flames at the place Stigandr had been standing a heartbeat ago.

The king extended his hand and jerked it to himself. Two of his spears returned to his hand. With a sweep of its wing, the dragon batted the third to the ground. It trampled the weapon, breaking the shaft with a sickening crack that made her flinch. One gone. They couldn't afford to lose any more.

Derya's fingers slid through the ashy soil. Its blackness made it nearly impossible to spot the peppercorns. *Where are they?* Her breath caught when she found a small pile of tiny, hard spheres.

She paused. Was this some animal's scat? Screwing up her face, she licked what she hoped was the peppercorn. Pepper mixed with ash. *Ugh.* She popped it in her mouth.

Stigandr darted back and forth on the opposite side of the clearing, shouting insults at the dragon. He hurled a spear. The dragon answered with a plume of flame. The spear turned to ash and drifted to the ground in tiny gray flakes.

Panic flared in her chest. She doused it before it could blaze out of control like a wildfire. Now they were down to one spear. No time to waste. She focused her magic on the dragon's left eye and pushed with all the heating power she had.

The beast growled and pawed at its eye. Its roving gaze landed on Derya, and the oval pupil of its eye narrowed. Without warning, it charged the princess, its tramping footsteps shaking the ground.

Stigandr scrambled to the beast's blind side. "Hey, over here!"

The beast roared and spewed flame in the king's direction. *Why won't its eye boil? The first had been so easy.* She screwed up her face and sent more magic, trying to heat the eye's fluid. The dragon spewed a torrent of flame, incinerating two pines that blazed like immense torches.

The king charged under the dragon's belly. He thrust his spear upward, slicing the soft flesh. A shower of black blood rained on his head.

The dragon howled and stomped furiously, like a man trying to destroy a nest of stinging ants. Stigandr rolled out from under its belly. The dragon stamped again, his hind foot grazing the king's head. Stigandr scrambled backward and tripped over a rut.

Derya took a deep breath. It was up to her. She intensified the magic she sent to the dragon's eye. The beast locked its gaze on her and opened its jaws. Smoky tendrils twisted from its snout.

Its eye burst in a spray of black blood. The beast howled and dropped to its knees, screeching and panting.

Stigandr seized a broken section of spear, ran to the dragon, and shoved the point into its ruined eye. He darted back as the dragon collapsed on the ground.

"Quick, princess."

Derya darted to him, unsheathing Hrathung as she ran. Dragons could heal themselves. Many a would-be hero thought they'd killed the beast, only to be shocked when it revived and slayed the slayer. This one was still writhing, howls mixed with steam pouring from its throat. She advanced and swung with all her strength, aiming her blow at the beast's neck. The magical blade bit deep into the scales but didn't go through.

She snarled and yanked the sword free. Grabbing the hilt with both hands, she struck again. The dragon lurched forward, the only marks of her attack a pair of scratches on its scales. It lowered its head, rubbing its eyes. In a handful of moments, its eyes would regrow. And it would come after them again.

Fury at herself surged up her throat. She wasn't strong enough. "Stigandr?"

He staggered toward her, limping. Silently, he took the blade from her hand.

With a yell, he struck the wound Derya had made in the scales. The blade cut through the bone. The dragon raised its head, roaring. It lashed its tail, threatening to impale them with its spikes.

Stigandr pulled Derya under the beast's throat. After taking a single breath, he jumped out and struck the dragon's neck. And again. The monster's head crashed to the earth with a thump like the sound of a falling tree. A torrent of black blood surged to the ground, forming a foul-smelling pool.

Stigandr lowered the blade, panting. "Nice work, princess."

"You too. You're limping."

He glanced down. "I'm clumsy, that's what. Tripped over my own feet. It's just a pull."

"And your arm?" She retrieved one of the dragon tree leaves from her bag. "Let me see."

He held out his arm, the skin red as if it had been scalded in boiling water.

"That's got to hurt."

"It does." His voice was tight.

She ripped a leaf and dripped the sap over his burn.

He let out a sigh. "What a relief." Already his skin was fading to its normal pale shade. "Are you hurt?"

"Not a scratch. Now. Where's the key?"

"I hope that beast isn't lying on it."

They searched the clearing, seeking a box, a chest, anything that would conceal a key. Stigandr used his wood magic to search for hidden nooks or vaults in the trees surrounding the clearing. Derya crawled over the ashes, probing for buried objects.

After a fruitless search, she flopped to sit on the ground, wiping sweat from her face.

Stigandr snickered. "You look like a chimney sweep. Or a coal miner."

Derya huffed and glared at him. "Where could it . . ." She burst into laughter. "We are blind."

"What do you mean?"

She pointed at the dragon's head. Twisted around its horns was a thin gold chain. Derya yanked the chain and found a golden key attached to it. "No wonder Kharan-Khuag wasn't afraid of anyone stealing it. Who'd try to stroke a dragon's head?"

"Let's get out of here," Stigandr said. He gathered the pieces of his broken spears and stabbed them into the dragon's head. Now she realized it was as long as Stigandr was tall. A shudder went through her. *Maybe we were fools to take it on.*

He extended a hand and moved it in an upward motion. The head lifted from the ground and floated in the air. "Lead on."

She frowned. "You're bringing it?"

"Why not? If you want your father to believe monsters are coming for his empire, don't you think showing him this will help make your case?"

He has a point.

Derya trotted through the forest, clutching Hrathung in her hand. Knowing the dragon's head was gliding behind her made her skin crawl.

As they hastened, a few birds chirped. *The birds know what we've done. Hopefully the forest fae do as well and will let us pass unmolested.*

A pair of moss-green eyes leered at her from the bushes. She waved Hrathung at the eyes. They vanished, leaving only the sound of mocking laughter behind. Her chest tightened. *There has to be a reason the forest fae aren't attacking.*

The tension behind her eyes relaxed when she saw the gleaming sand and heard the gentle roar of the waves. She sprinted to Bahadir, who was sitting up, sipping water. She knelt beside him. "Chiliarch, how do you feel?"

"I'll be fine, Kiral." He frowned. "These fools say they let you go alone with the barbarian to chase the dragon."

Derya glanced apologetically at Stigandr. "The barbarian is an impressive fighter, chiliarch."

Stigandr dropped the dragon's head on the sand. Puffs of dust rose up. "The princess is a brave warrior. I'll have to rethink my opinion of Cinarrians if that's how your women fight."

"Enough of this." Derya jumped to her feet. "We have

captives to free." She ran to the mass of prisoners, found the lock, and opened it. The golden chains disappeared like mist under a morning sun. But the people sat still, staring at her with blank, forlorn expressions.

"What's wrong?" Derya asked. "You're free. You can leave."

"No, we can't," a man shouted. "Look." He pointed at the sea.

Puzzled, Derya turned.

The landing boats she was counting on to return them to the ships were now crammed with mutant water fae. Groups of karcharia sliced through the waves, headed for the beach. How many more swam below the surface? Shouts from behind made her spin on her heel. Scores of mutant forest fae stood along the edge of the trees, their malicious boars' eyes fixed on the newly freed islanders.

Derya's heart sank.

We're trapped.

48

A KNOT HARDENED in Derya's stomach as she glanced from the advancing water fae to the leering forest fae. Of the hundred warriors who'd come on shore, it looked as though a quarter were dead or wounded. They were hopelessly outnumbered.

Sezgin was already shouting orders, and a brigade lined up to face the forest fae. The snarling fae charged, their long claws outstretched, poised to clash with the shining blades of the Cinarrians and Veletians.

Another brigade formed ranks on the shore, facing the water fae. A karcharia burst from the sea and closed its jaws over a soldier's knee. With a shriek, he toppled into the waves. Two more karcharia pounced on his thrashing body. Within heartbeats, the man was no more than shredded limbs spilling scarlet blood as they bobbed in the water. A karcharia raised its head from the man's torso, bits of intestines draping from its mouth.

Horror-struck, Derya froze. The sound of the surf mingled with the wail of an infant. A flutter of breeze skimmed Derya's heated face, drying the sweat and blowing away her despair.

Her shoulders stiffened, and she ground her teeth. Those monsters had attacked old people, babies, women, and children and driven them from their homes. Many bore bite marks on their limbs. Some had only stumps covered with bloody rags. This was an atrocity. Cetus may have conquered the islands, but he would not destroy these people. Whatever the price, she was going to preserve this remnant.

Stigandr touched her shoulder. "Any ideas?"

"You're a wood mage. Can you build a bridge?"

"If we ask nicely, do you think the forest fae will help me cut the trees?" He wrenched his spear from the dragon's head. "Can't you do something to the water?"

"Like poison it? No. Muddy it, yes. Would that make it hard for the water fae to breathe underwater?" She shook her head. "I could create waves and send the landing boats away. But then we still couldn't reach the ships."

"Do something!" an islander yelled. "Help us!" Many of the freed prisoners took up the cry.

"I could purify the water, for whatever good that would do."

Stigandr took in a quick breath. "Princess, stop shooting flies with a catapult."

"What?"

A karcharia lunged from the sea. Stigandr met it with the point of his spear. He thrust his hand upward. The speared karcharia flew twenty yards into the air. The king jerked his hand down. The struggling karcharia slammed into the waves and sank beneath the foam.

Stigandr gestured to his spear, and it returned to his hand. "What was I saying? Oh. Yes. A bridge. Of ice."

The ships were about one hundred yards away. She hesitated. "I could freeze the water. But all the way to the ships? I don't have that much power."

"Not even with an amplifier?"

"Dates? That would be a start . . ." A sudden memory

flashed in her mind. "Your brother told me about writing on the water. I tried it and broke one of Kharan-Khuag's spells. That's how I ended up with this." She patted Hrathung's hilt. "But that was a lake. This . . ." She waved at the tumbling waves. "This is . . ." Her hand dropped limply to her side.

"Use the dates and write on the water. I could help you."

"You'll feed me dates and prop me up when my legs go numb?"

A slow grin spread across his face. "Holding you in my arms and feeding you exotic fruit, while amusing, won't help. We could do that another time."

"That's not what I meant." Her face burned, and she glared at the approaching water fae so she wouldn't have to meet his gaze.

"Remember I talked about merging our powers?"

"Yes," Derya said slowly. "How does that work?"

"You draw on my power. When our magics combine, the power increases."

"Are you sure? I've never heard of that."

"Probably because few ever try it. It's dangerous. The person channeling the power could deplete the other without realizing it. Mages have been paralyzed, some even suffocated." He shrugged. "I heard a rumor the so-called civilized lands banned the practice."

Derya crossed her arms. "So you let me pull on your magic and add your power to mine?"

"Our powers don't add. They multiply. The power turns into the magic of the mage doing the pulling. You'd have your water magic multiplied by my metal and wood."

She nibbled her lower lip, glancing at the forest fae battling her soldiers. So far, her warriors had kept the boar-headed monsters from advancing. "That might be sufficient magic to freeze the bay long enough for us to get to the ships. But what about the water fae?"

"Maybe you can trap them in the ice. Once on board, we won't have to worry about the forest fae."

"And then we hope the water fae and karcharia just let us go?"

"If you keep them trapped in the ice, maybe we'll get far enough away they won't bother pursuing. The wind's blowing fair today. We'd make good headway once we set sail." He shrugged. "Or your men can try to kill them all."

Her hands went sweaty as she mulled over the idea of using forbidden magic that could get them both killed. Even if everyone got to the ships, they'd still have the water fae and karcharia to contend with. While fraught with risks, action was preferable to sitting on the beach waiting for the fae to attack. Or Kharan-Khuag to show up.

Derya shuddered, and a wave of frosty fear crackled through her veins. If they had one option, no matter how bad, she'd take it. "Well, if Cinar has such laws, I'll have to beg a pardon from my father." She swallowed the thought that if she committed a crime, it would be an easy way for one of her rivals to eliminate her. Nazif, she was sure, would waste no time bringing charges against her. "This means you'll have to trust me."

He nodded. "And you'll have to promise me if I say I can't breathe, you'll stop. No matter what."

"Even if it means we fail?"

"Even then. You and I need to survive to fight another day. We'll come back to avenge the ones we couldn't save."

His reasoning was sound. But her instincts recoiled from the thought of abandoning any of the western islanders to their fate, especially since they were so close to a rescue. "Let's see what the chiliarch says."

She strode to Bahadir, ignoring the pleading islanders, and laid out their plan. As she spoke, Bahadir's eyes grew wide and horrified.

"Kiral, you can't do that."

She recoiled. He'd never spoken so harshly to her.

The scars in his face spasmed. "Merging powers is a capital offense. The emperor would have you executed."

"So I should let these monsters kill us all?"

Bahadir sighed. "You know I have to report to your father."

Derya tipped her head to the side and raised an eyebrow. "Perhaps it will be a long time before you find a bird who can deliver your message?"

His lips twitched. "It will be difficult to find one, even if we return to Nafplio."

"Then get the men ready. Don't describe exactly what we're planning, just that they need to be prepared to move. Make sure all the prisoners who can't walk have someone to carry them."

"And have a few bring the dragon's head," Stigandr said.

Bahadir shot a hard look at him but nodded. He turned to Derya and gave her the Cinarrian salute. He raised his voice. "Sezgin, a word." He looked at Derya. "Do what you need to do, Kiral. We'll be ready."

Derya nodded and followed Stigandr to the water's edge. They stood on the damp sand, watching the waves break and roar as they rolled ashore. The mutant water fae were tearing arms and legs from the sailors who'd been manning the landing boats, tossing the bleeding limbs to the circling karcharia. The knot in her stomach expanded, forcing bile up her throat. *Those men died under my command.* She narrowed her eyes. "I don't care if my father executes me," she said. "We can't abandon these people."

"I agree. He can execute us both."

The heat in his words startled her. "Won't you return to Rorvik? I thought merging magic isn't illegal there."

"And leave you to face the consequences alone? What do you take me for, a barbarian?"

She snorted. "You're making me reconsider what that word means." She paused. "So, how do we do this?"

"We use the dates to amplify our power to chill things. Hold my hand and draw power from me. Then channel the combined power to freeze the water."

Derya gazed into his gray eyes and blushed under the intensity of emotion she saw there. He was staring at her as if she was the sun and moon and stars rolled up into one. She swallowed. *I must be imagining things. Nearly getting cooked by a dragon has addled my thinking.* She ignored how pleased she was by his look, and the thought that he found her appealing. A wave rolled up the beach and doused her to the knees.

She dug in her bag and found a packet of dried dates. She offered him one and bit into a second. The sweet of the fruit clashed with the sour fear in her mouth. What they were about to do terrified her. "Should we use the herbs too?"

"Why? This isn't exactly the time for healing."

"Not for you. For the ice. Don't your powers use herbs for mending metal and wood? Maybe that will help hold the ice together."

"It's worth a try. Which do you have? I don't like rue."

"Now you want to be fussy?" Derya snorted. "Don't worry, I have chamomile." He held out his hand, and she dropped a few tiny leaves into it.

She let the bitter taste mix with the lingering sweetness of the date. After a deep breath, she stiffened her spine. *If we die, we die. On our terms, not Kharan-Khuag's.* "I'm pooling my magic now."

"As am I," he answered. "I'll give you both at once, the metal and the wood."

"I'll try not to kill you."

"That's very kind, princess." He held out his hand, and she let him wrap his strong fingers around hers. The warmth of his grasp steadied her shaking fingers.

She reached with her magic toward him. To her surprise,

she sensed a pool of power brimming to overflowing. It held an earthy strength, alive and enduring, blended with a cold, sharp power, piercing and active. She pulled his magic toward her own.

The burst of power made her stagger. Stigandr gripped her hand, keeping her from tumbling onto the sand. She felt full to bursting, as if her body would shatter. Her head throbbed, spots danced before her eyes, and her knees wobbled.

"Quick, Derya," Stigandr said.

She stooped to the waves that caressed her ankles and wrote on the water. *Freeze.*

49

A s DERYA WROTE the final *E*, she could feel the water's icy bite. She stood and took a quick step back. The waves gentled, their pace sluggish, as if pushing against a restraining force. The briny green water close to Derya paled to white. A tiny hope, like the hint of a breeze, brushed against her fear. *This might actually work.*

A rolling wave splashed over the ice. Derya pointed at it and pushed harder with the magic. The relief in her head was immediate. The power no longer throbbed against her skull, begging to be released. She drew more of Stigandr's power and directed their combined magic at the waves.

"Am I taking too much?" she asked.

"No."

"Are you sure?"

"Worry about the ice, princess. I'll speak up before you kill me."

Unconvinced, she concentrated on the frozen path extending into the bay. The ice spread as quickly as water flowing down a hill. She watched wide-eyed as the rolling waves flattened into rippling humps, then stilled. The onshore breeze chilled and stung Derya's face.

Stigandr thumped the end of his spear on the ice. "Thicker. Make it thicker."

She shoved the power under the surface, pushing it down two, three, four feet, creating a thick layer of ice out of the surging sea.

Stigandr pounded the ice again and nodded. He took a few steps onto it, stamping his feet. The ice held. "Good."

Three water fae were twenty yards away. Before they could dive to escape, the expanding ice clamped around their necks like icy vises.

Stigandr chuckled. "That's one way to deal with them."

She tossed a wry smile at him. "Now for the others." Her ice spread toward the landing boats. Many fae dove into the water. When the ice reached the boats, she formed humps of ice over them, trapping the slower water fae inside. The sheet of ice raced toward the waiting ships.

Bahadir shouted, "Go! To the ships!"

The first of the freed islanders stepped onto the ice, the uninjured helping the others. The wind fluttered their ragged clothing, the gold embroidery sparkling in the sun. Cinarrian soldiers followed, carrying the smallest children, the aged, and those who'd lost legs to the karcharia. Bahadir staggered to the shore, waving off help.

Three of the islanders slipped and fell, their cries of pain piercing Derya's heart. "This isn't going to work," she cried. "They can't walk on the ice."

"Think of a metal fork etching it."

Derya tipped her head and frowned, unsure how that would help. But she imagined an immense metal fork scoring the ice. Gouges appeared in the surface, parallel lines crossing the pathway. Her lips parted in wonder. She could wield something akin to Stigandr's metal magic through the medium of her water magic.

She watched as a man slipped. A gouge in the ice stopped his slide. He stumbled but kept his footing. Reassured, Derya returned her focus to extending the ice sheet toward the waiting ships.

The sounds of shouting men and growling fae behind her diminished. Her heart skipped a beat. No. *I can't be losing my hearing already.* She glanced over her shoulder. A handful of the forest fae were loping for the trees.

Stigandr grunted. "Too bad they all aren't afraid of a little ice."

Sezgin barked orders. A brigade of Cinarrians charged a group of snarling forest fae. The fae lowered their boars' heads and raced to the Cinarrians, their tusks gleaming under the baking sun.

"Not our fight, princess."

She noticed Stigandr's breath came in gasps. "Am I taking too much?"

"Don't stop."

Sweat dripped from his forehead. Her face was damp too, and her toes were growing numb. It wouldn't be long before her hearing failed.

The first prisoners reached the nearer ship. The sailors draped the ratlines—the network of ropes that resembled huge nets the crew used to climb the mast—over the ship's side so the people could clamber aboard.

Derya squinted through the sun's glare off the ice. The first man grabbed at the dangling ratlines and missed. She hadn't let the ice touch the ships for fear of breaching the hulls, and the bobbing of the vessels made getting close precarious. A sigh of relief escaped her lips as the man grabbed the ratlines and helped a woman begin her climb aboard.

Triumphant yells forced her to jerk her head around. Two score of forest fae lay dead, pools of green blood spreading on the gleaming sand. A pair of Cinarrians sprawled nearby, their scarlet blood blending with the green to form a sickly brown.

Derya winced as grief clawed her. *How many more will die today?* The rest of the fae were in retreat, chased by a brigade of Veletians. The worry that had weighed on Derya's chest eased, only to be replaced with dread. "They must know something." She didn't want to guess. Kharan-Khuag could be watching, laughing at them. Her eyes scanned the beach. The sorcerer could swoop in and capture them all the minute they thought they'd found freedom. She swallowed the sour taste in her mouth and continued to push with her power.

People clambered up the ratlines on both ships. The last of the islanders were picking their way across the ice. Derya shuddered. Kharan-Khuag could melt the ice, and all those people would drown. She would have lured them to their deaths.

"How long do we stay here?" she asked.

"When the last reach the ships, we run." Stigandr grunted. "If we can."

"I can't feel my toes. You?"

He shook his head. "Nope."

They edged closer to the shore. Ten soldiers remained, forming a protective barrier between Derya and Stigandr and the watching forest fae. Derya could feel their malevolent gaze on the back of her neck.

Three water fae hacked through one of the ice domes. They continued to pound it with their hooked tentacles, sending chunks of glittering ice flying.

Derya scowled. Using her magic to refreeze that section would divert the power from keeping the ice sheet solid.

"Look." Stigandr's voice sounded weary. One of the karcharia had pulled itself halfway out of a hole in the ice. Gray blood dripped from its jaws.

"Did it bite through the ice?" Derya's voice shook.

Bahadir staggered to the flailing monster and stabbed it in the throat. It collapsed on the ice in a puddle of gray blood.

Bahadir kicked it, and it slid off the ice and sank beneath the waves.

Raging waters. At this rate, they'll free themselves just in time to meet us as we're passing by.

ERYA DABBED SWEAT from her face. Couldn't the
people hurry? A handful a stragglers remained on
the ice, but her numbing toes signaled she couldn't
keep the bay frozen much longer.

Grunts from behind made her whirl. Four forest fae leapt
on her soldiers. Stigandr waved his spear at them. Two of the
fae paused just long enough for the soldiers to wallop their
heads off. The other pair fled

Derya looked out to sea. A dozen men swarmed up the
ratlines on the near side of both ships. It appeared as though
most of the children and infirm were on the ships. She
squeezed Stigandr's hand. "Let's go now." *While I still can walk.*

He twisted his arm through hers. "You don't want to stay
and dance with a forest fae?"

She dug her elbow into his side and took a shuffling step
onto the ice. Instead of sensing the ice beneath her, she felt a
muted pressure in her foot, as if walking on a cushion rather
than solid ice. Moving her lower limbs was like trying to
control the legs of a puppet without the benefit of strings.

They stumbled to the track worn in the ice by the procession of islanders. That section had thawed slightly before

refreezing into a smoother surface. Derya skidded on a slick spot.

Stigandr's iron grasp on her fingers was the only thing that kept her from falling. He used his spear like a cane to keep himself upright. Her heart thudded in her chest as he steadied her.

"Try to skate."

To what?

He set one foot on the ice and glided, pulling her along. It took her a few tries, but she discovered he was right. The skating motion didn't require her to pick up her feet as high, and sliding was faster than walking. But would it get them to the ships in time? Her knees wobbled as her legs grew weaker.

Sezgin appeared at her elbow. "Kiral, do you need help?"

"Yes, please." She held out her free arm. Another soldier grasped Stigandr's arm. Supported on both sides, they made quicker progress for about twenty yards. Derya's knees buckled, and she fell, banging her knees on the ice. Had she not lost so much feeling in her legs, she'd be howling with pain. Stigandr had fallen as well but hadn't released his crushing hold on Derya's hand.

Sezgin whispered orders. *He must be shouting, but all I hear are whispers.* The kentarch scooped Derya up in his arms. "Let go of his hand."

"No." Her throat ached from the effort to yell, but her own words were muffled and indistinct. "I need to hold his hand."

Sezgin shrugged and motioned to two soldiers. They pulled Stigandr to his feet and draped his arms over their shoulders, positioning themselves so the king could maintain his grip on Derya's hand.

Sezgin edged toward the ship, allowing the others to keep pace. Through all this, the power Stigandr pushed to her hadn't wavered. *What impressive focus. No wonder he's so fierce in battle.*

She'd lost her concentration when she fell and needed to regain it. A spiderweb of dark lines spread in the ice, threatening to form wide cracks. *We're so close. I can't fail now. Ten yards to go.* She pushed more magic into the ice, pulling on Stigandr's power. His head lolled forward as he staggered. He stumbled, and the soldiers dragged him until he got his feet under himself.

With her free hand, she dug her fingernails into her palm, hoping the pain would keep her awake. The dark lines in the ice dimmed. They had time.

The gray head of a karcharia poked through the ice, the crack of breaking ice sounding to Derya no louder than the crumbling of a dry leaf. Another karcharia broke free. Arrows flew from the ship, one piercing a karcharia in the throat just where his shark's head ended and his human torso began. Bahadir had been right to wait. With most of the refugees on board, now the archers would have no fear of hitting one of them.

More rustling sounds. First one, then another landing boat's ice dome burst. Twenty water fae jumped out and sprinted across the ice, as sure-footed as if on wet sand. The seven remaining soldiers ran to engage them, slipping and sliding. A karcharia knocked one to the ground and bit his head off. Three more Cinarrians were struck down in quick succession, defeated almost as much by the slippery ice as the water fae's weapons. Derya's chest ached from her racing heart, and she tightened her grip on Stigandr's hand. He squeezed it and inched another step forward.

A mob of water fae surrounded two soldiers. The fae lashed them mercilessly with their hooked tentacles until they dropped to the ice. Their blood formed scarlet puddles that steamed and congealed.

Stigandr grunted and raised his spear as if ready to attack.

Derya knew neither of them could engage in combat. Her hearing was gone, and her legs were little more than numb appendages. The king's face was gray like the clouds over-head, and his footsteps were the shuffles of an old, dying man. If not for the soldiers supporting them, they would have toppled to the ice. When the fae turned their attention to Derya and the king, that would be the end.

One final desperate move could save them. It might kill her, it might kill Stigandr. But she would not let these monsters win. "Put me down."

Sezgin shook his head. If he said anything, she didn't hear him.

"Down." She squirmed in his arms, and he set her on her feet. Still clutching Stigandr's hand, Derya stooped and etched a word into the ice. As if in a daze, she tugged the bag hanging from her belt. "Kentarch, salt, please. For me and the king."

Sezgin gave her a startled look but put a pinch of salt in her mouth and Stigandr's. Then she pulled at her power, the cool water blending with Stigandr's earthy wood and prickly metal, hoping she wasn't draining him of all his magic. She extended her hand and jerked it upward, releasing the magic in one mighty burst.

Even with her muffled hearing, Derya could hear the ice groan like a wounded dragon. Her knees wobbled, but she continued to send power to the ice, as if sucking a well dry. The ice shattered into pointed shards like hundreds of swords. They stabbed upwards into the water fae and the karcharia, impaling them.

Derya released her power and collapsed to her knees. Stigandr twitched and convulsed. The soldiers staggered under the sagging king's weight. He still clutched his spear. *Or was that a death grip? Did I kill him?*

Sezgin knelt by her side and shook her arm. *What does it matter?* Derya thought. *The ice will melt, and the karcharia will eat us. I have nothing left to fight with.*

A stiff wind blew up and bumped the ice floe against the

ship. Stigandr's knees buckled. The ice floe bobbed with the motion. The soldiers grabbed the king, straining to keep him on his feet.

Sezgin shook her arm and pulled her upwards. Derya couldn't feel her feet to move them under her to even try to stand. She was a limp rag, wrung out and spent.

Sleep. I want sleep. She opened one eye. Sailors dangling from the ratlines were tying the unconscious, gray-faced Stigandr to the ropes, almost as if he was an enormous fish caught in a giant's net. A sailor climbed down to her, clinging to the ratlines with one arm, the other hand extended to grasp her.

Shadows fell over her face. A soldier stood over her, his sword drawn, while Sezgin tied a rope around her waist. She slumped onto the ice, her face pressed against the cold. She was so tired. If only she could sleep. But she needed to stay awake for a reason she couldn't remember.

The ice floe tipped. A water fae pulled itself up and grabbed Derya's boot. She cringed as a young soldier slashed at the beast. The water fae's tentacle knocked the blade from his hand.

"Take mine," Derya mumbled.

She felt him yank Hrathung from its scabbard. From under heavy eyelids, Derya watched his stroke send the fae's head sailing into the air. Ash-colored blood splashed the ice floe. It rocked as the dead fae slipped into the sea.

Sezgin slid his hands under her arms. Sweat beaded on his forehead, and his eyes bulged as he heaved her toward the ship. A waiting sailor wove her arms through the ratlines. When Sezgin released her, her knees folded, and she slid downwards. The dangling sailor grabbed her arms and yanked her up.

Had he pulled her off the ice? Her legs had no feeling; they were millstones attached to her hips. She had no sense if her feet supported her weight or not.

Something yanked on her hip. She looked down to see a karcharia with its jaws clamped over her boot. Panic rose in her throat. She couldn't feel its teeth pierce her skin. *Is the leather thick enough that it can't bite through?* She tried to yank her foot from the beast's jaws. But her leg refused to obey her mental command. Her breaths came fast and ragged, and terror gripped her heart with icy fingers.

The beast thrashed back and forth. Drops of red blood flew into the air. *Is that mine?* With no sensation in her legs, Derya wasn't sure. She tried to kick. But her leg responded no more than if it were a piece of wood.

Sezgin and the other soldier hacked the karcharia. The beast intensified its frenzied lashing. Its shark's head swiveled back and forth, its human body writhing in a contorted dance, seemingly oblivious to the wounds on its torso and arms.

The sailor on the ratlines yanked her. She shrieked with pain. Was he trying to pull her arms from their sockets? Then a stabbing burning agony seared up her spine, and all turned black.

51

T ARJA SHIVERED AND pulled her cloak tighter, rubbing her arms and listening to the ship's timbers creak and the waves slap the hull. She held a hand over her eyes to shade them from the sun and peered at the shore some hundred yards away. Derya had vanished into the forest with that barbarian who called himself a king, supposedly to kill a dragon. Dead forest fae littered the beach, along with many Cinarrians and barbarians. The gold chain binding the captive islanders glistened in the sunlight.

What is Derya thinking? She should leave those people to their fate. Only an arrogant fool would attempt to slay a sleepless dragon. Was Derya trying to get herself killed?

Tarja pursed her lips. If Derya died, Utku was next in line. Hearsay mocked him as a weak reed, blown about by the strongest wind. She smirked to herself. If she could finagle a way to marry him, she'd control the throne of Cinar. Then her father would regret ever planning to marry her off to an obscure nomad.

But what if Yildiz, the next in line, did away with Utku? And Nazif was after Yildiz. Either of them would be stronger than Utku. Maybe she should have killed Nazif when she had the chance.

Tarja's jaw slackened as a cheer rose from the soldiers on the beach. Derya strode out from between the trees, sword in hand. She darted to the chiliarch, who was sitting on the sand.

What was floating in the air in front of the barbarian king? When he neared the chiliarch, he dropped the massive thing on the sand, making a puff of dust rise. Tarja squinted.

When the dust cleared, she saw it. A head with a long, lizard-like snout, oozing black blood. *No. It can't be.* Tarja's eyes widened. Derya *had* killed the dragon. Tarja pounded a fist into her palm. Why did success rain from Derya's fingers? Was there nothing that could defeat her? The princess should have died when she fell overboard.

Tarja huffed. The knot of resentment and jealousy inside her would never ease until she killed Derya. Guilt over having failed, guilt over having tried, guilt over regretting having tried wrestled within her, cramping her stomach and tightening her throat. Her nostrils flared in irritation. *Why can't Derya just die already? Then I won't have to hate myself over whatever I decide to do.*

Farooq shouted for the archers. Tarja glanced at him, puzzled. She didn't see any fighting on shore.

Her heart lurched. Scores of the shark-headed monsters swam in circles around the ships. Fish-headed water fae swarmed the small boats. Tarja winced as the fae tore the arms from the men tending the boats. The spray of blood sent the karcharia into a frenzy. They fought over pieces of bodies, biting off legs and arms and heads. Tarja's heart pounded against her ribs. Derya and the others had no way of returning to the ships. Retreat was out of the question. Dozens of forest fae approached from the woods, their boars' jaws wide, their yellowed tusks menacing.

The Cinarrian and barbarian soldiers escorted the freed captives to the shore, carrying the children and those who didn't seem able to walk. Tarja frowned. *What good will tossing them into the sea do?*

Derya and the barbarian king approached the water, heads tipped together as if they were deep in conversation. Rows of soldiers with drawn swords lined up behind them, facing the forest fae and their tiger-like claws. Derya took Stigandr's hand. She stooped to the water, then stood and pointed at it with her free hand.

Tarja's jaw dropped. Ice formed in the sea, spreading from Derya's feet to the ships. Ice trapped the karcharia and water fae who'd been swimming on the surface. The landing boats were now mounds of ice, creating icy tombs for the water fae.

What magic could do this? Tarja's hands shook. Derya must wield an unusually immense power. Tarja gaped at the sight of Derya holding the king's hand. Were they melding their power?

Tarja pressed a hand over her open mouth. It was shocking enough Derya was wielding magic in public for all to see. But combining power with a man, one she wasn't married to? Tarja tapped a finger against her lips. Wasn't melding banned in Cinar? If she remembered correctly, Derya could be executed for this. She was taking an enormous risk, and for what?

It wasn't just to save herself. Half of the captives were on the ice, headed for the two ships. The captain ordered the sailors to ready ropes and drape the ratlines over the side.

They were going to a lot of trouble to rescue expendable people. A sudden flash of resentment came over her. While she'd been Nazif's slave, he'd thought of her as disposable. Yet here was his cousin, risking herself to save peasants who would be considered worthless in Pasargadae. What kind of person would do that?

She watched as scores of refugees climbed on board and were shuttled belowdecks. Derya and the barbarian staggered across the ice, slipping and sliding. *After using so much magic, how are they still conscious?*

Without warning, mutant fae burst from one of the ice domes where Derya had imprisoned them. In short order, they killed most of the men guarding her. The princess stooped down and touched the ice.

Derya stood straight and lifted her hand. A mighty crack like the cleaving of a mountain into two cut the air. The ice shattered and split into sword-like shards that impaled several water fae. Tarja stood with her jaw hanging open, barely able to breathe. This was power, indeed. Derya would be a formidable foe. No, she shouldn't ever rule Cinar.

Frantic shouts seized her attention. Sezgin was attempting to tie the sagging Derya to the ratlines. A karcharia leaped from the sea and seized Derya's foot in its mouth. Everyone around her was shouting. Derya screamed. Sailors grunted, and their muscles bulged as they hoisted the ratlines up.

Derya's scream ended, leaving an ominous void for a single heartbeat. Then the frantic shouting resumed. Tarja leaned over the side, blood thumping in her ears. Sezgin held Derya by the arms. Her left leg ended in a jagged stump just above her ankle. Blood poured in a scarlet torrent from Derya's leg into the sea. The bile in Tarja's stomach forced its way into her mouth.

Two sailors swarmed down the ratlines. One bore a spear and jabbed at the karcharia snapping at Derya.

The other dangled upside down, twisting his legs into the ratlines. He bound a leather cord around the stump of Derya's leg. By the time he finished, his hands were stained scarlet from the princess's blood.

A water fae lunged for a sailor's dangling foot, its hooked tentacles clawing at his boot. Frenzied shouting roused Tarja from her stunned state. *He shouldn't die for Derya's folly.* She palmed a knife, pooled her magic, and hurled the blade. It sank into the water fae's fishlike eye. With a twitch of a finger, Tarja recalled it. The dead fae splashed into the sea.

"Move! Pull!" Bahadir bellowed. Farooq and several soldiers joined the sailors hoisting the ratlines up. The captain shouted his own orders, commanding the crew to raise the anchor.

Tarja watched as Sezgin laid the limp, unconscious princess on the deck. A red puddle formed under the jagged stump of her left shin.

A few moments later, the barbarian king was hauled over the rail and dumped on the deck. He lay in a crumpled heap, seemingly no more aware of his surroundings than the princess.

Safiye raced to Derya's side and dropped to her knees. "Kiral!"

Derya didn't answer. Safiye wrung her hands and burst into sobs. *If it were me, would anyone mourn like that?* Jealousy tensed her jaw and regret tugged at her heart.

The sails overhead flapped as the sailors raised them. *Do they think we can escape the water fae?* She glanced back over the side. The empty landing boats bobbed on the swell. A lone trio of water fae tossed Derya's bleeding foot back and forth, their wide, toothy grins leering at the retreating ships. Tarja shuddered. It appeared the fae believed possession of the islands and the foot of their enemy were enough. She hoped so. She wrenched her gaze from the macabre spectacle and studied the crowd surrounding Derya.

Several healers clustered around Derya. One tightened the tourniquet. Others dabbed at the blood and cleaned the wound. Tarja winced at the sight of the crushed ends of bone and jaggedly torn muscle.

Bahadir limped by, his jaw clenched and the scars on his cheek twitching. He looked as grieved as if his own child had died. Even the soldiers and sailors were subdued. No one was celebrating the rescue of the islanders or their own escape. Everyone seemed distraught in the face of Derya's impending death. *They're mourning for her,* Tarja thought. *There's genuine affection and loyalty here.*

Perhaps this is my opportunity. She walked over to Safiye. "If you please," she said in as humble a tone as she could muster, "I might be able to help."

"How?"

Tarja repressed a frown. Where had that dour Kelebek come from? She bowed her head. "Oikeios, it appears the princess and the king have overused magical amplifiers. I know of a potion that can help counter the effects."

Kelebek folded his arms. "I've never heard of any such potion."

"Nor I," put in Safiye.

"A trader from Tinaxia sold the secret to my father." That was the exact truth. She held her breath, hoping they didn't ask awkward questions about who her father was and why Tinaxian traders would sell him valuable secrets. They didn't need to know the trader was a spy in Pasargadae's service, paid handsomely to steal Tinaxia's arcane knowledge.

Safiye picked up Derya's wrist. "Her pulse is weak and thready. Can't you do something?" Her tone sharpened into an agonized plea.

The grizzled healer shook her head. "She's lost a lot of blood." She pointed her chin at Stigandr. "If he breathes any slower, he'll be gone."

"Can nothing be done?" Safiye wailed.

The healer shrugged. "I've heard tales of Tinaxian brews. But no one knows the recipe." She raised her thick eyebrows at Tarja. "You might want to let this one try. Can't hurt."

Tarja studied the deck while Kelebek, Safiye, Bahadir, and the healer argued. *Can't hurt. Ha. I could heal the king and poison Derya. They'd never suspect a thing.*

But still. She surveyed the unconscious princess. What kind of ruler would she be? Derya cared about the expendable people. They had lives and loves and feelings of their own, something Tarja had never considered before she was sold as a helpless slave. *All this time, I thought she'd be no better than someone's puppet. But that's not true. Perhaps the world needs more rulers like Derya and less like my own father, the ruthless emperor of Pasargadae.* Or that odious tyrant who ruled Tinaxia.

Somehow Tarja didn't think that losing a foot would change Derya for the worse. If she survived such an injury. But she needed the side effects of overusing her magic to be countered immediately.

"Garzuli," Bahadir said. "How do you make this concoction?"

Tarja met his gaze. "First, chiliarch, I need to know which amplifiers they used."

"It's obvious, isn't it?" Kelebek said. "Dates. To freeze the water."

"And salt," Sezgin said. "Just before the end."

That made sense, to intensify the power when Derya shattered the sea. But what had held the ice together so well? They'd used herbs, she was sure of it. But it wouldn't do to question the kentarch. She didn't want to raise any suspicions. "Please bring me hot water and honey and samples of all the amplifiers, except salt and dates."

The concoction called for a brew made of the amplifiers that hadn't been used. So no salt or dates. But what about the herbs? If they hadn't used any, leaving them out would be fatal. As would including them if they had. She needed to be sure.

While she waited, she sat against the rail, watching Safiye tenderly wrap Derya in a blanket. She removed the princess's damp boot and massaged her remaining foot, her fingers stroking the white, waterlogged skin. The woman seemed to really love Derya. Bahadir's eyes glittered, and his shoulders slumped, and even Kelebek, who Tarja had always thought despised Derya, looked sad, his lips pressed together in a thin line, his brows pinched together.

Farooq sat next to Safiye and pulled the boots from the barbarian king's feet. He burst into laughter. "Look, the king needs new socks." Stigandr's big toe stuck out of his brown woolen sock.

A chuckle slipped from Safiye's throat before a frown darkened her face. "Have a little respect," she snapped. "The man almost died saving the kiral."

Bahadir snorted. "Just warm up his feet, kentarch. And thank you for volunteering. It's not a job I'd ever order someone to do."

Tarja drew her eyebrows together and stared at Farooq. This was getting stranger and stranger. In Pasargadae, only a slave would provide such a menial service. And the barbarian king would have been ignored, left to recover on his own.

A soldier set a tray on the deck next to Tarja. It held a steaming teapot, a tiny jar of honey, and small vials that contained the amplifiers. She eyed it warily. Now what? Should she try to heal? Or kill?

Derya wasn't the obnoxious princess she'd imagined her to be. She'd been valiant and compassionate, despite her act when she pretended to be either frivolous or imperious. And she possessed a sense of fun that would make her a good friend. On top of her obvious loyalty to her attendants.

But healing Derya would earn Tarja the wrath of her father. Tarja shivered, thinking what punishment her father would mete out for that act of treason if he ever heard of it. His network of spies would track her down and drag her home to face her father's rage. No, better kill Derya. For all her admirable qualities, she was still an enemy of Pasargadae.

Safiye's muffled sobs and Bahadir's cough prompted her to get to work. Tarja knelt by the steaming pot and searched her memory for the proper order for adding the amplifiers. Carefully, she added a drop of lemon juice and a peppercorn.

Drops of wine, beer, and vinegar followed. Then she dropped a single dried berry into the water. She didn't recognize it, a cluster of tiny reddish-pink balls forming a hollow half-sphere.

She crushed a dried leaf between her fingers, thinking it to be marrubium from the minty medicinal smell. Even though no one had mentioned herbs, Derya and Stigandr must have used them. That was how they kept the ice intact. Adding a touch of herbs would free her of the girl she'd long hated.

The image of Derya soaring from the sky on the back of a winged horse burst into her mind. An old Pasargadian legend told of heroes favored by the gods. Only they could tame a winged horse. Could that god the Cinarrians worshipped, the Rider of the Ancient Skies, be helping Derya? Or had Tarja's own gods blessed her hated enemy?

Either way, Derya was a powerful water mage, the most likely one to be able to fight Cetus and win. If Cetus defeated Cinar, Pasargadae would be next. Tarja's heart quailed, thinking of her homeland overrun by mutant water or forest fae. Or even more fearsome monsters. *Saving my enemy might be the best way to protect my country.*

She pressed her lips together. *Which means I should help her.* Tarja rubbed her aching forehead and curled her lip. *As much as I hate her, I have to help her defeat Cetus. If Derya finds the crown, I'll give her the band.*

Tarja let the herbs trickle through her fingers into the icy breeze that blew them away. With deliberate care, she added one drop of honey to the steaming brew. *Time to see if this potion will actually work.*

52

Chorokha

Ninety-five days after the winter solstice in the Year 999 (Chorokhese reckoning) and in the 29th year of Emperor Vural Tzimiskes of Cinar

ELIANA PRESSED A HAND against the stitch in her side, gasping for breath. She leaned her sweaty forehead against the cool, damp passage wall. Hours ago, she and Adakizh fled the battle with the Alaf-Shilams and the water fae, and they'd been sprinting through tunnels ever since. Every so often, Adakizh paused and created another cave-in. If anyone was pursuing them, they'd have piles of broken stone and rubble to dig through.

But in their efforts to confuse any pursuers, they'd strayed from the route that led to Qala Khatavian. Anxiety for the warriors they'd sent ahead drove her to keep running. But her shaking legs begged for a rest.

Adakizh laid a hand on her shoulder. "Why don't we take a break?"

She opened her mouth to agree when she heard a clicking sound in the tunnel behind them. Her heart lurched, and she froze. A low, guttural snarl filled the cavern. Its echoes bounced from the walls and assaulted her ears in a cacophony of growls and threats.

Adakizh grabbed her arm and dragged her into a run. The snarls turned into a roar. Instead of their allies, they'd found a vishapion.

They tore along the tunnel, stumbling over fallen stones, sending the loose pebbles skittering. The corridor made a sharp bend, and they skidded to a halt. Twenty feet in front of them was a solid wall of stone, lit by a handful of blue mushrooms. Adakizh's fingers tightened on Eliana's arm. "Can you hold it off?"

Unable to force words through her tight throat and desert-dry mouth, she nodded. She'd faced down a vishapion before. She could do it again. With a hand over her heart, she pulled at her magic, sensing he was doing the same.

A crash and a thud told her she guessed right. Adakizh had cut away a chunk of stone, making a narrow opening in the rocky wall. Another thud.

Eliana squared her shoulders and paced half the distance to the bend in the tunnel. Taunting echoes magnified the vishapion's roars and shuffles.

Please, forget about us. Or try another tunnel.

More cracking sounds reverberated through the cavern. She glanced over her shoulder to see Adakizh stick his head into the rift he'd carved through the wall.

The snarls grew louder. *Slow breaths, Eliana. Wait for it.* Part of her wanted to run toward the monster, to fling her magic at it and end this horrible waiting.

"I'm almost through," Adakizh yelled. "There's blue light."

That's one mercy. At least they wouldn't escape the vishapion only to fall into a nest of stinging worms.

More clicking, more grunts. Her hammering heartbeats obscured every other sound. After another roar and more thudding footfalls, the monster's boar-like snout flanked by long horns appeared around the corner.

With a wave of her hand, she hurled light into the monster's eyes. It shrieked and backed away.

She took a step back. Broken stone rattled on the cavern's floor, and the scent of hot minerals stung Eliana's nose. Adakizh must be heating the rock to crack it faster.

The vishapion roared and charged. Eliana hurled herself to the side of the tunnel, just missing the beast's gaping mouth. She crouched behind a rock. The vishapion's massive tail grazed her head, and she hissed in pain. Hot wetness trickled down her cheek. *So, light didn't work.* She formed an air spear and drove it into the beast's ribs.

It roared, the sound shaking the stone cavern. A few stones clattered as they tumbled down the wall. Eliana hurled another air spear. It grazed the beast's horn. The monster lunged toward her.

"Eliana, now!"

She didn't give herself a heartbeat to hesitate. She flung a burst of light at the vishapion and darted to Adakizh. He pushed her toward the crevice in the wall.

The vishapion bellowed and charged. Eliana created an air garrote and twisted it around the beast's front legs. She yanked it tight. The vishapion tripped and fell on its face, smashing its jaw onto the floor. It growled and fixed a malevolent glare on Eliana and Adakizh.

"Go!" Adakizh yelled.

Eliana squeezed through the crack, the sword at her waist clanging against the rock. Once through, she turned, breathlessly watching the stalking beast. Adakizh backed up, halting just before the opening.

The vishapion opened its jaws, ready to clamp them on

Adakizh's head. A stalactite dropped on its snout. With a howl, the beast lurched back.

Adakizh spun and threw himself into the crevice. Once he had an arm through, Eliana grabbed it and tugged. He popped through and they tumbled into a pile on the ground. Pain shot through her abdomen, forcing a groan from her lips.

Adakizh grunted and picked himself up. Eliana scrambled to her feet. He was already magically piling up rock in the crack, heating it so the crystals would melt and seal them in.

The vishapion scratched and clawed the piled rocks, scrabbling to get through. It tore down the stone as fast as Adakizh could pile it up.

Gulping, Eliana created a new air garrote. With a shaking hand, she guided it around the beast's throat and wrenched it tight. The vishapion's shriek ended in a cough and a gurgle. The echoes of its agony multiplied its pain. It toppled with a loud crash that shook the floor. A few loose stones skittered down the cave's walls.

Adakizh finished sealing the crevice and wiped his forehead. "I hope it's dead."

"What if it's not?" Eliana edged away from the newly-sealed crack. "We should go."

"To where?"

Her eyes flared wide when she took in her surroundings. They stood in a crystal-walled chamber the size of a large kitchen, bathed in the glowing mushrooms' blue light. Metal doors were centered on the other three sides of the room. Swirling patterns of diamonds, flowers, fish, goats, and flowing water were etched into their surface, along with lines of words in what Eliana recognized as Old Malkhian.

Adakizh turned to her and gasped. "You're hurt."

"Its tail grazed me." She put her fingers to the still bleeding wound.

Adakizh raised a hand and muttered a few words.

The stinging pain in her head ceased, and she smiled at him in relief. "Thank you."

"Guess you'll keep me around then? For my healing abilities?"

"And a few other talents. But we should get out of here."

Adakizh walked to the far door and pointed to the etching of a dolphin leaping from surging waves. "This is the ancient crest of the Alagatas. But why would it be here? I never heard of my family ever living this far south."

"It looks ancient."

He shrugged. "It does. But I'm more interested in getting out. I don't suppose we'll be able to open these doors," he said. He depressed the latch of the right-hand door. It didn't budge.

"What about this one?" Eliana tried the left door. It didn't open. Neither did the center one.

Adakizh rubbed a hand over his head and stamped his feet. "I need a moment to rest. I can't feel my toes." He glanced at the crack in the wall. "I don't think the vishapion will bother us anymore." He sank to the ground and leaned against the left-hand door. With a grunt, he bent his knees and rested his face on them. She settled next to him, sliding under the edge of his cloak and snuggling against his side.

They sat without speaking, the only sounds their own breathing and the faint trickle of water.

Adakizh let out a long breath. "It's starting to seem hopeless."

"It kind of does," she says. "But we're not done yet."

"We've destroyed two kingdoms, led the Zhilakhurs into defeat, allowed the Alaf-Shilams to destroy the Minarilis, oversaw the fall of Qala Kambada and lost Qala Bisen. The Saumarotas may or may not have defected to the enemy. And Bednieri—" His voice hitched.

That was what was pulling him down. Not the military setbacks or the bickering clans. Those were nothing new. And while disappointing, not insurmountable. It was the personal loss of one of his closest friends that was crushing his soul.

She had no words. One more person had been ripped from him while he was still mourning the deaths of those he'd loved before his enchanted sleep. "I'm sorry."

He pressed his forehead against her hair and took a shaky breath. "It's all too much."

She put a hand on his face. "You loved him. And he loved you. He died defending you. Please don't blame yourself."

"Oh, to be a normal man, not the tagavoi who holds life and death in his hands."

Now he was getting maudlin. "What fool poet said that?"

He snorted. "I don't know."

"But I know you are the tagavoi, the leader the Rider chose to serve in this time. Which means you will overcome Kharan-Khuag."

He tugged at one of her braids. "That's my queen. Don't ever let your light go out. I'd blunder in the dark forever." He pulled her into a tight embrace.

Don't you ever stop being my strength.

"Eliana."

She waited, but instead of his voice, heard only her own breaths. When he didn't continue, her heart sank. Maybe he was succumbing to his black mood. What could she say to keep him from brooding? She needed him active and fighting, not passive and melancholy.

"Eliana, you're right." His voice took on a confident tone. "We broke the dark."

She patted his cheek. "How quickly you forget."

He kissed her softly. "I hope you haven't forgotten this." He covered her mouth with his.

When he released her, she was gasping for air and her toes tingled. "No danger of that." She tipped her head to the side. "I take it you're feeling better. Want to break us out of here?"

He shook his head. "My toes are still numb. Besides, see

those cracks in the roof? Breaking through the walls might bring it down. It's not a job you want to do in a hurry."

Her hands were damp, and she found it hard to breathe. They were trapped in a tiny room. The ceiling could cave in, rocks could tumble down, trap her, crush her . . . Her chest tightened, and her shoulders tensed. She buried her face in his shoulder. Pressing her lips together, she took slow breaths through her nose.

A whisper of a thought, a tendril of suggestion slid into her mind. Something was thrumming, plucking, calling to her. She jerked her head up.

"Do you feel it too?" he asked. "What's calling to us?" He stood up and helped her to her feet. With a frown, he grasped the door latch and yanked. It didn't move. "No surprise there. I suppose it's pointless to try the other doors again."

"I'm not so sure." Eliana gripped the latch of the center door and squeezed. It gave a little, but not much. She brushed aside the anxiety that screamed they were sealed in a chamber destined to become their tomb. "Maybe you try."

After several tugs, he had no more success than she did. He wrinkled his brow. "There's something magical in there."

She sensed it too, something thrumming that tugged at her magic. Something that demanded to be found. She nibbled her lower lip. "Should we disturb it? What if it's evil?"

"Fair question." He drummed his fingers on the door. "But it's calling me."

"Me too. Which is making me nervous. Whatever's in there could be dangerous."

He sucked in a breath. "Or be useful."

She snorted. "Since when are you the optimist?"

"You're rubbing off on me." He gave her a smirk and wiggled his eyebrows. "But don't worry, I haven't given up on pessimism yet. We're most likely going to die in the next few months anyway. I say let's at least satisfy our curiosity. Seize what happy moments we can."

"And if this thing kills us, we put ourselves out of our misery?"

"Something like that." He stared at the door. "I guess one of my ancestors hid a magical item here. And maybe we need it."

Eliana shrugged and gripped the latch. It gave a hair's breadth. "I'm just not strong enough."

Adakizh put his hand over Eliana's. "Let me help." Together, they squeezed. The latch clicked, and the door shifted.

Eliana held her breath, her heart beating a rapid cadence.

No roaring beast emerged. No evil magic flooded out.

Adakizh shoved the door with his shoulder. Its hinges gave a protesting squeal. A few more shoves and the door scraped half open. Nothing illuminated the darkness, so Eliana created a ball of light and floated it into the gloom.

Hundreds of sparkles met her gaze. She gasped. They'd opened a door to a tiny room whose walls were covered with gemstones. But instead of the raw stones found everywhere in the tunnels of Chorokha, these had been cut, each one with multiple facets that glittered and reflected brilliant colors.

A short pillar dominated the room's center. An ornate crown perched atop it. Heavy gold arches curved over a thick circlet, all studded with emeralds, lapis lazuli, turquoise, and onyx. There was an empty setting in the center of the crown's front where a massive gem should have rested.

"What is this?" she asked. "The crown of ancient Malkh's tagavois?"

"If it is, why would they hide it?" He picked it up, running a finger over the edge of an emerald. He shook his head. "It looks nothing like my father's crown." A puzzled expression crossed his face.

"Someone went to a lot of trouble to conceal it here."

"So, it was important to them. But I don't see a use for it."

"Neither can I, even though it holds magic of some sort."

He handed it to her. "Do you feel it?"

Her eyes widened. She sensed something plucking her magic like a musician strumming the strings of a lyre. But the magic felt off somehow, like rancid oil. She thrust it back at him. "It's wicked. Let's leave it here."

He replaced the crown on the pillar and rubbed his hands on his trousers. "It does feel evil. Maybe that's why it was hidden."

They closed the door after them and returned to the central chamber. Eliana glanced at the room's other doors. "Now, how do we get out?" She studied the words etched on the wall. "Adakizh, can you read Old Malkhian?"

"A little." He frowned at the words. "I think it says 'multiply necessary to open.' Does that mean many people? Or weapons?"

Eliana pursed her lips. "It can't mean we have to perform a mathematical calculation. Maybe it just means more than one person."

He tapped a word with a finger. "If this means 'two' instead of 'multiply,' you could be right." He scoffed. "It can't be that easy."

"It worked on the center door."

He gripped the latch of the left-hand door, and she covered his hand with hers. When it swung open, it revealed an empty chamber.

"That worked." Eliana shook her head. "But didn't help."

They moved to the right-hand door. Adakizh gripped the latch with Eliana's hand on his. The latch didn't move.

Her breath came faster. *No. We can't be trapped. We can't.*

They made several other attempts. Adakizh huffed and knocked his head against the door. "I truly have mushrooms for brains."

She stared at him.

"You put your hand first." She did, and, with his large hand covering her small one, depressed the latch.

With a protesting groan, the door swung open. Damp, cool air rushed in. The tunnel was dark, illuminated by a few scattered blue mushrooms. In the distance, a thin shaft of sunlight cut through the dark.

Relief flooded Eliana, loosening her tight shoulders. They weren't going to die in a stony tomb, at least not there. "Well, let's find the Khatavians."

"Before another vishapion finds us first."

53

Ninety-eight days after the winter solstice in the 29th year of Emperor Vural Tzimiskes

ERYA SAT UP AND extended her hands. "Please, Safiye, I beg you. I can't stay in this cabin one more moment." Her entire left leg ached, and her foot and shin throbbed and burned. "I'm suffocating in here." She turned her face to the open porthole. Bright sun and puffs of ocean breeze made her yearn for light and fresh air. Walking on deck and feeling the wind in her hair would provide distractions from the pain and shake off her grogginess. "If I could just walk a bit, I wouldn't feel so stiff."

A shadow flickered across Safiye's face. "You only woke up an hour ago. Have something else to eat." She held out a bowl of steaming stew.

Derya scowled. "You say I slept three days? That's sufficient time to recover. My hearing is back." True enough, but she had to strain to understand voices. She heard the ship's timbers creak, but the sound was muted, as if far away. "I can feel my toes." She sighed. "Such a relief to have warm feet, even if the left one still hurts. The next time someone wants to send me on a quest, I'm not going in winter. Unless it's to someplace warm."

Safiye's face tensed.

Derya gave her a puzzled frown. *What was wrong with her danisman?* "Besides, King Stigandr will think I am a weak southerner if I loll in bed longer than he does."

"He wasn't the one channeling the power. Besides, he's a man. He'll assume it was normal he recovered faster."

"Is he up?"

Safiye looked at the bowl in her hands. "Yes."

"Has he been to see me?"

"We thought it wise for you to rest."

Derya stifled a pang of disappointment. "I've rested. So why can't I go on deck?"

There was a rap on the door. Safiye turned to it so quickly stew sloshed onto her tunic. She opened the door to admit Bahadir and Kelebek. Kelebek's severe expression was even more stony than usual, and the scars on Bahadir's face were twitching.

"What's wrong?" Derya asked. "Are we about to be attacked?"

Bahadir and Kelebek exchanged glances. The two men filled up the space between the bunk beds on one side and Derya's narrow cot on the other, making it feel overcrowded and stuffy. Bahadir took a deep breath before closing the door. "Kiral, we've been debating where to sail next."

"It's obvious, isn't it?" Derya gave him a puzzled frown. "We sail for Tulgutalp to give my father and everyone else proof that no matter what lies they heard from Nazif, I am alive." She waved a hand at them. "Oh, do sit down. You're making me nervous looming over me like that."

Kelebek, Bahadir, and Safiye perched on the edge of Safiye's bed, leaning forward to avoid hitting their heads on the upper bunk. To Derya, they looked like three guilty schoolchildren awaiting punishment.

"Out with it," she said.

Kelebek gave the others a warning nod. *Oh, no*, thought Derya. *This isn't going to be good.*

The oikeios clasped his hands, resting his forearms on his thighs. "Kiral, we felt it best to sail for M'Diq."

"M'Diq?" Derya pursed her lips, scrambling to remember all she knew of Axum's largest port. It clung to the country's west coast, seated just south of the tip of a pointed peninsula. Cinar's navy guarded the port, which was known for its cobalt-blue houses, sweet mint tea, and night souks filled with snake charmers, musicians, food stalls, and vendors of everything imaginable. "Why M'Diq?"

"Since we don't know the situation in Tulgutalp," Kelebek said, "we thought it was more prudent to go where we could obtain some news."

"What news?" Derya said. A knot formed in her belly. "About my father's health?"

"That," Kelebek said, "and if he's named a new kiral."

He said the words blandly, as if discussing the weather. They hit Derya like an icy wave to the face. "You mean after Nazif told him I'd gone overboard?"

Bahadir nodded. "If the new kiral is at all ruthless, he could denounce you as a fraud."

Nazif wouldn't do that, Derya wanted to say. Or would he? But he wasn't next in line. Utku, or whoever was pulling his strings, would kill her to get her out of the way. As would Yildiz. "So, what do you suggest? Send a bird to my father telling him I'm alive?"

"That might not be wise," Safiye said softly.

Derya crossed her arms as she raked an angry glare over the faces of her advisers. "Raging waters, what is it you're not telling me? The three of you treat me like an invalid and act like I'm about to break. What is going on? Why can't I return home and claim my position? It's not like you've heard any news, not this far out to sea. Or have you?" She narrowed her eyes.

"No, Kiral," Bahadir said. "We sailed south from the islands rather than east, hoping Cetus would assume we'd head for Tulgutalp, and if he sent any fae or karcharia after us, they'd head in that direction. We won't know anything about events in Tulgutalp or anywhere else until we make port."

"So that's not what's bothering you. Out with it. Or I get up." She moved to fling the blanket off her legs.

"No!" three voices exclaimed in unison.

Derya stared at them. "Why not?" She didn't bother to keep the frustration from her voice.

Safiye knelt beside the bed and took the princess's hand. "Derya, you can't. Your leg—"

"It hurts, but that doesn't mean I can't walk."

"Your injury," Kelebek said, "has some complications." His dark eyes landed on hers.

Derya noted with a start that his usually inscrutable expression held a sadness she'd never seen before. The downcast mien spread over his wrinkled face made him look closer to sixty than fifty.

"What complications?" Derya ground out the words through her clenched teeth. "Tell me."

"Kiral." Bahadir's voice was strained. "The karcharia bit your foot off."

She gaped at him, jaw slack. "No. You're lying."

He met her gaze and shook his head regretfully. "I'm not."

"That can't be. I feel it, and it hurts." She jerked her hand from Safiye's and yanked the blanket off her left leg. It ended a few inches above her ankle and was swathed in a thick roll of bandages. She glared at Safiye. "Why didn't you tell me?"

A tear dripped from Safiye's eye. "We wanted to. But we thought it best you healed from the effects of overusing your magic first."

"What trickery is this? My foot has to be there." Even as she uttered the words, a lump formed in her throat. The horrifying truth shredded her insides, gouging the hard knot in her stomach.

"I'm sorry," Safiye said.

Anger surged through Derya, heating her face so that beads of sweat dampened her forehead. "You're sorry? How dare you keep this from me?" She wanted to scream, to throw something. Now she understood the burning and throbbing around her shin. And why she could move the toes on her right foot but not the left. What didn't make sense was why she felt stabbing pain where her left foot had been. Or cramping of the missing toes.

Air punched from her lungs, and she struggled to inhale. Now she was panting, gasping in shallow breaths that made her feel she was suffocating. "No. This can't be." She clutched Safiye's tunic in a desperate grip. "Heal it!"

Safiye shook her head. "The healers did all they could—"

"My bag. My amplifiers."

"They won't help."

"You don't understand!" Derya pounded the bed with her fist. "Before we killed the dragon, we found a dragon tree. I took some of its leaves. They have magical healing . . ."

She stopped talking when she noticed the regretful nods of the others. Safiye wiped her eyes and sniffed before answering. "The king told us. We used them, and they helped heal your wounds. But, Kiral, you know no magic can regrow a limb."

Derya stared into Safiye's watering eyes, then into Bahadir's resigned face and Kelebek's grim visage. The princess slumped against the pillows with a shriek. "No, no, no, no, no. This can't be happening." Her jaw tightened. "No matter what it takes, I'm going to end Cetus. He deserves a long and agonizing death." She covered her face with her hands. "But I can't. I've failed at every turn." Memories of her missteps collided in her mind. "I should have shattered the sea sooner. It's all my fault."

The others were murmuring. *Let them.* They were just muttering calming platitudes to pacify her. There was no hope. None.

Now she understood. Why the long faces. Why the reluctance to tell her. If her father hadn't already named a new kiral, he would now. It was bad enough she was a girl. Many of the nobles made no secret of their disdain for her and the idea of a female heir. But a maimed cripple? It wasn't many years ago that children born with missing limbs were tossed into the sea. No one would want her as empress. There were laws that would bar her from the throne. Despair seeped through her bones.

She surveyed her advisors' faces. Kelebek's thick eyebrows met over his nose, and deep furrows crossed Bahadir's brow. Safiye was pale, and her lips trembled. They all knew the fate of those who'd been named Heir of Cinar and failed to ascend to the throne. The new emperor usually had them and their closest associates hung for treason on charges that were all or partially fabricated. Shame stabbed through her depression. Safiye, Bahadir, Kelebek. Their lives were at risk because of her incompetence and folly. They should throw her overboard and end her misery—and theirs.

Kelebek might weasel his way out, pretending that he was spying on her for another. He could work out an arrangement with Nazif. Or even Yildiz. But Safiye, Bahadir, and her entourage? If the new emperor didn't kill them, he'd punish them for serving her. Or maybe banish them to remote outposts. And her father was rumored to be in ill health. A new emperor could take the throne far sooner than she'd expected.

She slumped against the pillows, letting the tears trickle down her face. She'd failed. Failed her father. Her loyal supporters. And herself. All those who whispered she was an inadequate, worthless snip of a girl—they were right. Cetus's taunt rang in her ears. *Little water mage. He knew that's all I am.*

And Stigandr. Once he learned of her deformity, he'd have no use for her. The barbarians probably fed anyone who lost a limb to the wolves. Or the wyverns. Her face burned at the memory of his arms around her. Any hopes in that direction melted away like ice under a summer sun.

As did any hope for a full life. She should have died once she saved the islanders.

Derya turned and buried her face in the pillow. "You can all go now."

"Derya—" Safiye's voice cracked.

"That was an order. Unless you've deposed me yourselves?" If they didn't leave soon, she'd have to bite the pillow to keep from shrieking. "Get out."

D ERYA SCREAMED INTO the pillow and pounded her fist on the mattress. Jagged sobs wracked her, bursting from her in guttural wails. She'd lost a foot, and with it, everything she'd ever wanted. She was doomed to suffer as a cripple, dependent on others even to move from bed to bath.

And she'd never be the empress. The rock in her stomach grew into a boulder, and bitterness stung her mouth. It was no secret how the Cinarrian emperors kept their empire intact. Physical perfection in the emperors, along with wily strategy and cunning statecraft, convinced the vassal states they were inferior to their imperial overlords. An emperor without a foot might provoke questions about how powerful the Cinarrians were. Then the entire empire would crumble. Just like her own aspirations. She clawed the pillow and gasped for breath.

I'm going to have to disappear. Hide my identity so no fool wrongly accuses me of defying our laws and plotting for the crown. Or tries to stage a coup in my name.

She rubbed her fists in her eyes. *My life is over. Why did they save me?*

A pair of arms wrapped around her, and she caught a

whiff of cinnamon. *Safiye*. The danisman pulled Derya into an embrace and rocked her until the sobs ebbed.

Derya wiped a tear from her stinging eyes. "I ordered you to go."

A faint, low murmuring filled the room. It sounded like Bahadir and Kelebek. She clenched her jaw. How had they dared disobey? She assumed they'd left. Her face, already hot, heated more when she realized they'd witnessed her paroxysm of despair. Her lower lip trembled. Hadn't she suffered enough humiliation? "Go away," she snarled, her voice raspy and sore. She pulled away from Safiye and glared at her. Safiye stood up and shuffled back a step, her face as gray as her hair.

"No," Kelebek said.

Derya's missing foot throbbed and her head ached. "Get out."

"I will once you hear me out."

She draped the blanket over her head. "I don't want to."

"Then listen to me," Bahadir said.

She didn't answer. Maybe they'd all go away and leave her to her misery. Or offer drugged tea so she could slide into oblivion.

"Kiral," Bahadir said. "You know many of your entourage could have parted from you in Nafplio and returned to Tulgutalp. Everyone wanted to stay in your service. Not because you were the kiral. But because people *want* to call you the kiral. You lead with compassion and courage. And laugh in the face of danger. That's the kind of person they believe should be trusted with the empire."

Derya lay still. Was he saying this to make her feel better?

"If anyone thought you were unworthy to lead Cinar's military, you proved them wrong when you rescued the western islanders and led them to safety."

Did it matter what anyone thought? Her days as Heir of Cinar were over. They'd best think about how they were going to survive, the followers of the disgraced and maimed former kiral. "You don't understand." Without a foot, she couldn't be the kiral.

"I do, more than you know," Bahadir said gently.

She curled her lip. "How can you possibly understand?"

"Have you never wondered why I was a kentarch so long?"

Derya frowned and moved the blanket from her face to stare at him. He'd been her guard for ten years, and all that time a kentarch, until her traveling entourage was formed and he was promoted to chiliarch.

He tapped the three scars on his cheek. "Once you get past the rank of kentarch, promotions become political. An officer with a scarred face wouldn't fit the ideal of Cinar's perfection. Leading your entourage was the only way I could become a chiliarch."

"So you took the position no one wanted solely for your own gain?" Shame twisted her bowels. How could she be so naïve? All this time she'd thought he respected her.

Bahadir looked down and shrugged. "It was my only chance for promotion." He brought his gaze back to hers. "But I'm not saying I didn't want the job for other reasons."

She gave him a puzzled frown.

Bahadir continued. "When I was wounded in a battle with a Tarhuntassian lord, I was one of hundreds of casualties. Our healers were overtaxed. I refused help until all my men were out of danger. That took four days." He shrugged. "By then, it was too late for healers to repair my face without leaving scars. On returning home, I thought I'd be pushed out of the military."

A challenge glittered in his eyes as he fixed his gaze on Derya. She stared at him, stunned into motionlessness. His act of sacrifice, of putting duty over his own ambitions, nearly ended his career.

As if perceiving she'd understood him, he continued. "Instead, they offered me a place in your guard. Rumor whispered you were spoiled, frivolous, and empty-headed. At first, I thought rumor was correct. I observed a girl inform noblemen she couldn't be bothered to remember the days of the week and decided there were too many letters in the alphabet. But I also saw someone who knew the names of every person in her guard, their wives and children, and sometimes even parents and siblings, and never failed to send food and money when someone was ill."

He chuckled. "It took me a while, but I concluded that rumor lied about you. So when the chance came not only to rise in the ranks but to travel with the new kiral, I saw an opportunity to find out what else the gossips had gotten wrong about you.

"These past few months, you were brave, clever, and kind to all, even the lowest ranking. And you learned from your mistakes. You demonstrated you are worthy to rule the empire, but you also earned my loyalty, and that of all under my command."

Derya was still gaping at him, unable to comprehend what she was hearing, when the bed shifted as Safiye sat down. "Kiral," Safiye said, "when your mother died, she begged me to help you grow into the role thrust on you. The task has been easier than I anticipated. Even at your worst, you sought the best for the empire and the people you were responsible for. You've grown into a leader with sound judgement and the ability to rely on others to make you stronger."

Tears leaked from Derya's eyes. After all her blunders, Safiye had confidence in her? "But the only place I can lead you is into exile."

"That, Kiral," Kelebek said, "may not be true."

Derya fixed him with a hard stare. "Why, oikeios, have you stayed with me? Don't deny you despised me for years."

Kelebek's olive skin reddened, but he didn't flinch. "Do you blame me? But that was years ago, and you are much altered from the willful child you were." He met her gaze steadily. "After my escape from Ptolemaida, I was grateful to join your entourage and assumed I would travel back to Tulgutalp with you as planned.

"Then the emperor commissioned you to find the scepter. After long discussions with Ambassador Zeki, we decided you needed someone to ensure you conducted yourself properly and to clean up any diplomatic crises you might precipitate. The empire needed that scepter, and we had scant hope that you would succeed."

Rage choked Derya so she couldn't hurl the curse at him that he deserved.

Kelebek held up a hand. "Yes, you made errors in Ethkarpia. But the way you made an ally of the queen impressed me. It was obvious that the empty-headed flirtatiousness had been an act. It was a clever one to keep factions from forming around you. Your mother's idea?"

Derya nodded.

"The way you maintained that deception for years was remarkable. As was the way you secured the scepter." He shook his head. "None of us expected you to survive falling into the sea. Yet you did, through your resourcefulness and ability to make an ally out of someone who could have remained an enemy." He shifted his weight, making the floorboards creak. "And befriending a winged horse, well, that's a mark of the Rider's favor. I decided you were the worthiest contender for the throne, and I was going to do all in my power to help you keep your position as kiral and, in time, become empress."

Tears trickled down Derya's face. Her jaw quivered. She had much to say, but words eluded her like smoke blown by a spring breeze. Kelebek had never made a secret of his disdain for her. Now he supported her? A few days ago, praise from Kelebek would have been priceless. Now, while pleasant to hear, it was worthless. He was going to have to find someone else to serve.

Bahadir coughed. "We tell you this because we have decided. We will serve you as long as you will have us."

Derya's jaw went slack. Was she hearing correctly? Bahadir's steady gaze told her she was. "Thank you," Derya gasped. "Thank you all." She had no other words for the gratitude swelling her heart and leaking from her eyes. *I didn't retrieve the crown, but I've gained much more.*

Safiye stood up. "You need to rest." She ushered the two men from the cabin. "I'll bring you some tea."

No sooner had she left when the door opened. Instead of a maid, it was the king of Rorvik holding a tray with a teapot, mug, and a bowl of steaming stew. The odor of pepper tickled Derya's nose.

"I heard you were up," he said.

Derya winced, hoping that didn't mean he overheard her despairing sobs. She rubbed her face, attempting to erase any traces of tears. "I'm awake, not up. How are you?"

"I'm up and not crying."

"That's cold." She clenched her fists. "You're not the one who lost a foot."

He set the tray down, shaking his head. "I'm sorry. I didn't mean it the way it sounded." He raised his eyebrows. "If I give you some tea, will you drink it or throw it at me?"

Her desire to punish him lost to her thirst. "I'll drink it."

She struggled to sit up and lean against the wall while he poured a cup of the steaming brew.

He handed the cup to her and sat on the edge of her bed. Derya pulled her legs away from him. Really, he had no business encroaching on her. She eyed him. "You look well."

He shrugged. "But I'm hungry all the time."

Derya gave him a mocking smile. "Food not to your liking?"

"No, just lost my sense of taste." Stigandr grimaced. "The first day was bad. Everything had no more flavor than paste.

On top of that, I burned my mouth twice. And tripped over my own feet."

Yes, wood mages lose taste, metal mages touch. Funny how the loss extended to everything, that he couldn't feel the floor under his feet. "But you can feel again, right?"

He nodded. "Since my senses returned, I can't eat enough. You?"

She gave him a sympathetic shrug. "I can move my toes again. As long as people speak up, I can follow what they're saying." His resonant baritone was a lot easier to understand than Safiye's soft alto.

He leaned toward her. "You seem a bit under the ice. How are you, really?"

"How should I be?" More bitterness and self-pity poisoned her tone than she'd intended. "I failed to find the crown. Scarcely a remnant of the western islanders escaped. And I'm missing a foot." There. She'd admitted her quest had ended in a humiliating debacle, coupled with the ruin of her hopes. And uttered the words without a tremor in her voice.

"The islanders on board haven't stopped thanking me. They don't think rescuing them was a failure."

"I should have saved more."

"You saved the ones who were there."

"It doesn't feel like enough."

"You did more than anyone else could have. When we combined our magic, I was astounded. I'd never tried that with a mage as powerful as you. We're about evenly matched, but if I wasn't careful, you'd have easily been able to deplete me."

"I tried not to."

"I could tell. Your control was astonishing. And shattering the sea? Brilliant."

He'd talked of her courage, her magical power, her cleverness. Things he'd say to the Heir of Cinar. But not what he'd murmur to a woman he desired. She swallowed a lump in her throat. *I'll never be desired. Not now.*

Stigandr glanced out the porthole. "They tell me we're headed for Axum. What are your plans?"

She stared at him. "Plans?" She stabbed a finger toward the lump under the blanket where her stump ended. "Assuming Cetus doesn't kill us all first? Try to keep the next kiral from killing me and all my supporters. Find somewhere to hide to live out my life in peace."

"Why would you do that?"

"They didn't tell you? Without a foot, I can't be empress. It's a law."

"Who came up with that?" He snorted. "Someone who doesn't have all his hens at home."

"Suppose you lost a foot. Would you still be king of Rorvik?"

"Of course. We don't let a little thing like losing a hand or foot bother us."

His words hit her like a wave that threatened to capsize the flimsy boat of her equilibrium. "Little thing?" Her voice rose in a screech.

"Every winter, quite a few people lose toes or feet to frost-bite. Or hands and fingers."

"What happens to them?"

"Our wood and metal mages create artificial limbs. As long as they're magically infused, they work rather well. With the advantage that they are impervious to cold."

Derya stared at him. "You mean," she said slowly, "if I went to Rorvik, someone could make me a foot?" *That's impossible.*

"They might," he said. "But I'm sure Kharan-Khuag is looking for you. It might not be wise for you to sail those waters right now."

The hope that was rising within her shriveled like an autumn leaf.

He rubbed his jaw. "But if you like, I could try to construct one."

Derya jerked upright, her eyes wide open. She grabbed his hand. "Could you?"

He held her hand between both of his own and fixed his gaze on her face. "I'm not going to lie. I've never built any, just watched our mages and seen the feet they made. It might take a few attempts."

A new foot. At least publicly she'd appear whole. Gratitude lifted her chin, and hope diffused her despair. "Thank you. I mean it. Do you need help?"

"I was thinking of Garzuli. She's a clever one, and a capable metal mage."

"She is," Derya said thoughtfully, remembering how Garzuli had repaired the scepter and infused the fakes with magic.

"It might be helpful for her to understand how to construct and infuse the foot. That way, you'll have someone to keep it working after I leave."

Derya froze. He was leaving? Tears pricked her eyes, startling her with the intensity of her sadness at the thought of his departure. She stifled a huff of irritation. Of course he'd leave. She'd rescued him, he helped her with the islanders, and he owed her nothing. And any attraction he had for her was gone. Who would love a girl with a stump?

"I could stay for a while, you know," he said idly. "As long as you keep the Axumians from lynching me for being a barbarian." He shot her a guilty smirk. "I may have raided those shores once or twice."

She rubbed her still-damp cheeks. That could get complicated. "I'll make sure they understand we need you alive to defeat Cetus."

"Thank you." He paused. "I'm not certain what he meant about all his plans being ready in a year, but that gives us a little time." He offered her a small smile, his gray eyes twinkling. "And I believe you and I have unfinished business."

Derya knew what she wanted him to say but feared he wouldn't. She stiffened her spine. "You mean with a certain sorcerer who deserves death?"

"Well, that too." He reached up and brushed a lock of hair from her face. "I had something more pleasant in mind. But it can wait. I don't want to overtax you."

Her heart was fluttering, and she nearly flung her arms around his neck. But she would not risk humiliating herself by showing him what she was feeling. "I'd like that very much, King Stigandr. The Heir of Cinar is grateful for your offer of service."

He let out a bark of laughter. "Oh, princess. I must not be as charming as I think if a little flirtation makes you go all imperial. Save that for Kelebek. He'll enjoy it much more."

Stigandr trailed a finger down her cheek. "I should leave before I do something barbarically improper." His eyes bored into hers. He dragged his hand back, seemingly as reluctant to remove it from her face as she was for him to move away. "Perhaps I'll come up with some exotic entertainment for you."

She couldn't keep the smile from her face or the blush from spreading across her cheeks. "Then I have something to look forward to."

WANT to find out how Derya rallies and leads the defense against Cetus? Read on for a sample of **The Girl Who Cracked the Sky**!

Chapter 1

A MISSING FOOT was more than just a missing limb. Derya

stared at the empty space where her left foot had once been, still barely able to believe it was gone. A shudder wracked her slim shoulders. She was maimed, crippled, and so powerless she could barely get out of bed.

Meanwhile Cetus was plotting to enslave the continent. She shivered and wrapped her arms around herself. If he succeeded, the ancient sorcerer's delight in torture and abuse would have countless millions of new victims. Her best hope at stopping him vanished when she'd failed to find his crown. And lost her foot. She screwed her eyes closed to block out the sight of her stump.

But that didn't erase the memory from sixteen days ago. The karcharia's jaws crunching through her shin. Blood streaming, gushing into the sea. Her own screams sounding far away.

And the searing, agonizing pain.

She squirmed to find a more comfortable position on the hard, narrow bed. Her throat tightened as she studied the place her shin ended, a few inches above where her ankle used to be. Three water mages, or so they told her, had worked day and night for three days to heal the torn flesh and splintered bone. They knitted her shredded skin back together, accomplishing what would have taken weeks without magic. But no amount of magical healing could replace what had been torn off by the karcharia's jaws. Not even dragon tree leaves. All they'd done was hasten the healing and dull the pain.

The bed rocked with the ship's motion. Derya clenched her jaw to suppress a whimper.

The ship creaked and she added her own moans to the sound. Her missing foot throbbed and the muscles of her missing toes cramped. Why the pain? The foot was gone; she should feel nothing.

A gust of wind blew through the window and the ship rocked. Derya swayed with the motion. *I'm letting being stuck in this cabin depress me.* If only she could ride the wind and be free of all her woes. She scoffed. *There's no escaping that way. Cetus will hunt me down wherever I go.*

The ship's timbers groaned like a dying man. Cetus's words resounded in her mind. *Princess of a dying empire, you're just like me. Claiming you want to protect the people, when all you crave is power.*

Three sudden raps on the door jolted her from her horrifying musings and she jerked the sheet over her wounded leg. The door burst open and her danisman Safiye sidled in, carrying a pitcher of water, Stigandr right behind. His head nearly brushed the ceiling and he seemed to fill the tiny space between her bed and the bunk beds opposite with his bulk.

"Kiral," Safiye began. "We need to change the bandages."

Derya screwed up her face. Any touch on her wound was painful. Worse was sensing someone's gaze on the stump and seeing the pity in their eyes. And even after a fortnight, she still hated for anyone—especially Stigandr—to see her deformity. She crossed her arms. "If you must."

"We must," Safiye said. She placed the pitcher next to a bowl on the table and chose a cloth from the pile. She picked up the pitcher and began pouring water over the cloth. "You don't want to—" Her words ended in a scream that cut through Derya like a burning blade.

Safiye dropped the pitcher. Stigandr grabbed it before it toppled to the floor. Safiye's hand blazed crimson, and puffy blisters formed on her fingers. She shrieked, clutching the wrist of her scalded hand.

Derya's heart raced and sweat dampened her face. What had happened to Safiye? "Let me see. I'll heal you."

"Not you," Stigandr growled. He jerked the door open. "You," he said to one of the guards. "Take her to a healer. Then find the chiliarch." He ushered the moaning Safiye out of the room.

Derya watched her go, anxiety drying her mouth like a hot wind over a desert. Stigandr was right; she had no magical reserves to try to heal anyone. "What happened?" Derya asked.

Stigandr sniffed the contents of the pitcher. His face hardened and he dropped into the room's lone chair. "There's quicklime in the water."

Derya frowned. "Isn't that used to purify water?"

"In small amounts. Too much, and it's poisonous. And burns." He shook his head. "Whoever did this was clever. If they were caught adding the quicklime, they could say they were making mortar to patch a leak. In any case, it would've been easy enough for someone to add it to the water without Safiye noticing."

The enormity burst over Derya like a raging storm. "Someone is still trying to kill me."

AFTERWORD

I hope you enjoyed **The Girl Who Shattered the Sea**!

If you'd like to receive updates about upcoming releases, book recommendations, bonus content and sneak peeks of my work, please subscribe to my newsletter at:

www.evelynpuerto.com

And if you did enjoy **The Girl Who Shattered the Sea**, I would be deeply grateful if you would leave an honest review on BookBub, Goodreads or your favorite online retailer. A sentence or two giving your opinion is enough.
Book reviews mean a huge amount to a self-published author like myself. More reviews help my books get better visibility and perform better in search algorithms. Your review will help other readers find my work and will make my day!

Even one sentence will help a lot.
Thank you!

ACKNOWLEDGMENTS

FIRST, A BIG THANK YOU to you, my readers, for continuing to follow Derya and Eliana and their adventures. I'm especially grateful to those of you who read my earlier works (The Outlawed Myth series) and continue to read and enjoy my stories.

Special thanks to Joe Bunting and the gang over at the Write Practice. Lyn Blair, John King, Antonio Roberts, Robert Harrell, Lori Palmer, Monica MacKinnon, Wendy Pearson, Sharon Markey, Sandy Juker, and many others faithfully read and critiqued early versions of this book. Your feedback was priceless, as was your encouragement and enthusiasm about this story. The science fiction and fantasy chapter of the South Carolina Writers' Association also provided excellent suggestions for making the story more exciting. Barbara V. Evers offered valuable comments as well.

Others who contributed their thoughts include Alejandra Cue, Irene Rostas, Diane Varnadoe, Carissa Fairchild, Valeria Herrera-Rodriguez, and Michael McIntyre. I'm grateful for each one of you sharing your opinions.

My editor from Ebook Launch patiently corrected my sometimes chaotic punctuation, pointed out inconsistencies and smoothed out the rough spots in the prose.

Sebastian Breit of Foreign Worlds Cartography did an outstanding job taking my scribbled notes of Ardebil and turning them into a wonderful map.

Most of all I'm grateful to my husband Tony, whose

support, encouragement and love keep me going when I can't find the words. And thank you for giving me space to work, and for holding my hand when it's not going well.

And thanks be to God, who gave me what ability I have to string words together into a story.

ABOUT THE AUTHOR

EVELYN PUERTO entered the world around the time of the unveiling of the microchip, the introduction of Japanese cars to the US, and postage stamps that cost four cents. Her Saturday morning friends were Mighty Mouse, Dudley Do-Right and the Jetsons.

Growing up, school was merely an interruption of her exploration of the worlds of Grimm's Fairy Tales, Louisa May Alcott and, later, JRR Tolkien.

When she married late in life, she inherited three step-daughters, a pair of step-grandsons, and a psychotic cat. Currently she writes from South Carolina.

She's the author of the award-winning **Beyond the Rapids** and the multiple award-winning Outlawed Myth series, as well as the award-winning first book of the Royal Mages series. To learn more or to check out some of her short fiction visit evelynpuerto.com. Or keep up with her on social media.

tiktok.com/@evelyn.puerto.aut

instagram.com/theevelynpuerto

bookbub.com/profile/evelyn-puerto

facebook.com/Author.Evelyn.Puerto

ALSO BY EVELYN PUERTO

The Outlawed Myth Series

Flight of the Spark

Fifteen-year-old Iskra never questions the Prime Konamei's rules—until a Risker rescues her from a bandit attack, shattering everything she believes about their kind. When her friend Tavda vanishes after challenging the truth, a guilt-ridden Iskra seeks answers.

Defying the law, she visits the Riskers and is drawn to their fearless way of life—and to the fearless and handsome Xico. But when the village ruler threatens her into silence, Iskra stands her ground, unaware that her defiance may trigger an ancient prophecy that foretells the end of the realm—and cost her life.

Flicker of the Flame

When Tereka's mother turns violent, a shocking revelation forces Tereka and her father from their home. As she uncovers the truth of her parentage, Tereka is caught in a deadly web of prophecy, magic amulets, and would-be assassins. As threats close in and the mystery of her birth unravels, Tereka must make an impossible choice: embrace a scandalous truth and a destiny she never wanted—or risk being destroyed by the past.

Sting of the Scorpion

After witnessing the slaughter of her clan, Damira vows never to feel powerless again. She, her brother, and a friend surrender to a warlord, pawns in the grip of the Endless War.

But when the ruthless Wei Fang—armed with deadly magic amulets—threatens everything, Damira must decide: will she claim the amulets' power to fight back, or be destroyed by it?

Flood of the Fire

After leading her friends to freedom and surviving as fugitives, Tereka is determined to fulfill her vow to overthrow the corrupt rulers—starting with her evil aunt, Juquila.

When an invading army seizes the south, Tereka dares to hope: is this the prophesied savior, or a new threat? Caught in rising chaos, she must decide her role. The wrong choice could be deadly for her—and the peoples of two warring nations.

www.ingramcontent.com/pod-product-compliance
Lightning Source LLC
Chambersburg PA
CBHW021841010726
47493CB00005B/1507